LASSOE

Cat reminded Logan of his promise by the corral, his jest that his hands could teach her about all sorts of things.

Logan tried hard to keep his mind on what she was saying, not what she was doing, as she kissed each of his fingertips. "I . . . I don't think that would be a very good idea," he whispered breathlessly. But more and more what she was saying only fueled the fire of what she was doing. This wasn't right. It would only complicate an already enormously complicated situation.

But his body didn't seem to care. Nor did his heart.

Cat burned with the need to touch and be touched by this man. "Logan, please . . ."

He groaned low in his throat, his hands tracking the curves of her. "We can't, we can't." He said the words, but his body betrayed them. Cat could feel his desire and gloried in it.

Gloried, yet feared it. She had never been with a man before, not this way. To be with a man as practiced and bold as Logan Blackstone . . . What if he found her wanting?

But then it didn't matter. Nothing mattered as the practiced, bold Logan Blackstone guided her down to the soft layering of clean straw scattered across the stall floor.

FIERY ROMANCE
From Zebra Books

AUTUMN'S FURY   (1763, $3.95)
by Emma Merritt

Lone Wolf had known many women, but none had captured his heart the way Catherine had . . . with her he felt a hunger he hadn't experienced with any of the maidens of his own tribe. He would make Catherine his captive, his slave of love — until she would willingly surrender to the magic of AUTUMN'S FURY.

PASSION'S PARADISE   (1618, $3.75)
by Sonya T. Pelton

When she is kidnapped by the cruel, captivating Captain Ty, fair-haired Angel Sherwood fears not for her life, but for her honor! Yet she can't help but be warmed by his manly touch, and secretly longs for PASSION'S PARADISE.

LOVE'S ELUSIVE FLAME   (1836, $3.75)
by Phoebe Conn

Golden-haired Flame was determined to find the man of her dreams even if it took forever, but she didn't have long to wait once she met the handsome rogue Joaquin. He made her respond to his ardent kisses and caresses . . . but if he wanted her completely, she would have to be his only woman — she wouldn't settle for anything less. Joaquin had always taken women as he wanted . . . but none of them was Flame. Only one night of wanton esctasy just wasn't enough — once he was touched by LOVE'S ELUSIVE FLAME.

SAVAGE SPLENDOR   (1855, $3.95)
by Constance O'Banyon

By day Mara questioned her decision to remain in her husband's world. But by night, when Tajarez crushed her in his strong, muscular arms, taking her to the peaks of rapture, she knew she could never live without him.

SATIN SURRENDER   (1861, $3.95)
by Carol Finch

Dante Folwer found innocent Erica Bennett in his bed in the most fashionable whorehouse in New Orleans. Expecting a woman of experience, Dante instead stole the innocence of the most magnificent creature he'd ever seen. He would forever make her succumb to . . . SATIN SURRENDER.

Available wherever paperbacks are sold, or order direct from the Publisher. Send cover price plus 50¢ per copy for mailing and handling to Zebra Books, Dept. 2526 475 Park Avenue South, New York, N.Y. 10016. Residents of New York, New Jersey and Pennsylvania must include sales tax. DO NOT SEND CASH.

TEXAS WILDCAT

LINDA BENJAMIN

ZEBRA BOOKS
KENSINGTON PUBLISHING CORP.

ZEBRA BOOKS

are published by

Kensington Publishing Corp.
475 Park Avenue South
New York, NY 10016

First printing: December, 1988

Printed in the United States of America

To my parents, Lorraine and Doug . . .
and their other four delightful offspring—
Tom, Paul, Carol, and Patti

and

To JoBell, for her timely
inspiration.

Chapter One

Shadows.

Voices. Voices shouting, screaming.

The tiny girl shrank back, cowering, terrified. The shadows shifted, drifted closer. She tried to hide, tried to be quiet. No one must know she was here. She should be in bed, she knew. But she couldn't sleep. She had come out to the barn to pet her pony.

But Princess wasn't there. Only the voices and giant shadows.

Quiet. She must be quiet as a mouse. On tiptoe, she crept toward the gaping blackness of the barn door flung open to the night.

It was then she heard the muffled sobbing, saw the boy crying. She knew the boy, liked him. He was her brother's friend. She would give him a hug. He would feel better.

Then the shadows came again, and she ran.

No one must know. No one.

Know what?

Know what . . . ?

Cat Jordan kicked at the linen sheet tangled at her ankles, sitting bolt upright in bed. Her body trembled, as she fought to remember. But already the shadows receded, their identities shrouded in mist. She had been only four years old that long ago August night. And try as she might, she could not piece the memories together.

The voices. The shadows.

Fifteen years ago.

Fifteen years that lately seemed no more than yesterday. She rubbed her arms, soothing the gooseflesh, though she wasn't cold. No one could be cold in mid-July in north central Texas. Yet still she shivered, the aftereffects of the nightmare staying with her.

Fifteen years. A hot August night. And a twelve-year-old boy named Logan Blackstone. She could never remember any more than that, never make sense of the dream. And she was tired of trying.

It hurt too much. Everything hurt too much these days. The nightmare had begun five weeks ago. The night her father had been late coming back from town.

The next day he was dead.

His horse had stumbled in a prairie dog hole. So sad, everyone said. So tragic. Hadley Jordan was such a good man. A good husband. A good father.

Cat took a deep, steadying breath, her gaze trailing to the gingham-curtained window across the room. She would need all her wits about her today. Though the first hints of dawn portended nothing out of the ordinary, this day would be anything but.

An accountant was coming to handle the final arrangements for the ranch. *For the best* to foreclose on the Circle J. *For the best* the family move east and begin a new life.

8

"No!" Cat slapped a hand against the feather-tick mattress. The Circle J wouldn't die. She wouldn't let it. No stone-hearted Boston banker was going to put an end to her father's most cherished dream.

"The Blackstones!" She spoke the name like an epithet. How could her father have signed loan papers with a family whose very name had been villified in the Jordan house these past fifteen years?

She grimaced. That her father had been desperate, Cat had no doubt. It was common knowledge he'd over-extended in buying breeding stock last fall. The bank in Red Springs had been ready to foreclose. But the Blackstones had bailed her father out. Why? It didn't make any sense.

But then nothing had made much sense these past few months. Her boisterous, ever-optimistic father had become secretive and withdrawn. Her mother, never fond of ranch life, had taken on a zealot's fervor in her efforts to get Hadley to sell off the Circle J and move the family back east.

And Matt . . . Even thinking her brother's name darkened her mood. Cat would do everything she could to save the Circle J. Matt would do nothing to help her.

Shaking off her brooding thoughts, Cat clambered out of bed and stalked to the washbasin across the room. A cloying warmth hung heavy in the air, promising another day in the mid-nineties.

Dim sunlight glinted off the frameless looking glass above the basin. The bleary eyes staring back at her offered no hint of the mischief usually evident in their emerald depths. Her shoulder-length tawny gold hair more closely resembled a wind-tossed haystack.

The last thought, at least, brought a ghost of a smile to

9

her lips. It would serve the witling Boston accountant right if she showed up to greet him at the stage depot in Red Springs this afternoon looking like something that had tangled with a puma and lost.

Her expression sobered, her bedraggled reflection suddenly conjuring an unwelcome but all too familiar maternal refrain. "You really should take more care with your appearance, Cordelia. Sometimes I can't tell you from the cowhands." Cat's nose wrinkled at how precisely she had captured Olivia Jordan's long-suffering tones.

"A gentleman," Olivia Jordan had assured her on more than one occasion, "wants a woman who looks like a woman."

Not a woman who could outrope and outride him. Not a woman who could outshoot him. Not a woman who could outcuss him. "A gentleman," Olivia Jordan was so very fond of saying, "wants a lady."

A lady. With a wry irony, Cat dug beneath several of her more serviceable cotton nightrails to pull free the delicate garment hidden beneath them. For a long minute she stood there, caressing the satin ribbons of the pale ivory peignoir. How astonished her mother would be to know Cat even possessed such a piece of feminine frippery.

Cat was astonished herself sometimes. She wondered what kind of spell she'd been under when she'd bought the thing at Smithson's Mercantile in Dodge City at the end of last fall's cattle drive. Wrapped in brown paper, it had been secreted away in her saddlebags lest any of the drovers see it. But in truth it was her mother's judgment she most feared. Perhaps even the pale ivory peignoir would have been found wanting.

"Enough!" Cat snapped, grabbing up a well-worn pair of denims and a pale blue chambray shirt. Quickly she got into the shapeless garb, assuring herself she chose the attire for solid, practical reasons. After all, she would be traveling to Red Springs on horseback. How else could she dress?

You could wear a riding skirt, a voice taunted. *And the blouse Maria made for you last Christmas.*

Thoughts of the blouse made her cheeks heat. Maria had meant well. The seventeen-year-old daughter of the Circle J's head wrangler, Maria Hidalgo had long been Cat's closest friend. Cat could still remember the glow in Maria's wide brown eyes when the lovely garment spilled out of the gaily wrapped package into Cat's work-roughened palms. Maria had urged her to try it on at once.

Much against her better judgment Cat had hurried into her bedroom and done just that. Its provocatively low-cut neckline had fired a blush that began at the top of her head and didn't stop until it reached her toes, yet her heightened color had only served to enhance the lovely garment's effect on her. For an unguarded moment Cat Jordan had dared to think of herself as pretty.

Almost as if in a dream, she'd returned to the living room, reveling in the delighted gasps of her mother and Maria. But another pair of eyes had alighted on her as well. Ryan Fielding, owner of the neighboring Rocking R, had grown suddenly tense, his hazel eyes blazing brighter than the candles on the Christmas tree.

"Why don't you pour Ryan a little more eggnog?" her mother had urged, all but shoving Cat over to the punch bowl. A none-too-subtle nudge with an elbow, accompanied by a meaningful look directed toward the kitchen

11

archway, had sent a shocked gasp bolting from Cat. Her mother wanted her to maneuver Ryan under the mistletoe!

But Ryan had already read Olivia's mind. He was beside Cat in an instant. With holiday tradition's full blessing, the blond rancher had pulled Cat into his arms and kissed her.

Cat was certain her mother had seen only a seemingly friendly bear hug from a respected friend. What Olivia hadn't seen was Ryan Fielding's right hand creep up to graze suggestively across Cat's left breast. Nor had Olivia heard the crude words whispered hotly against Cat's ear.

Cat had brought her booted foot down hard on Ryan's instep. He'd grunted and stepped back, making it look for all the world as though Cat had stumbled. The Rocking R owner had then affected a look of amused tolerance. "Too much eggnog, my dear?"

Cat had pursed her lips in fury. "Be glad it's Christmas," she'd hissed, so that only he could hear. "Because that's the only reason I'm letting you keep your teeth." Spinning on her heel, she'd stomped back over to the hearth, wishing to heaven her father hadn't ridden out earlier to check on the stock. Hadley Jordan would've broken Ryan's jaw for even an imagined insult to his daughter. But the stinging disapproval in her mother's eyes silenced any thoughts Cat might have had about confiding in her.

"You have to admit, Cat," Ryan had offered cajolingly a short while later, "you sure do look different. Like a woman."

Cat closed her eyes, trying hard to convince herself that Ryan's words hadn't stung. She lived her life the way she wanted to live it. Fancy clothes and even fancier manners were for supercilious females like Chastity Vincent, who spent more time primping and flirting than doing any work in her father's bank in Red Springs.

And if being dressed up meant someone like Ryan acted like a savage, then Cat wanted none of it. Even though he'd taken her aside and apologized just before he'd left, he'd made sure to lay most of the blame for his behavior on her blouse and the eggnog. "A little too much whiskey," he'd murmured. "Besides"—his hazel eyes had trailed suggestively to the valley between her breasts—"a woman who doesn't want it shouldn't tease a man into thinking she does."

She had been too stunned even to respond. After the Rocking R owner had ridden off, Cat had gone to her mother, hoping for help in sorting through the odd mix of emotions roiling through her. But her words had died on her lips.

"Why did you change back into those infernal pants?" Olivia Jordan had snapped. "For heaven's sake, can't you see Ryan finds you attractive. Though goodness only knows why, when you bury every curve you have under those hideous clothes. Would one smile hurt you? I think the man might even be thinking marriage."

"Or thinking how much bigger the Rocking R would be if it merged with the Circle J," Cat had returned acidly. "Pa told me Ryan made him an offer."

Olivia had tried to hide the surprise showing in her brown eyes, but Cat had not missed it. Obviously, Hadley Jordan had not shared Ryan's offer with his wife.

"I just want what's best for you, Cordelia," Olivia had managed to say softly. "To get a man you sometimes have to play by his rules. Treat him like a king, and he'll make you his queen."

13

Cat had no desire to be any man's queen. In fact, she'd intimidated the hell out of most of the men she had ever met because she *could* outrope and outride them. And outshoot. The cussing, Cat conceded, was open to debate. Dusty Yates, Circle J's grizzled foreman, could raise a blush on the devil.

But her mother remained undaunted. Olivia Jordan considered it a maternal priority to find a husband for her daughter. And nothing, most especially not Cat's objections, was going to stop her.

For over a year now Ryan Fielding had topped her mother's list of suitable prospects. Wealthy, ambitious, and capable of a captivating charm, Ryan could do no wrong in Olivia's eyes. Even his being a rancher was not a drawback, because the man openly indulged in an often lavish lifestyle and made no secret of his future political aspirations.

Even so, Cat thought, her mother would prefer a Philadelphia lawyer. Or a Boston banker.

Cat laughed without humor. No, not a Boston banker. There even Olivia Jordan would draw the line. A Blackstone would be the last man on earth her mother would want her to marry.

With a sigh, Cat crossed to the open window that faced east into the rising sun. Tugging back the blue-checked curtain she gazed out at the purple haze hanging low on the distant horizon. The grassy plain stretched on endlessly, broken only by occasional slashes of cottonwoods bordering creeks she could not see.

But as far as she *could* see—in all directions—lay Circle J land, a ranch carved from the sweat and blood of Hadley Jordan. Her legacy. And she wasn't going to lose it. Not ever.

14

In her mind's eye, she saw her father as he had been that last day she'd seen him alive. The sentencing had been handed down in the trial of a man Hadley had caught rustling Circle J beef. The rustler, a no-account named Barney Jackson, had also killed a Circle J ranch hand. The judge had sentenced Jackson to hang.

"That should send a message to anyone else thinking of stealing what's ours," Hadley had said, his green eyes blazing.

Cat had believed him. And she'd believed him when he'd told her that now he could concentrate on getting the loan extended.

Dusty had brought his body home the next day. Hadley had never made it back to town. Never sent for the extension.

Now it was up to her to make sure Blackstone's emissary understood that she meant business, that she was just as determined as her father had been to save the ranch. She leaned her forehead against the warming pane of glass. All she needed was a plan.

"You have to play the cards life deals you," Hadley Jordan had told her time and time again. "But a good bluff and a grin can beat a chicken-livered pat hand every time."

A bluff and a grin was all she had for now. She would make it be enough.

The variable she couldn't predict was the Blackstone family.

She bit her lip. She'd never learned the full truth of what had caused the rift between the Jordans and the Blackstones. Over the intervening fifteen years she'd often heard her mother's version of what had happened, and Matt's. But she had never heard the Blackstone version. And whenever she had broached the tender subject with her father, he had refused to speak of it.

Fifteen years. So much bitterness, so much pain—over a foolish mistake made by a twelve-year-old boy.

Logan Blackstone.

Dark tousled locks spilled across her memory, as surely as they had spilled over too-serious gray eyes. Logan Blackstone, the quiet boy her brother's own age, had come to spend the summer at the Circle J. Her own half-remembrances vied with the more vivid tales told her by Matt and her mother, but never had Cat forgotten an indulgent smile for a friend's tag-along sister. Nor the spray of wild violets pressed into her tiny hand and the red bandana that had dried away her tears when her favorite puppy had died.

But the idyll had ended, shattered into nightmare . . . and shards of memory Cat had yet to piece together.

Nor would she attempt to do so now. She'd wasted enough time on memories. It was time to face this most unpleasant day. She stalked to her bedroom door, turning back once to gaze longingly toward the open window. How much easier that less orthodox, but more expedient, exit would be. How much easier to avoid further confrontation with her mother and her brother.

With a resigned sigh, she opened the door. The aroma of frying steak drifting toward her from the kitchen told her Maria was up and about as usual before the rest of the family. Cat smiled. If anyone could lift her spirits on this bleak day, it would be Maria.

"Cordelia!"

Cat frowned. Her mother's voice—coming from the kitchen, followed at once by the sounds of pots and pans being banged about. Maria would never make so much

16

noise. Olivia Jordan was making breakfast. Olivia Jordan despised cooking, almost as much as she despised the Circle J. Things were not looking up.

"Cordelia, is that you?" Olivia called again. "Come in here, please. I could use some help with Matthew."

A quick flush of resentment rippled through Cat. She instantly regretted it. Matt couldn't help the way he was.

"Cordelia, now!"

Years of familiarity made Cat give little note to the Spartan furnishings as she crossed in front of the fireplace in the main living area and headed for the kitchen. Plain pine furniture, braided rugs, and virtually no adornments on the walls gave the place an austerity that belied its careworn homeyness. The extra money that could have bought the feminine touches that would have so pleased her mother had more often been put to what her father termed "more sensible use"—upgrading the herd.

In the kitchen, Cat skirted the heavy oak table and headed over to the cast-iron stove beside which her mother stood, vigorously stirring a panful of eggs.

"Where's Maria?" Cat asked.

"I'll be taking Matthew's meals to him from now on."

Cat didn't miss the undercurrent in her mother's voice. "Keeping Maria from fixing Matt's meals isn't going to keep Maria from Matt."

"Please, don't start." Olivia turned to face Cat. The tiny wrinkles around her mother's eyes seemed more pronounced than usual. Her coffee brown hair, normally pinned up in a plaited crown, hung in straggling disarray. "And please," she continued, her gaze tracking Cat from boots to bandana, "do not tell me you're wearing *that* to meet the stagecoach this afternoon."

"I'm riding Nugget," Cat said, "and you're changing the subject. Where's Maria?"

"I'm sure she's out cooking for the hands," Olivia said. "I didn't say she was no longer the cook, only that she was no longer cooking for Matthew."

"She loves him, you know," Cat said softly. "And heaven knows Matt could use—"

"*I* know what's best for my son."

Cat knew further argument was useless. On the subject of Matthew Jordan, her mother yielded to no one. Instead, Cat picked up a plate and held it close to the skillet. "I can take Matt his breakfast."

Olivia heaped the plate full of steak and eggs. "Just make sure you don't bother him about this loan business."

"I won't need to *bother* him about that," Cat said slowly. "I'm going to be taking care of it."

Olivia slapped the spatula back into the pan, then took a deep breath. "We've all been on edge lately, Cordelia. I know that. But please, for the love of heaven, let it go."

Cat felt for the hurt in her mother's voice. Part of her felt responsible for it. Hadley Jordan had left controlling interest of the Circle J to his daughter, not his wife or his son. Hadley had done it because he knew Cat would do everything she could to save the ranch. But the pain Hadley's decision must have caused her mother and brother, Cat could only imagine.

"I have to try," Cat said. "Please understand."

"No woman can run a cattle ranch."

Though the Circle J cowboys were her friends, Cat had to be brutally realistic. They might well balk at working for a woman. "Matt could give the orders."

Olivia blanched. "You know he could do no such thing."

18

"He could do anything he set his mind to, if you'd—"

"We're finished with this ranch!" Olivia cut in. "Finished, do you hear me? It killed your father, crippled your brother."

Cat's eyes widened. "You always told me it was Logan Blackstone who crippled Matt."

"I don't want to hear that name in this house."

"Mother, please," Cat said, choosing her next words carefully, "I know there are a lot of bad feelings between the Jordans and the Blackstones. But I'm going to need their cooperation on this loan. After all, Pa was once best friends with Logan's father. And the man did come through on the loan when Pa needed it."

"I'm sure the advantage was Jeremy's."

"Why would Jeremy Blackstone want to involve himself financially with a Texas ranch?"

Her mother jabbed a fork into another piece of meat and flipped it into the frying pan. "I'm sure I don't know."

"You were friends with the man's wife, once, weren't you?" Cat probed. Any insight she could gain into the Jordan-Blackstone feud might be the edge she needed in getting the extension.

"Elizabeth and I were traveling abroad back in forty-six," Olivia conceded, a faraway look coming into her eyes. "We were in Paris. That's where we met Jeremy and Hadley. They were on their grand tour." She stopped, her tone shifting abruptly. "This is no time for reminiscing. If it weren't for Jeremy Blackstone, his son would never have come here. Matthew wouldn't be a cripple."

"But it was an accident."

"Do you think that matters to your brother?"

"I don't think that Matt knows what matters. If he'd

19

get out of bed more often, see the ranch, work it, I know he'd love it as much as I do. And he'd fight for it, just as I intend to do."

"This ranch!" Olivia said bitterly. "How can you defend it? It wasn't just Logan Blackstone who crippled your brother. It was this place. If we'd stayed in Boston, it never would have happened."

With a sigh, Cat strode over to the storage cupboard. She might as well argue with a stone. Olivia hated the ranch and nothing would change her mind.

Returning her attention to Matt's breakfast, Cat pulled down a jar of peaches from the cupboard. Sudden tears burned her eyes. Peaches had been her father's favorite.

Swallowing hard, Cat spooned some of the fruit into a bowl and settled it on the tray that held the rest of her brother's breakfast.

Heading down the hallway, leading off from the kitchen, she halted at the first door on the right. Balancing the tray against her body, she knocked on the door. A muffled grunt from within was all the permission Cat needed to enter. Inside, her nose wrinkled at the smell of whiskey and sweat. The windows were closed tight. So typical of Matt. Shut out the world. She set the tray on the bedside table and marched over to one of the windows, throwing it open.

"Close it!" The growled words came from the bed.

"Fresh air is good for the spirit." Cat kept her voice even. She loved her brother, but he so tried her patience.

"Where's Maria?"

Cat noted the reluctant interest in Matt's voice. "Ma decided to do the cooking this morning."

If such an oddity aroused Matt's curiosity, he made it a point not to show it.

20

Cat studied her brother. Most women would consider him handsome, with his high cheekbones and aristocratic nose, his sandy-colored hair a shade or two darker than her own. But when their scrutiny reached his eyes, a deep brown color, their interest would come to an abrupt end. Cat held only the vaguest memories of laughter and light in those depths. Red-rimmed and bloodshot, they often sparked with bitterness or, more frightening still, revealed nothing at all. His sallow color bore quiet witness to a life spent too much indoors; the muscles of his arms and upper body lacked the honed toughness of a man who lived on a Texas ranch.

Matt's hands, though, she almost envied. Slender fingers, uncallused. Her own hands were often red and rough, even though she wore gloves when working the cattle. Inevitably, her gaze trailed to the blanket covering the lower half of Matt's body, settling on the silhouette of his right leg and then on the left that ended just above the knee.

Logan Blackstone's legacy.

"I'm meeting the stage this afternoon," she said. "I don't suppose you'd like to ride along."

He scowled darkly.

Cat tried to swallow her exasperation. Though her words were meant to be cajoling, her voice sounded sharper than she'd intended. "It would do you good. You never get out. I could even ask Maria to go along."

"Thanks for bringing my breakfast. If you don't mind I'll eat alone."

"You know, if you'd put half the energy you use feeling sorry for yourself into learning to get around on your crutches—"

"Cordelia!" Olivia Jordan stood framed in the

21

doorway. "That's enough. You know your brother is in constant pain. How can you badger him so?"

Cat conceded defeat and started for the door. She turned to give her brother one last chance. "If you change your mind about coming along, I'll hitch up the buckboard. I'll be leaving in half an hour."

"You're still going to try and work something out with that damned accountant this afternoon, aren't you?" Matt gritted out.

"I am."

"Then you're a bigger fool than Pa," he said. "The Circle J is finished. Pa knew it even before his horse fell on him. And you'll know it, as soon as you try to deal with anyone connected with the Blackstones."

"You may not give a damn about this place, but I do."

Matt struggled to sit up, a strange light in his brown eyes, and an emotion she couldn't read. He was about to say something when a spasm of pain rocked him. He sucked in a deep breath, his hands twisting in the bedcovers.

"Laudanum," he gasped. "Ma, please, get the laudanum."

"See what you've done!" Olivia cried, rushing over to the bed. She nearly upset the contents of the brown bottle on the bedside table, as she forced the cork free with shaking fingers.

"There, there, Matthew," she soothed, as she poured a dose onto a spoon and held it to his lips. "Cordelia didn't mean to upset you. Everything will be all right. You'll see." She shot an accusing glare toward Cat, then immediately returned her attention to Matt.

Cat fought back tears as she watched Matt struggle to control his pain, knowing he might win the battle, but never the war. The stump hadn't healed properly, never would, according to the doctor in Red Springs.

No wonder her brother hated Logan Blackstone. How could he not? They may have been boys, but it was Logan's carelessness that had left her brother with a lifetime of pain while Logan went back to his life in Boston, the dimness of time no doubt erasing any twinges of conscience that may or may not have beset him over what he had done.

"I'm sorry, Matt," she mumbled, backing out of her brother's room. "I'm sorry." Bolting for the front door, she flung it open and rushed outside, the heat of the early morning sun suddenly welcome, necessary, its presence assuring her that, even in the face of family disapproval, she was doing the right thing. That, for her father's sake and her own, she had to do everything she could to save the Circle J.

"I owe it to you, Pa," she murmured. "I owe it to us both."

Hadley Jordan had lived and breathed the Circle J ever since he'd brought his pregnant wife to Texas back in '52. He'd brought up his children to do the same. It was Matt's self-pity that kept him from fighting for what was as much his as it was hers. But Cat would never deny her birthright. If she had to, she would travel to Boston and face the Blackstone family head-on.

That decided, she crossed the main ranchyard to the barn. The palomino mare in the near stall whinnied a greeting. Cat couldn't resist rubbing Nugget's velvety nose. "I don't know about you, girl," she said, "but if this afternoon ends up anything like this morning . . ." She shook her head, not finishing the thought. Somehow she would convince the Blackstone accountant to wire his employers for more time. And maybe it wouldn't be just a bluff and a grin. The Circle J might be cash poor at the moment, but they had their biggest head count of four- and five-year-old cattle ever. Those were the beeves that would be driven to market this fall. If the Blackstones could wait until then, Cat could pay them back half again what she owed them. Surely, a banker could wait three months for a fifty-percent profit. It was her best hope.

As Cat led Nugget out of the barn, she thought about stopping by the cookhouse to see Maria, then decided against it. Maria would more than likely ask Cat to intervene in Olivia's decision to take over the cooking chores for Matt. Cat wanted to help her friend, but right now she couldn't involve herself in the matter. She and her mother were on fragile enough ground.

Almost against her will, Cat found herself walking toward the massive cottonwood that stood sentry over the creek some two hundred yards to the rear of the house. Beneath the tree a white stone cross marked a mound of scarred earth. Kneeling, Cat tugged at the new shoots of buffalo grass at the base of the cross.

"I miss you, Pa," she whispered, trailing her fingers lovingly over the stone's simple markings—Hadley Jordan 1825–1880. "Sometimes I don't know what to do without you." She hadn't intended to cry, yet she couldn't seem to stop herself. Tears tracked unchecked down her cheeks. "I don't want Mama to hate me. And God knows I don't want to hurt Matt." She sobbed brokenly, feeling more alone than she'd ever felt in her life. "What am I supposed to do, Pa? What am I supposed to do?"

For long minutes she sat there, listening . . . to the

24

creek, barely more than a summer trickle; to the horses milling in nearby corrals; to the flies droning endlessly, everywhere. The Circle J—her home.

She looked up, her gaze shifting toward the bunkhouse, a clapboard structure just east of the main house. She had forged some of her fondest memories in that whitewashed building. With her father and Dusty and Esteban Hidalgo and the rest of the hands she had learned to play poker, brew mud-thick coffee, and swap some of the tallest tales ever told.

Dusty had once even shown her how to roll a cigarette. On a dare she'd smoked it. She would have died before she'd let any of them see its effect on her. But once outside, she'd thrown up for half an hour. She was certain her complexion was green for a week.

Cat rose to her feet, her chin set in the stubborn line that had given her father more than one gray hair. "I'm going to do it, Pa," she said. "I'm going to make you proud of me."

She gathered up Nugget's reins, threading the leather through her fingers. No matter what it cost, the Circle J would be hers. "And nothing and no one is going to stop me," she muttered.

Cat checked the position of the sun. The stage would arrive in Red Springs at four that afternoon. She would time her arrival so that she appeared neither overanxious nor indifferent to the Blackstone's representative. She would buy him dinner at Pritchard's Cafe, and they would come to some kind of understanding.

Unbidden, the image of a likely Blackstone accountant came to her mind—a simpering milksop who feared his black-hearted employers almost as much as Cat did.

Grimacing, Cat swung into the saddle. She would find

25

out soon enough. She nudged Nugget forward with her knees, but pulled back at once. A rider was thundering toward the house. Cat rode to intercept him, but she was too late. Her mother stood in the doorway. She and the man exchanged words Cat could not hear; then he handed Olivia a folded slip of paper, tipped his hat, and continued on his way.

Cat rode up and dismounted, unaccountably ill at ease. As she watched, her mother's face paled, the message falling from nerveless fingers. Cat rushed over, snatching it up before it hit the ground. Her own heart pounded as she read.

Olivia,
    I can't tell you how saddened I was to hear of Hadley's untimely death. It grieves me to think of the friendship we once shared and how it ended. The pain you must be feeling is probably much the same as my own four years ago on the passing of my beloved Elizabeth. When I mentioned the unfortunate circumstances to Logan, he insisted he be the one to handle the final details of the loan personally. . . .

Cat scarcely noted the condolences that followed. "My God," she murmured, her imagined accountant suddenly infinitely preferable to cold-blooded reality.

Logan Blackstone was coming back to the Circle J.

Chapter Two

Logan Blackstone eyed the stagecoach that would take him the last leg of his journey, and tried to shake off the disagreeable notion that he was behaving like a coward. If he had hired a horse, he could've traveled cross-country and been at the Circle J by now. By taking the stage, he wouldn't even arrive in Red Springs until late this afternoon, leaving an additional four hours for the trip to the ranch.

Of course, he reasoned, the latter was precisely what the Jordans expected. And he tried hard to convince himself that that was why he didn't want to change his plans. Except that he knew better. The longer the journey took, the longer it would be before he had to face Matt Jordan.

"You gonna board, mister?" a voice called.

Logan looked up to see the bowlegged, buckskinned stage driver ambling toward him. The sweat dripping from Farley Jessup's beard-stubbled face offered mute testimony to both the day's sweltering temperature and the fact that he'd just single-handedly hitched up the

27

fresh team of six horses that would take the stagecoach the next leg of its journey.

"On my way," Logan said, threading his fingers through hair the dusky black of a moonless night. Slate gray eyes seemingly tinged with a perpetual aloofness added an air of reserve to a man already inclined to keep a deliberate distance between himself and the world.

"I just cain't get over them purty clothes, mister," Jessup said, the tobacco-stained whiskers surrounding his mouth wriggling in such a way that Logan could only presume the man was grinning at him.

Logan responded by swatting at the dust that had settled in a thin layer across the shoulders of his finely tailored frock coat. The equally fine cut of his trousers accentuated lean hips and long legs that ended in highly polished black leather boots, now also layered with the ubiquitous Texas dust.

"I'll leave you the name of my tailor, Mr. Jessup," Logan said, checking the gold watch nestled in the pocket of his silver brocade vest, vaguely disappointed to discover the stage was still on schedule.

Jessup hooted gleefully, then climbed into the driver's boot. Logan hefted his gold-handled walking stick in his right hand and settled his black derby hat atop his head with his left. He pulled open the stage door and was about to board, when he caught the sound of feminine voices coming up on him from behind.

He backed up a step and removed his hat, smiling politely at the two approaching women. They'd alighted from a southbound stage some minutes earlier and had waited in the shack out of the sun until Jessup readied the westbound Red Springs coach. The younger of the two, an ebony-haired beauty dressed in an outrageously

28

impractical pink taffeta gown, tittered coquettishly and batted long dark lashes at him from under her pink parasol, while the older woman looked on approvingly.

"Ladies," Logan said, offering a hand to assist them into the stage.

"My, my! What an exquisite cane!" the older woman exclaimed, taking Logan's proffered hand. "I've never seen anything like it."

Distractedly, Logan fingered the leonine head of the cane. "A gift from Lord Harcourt, baron of . . ." He swallowed the rest when both women's eyes lit up with keen interest. Logan could almost hear them calculating the cane's worth—and his own.

Inside the stage, he took the seat facing the front of the stage, while the women sat together on the seat opposite.

Logan knew he should introduce himself, but he was not in the mood for conversation. He had too much on his mind. He was grateful when Jessup cracked the whip and the stage lurched into its normal bone-rattling motion. Within minutes the six-horse team settled into a ground-eating canter, heading for what the driver had told Logan was the Henderson relay station, the final stop before Red Springs.

He found himself wondering if Matt would be in town to meet him. He hoped not, deciding he would rather ride to the Circle J alone. It would give him time to consider again just what he was going to say to the man who, for one adventure-packed boyhood summer, had been his best friend.

Until everything had gone wrong . . .

"If I may be so forward, sir . . . Sir?"

Logan shook himself back to the present, aware now that the older woman was addressing him. From the

29

vaguely indignant look on her face, Logan discerned she may have been trying to gain his attention for several fruitless seconds.

"I beg your pardon, madam," he said. "You were saying?"

She beamed graciously, obviously pleased by his apology. "I was only saying that it is going to be a journey of several hours and I thought, well . . . if I may be so forward: I'm Leona Vincent and this is my daughter Chastity."

Logan curved his mouth into an acceptable smile. "Logan Blackstone."

"I'm so pleased to make your acquaintance, Mr. Blackstone," Chastity Vincent trilled in soft accents. "It's so rare to meet a gentleman of distinction on these desolate plains." She waved a pale pink hankie above the creamy flesh of her décolletage. "Aren't these traveling coaches just an abomination?" She gave him no time to respond, continuing, "Why the one we were on yesterday threw a wheel, or we would already have been home by now. The whole experience has been such an ordeal."

"A train would be preferable," he said. "But then the railroad hasn't quite reached Red Springs yet."

"Oh, is that where you're going?" Leona exclaimed. "How delightful! That's our home, you know. My husband, Abner Vincent—you may have heard of him?" She looked expectantly at Logan.

He shook his head.

"Well, Abner is a banker. And a very successful one at that. Very prominent, very well thought of, if I do say so myself. He owns the Red Springs Bank."

Logan considered mentioning he was a banker himself,

but decided against it. Perhaps the conversation could die a natural death if he didn't hold up his end of it.

He hadn't reckoned on Leona's tenacity. "Poor dear Abner is probably beside himself with worry, since Chastity and I didn't arrive this morning as planned. Chastity and I have been visiting my sister in Memphis. Have you ever been to Memphis, Mr. Blackstone?"

Again Logan shook his head.

"My, my, my, what a time!" Leona said, launching into a ten-minute discourse on the best hotels and finest restaurants in the city and reciting the menus of each. "We dined with some of the wealthiest families in the country. Of course, it was the young gentlemen of those families who insisted. After all, I do have the most beautiful daughter in the entire South. Don't you agree, Mr. Blackstone?"

"Without a doubt," Logan deadpanned, his gaze flicking to where Chastity trailed a finger along the lace that bordered the low-cut bodice of her gown. He found the girl's outlandishly brazen flirting almost comical. But when she stared straight at him and gave that same finger a tiny kiss, Logan wished grimly that he'd given more thought to hiring a horse.

"Why, it was all poor Chastity could do to keep up with all of her gentlemen callers." Leona sighed sympathetically, giving her daughter's wrist a tender squeeze.

"Very tiring, I'm sure," Logan said.

"It's just unfortunate my husband was unable to accompany us," Leona continued. "We've only been in Red Springs for two years, and Abner still doesn't feel he can trust things to the help, you know."

Logan grunted noncommittally.

"Are you visitin' someone in Red Springs, Mr. Blackstone?" Chastity inquired sweetly.

His gaze shifted, his gray eyes focusing on nothing in particular. "A business matter," he allowed. "Not a pleasant one."

In the next instant the stage lurched violently to the left, sending Chastity catapulting onto Logan's lap. "Oh, my heavens," she squealed, "are we going to crash?"

"We hit a rut," Logan said, trying to extricate himself from the girl's death grip on his neck. "We're fine."

She snuggled her head under his chin. "Are you sure? I'm so frightened."

"We're fine," he repeated, again trying to ease her away from him. When she wouldn't budge, he decided wryly that having a lovely young woman's breasts crushed against his chest wasn't the worst way to spend a tedious morning in a stagecoach. It might even take his mind off other things.

"Chastity, dear," Leona clucked, "I do think Mr. Blackstone needs a little more room."

"Yes, Mother," the girl said, more than a little breathless. She didn't take her eyes from Logan, as she settled herself back onto her own side of the coach. "Please, forgive me," she murmured.

"No harm done."

Chastity giggled.

"I'm just hoping Chastity will be able to rest a bit now that we'll be getting home," Leona said, giving Logan a conspiratorial wink. "Breaking a new heart every night can be so wearing on such a tiny little thing."

"Now, Mother . . ." Chastity chided.

"It's the same for her in Red Springs, of course." Leona sighed. "Though I think she's narrowed her

32

choice just a bit of late, haven't you, dear?"

"Mother, really, you mustn't go on so." But Logan noted a look of satisfaction, not embarrassment in the girl's wide blue eyes.

"Ryan Fielding took you to the cattlemen's ball this past spring, did he not? And he's called on you several times since." To Logan she said, "The man is very well off and very handsome."

For the first time a hint of displeasure clouded the girl's eyes. "Sometimes I think Ryan is more interested in that . . . that hoyden—what is her name?" Before her mother could answer, Chastity managed to cheer herself, saying, "I doubt the girl even owns a petticoat, let alone a dress."

"Hush now, darling," Leona said. "Mr. Blackstone would hardly be interested in hearing about petticoats and hoydens." She returned her attention to Logan. "Of course, Chastity hasn't given Ryan Fielding a definite answer. She's still quite . . . available."

"I'm sure she is," Logan said dryly, watching as Chastity adjusted her position on the seat, using the movement as an excuse to lift her skirts just enough to display a shapely ankle.

Thankfully the continual dust swirling in the coach eventually proved too much even for the loquacious Mrs. Vincent. She soon settled back and closed her eyes, insisting that Chastity do the same. Logan grinned. Mama wasn't foolish enough to leave Chastity to her own devices.

In any event, Logan was thankful for the respite. Creaking leather, hoofbeats, and the occasional crack of Jessup's whip became the only sounds as the miles rolled by. Logan used the time to study the passing terrain,

terrain that somehow looked different when viewed by a man, instead of a boy on his first trip away from home.

Occasional hills were broken up by the expansive prairie. Clumps of buffalo grass and blue grama fought for life under the blazing summer sun. The soil itself boasted the reddish cast that had given Red Springs its name. Had it really been fifteen years since he'd last seen this land? Fifteen years—a lifetime.

"A visit with Hadley will do wonders for you," Jeremy Blackstone had said, settling his only son onto a private train car that would begin his trip west.

"Yes, Papa," Logan replied, unable to suppress the tremble that rippled through his too-thin body. He was twelve years old. He wasn't supposed to be afraid. But he couldn't seem to help it.

Jeremy Blackstone sat down next to Logan on the plushly upholstered velvet seat. "A little nervous, son?"

Logan nodded.

"I would be too," his father reassured him. "But you'll have a fine time." Jeremy glanced out the window to where Elizabeth Blackstone stood pensively wringing her hands. "Your mother couldn't bear this final good-bye. That's why she didn't come on board."

"She worries about me a lot."

"That she does. Maybe I do, too." His father had gotten a faraway look. "You know she lost four babies before you. She can't help fussing. It's just that she loves you so much."

"I know, Papa."

Jeremy smiled. "You're a good boy, Logan. The best. I know you'll take to Hadley, take to Texas. And remember, your mama and Mrs. Jordan used to be real good friends once. I'm sure Olivia will look after you, too. And when you get back, you'll tell your mother and me all about being a cowboy. You'll be healthy and strong and . . ." His voice trailed off. "You'll do just fine."

"I'll do you proud, Papa. And you'll see, Mama won't have to worry about me so much anymore."

Jeremy Blackstone gave his son a fierce hug. "You do what Hadley tells you. And take care, you hear?"

"Yes, Papa." Logan swallowed the tears that threatened to spill down his cheeks. He wasn't going to let his father see him crying like some little baby. Papa wanted him to go to Texas. Papa wanted him to get tough and strong. And that was what he was going to do.

Tough and strong. Logan had done that all right. In three months his underused muscles had been honed to a steely toughness he would never have believed possible. His sickly pallor had been replaced by a healthy Texas tan. He had reveled in being a cowboy, reveled in being Matt Jordan's friend.

Logan shook off the memories, forcing himself to doze as Farley Jessup's stage rambled on. But it was a day for memories. He knew they wouldn't be the last.

The stage paused once for nature's necessities, but otherwise journeyed on until well past noon, when Jessup pulled up at a small ranch house that seemed much more Logan's idea of a stage stop than the dilapidated shack had this morning.

Farley Jessup opened the stage door, assisting the two women to the ground. "Mrs. Henderson sets a good table," he said. "Go on in and say howdy."

Logan lingered a moment, looking east. "We've had a couple of riders following."

35

"I noticed. Started about five miles back."

As if on cue, the two riders rode in. Quick introductions labeled the first one Yerby, a bullish-looking man well past forty with close-set eyes and an unkempt graying beard. The other, a smallish terrier of a man, called himself Doakes. He seemed secure only at Yerby's side.

"Spare us some grub?" Yerby directed the question toward Jessup, though his gaze tracked Logan's attire with obvious contempt.

"Ain't my place to say," Jessup said, gesturing toward the house. "Have to ask the Hendersons."

A man had appeared at the door to admit Mrs. Vincent and her daughter. Now the man stepped past the women and headed toward the stage.

"Doug Henderson," Jessup said to Logan. "Owns the place. Real neighborly fella."

Logan accepted Henderson's handshake. "You've got a nice home here, Mr. Henderson."

"Call me Doug," he said, striding over to help Jessup unhitch the team. "You fellas go on inside," he said to Logan and the two drifters. "Have the missus set you a place for lunch. She's a real good cook. You won't be sorry."

Logan headed toward the house, removing his hat and reaching the door at the same time Yerby and Doakes did. From horseback the two men had seemed disreputable enough, now Logan's nose confirmed the fact that neither one of them had strayed near a bar of soap for months. The prospect of a pleasant meal had just dimmed considerably.

"Them's real fancy duds, mister," Yerby said, his bear-sized body taking up most of the entryway. "You must do real well for yourself."

"I manage," Logan said, stepping around the man and into the house. The main room seemed to be one big kitchen with a long oak table in its center and bench seats of equal length on either side of it. A handsome woman stood tending the three pans of food simmering on the stove, while four racketing youngsters of varying sizes gallumphed around the room.

"I'm hungry," the younger of two towheaded boys screeched.

"Patience, Paul," the woman said, looking up to see three new arrivals in her kitchen. "Three more plates, Carol Ann," she said at once, gesturing to one of the girls, who looked to be around eight years old. The woman gave the three men a cheerful smile. "Welcome, gentlemen. I'm Lorraine Henderson."

Yerby and Doakes grunted, but otherwise made no reply. Without going near the washbasin they sat down at the table next to the Vincents. Leona and Chastity immediately rose and moved to the table's opposite side.

"Logan Blackstone, ma'am," Logan said. "You've got a fine-looking place here, a fine-looking family."

"Thank you." She pointed toward each child individually, somehow managing to differentiate them for Logan. Carol Ann, the cherub-cheeked older girl. Patricia, smaller, quieter. Paul, the hungry one. Tom, the oldest, tinkering with the pump handle on the sink.

"Our eldest ran off last spring with some drifter named Luke," Lorraine said, the tone of her voice indicating she didn't exactly approve. Her husband came through the door just then with Jessup. His grin suggested that Luke had been an acceptable choice.

When everyone was seated, Lorraine and Carol served

37

up heaping plates of beef stew, Indian pudding, and black-eyed peas. Chastity turned up her nose, but her mother's less than discreet jab to the ribs encouraged her to remember her manners.

"Thank you, Mrs. Henderson," Logan said, as the woman poured him a cup of coffee. "If everything tastes as good as it looks, I may still be sitting here come supper time."

The woman brushed back a strand of brunet hair, flushing warmly under Logan's easy grin. "Why thank you so much, Mr. Blackstone. It's a pleasure to cook for a man who appreciates a good meal."

"I appreciate more than your cookin', woman," Doug Henderson said, grinning.

"Go on with you now!" Lorraine said, blushing prettily.

The boisterous youngsters kept the conversation lively throughout the meal, only Yerby and Doakes saying nothing as they stuffed their faces with four helpings each of Lorraine Henderson's buttermilk pies.

With the meal finished, the children quickly began clearing away the dishes, while the adults enjoyed a second cup of coffee. But when Leona Vincent launched into another recitation on Chastity's irresistibility, Logan stood abruptly. "If all of you would be so kind as to excuse me, it's been a long morning. I think I'll go out and stretch my legs for a while."

"Don't get lost," Yerby grunted. "A tenderfoot like you, you never know what can happen."

"I get his pie," Doakes said, reaching across the table.

Logan again thanked the Hendersons for their hospitality, then headed outside. Crossing the yard, he wandered over to the corral, where a half-dozen horses stood dozing in the afternoon sun, only their tails switching at an occasional fly.

In a few more hours Logan would be in Red Springs. Not long after that he'd be face to face with Matthew Jordan. He had no delusions about what his reception would be like. Not even after all these years.

Reaching into the inside pocket of his coat, he pulled free a battered envelope. The letter inside it—his only communication with the Jordan family in thirteen years—was from Hadley Jordan. The rancher's message had been brief, the words cryptic lest anyone else had chanced to read it. But no one ever had. Not even the one person Hadley had feared most would see it—Jeremy Blackstone. Logan unfolded the aging blue stationery.

Dear Logan,

Many times these past two years I have begun this letter, many times I have burned it.

I never asked for, nor even expected you to keep silent about what happened. The fact that you so obviously have proves you're more of a man at fourteen than many men three times your age. You have spared my family more pain and grief than you can know.

In return, it is you who've suffered. Your mistake was a boy's mistake. I wish there were some way to undo it. But, of course, there isn't. Matt is bitter. Olivia daily exacerbates that bitterness with a bitterness of her own. I fear what will become of him.

Just know that I don't hold you to blame for any of it and never will. Take care,

Hadley

Logan tucked the letter safely back into his pocket. Could even Hadley Jordan have known the impact his unexpected compassion would have on its recipient? Until it had arrived, Logan had been consumed by guilt, a guilt he couldn't share with anyone. After the letter, he'd made peace with himself, gone on with his life. That he'd never heard from Hadley again made him certain Matt had not gone on with his.

Logan twisted a hand around the top rail of the corral, the rough wood spinning memories of a city boy's dream before it had become the stuff of nightmares. He recalled the June day spent trying to lasso Matt's ever-patient pony, Jingles, in the Circle J corral. From tossing the rope until well past dusk, Logan's hands had become blistered and had bled. But the next day he'd been out there to do it again.

For three months he and Matt had hunted and fished, pretended to track murderous outlaws, even sliced open their palms to press them together—blood brothers forever.

"Dammit, Matt," Logan murmured, tracing the faint scar still visible on his palm, "it didn't have to end the way it did." Logan's own sheltered existence had led him to make a hero of Matt from the instant they met, to be in awe of Matt's devil-may-care attitude toward life. Even when Matt's recklessness too often landed both boys in hot water with Hadley Jordan, Logan had rarely held his friend accountable.

Logan grimaced. Except for the time Matt had accidentally shot one of Hadley's best mares thinking it was a deer. Matt had concocted an outrageous tale of how they'd had to put the horse out of its misery because it had been snake-bit, even going so far as to kill a rattler and place it beside the dead horse.

"We can't lie to your pa," Logan had said. "It isn't right."

"If we tell him the truth," Matt had reasoned desperately, "then I won't get that big Appaloosa Pa promised me this fall when roundup's over. I'm tired of riding a pony."

With extreme reluctance, Logan had gone along with Matt's story, wincing at the disappointment in Hadley Jordan's eyes. The man hadn't been fooled for a minute; he knew the horse had not been bitten. But it was the lying more than the accident that had disappointed the sometimes formidable, but always fair, rancher. He forbade either boy to go hunting for the remainder of Logan's visit. And he told Matt a boy who lies doesn't deserve to ride like a man.

Logan closed his eyes, shutting his mind to what happened those final days at the Circle J, but unable to shut out the memory of Matt's agonized screams when the doctor told him he would lose his leg.

With an oath, Logan stepped away from the corral and headed back toward the house. It was time to be moving on, time to face his past, face Matt. Jessup should be ready to head out. Logan reached the door, raising a hand toward the latch.

Inside the house, a woman screamed. Startled, Logan slammed open the door, only to find himself looking down the barrel of a Colt .45.

"We been waitin' for you, mister," Yerby said, thumbing back the hammer on the six-gun. "Come on in; join the party. It's the same for you as I told these folks. Don't do nothin' stupid, and maybe you won't get hurt."

Logan swore inwardly. He should have tried to find out

41

what was happening, instead of bolting inside like a green fool.

Across the room, Lorraine Henderson was kneeling beside her husband, the children huddled around them both, wide-eyed and silent. A cut along the back of Henderson's head bled freely, where Yerby had likely clipped him with the pistol butt.

"He tried somethin' stupid," Yerby said.

Mrs. Vincent and Chastity sat transfixed at their places at the table. Farley Jessup stood just to the left of the Hendersons, his hands in the air.

Logan took it all in in an instant, assessing his chances, then raised his own hands, being careful to make no threatening gesture with his cane as the stocky thief stepped closer. Quickly Yerby patted down his clothes.

"Nothin', Doakes," he snorted. "Not even a hide-out gun." He dug eagerly into Logan's vest pocket. "But lookit this! One damned purty watch, huh?" He held the gold watch up to his ear. "Ticks real good, too." Poking the Colt into Logan's ribs, he growled, "What else ya got?"

"Take anything you want," Logan said. "Just don't shoot me, please." He thought the quaver in his voice was a nice touch. Mrs. Vincent's disdainful look told him he'd been successful. Chastity looked crushingly disappointed.

Yerby snorted, guffawing loudly. "So much for your big *hee-roh*, ladies." The man sneered and stepped over to Leona and her daughter. "Your fancy Dan is shaking in them fancy boots of his like to bring the house down." He cast a glance back toward Logan. "These little ladies were almighty sure you were going to swoop in here and rescue 'em. What was it you said, missy?" He lifted Chastity's

42

chin with the barrel of his gun.

"N-n-nothing!" she sobbed.

"Oh, but I recollect it real good," Yerby said. "You were tellin' me and Doakes that this dandy was gonna chew us up like vermin. That was it, wasn't it? Me and Doakes was vermin."

"N-no, no," Chastity choked, "I didn't mean . . . I . . ."

"Oh, now, missy, there's no need to get all scared. Me and Doakes would never hurt a purty thing like you." Yerby gestured toward Doakes, who was guarding the Hendersons and Jessup. "We wouldn't hurt her, would we, Doakes?"

"Naw, we got lotsa better ideas fer such a sweet thing."

"You're gonna get a chance to watch real men, Blackstone," Yerby leered. "Make you wish you never left home. Make you in a real hurry to get back there, I'll bet." He rubbed the gun's barrel along the trembling girl's jawline.

Logan's hand tightened imperceptibly on the shaft of his cane, waiting.

"Leave the girl be," Jessup hissed.

Doakes whirled, slamming his gun butt into Jessup's midsection. The stage driver grunted and collapsed to his knees.

Paul wailed. His sisters joined in.

"Shut those brats up," Yerby gritted out. "Or I'll do it for you."

Mrs. Henderson began to sob.

Logan saw his chance. With the cane in his left hand, he twisted the gold lion's head with his right. In one fluid motion he pulled it free of its shaft, revealing the tempered steel of a three-foot-long rapier.

"What the hell . . . ?" Doakes yelled.

But Yerby had no time to react before Logan was across the room. With a lightning movement he slashed at the outlaw's gun arm. Yerby yelped in pained surprise, blood spurting from the path the rapier had sliced across his arm. The Colt dropped free of his now useless hand.

Even before the gun hit the floor, Logan wheeled, disarming Doakes with the same slashing movement.

Jessup immediately pounced on both guns, leveling one at the outlaws and stuffing the other into the waistband of his pants. To Logan he hooted, "Never seen nothin' like that in all my days, mister."

"Just keep an eye on them," Logan said, hurrying over to Mrs. Henderson. Quickly he checked the wound on her husband's head. "It's not too bad," he reassured her. "Do you have some clean cloths I could use for a bandage?"

"Of course," she said, dabbing at her tears with the hem of her apron. Before she moved away, she caught Logan's wrist. "I want to thank you—"

"If you could get those bandages . . ." he prompted.

"Of course." The woman rose and hurried off, her children trailing after her like ducklings.

"Mr. Blackstone," Leona Vincent called quietly from where she still sat hugging her sobbing daughter. "We'd also like to thank you."

"I'm glad I could help," he said. "Is your daughter all right?"

Leona nodded. "But I'd hate to think what would've happened if—"

"Then don't think of it," Logan said, accepting the cloths Lorraine Henderson handed him. Working swiftly he cleaned and dressed Doug Henderson's wound,

44

vaguely aware that Farley Jessup was gathering up a couple of lengths of rope and tying up Yerby and Doakes.

"We'll deliver these two owlhoots to Sheriff Fletcher in Red Springs," Jessup said. "Toby will see to it that they don't bother no one else for a long time."

Logan stood, striding over to the two trussed-up thieves. Doakes's wound was superficial, but Yerby was still bleeding freely and the outlaw looked pale under the layer of grime that covered his face.

"I should just let you bleed until you run dry," Logan said. "But I guess it's not my day to let that happen." He turned to Lorraine Henderson. "Do you have a needle and thread, ma'am?"

The woman brought it to him.

Logan used a knife to cut away the wounded man's shirtsleeve. He then picked up a bottle of whiskey he found on the counter.

Yerby's eyes widened. "You're not gonna waste . . ." The outlaw's words skewed into a string of profanities as Logan poured the whiskey on the open wound.

"Mr. Yerby! There are children present," Lorraine Henderson scolded.

When Yerby wouldn't stop, Logan gagged him. He then took up the needle and thread, dipped them into the whiskey he'd poured into a bowl, and began to work on sewing together the two edges of flesh.

The Henderson children gathered around and watched in wide-eyed fascination. "Can you show me how to do that, mister?" Tom demanded eagerly.

"Maybe someday."

Jessup whistled his admiration. "You a doctor, mister?"

Logan hesitated only a moment before quietly

replying. "No."

"Well, I seen me plenty of sawbones who done worse." The stage driver offered Yerby's gun to Logan, butt first. "Keep your eye on 'em, will ya. I want to go out and check the team. Then we'll be headin' out."

Logan didn't take the gun. "They aren't going anywhere."

The driver shrugged and left.

Fifteen minutes later, he returned to tell the passengers the stage was ready to go.

Chastity Vincent rose with her mother, but she didn't follow Leona outside. Instead she lingered, waiting for Logan who was escorting the two prisoners to the coach.

"You saved my life, Mr. Blackstone," she said. "I can't thank you enough."

"You don't have to."

"Oh, but I want to. Please, you simply must let me make dinner for you while you're in Red Springs."

"That isn't necessary," Logan said.

"It would be my pleasure, Mr. Blackstone."

"Logan."

The girl beamed. "Logan. Please, say you'll come. Folks say I make the finest peach cobbler in all of Texas."

"We'll see," he said, keeping his eyes on Yerby and Doakes as they climbed into the stage. Leona and Chastity followed warily, sitting on the opposite seat. Logan could tell both women were still terrified.

"Not much room in there now, Blackstone," Jessup said. "You could ride up top with me."

Logan knew it was considered an honor to be invited to ride in the driver's boot. "I appreciate the offer, Jessup," he said. "But I doubt the ladies would be too comfortable in the coach with two outlaws."

46

"I guess you're right." The grizzled driver stuck out his hand, which Logan accepted. "You may look like a tenderfoot, but let me tell ya, you could ride the river with me anytime."

Logan's smile was genuine. "Thank you."

"Whereabouts in Red Springs you headed anyway?" the driver asked, as he clambered up to his perch.

"The Circle J."

"Gonna buy 'em out now that Hadley's dead?"

Logan hedged, unwilling to discuss the Jordans' financial difficulties. "I don't know."

"Hadley was a good man. Two women and a cripple can't keep the place up."

Logan winced inwardly at the reference to Matt. "Maybe I can do the whole family a favor. Give them a chance to set things in order so they can move into town, get on with their lives."

Jessup chuckled.

"Something funny about that?"

"No," the driver said. "Just tryin' to picture Cat Jordan livin' in town."

"Cat?" He frowned, puzzled.

"Hadley's daughter. Or at least I *think* she's female."

Logan's frown deepened. "You don't mean Cordelia? The Jordans' little girl?"

Jessup slapped his knee, chortling. "I can't picture that wildcat ever bein' a little girl. And God help the man that calls her Cordelia. Cat—" he shook his head— "hellcat would be more like it. You try to buy up the Circle J, you'd best be on the lookout for some damned sharp claws."

47

Chapter Three

The stage was late.

Cat stalked the length and breadth of the small Butterfield office and fumed. Late! Of all the days for Farley Jessup to be behind schedule, why did it have to be today?

"What kind of operation are you running here, Cyrus?" she grumbled, piercing the bespectacled ticket agent with yet another killing glare. "If Butterfield can't get their stages here on time, maybe Red Springs should bring in a company that can."

"See here, Miss Jordan," Cyrus Winslow huffed from behind his glassed-in counter, "I don't think you should cast asperions on the entire Butterfield stage company because one coach is late. We keep a very tight schedule, and I find—"

"Bah!" Cat stomped over to the bulletin board where the timetable was posted. "Four P.M." She jabbed the paper with her index finger. "According to your *tight* schedule. But if you'll notice that clock above your head"—she made a sweeping gesture toward the back wall—"the big hand is on the three and the little hand is on the six. What does that tell you?"

"That it's past your supper time?" The lazy drawl intruded through the door opening behind her. "I hear cats get real testy when they don't get fed."

Cat whirled, prepared to dress down this new wiseacre, but chagrin instantly became delight. With a shriek of joy, she bounded across the room and threw herself into the wide-stretched arms of Sheriff Toby Fletcher.

The barrel-chested lawman spun her around twice before setting her back on her feet.

"I'll take me a welcome-home like that anytime," the sheriff said.

"Your deputy said you were out of town," Cat responded, grinning. "If I'd known you were back, I wouldn't have been cooling my heels in this place."

"I only rode in about an hour ago." He doffed his Stetson long enough to run a hand through chestnut hair graying at the temples. "And I spent most of that hour peelin' trail dust off'n me over at Maude Dancey's boardinghouse."

"Was Maude helping with the peeling?" Cat giggled.

Fletcher gave her a friendly swat on the behind as he followed her over to the row of straight-back chairs lining the bay front window. "Your pa would have your hide for that kinda talk."

"He'd have said it first!"

Fletcher laughed, tiny lines crinkling around gray-green eyes. "I suppose he would." He leaned back, his expression growing more serious. "I miss him, Cat. He was one helluva man."

She managed a wan smile. "I know." Shaking off a surge of melancholy, she gave the sheriff a friendly poke in the arm. "So, where've you been anyway? Gallivant-ing around on taxpayers' money?"

Fletcher looked away.

"What is it, Toby?"

"I went to the county seat."

Cat's brows furrowed in confusion. "Is that supposed to mean something to me?"

"I went to Barney Jackson's hanging."

"What?" she cried. "I thought that snake was supposed to hang weeks ago!" The outlaw had been convicted of rustling Circle J beef, and of killing line-rider Tod Hughes. Her father had found the seventeen-year-old ranch hand with a bullet in his back, six feet from where Jackson was skinning a Circle J carcass.

"Jackson's lawyer tried to raise a stink after your pa died," Fletcher said. "Something about an appeal not being fair with a key witness dead. For a while I thought he was going to get the verdict overturned."

"Pa's death might have gotten Jackson off? Why didn't I know about any of this?"

Fletcher shifted uncomfortably.

"Toby," she said slowly, her imagination leapfrogging ahead of reason. "What else haven't you been telling me?"

"Nothing," he said too quickly. Glancing toward the back wall, he rose abruptly. "Look at that time, will you?"

"Toby, for God's sake," Cat said, a nameless fear clutching at her insides. "Talk to me."

The lawman stared at the floor. "I'm doin' this all wrong, Cat. I'm sorry. I shouldn't have said anything."

"It's too late for that now."

"Maybe I'd best talk to Matt. He is the man of the house."

Cat bristled. "If this has to do with my father's death, you tell *me* now."

Fletcher tipped his hat back, shaking his head in consternation. "It's probably nothing. But Jackson said something to me before they led him up to the gallows, something that when I piece it together with . . ." He stopped, his gaze flicking to Cyrus Winslow, who seemed to be absorbed in his ledger books behind the counter. "I have rounds to make. Stop by the office after your stage comes in, we'll talk. All right?"

"Why can't you just tell me now? I—" She followed his gaze to Cyrus and understood. Whatever it was, Toby didn't want anyone else to hear. "I'll be there as soon as the stage arrives."

Toby nodded and started toward the door. "Who are you meeting on the stage anyway?"

"The polecat who owns the note on the Circle J."

"He's going to foreclose on you?"

"He's going to try," she said, "but I'll be damned if he's going to get away with it."

"Now, Cat," Toby cautioned, "you're not thinkin' of doin' anything . . . illegal to persuade this gentleman, are you? I'd hate to have to get involved in this on a professional basis."

"I'm not going to put a gun to his head, if that's what you're suggesting, Tobe," Cat grumbled. "Although, the thought does hold a certain appeal—"

"Cat Jordan."

"I won't shoot him, all right?" she snapped.

The door burst open, a wild-eyed cowboy Cat didn't recognize rushing through it and over to Fletcher. "You gotta come, Sheriff," the man said. "Latigo's bustin' up the Double Eagle again."

The name Cat recognized. Rafe Latigo was Ryan

Fielding's foreman at the Rocking R.

"Can't that hardcase ever learn to hold his liquor?" Fletcher groused. Bidding a hasty good-bye to Cat, he followed the cowboy out the door.

Cat didn't like having to wait to pursue her conversation with Fletcher. But he'd given her no choice. She tried sitting down again, but any patience she may have had was gone. Besides, she supposed she'd terrorized poor Cyrus long enough. Maybe some fresh air would help her mood.

Outside, the sun was dipping westward, but the temperature still hovered near ninety. Wiping the sweat from her face with her shirtsleeve, Cat started toward the Double Eagle. What she wanted was a cold beer, but in this heat it might go to her head. She would settle for a sarsaparilla.

A quick glance up the street told her there was still no sign of the stage. What if they'd had an accident? What if they'd been robbed? Logan Blackstone could have been kidnapped. Maybe he was even now being held for ransom.

She'd save him! Jeremy Blackstone would be eternally grateful, forgive the Jordan loan, and then . . .

Saints alive! Where was this fantasy coming from? Maybe she would have that beer. She needed to calm her jangling nerves. Her dealings with Blackstone would be straightforward, strictly business. Neither family's past history need be involved. She would request a simple extension until the herd was sold this fall.

Walking briskly, she continued toward the saloon. As she passed the bank, the door opened, a huffing Abner Vincent all but barreling into her.

"I beg your pardon, madam," the portly man

blustered, his gaze skating past her up the street. "I was in a rush, I . . ." He redirected his gaze, peering at her over the wire rims of his spectacles. "Oh, it's you, Miss Jordan."

She wondered if he was going to take back his apology. Heaven knew she had little use for the man. It was Vincent's refusal to extend her father's note last fall that had forced her father to approach the Blackstones.

"What's the rush, Mr. Vincent?" she asked coldly. "You have a chance to foreclose on an orphanage?"

"Such a delightful sense of humor," the man said, wrinkling his nose. "Just like your father."

"I consider that a high compliment. Thank you."

"Then I withdraw it." His gaze again traveled past her as he nervously smoothed a hand over what little hair remained atop his balding pate. "You haven't seen the four o'clock stage, have you?"

"As a matter of fact, I'm waiting for it myself." She frowned at the look of real concern creasing the man's high forehead. "Is something wrong?" She wondered that she should even care.

"My dear wife and lovely daughter were due back this morning," he said, reaching into his pocket to extract a silk handkerchief, then using it to pat at the rivulets of sweat seeping into the starched white collar of his shirt. "A rider came in awhile ago saying the stage threw a wheel and the passengers had been rerouted to this afternoon's coach. But it hasn't arrived either."

"I'm sure it will be along anytime," Cat said.

He tucked the handkerchief back into his pocket. "I do hope so."

"No more than I do, Mr. Vincent."

He assumed a look of such feigned sympathy that Cat

53

almost laughed. "You must know I'm sorry about all your troubles, Miss Jordan," he said. "But at least you'll be getting all that nasty business settled. You and your lovely family can then get on with your lives."

"And what would you know about my business, Mr. Vincent?"

"Oh, my dear," he said, as though he were talking to a dull-witted child, "I'm certainly aware of your father's financial difficulties. And as a banker, when a ranch the size of the Circle J comes up for sale—"

"The Circle J is not for sale!" she snapped.

"I doubt the note holder will see it that way. Your father should have given up last fall. I told him it was foolhardy—"

"I'm sure you told him quite a few things, Mr. Vincent," Cat said. "Now I'm telling you—the Circle J is my ranch and it's going to stay my ranch. You mark my words."

She stomped off, leaving the pompous oaf to tut-tut about her foolhardiness all he liked—to himself. It took several angry strides before she could again slow down to a walk.

She bypassed the first saloon—the Longhorn—when she heard its player piano tinkling a merry tune. She was not feeling in the least merry. Yet all around her Red Springs burst with the energy of a thriving community. Hammer clanged against anvil in the blacksmith's shop, the aroma of baking bread drifted out the open door of Pritchard's Cafe. Buckboards and lone riders clattered past in the street.

All up and down the main street she saw and heard the pulse beat of the town. A hotel, a boardinghouse, the mercantile, several saloons, a church, and school made

54

up most of the business section, with single family dwellings lining the town's outlying streets. She had always loved to visit here—with her father to pick up supplies, or with the men whooping it up on payday. But she couldn't imagine living here, couldn't imagine living anywhere but on the wide-open range of the Circle J.

City life was no life for Cat Jordan.

She reached the batwing doors of the Double Eagle just in time to watch several men carrying out a bloodied body. Toby Fletcher brought up the rear of the grim procession.

"Latigo cut him up pretty bad," Fletcher told her, "but he'll live. They're takin' him to Doc Sanderson's."

"Did you arrest Latigo?" Cat asked, peering past Fletcher into the saloon's murky interior.

"I've talked to every manjack in the place. Every one of 'em says it was a fair fight."

"You don't look convinced."

"There's not much I can do without witnesses."

"Where's Latigo now?"

"I told him to get back to the Rocking R and sober up. I may not be able to put him in jail, but I can send him the hell out of town." Fletcher blew out a disgusted breath. "I don't know why Ryan Fielding keeps that no-account on his payroll. You'd think a big rancher like that would have more sense."

"Ryan says he's a good foreman." Cat had her doubts on that score, but it wasn't her business to question Ryan's choice of hired hands.

"I'm going to head up to Doc's, see how that fella's doin'," Fletcher said. "Meet you at my office . . . say half an hour?"

"Fine." She felt nervous all over again, wondering

55

what Fletcher was going to tell her. But the street was no more of a place to press him for information than the stage office had been.

"Still no stage?" he asked, frowning.

"No sign of it," Cat said. "But I'll wait all night if I have to."

"I may have to send a posse out lookin' for it before then," Fletcher said.

"Then I'll ride along."

"The only thing you're going to do is be in my office in half an hour."

She nodded, then watched as the lawman disappeared down the street toward Sanderson's place. As she turned to head into the saloon, an odd lurching movement caught from the corner of her eye snagged her attention. A buckskin-clad man was stumbling out of the Lady Luck saloon across the street.

Latigo.

Obviously, he'd taken a wrong turn on his way out of town.

Cat waited, hoping to see him mount and ride out. The black gelding at the hitchrail rolled its eyes and tried to back away at Latigo's approach. Latigo caught the reins and yanked hard, seeking to jerk the horse closer. Stumbling again, he made a grab at the saddlehorn and missed.

Cat started across the street.

Latigo shoved his left hand tight against the horse's mouth, twisting the bit until the horse whinnied in pain. Cat ran.

Her stomach turned at the jangle of spurs on the man's boots—big Mexican spurs with rowels the size of a man's fist, one of which had a point missing. Cat was close enough now to see the scars on the gelding's flanks and barrel. Her lips thinned as she imagined the spur point still imbedded in the horse's flesh.

The gelding reared. Cat launched herself at the man. Throwing herself body-long against his arm, they both slammed into the terrified gelding. The horse tore free of Latigo's grip and thundered down the street.

Latigo turned on Cat, the rage he'd loosed on the horse now totally focused on her. His dark eyes burned black, the beard stubbling his cheeks making his swarthy features seem darker still, sinister, cruel.

Cat took an unconscious step back, barely noting the sudden dust cloud swirling around her. The stage was arriving.

Latigo caught her arm. She tried vainly to twist away. "Leave me be, Rafe," she said. "The horse is gone and you're drunk."

"You owe me for that, bitch. Maybe I'll get me some." He caught her in a revolting embrace, crushing her against him.

Cat struggled, slapping, scratching. Her fingernails gouged his cheeks.

Latigo swore, viciously twisted a handful of her hair. Involuntary tears stung Cat's eyes. She tried to kick out, but she was off balance. Latigo raised his fist. She closed her eyes, expecting the blow.

It didn't come.

She opened her eyes to see Latigo's wrist manacled in a grip of steel. A man dressed in black held the drunken foreman immobile.

"Let me go!" Latigo yelled.

Cat stared at hard gray eyes and heard a voice that matched. "I think you'd better apologize to the lady."

"And I think you'd better mind your own business."

"What's going on here?" another voice demanded.

Cat turned to see Rocking R owner, Ryan Fielding, striding toward them.

"Your foreman was abusing his horse," Cat said, her censure meant as much for the man who had hired an hombre like Latigo as it was for Latigo himself.

Ryan straightened, glaring at Latigo. "I am getting damned tired of your inability to hold your liquor, Rafe. I just had a run-in with the sheriff about you, and now I find this." He jabbed a finger at Latigo for emphasis. "One more brush with the law and you're through at the Rocking R, you hear me?"

"Yes, sir." His voice was sullen.

"Go to the hotel and get cleaned up," Ryan continued, "and don't bother to come back to the ranch until you're sober."

Latigo lumbered off, grumbling obscenities under his breath.

"I'm sorry," Ryan said, speaking to Cat. "He really is a good foreman, when he isn't drunk."

Cat slapped at the dust on her shirt, saying nothing.

"Did he hurt you?" Ryan asked.

"I'm fine." She didn't want to discuss it any further. She was painfully conscious of gray eyes boring into her back. "Maybe you should follow him, make sure he doesn't draw any more blood today."

With apparent reluctance Ryan acquiesced. He tipped his hat, flung a curious glance toward her rescuer, then headed after his foreman.

Cat turned toward the gray-eyed stranger and jutted her chin forward. She was determined not to seem foolish for having attacked a drunken cowboy. "I suppose you expect me to thank you."

"Most people might," he said.

"I'm not most people."

He allowed a slow smile. "I can see that."

She bristled, slapping at more dirt on her shirt and pants. "Well, thank you."

"You're welcome."

He flashed her a thoroughly enchanting grin, and she was unaccountably warmed by it. She gave herself a mental shake. The man was dressed like some dandified prince, and was no doubt secretly looking down his royal nose at her. "You'll have to excuse me," she said, suddenly recalling that she'd almost been run down by the stage. "I've got me a polecat to meet."

Spotting Farley Jessup, who was heading toward the Lady Luck, she hollered out to him. "Farley, I'm lookin' for one of your passengers. A skunk named Logan Blackstone."

Farley hooted wildly.

Cat stamped her foot. "Well, did he come in on the stage or not?"

"Yup."

She planted her hands on her hips. "So where the hell is he?"

"You're standing next to him."

Heat fired in her cheeks and an unaccountable fury seized her. She turned, fully expecting to face the man's wrath. He was chuckling.

"Which was closer?" Logan asked. "Polecat or skunk?"

Her lips thinned. "They're the same thing actually."

His eyes sobered. "I take it you're from the Circle J."

She thought of offering the man her hand, but decided

59

against it. "Cat Jordan."

He started. "Corie?"

No one had called her that for a very long time. Years ago her father had tagged her with Cat for her boundless curiosity. Corie triggered a memory, just out of reach, memories dusted with shadows . . .

But Blackstone gave her no time to think. He was all business. She shook herself, listening.

"I take it you're to escort me to the ranch?" he asked, then went on speaking, allowing her no time to answer. "Lead me to your carriage. I want to get this business with Matt over with as soon as possible."

"What business with Matt?" she asked, confused. The man's whole demeanor had taken her off guard. He looked exactly like the milksop accountant she had conjured up that morning, yet his every move, every action, belied his dandified appearance.

"The ranch," Logan supplied. "The loan."

"You're not dealing with Matt on that," she responded indignantly. "You're dealing with me."

"What are you talking about?"

"I mean my father left controlling interest of the Circle J to me."

This bit of news clearly surprised him.

"I'll still want to travel out to the ranch, Miss Jordan."

She bit the inside of her lip, oddly hurt by the distance he'd just put between them by addressing her formally. And then it struck her. She had expected to hate this man. She was *supposed* to hate this man, as her mother and brother so virulently did. Yet she had never been able to fully accept their reasoning. True, Matt's life had been irreversibly altered by the loss of his leg, but he hadn't lost his life. He'd given that up of his own accord.

60

No, she wasn't sure what it was she was feeling toward Logan Blackstone just now. But it definitely wasn't hate.

Still the thought of what her mother's reaction would be if she brought the man out to the ranch—even though Olivia fully expected her to do so—prompted Cat to try again to dissuade him. "I really think we can settle everything here in Red Springs. I have all the papers. We could go to the cafe, have something to eat—"

"I'm sorry, Miss Jordan, but I'm going to have to talk to your brother."

Cat's nervousness vanished, her pride rankling. "There is nothing you can learn about the Circle J from Matt that I can't tell you."

"I'm sure that's true," he said. "But I didn't come all this way not to see your brother."

Cat started to protest, then stopped. Though she knew the likely outcome of such a meeting, she had to admire Blackstone's determination to face Matt.

Instead she said, "It's too late tonight. We wouldn't be able to make it back to the ranch until well after nightfall."

"I don't mind, if you don't."

Actually she did. She wanted to stay in town, at least overnight. Better to face her mother and Matt fresh in the morning than dead tired from an exhausting day. But she could scarcely admit that to Blackstone. "All right," she said. "We'll go. But first I have to stop by the sheriff's office."

"Lead the way," Logan said.

They made the short walk in silence, Cat quashing her churning curiosity about Blackstone, even as she refused to speculate on what Fletcher had in store for her.

The bell above the jamb jangled noisily as she opened

61

the door to Fletcher's office. The lawman rose at once to greet them, stepping from behind his small oak desk.

Cat introduced Logan, then focused her attention on Fletcher. "You said Barney Jackson told you something before they hanged him. Something that made you think about my father's death." She couldn't believe how calm her voice sounded, as though she'd just asked him to comment on the weather.

Toby nodded, obviously reluctant to repeat it, or perhaps, she guessed more rightly, reluctant because of Blackstone.

"You can talk in front of him," Cat said, gesturing to Logan. "He can't know anything. He's from Boston."

Logan snorted, though his eyes sparked with a genuine humor that again made Cat unaccountably warm. Only then did she realize her choice of words had been less than flattering. She grimaced. "Get on with it, Toby. Please."

"It wasn't so much what Jackson said—"

"Blast it, Toby!" Cat snapped, her façade of feigned control crumbling more with each passing second. "What did he say?"

"He said he found it real interesting that your father didn't live to see him hang."

"Jackson was a vile, lowlife piece of scum," Cat gritted out. "What would you expect him to say?" She put her hands on her hips. "Now if that's all . . ." But it wasn't. She had known it wasn't. Her heart thudded as she watched Fletcher go behind his desk and open the locked lower drawer on the left. He pulled out a walnut-handled Navy Colt.

"That's my father's gun," Cat said, crossing the room in two strides. Until this minute she hadn't even realized it was missing. She'd just presumed Dusty had taken possession of it as she'd asked.

"Dusty brought it to me," Fletcher said.

"Who's Dusty?" Logan asked.

"My foreman," Cat said, irritated to be sidetracked.

"Would that be Dusty *Yates?*"

Cat frowned. "How did you know?"

"He was there the last time I . . . visited."

Cat didn't miss the ironic inflection on the word *visited.* Why hadn't she made the connection before? Of course, Logan would know Dusty. Dusty had been with the Circle J almost since the day her father had rounded up his first steer. He had certainly been there fifteen years ago. But, like her father, Dusty had never spoken of that time.

"Why would Dusty bring you my father's gun?" Cat asked. "And why wouldn't he tell me he'd brought it to you?"

"First and foremost, he didn't want to upset you, especially if there was no reason."

"Toby," she said slowly, carefully, "why did he bring you my father's gun?"

"He said there was something about it that bothered him. He found it in your father's holster the day he found Hadley's"—he'd stumbled over the word *body*, Cat was certain—"found him."

"And . . . ?" Cat prodded, though her every instinct pleaded with her not to ask.

"There were three spent cartridges in it."

"So?" Logan asked.

"So," the sheriff said, "according to Dusty, Hadley Jordan always reloaded his pistol the instant he had a chance. He would never have been riding with three spent shells in a holstered gun."

"It doesn't mean a thing," Cat said, failing miserably in convincing even herself. "My father must have taken a shot at something before he died. A rabbit, a snake." She couldn't seem to stop trembling. She had to fight the overwhelming urge to bolt out the door.

"Maybe not some*thing*," Fletcher said gently. "Maybe some*one*."

Cat's mind screamed a denial, even as Logan Blackstone said the words.

"Sheriff," Logan asked, "are you suggesting Hadley Jordan was murdered?"

Chapter Four

Murdered. The word hung in the silence of Toby Fletcher's office. Her father murdered? Cat couldn't breathe as she waited for the lawman to respond to Blackstone's question. When Fletcher did, he seemed to weigh each word with extreme care.

"When Dusty first told me of his suspicions," he said, "I dismissed them completely. I figured he was upset over the death of a man who'd been his boss and his friend for nearly twenty years."

"And now?" Cat asked shakily.

"Now I don't know, Cat," the lawman admitted. "I just don't know." He stepped around his desk and returned Hadley's gun to the lower drawer. He sat there for long seconds afterward, thrumming his fingers on the desktop, debating, Cat was certain, whether to say anything further.

It was Logan Blackstone who pressed the issue. "You didn't think much of the three missing cartridges," he said. "And a convicted murderer would seem just the type to be happy the man who sent him to the gallows is dead."

"There's more, isn't there?" Cat prompted.

Fletcher sighed, reaching into the desk drawer to extract a folded sheet of paper. "This was on my desk, when I got back here ten minutes ago."

With trembling fingers, Cat unfolded it. On the paper was a scrawled letter J with a circle around it. "It's our brand," she said, confused. In the center of the brand a slit had been made.

Fletcher pointed to a deep gouge in his desktop. Then he pulled yet another object from the bottom drawer. It was a dried rattle from a rattlesnake. He also pulled out a six-inch ivory-handled dagger.

Cat watched, fascinated, as Fletcher placed the paper on the desk atop the gouge, then set the rattle on top of the scrawled Circle J. She jumped, startled, when Fletcher took the knife and plunged it through both. "This is how I found it," he said.

"And you think it's some kind of warning," Logan said.

"A warning or a threat," Toby said.

"But why?" Cat demanded. "Why would anyone kill my father? Why would anyone threaten the Circle J?"

"I don't know," Fletcher said. "That's why I wanted to talk to you. Has anything unusual happened out at your place since your pa died? Any accidents? Anything?"

Cat shook her head, unable to take her eyes off of the dagger. "Should I be expecting something to happen?"

Fletcher shook his head. "I don't know, Cat. I honestly don't know. None of this makes any sense to me. Jackson was a two-bit cattle rustler, who'd been in and out of prison since he was fifteen. I can't imagine he'd have anyone loyal enough to him to be making threats now that both he and your father are dead." He jerked the knife free and put it, the rattle, and the paper back into his desk. "I wanted you to know. I wanted you to be careful."

She nodded, more confused than ever. If her father truly was murdered, then his murderer was out there somewhere, free. "You have to find out more, Toby," she said. "If my father's death wasn't an accident, I want the person responsible standing on the same gallows that put an end to Barney Jackson."

"I'll do everything I can," Fletcher said. "You know that. But you be careful."

"I will," she promised. She turned to Blackstone, her voice as subdued as her spirit. "We'd best get going."

"Are you all right?" Logan asked. "We can stay in town if you like."

"I appreciate that," she said, and meant it. "But you want to see my brother. And there's no sense putting it off."

Logan straightened. "No, no sense putting it off."

Cat headed for the door, Logan following. She wasn't going to think about this anymore, not tonight. Maybe someone was trying to scare her off the Circle J, but surely it had nothing to do with her father's death. Some vulture saw his chance and wanted the Circle J for himself. It was absurd to think her father had been murdered. She would talk to Dusty when she got home and it would be straightened out. Dusty didn't want to believe her father had carelessly forgotten to reload his gun, but Cat knew that Hadley had had much on his mind that day.

Outside, she headed toward the livery stable, Blackstone falling in step beside her.

"Was there some trouble with the stage?" she asked, hoping the small talk would soothe her fraying nerves.

"There was a little delay at the Henderson relay station," Logan said.

"Horse throw a shoe?"

"Not exactly."

They arrived at Robinson's Livery only to find that the hostler had shut down for a late dinner. The sign he'd left said he would be back at seven-thirty.

"Twenty minutes," Logan said, flipping open the gold watch he'd extracted from the pocket of his brocade vest.

Cat stalked over to sit on a bale of hay butted up against the barn. Blackstone surprised her by doing the same, his right leg barely inches from her left. She cleared her throat self-consciously. "Did you . . . have a nice trip?"

"It was fine."

Cat ground her teeth together. The man was a veritable chatterbox. Couldn't he guess how nervous she was? Couldn't he make more of an effort to keep the conversation light, innocuous? She watched him angle his cane against the hay bale, then settle his derby hat atop the leonine head. Long fingers brushed at a mane of dark hair, but several strands spilled back across his forehead.

Cat stared at him, her heart seeming to skip a beat. She felt as though she were spinning back through time, odd jolts of memory sparking through her. The musty scent of fresh hay, the stamp of a horse's hoof, a young boy sobbing . . . She stepped toward him, toward him. . . .

"Corie? Miss Jordan?"

She felt the less than gentle shake on her arm, felt the triphammer beat of her own heart thundering in her chest, and became aware of the clammy feel of sweat that

68

had nothing to do with the day's temperature. Only then did she sense the urgency in Logan Blackstone's voice. She stared at him, a man's face, not a boy's. A handsome face with slate gray eyes now narrowed with fierce concern. "What is it?" she murmured.

"What is it?" he demanded. "I thought you were going to faint."

"Faint?" she snapped. "I never faint."

"You could have fooled me."

She drew in a long, shuddering breath. "I . . . I was merely thinking of something that happened once. It was nothing."

He didn't seem convinced, but he let the subject drop.

"Are you glad to be back in Texas?" Her attempt at banality failed utterly. She could have bitten off her tongue. The man was not here on a holiday! Nor would his previous visit exactly evoke fond remembrances.

He deflected the question by asking one of his own. "How's your mother?"

So much for light and innocuous. "My mother isn't . . . I mean, she doesn't . . . she . . ." Oh, blast, what could she say?

"Your mother isn't too happy at the prospect of seeing me," Logan supplied dryly.

"Look, I don't pretend to understand all of this, but"—she looked at the ground—"I'm sorry."

"It's none of your doing."

Cat slapped a hand on the bale in frustration. "I think we should just be on our way. I have my mare up the street. You could take the bay in the corral."

"I prefer a buggy."

"Why doesn't that surprise me?" she muttered under her breath. At least in the buggy she supposed she would have a better chance of bringing up her proposal for the extension.

"Logan!" a feminine voice called. "Logan, I've been looking all over for you. I thought I'd missed you."

Cat felt her hackles rise as Chastity Vincent flounced up to them, dressed exquisitely, this time in a tiered yellow taffeta that somehow managed to look crisp and fresh in spite of the sweltering heat. Couldn't the girl at least have the decency to sweat?

"Thank heavens I caught up with you," Chastity gasped breathlessly. "You're not leaving already, are you?"

"I have business outside of town."

"Circle J business," Cat put in.

Chastity looked at Cat, only grudgingly acknowledging her presence. "Oh, yes," the ebony-haired beauty clucked with exaggerated sympathy. "My father mentioned something about it."

"I'll just bet he did," Cat ground out. "But maybe it isn't going to turn out the way he thinks."

Chastity appeared totally disinterested. She turned to Logan. "I just wanted to remind you of that dinner I promised you." She insinuated herself on the hay bale between Cat and Logan, half of her rear end finding a perch on Cat's left thigh. Clenching her teeth, Cat jerked herself free and stood up. Chastity smiled, hooking her arm around Logan's.

"He was so brave, Cordelia." Chastity sighed. "He fought off those two dreadful robbers single-handed."

"Robbers?" Cat looked at Logan. "The stage was robbed?"

"They tried," he said. "They didn't succeed."

"Thanks to you, Logan," Chastity purred. "Oh, when

70

I think what those horrid men might have done to me."
Huge tears formed at the corners of Chastity's blue eyes.
She dabbed at them ever so daintily with her yellow silk
hankie. "Father was so upset. He just insists that you
come to dinner, so he can thank you personally."

Cat couldn't believe the man had said nothing about
the stage being robbed. "Was anyone hurt?" she asked.

"A few bruises," Chastity said, dismissing Cat utterly.
"Isn't this heat just dreadful, Logan. Mama told me to
take my parasol, but I thought my lovely new bonnet
from Paris would do just as well." She straightened the
perfectly tied bow beneath her chin. "I would certainly
never take any chances with my delicate skin. Lord
above, I don't know what I'd do if it began to resemble
cowhide."

Cat shoved her tanned hands into the pockets of her
trousers, wishing she hadn't left her gloves in her
saddlebags. She glared at Chastity as the girl simpered
over Blackstone.

"Well, don't just stand there," Chastity said, gesturing toward Cat. "While Logan and I are chatting,
shouldn't you be getting his conveyance ready?"

"I beg your pardon?"

"Aren't you working at the stables to make a little
extra money these days?"

"I am not," Cat replied thinly, though her cheeks
burned.

"Oh, do forgive me." Chastity tittered. "I just thought
from the way you were dressed that you'd taken on the
extra work of cleaning out the stables."

For one delicious moment Cat stood there and
wondered what Chastity would look like with a bloody
nose. Yet even as she thought it, she found herself

making a half-hearted attempt to smooth her wind-tangled hair. Thankfully, Gus Robinson chose that moment to return to his livery. Cat quickly hurried up to him. Though Gus didn't ask, Cat helped him hitch up the buggy she'd hired. She didn't care what Chastity had to say about that either, only that she not be near enough to hear it.

"Ready, Mr. Blackstone?" Cat asked testily, leading the buggy horse over to the hay bale where Logan seemed to have taken root next to the prattling Chastity.

"Whenever you are," he said, rising at once.

Chastity kept her arm linked to his, as he strode over to the buggy. "Don't you forget now. Tomorrow night. And I'll make my peach cobbler just especially for you."

"I'll look forward to it," he said, extricating his arm. He held out his hand to assist Cat into the carriage.

She took great pleasure in ignoring the gesture, and clambered into the buggy by herself.

When Logan climbed in after her, Cat made the unsettling discovery that the seat in the buggy was a lot smaller than it had looked when she'd told Gus it would be fine. She was closer to Blackstone now than when they'd first sat on the hay bale. His right thigh pressed intimately against her left thigh.

"Tomorrow night. Don't forget!" Chastity called.

Logan lifted the reins.

"I should drive," Cat said.

"I can manage."

"You don't know the way." This tenderfoot was liable to send them over a cliff.

"I've driven a carriage or two."

Cat decided not to make an issue of it, and Logan clicked the chestnut gelding into motion. They headed down main street, stopping only to retrieve Logan's valise from the stage office and to tie Nugget to the back of the buggy.

"I suppose you think she's beautiful," Cat said, kicking herself the instant the words were out of her mouth. Why rub salt into a wound?

"Your horse?" Logan asked distractedly.

"Chastity," Cat snapped.

"Oh, yes, I suppose she is. It was hard to tell," he said, his lips curving into a wry grin, "with her mouth open so much of the time."

Cat blinked, not certain she'd heard him correctly. But she couldn't misread that smile. And then she was laughing, really laughing, as she hadn't done in a long, long time.

"I'm sorry," he said, when she'd quieted. "I shouldn't have said that."

"No," she agreed primly, "you shouldn't have." And then she was laughing again.

The tension between them drained away. For the next hour Cat could scarcely believe how easily she and Logan talked. About Texas, about horses, about how President Hayes was running the country. She was feeling almost giddy. Like she should pinch herself.

And then she did. She had to remember who this man was. Logan Blackstone. He had come to Texas to foreclose on the Circle J. He might be being kind to her for that very reason.

Besides, he was extremely handsome. Making idle conversation with doe-eyed females was likely second nature to him.

Doe-eyed? Had she actually referred to herself as such? As if *she* were being taken in by him? By his wit, his

73

charm, his devastating good looks.

Stop it, Cordelia Jordan, she silently chided herself. And then she *knew* she was in trouble. She *never* referred to herself as Cordelia.

"I was really sorry to hear about your father," Logan was saying. "He was a fine man. Tough but fair."

"Thank you," Cat said, seeing a chance to steer the conversation back to business. "This ranch was really his life, you know. He loved it so much. He wanted it to go on forever."

"Sometimes dreams just don't come true."

Cat's brow furrowed. There had been an undercurrent of regret in Logan's voice that went beyond her father and the Circle J. Her curiosity about this man and the boy he had been, never fully satisfied, pressed in on her.

"I know I was only four when you were here before," she said slowly. "But I remember it a little. . . ."

She felt him tense, and she hesitated. If she made him angry, he would never listen to her proposal to save the ranch. But for once, just once, she had to hear the Logan Blackstone version of what had happened that long ago night.

"Mother filled in some of it, of course," she said. "And Matt."

"And what did Matt say?"

Cat chewed her lip, trying to merge the story she'd been told all her life with the reality of this imposing male sitting next to her. Even as a boy of twelve she could not believe Logan Blackstone would have run from responsibility. "He told me that you pushed him down. By accident. You were roughhousing in the barn. Matt cut his leg on a pitchfork.

"You and Matt had just been in trouble not too long

74

before about a horse or something. So you were scared to death that my father would send you packing. You swore Matt to silence. And then the leg festered. . . ." She let her voice trail off.

Logan's hands tightened on the reins, the only outward sign that he was even listening. She didn't dare look at his face.

"I . . . I know you were only a boy. I'm sure you didn't mean for Matt ever to . . . suffer so. I mean . . ." Blast! What did she mean?

Cat dared a sideways glance at him. His earlier congeniality was gone, replaced by a stony silence. "Is that what happened, Lo— Mr. Blackstone?"

"Does that question mean you doubt your brother?"

"Actually, yes," she admitted, astonished that she would say so to this man. "You just don't seem like someone who would . . . do such a thing."

"You don't know me, Miss Jordan," he said, a new icy tone in his voice. It frightened her, because it seemed devoid of any feeling at all, even anger. "You don't know what I could have done then. Or now."

The sun was gone, and though it was still warm, Cat shivered.

"Would you like my jacket?" he asked, his concern seeming genuine, even though he was still angry.

"No," she said too quickly. "I . . . I'm not cold." But the chill persisted, brought on by the unaccountably unsettling presence of this man and by something else. She gazed off to the right in the descending darkness.

"What is it?"

"There's a prairie-dog town a half-mile west of here. That's where . . ." She stopped.

"Your father was killed," he finished.

75

She nodded.

"Do you think it was murder?"

She winced at his bluntness, yet oddly welcomed it. "I don't know. I'm going to talk to Dusty, ask him just exactly what he found that day. Obviously, he kept the business about the gun from me. I want to know if there's anything else."

"Your father was heading to town that day?"

"Yes." *He was going to write your father for an extension on the loan,* she thought, but the words caught in her throat. What if he turned her down?

No, she couldn't think that way. She had to just say it straight out. "As a matter of fact—"

A wild crashing sound distracted her, echoing from the brush on the right and followed at once by a fearsome bellow. The gelding shied violently, a huge shadow lurching across the trail bare inches ahead of the buggy. Cat felt herself being jerked forward and back, as Logan sawed back on the reins.

"What the hell was that?" Logan demanded, when he finally fought the gelding to a standstill.

"A steer," she said. "Likely a Circle J longhorn strayed off the range. He must have had a six-foot span on those horns. If he'd been a second or two later . . ." She rubbed her side, imagining that horn slicing through her flesh instead of air.

"Get out your gun," Cat hissed. "He might be back."

"I don't have a gun."

She started to climb out of the buggy, but Logan caught her arm. "What are you doing?"

"I'm going to get my rifle from my saddle."

"If he does come back, you're not going to be on foot." He gigged the horse forward, the momentum forcing her

76

to sit back down.

"This is Texas, *Mister* Blackstone. You can't be riding around without a gun."

"I've managed so far."

"I'll get you one when we get to the ranch."

He hefted his cane, twisting the head and pulling the rapier free.

She whistled softly. "Now that's something."

"I'd rather look a man in the eye if I'm going to fight him."

"That's all well and good," she allowed, "if it's men you're fighting. Loco steers are a lot harder to skewer than they are to shoot."

He chuckled, and for a moment she felt some of their earlier camaraderie returning. But it was an illusion. The tension remained in him. And when she looked ahead she knew the reason.

Four hours had passed much too swiftly. She was furious with herself for not asking him about the extension. And now it was too late.

In the moonlight she could see the outbuildings of the Circle J.

Chapter Five

Matt Jordan struggled to sit up, ignoring the pain that sliced through the stump of his left leg. Logan Blackstone was here, at the Circle J. And Matt wasn't going to face him for the first time in fifteen years lying flat on his back in bed.

Cat had come in five minutes ago, saying Logan had insisted on currying down the livery horse they'd hired. When he'd finished that, she said, he would come inside.

Matt knew better. Logan had sent Cat ahead of him to give Matt fair notice of his arrival. But was it courtesy or warning? Matt couldn't decide. A shudder rippled through him that had nothing to do with the pain. What was Logan going to say after all these years?

What if he told the truth?

Matt gathered his strength and grabbed at the wheelchair next to the bed, cursing when it rolled away a few feet. A thin sheen of sweat broke out on his forehead. Stretching low he caught the rim of the near wheel and tugged the chair toward him. Hitching it around, he positioned it so he could maneuver himself into it.

He should call his mother, he knew. She would be in here in a rush, in spite of the fact that she, too, had been on edge all evening awaiting Blackstone. For a while Matt had wondered if Cat had decided to stay over in Red Springs, to deal with Blackstone there. But then he'd thought about Logan. Logan would never settle things—one way or the other—without coming out here, without looking Matt straight in the eye.

Matt reached again for the wheelchair. He would do this alone. He needed to do it alone. Though he nearly passed out from the pain, he pushed and pulled and finally dragged himself into the chair. His whole body trembled from the effort.

Not one day, not one, had passed in fifteen years when he didn't feel pain. There were days when he thought he would go mad from it. But other days, when the pain was only a dull throb, he allowed himself to believe that a day could come when he would be able to function using only the crutches his father had fashioned. One day maybe he could even sit a horse.

For now he adjusted the stump on the narrow board that jutted from beneath the wheelchair's seat. His gaze tracked to the bedside table on the opposite side of the bed. Just looking at the bottle of laudanum seemed to set the pain jumping tenfold in his leg. But he closed his eyes and fought it off. He would not face Logan Blackstone with a mind dulled by painkiller.

A knock sounded at the door to his room. Matt's heart thudded. He knew without even calling out.

Maria.

"Go away."

"*Por favor, Mateo*," she called, her voice soft, cajoling.

"Not now, Maria."

As had been her habit of late, she opened the door in spite of his protest and swept into the room. She's spending too much time with Cat, he thought grimly. But he wasn't angry. He could never be angry with Maria.

She remained in the open doorway, her dark eyes brimming with sympathy. "Your mother is most unhappy, Mateo," she said. "I fear this Señor Blackstone worries her terribly."

"Is he here? In the house?" Did he sound as nervous to her ears, as he did to his own?

"No, not yet. Cat said she will go out and fetch him if he doesn't come in soon."

"Listen, Maria, if you don't mind, I'd really like to be alone for a while."

"Is there nothing I can do for you? Help you shave, change your shirt—"

"No!" His voice was more curt than he'd meant it to be, and he winced at the hurt in her wide brown eyes. But though he indulged in it far too often himself, one thing he could not abide right now was any allusion to his helplessness.

"I did not mean to upset you, Mateo."

Matt sighed heavily. "I know." He studied the perfect oval of her face, the gentle features set in warm bronze skin, the cascade of ebony hair that fell past her shoulders. It seemed only yesterday she had been a gangly child, all arms and legs. But that had all changed. He remembered the day clearly, two months ago, when she had been bending over his bed, fluffing his pillows. He had lain back and looked at her, really looked at her for the first time in a long time. Girlish thinness had given way to soft curves, and he hadn't missed the ripe swell of her bosom beneath the gathered neckline of her off-the-shoulder blouse. The same blouse she was wearing now. The girl had become a woman.

"Please, Maria, just go." He wanted to be patient, to explain that he didn't want her fussing over him, especially when it was evident that she no longer did so as a nursemaid. But he had no patience tonight.

And though he would never have admitted it to Cat, he was grateful that Maria would not be bringing him his meals anymore. Not for the reason his mother had ordered a halt to the practice. But because, in spite of the ever-present pain in his leg, Maria was stirring to life feelings he hadn't thought he could possess. And it terrified him that he would never be able to act on those feelings.

"Mateo?"

"I'm fine, Maria," he said, straightening in the chair as best he could. "Please go."

Instead, she stepped closer. Matt's pulse quickened. He no longer looked at her. She brought over the small quilt he used to cover his legs. With great care she tucked it around his waist. It was all he could do not to touch her. It was all he could do not to fall in love with her.

Her concern, her caring were never the oppressive hovering of his mother. She encouraged him to sit up more, to get out of the house in the wheelchair, to stop being a recluse in his own house. She encouraged him to be a man.

And he couldn't bear it.

He wanted her. God help him, he wanted to make love to her, to have her naked in his arms. And knowing that he never could tore at his heart, his soul, as nothing ever had before. How could he be the man she deserved, when so often he didn't feel like a man at all?

"Will you help Cat in her fight to save the ranch?" Maria was saying.

"There's no point," he said bitterly.

"You try so hard to hide it. But I do not think you want to leave here either. It is your home."

"Maria!" Olivia Jordan's voice was sharp with disapproval, as she stepped into the room.

Maria whirled, startled. "Mrs. Jordan."

"I thought I told you not to come in here."

Matt watched Maria's expression change from guilty to defiant. But she said nothing, perhaps hoping Matt would take her side. When he did not, Maria quietly left the room.

"I'm sorry, Matthew," Olivia said, crossing to his wheelchair. "I'll speak to her again." She bent to straighten the quilt on his lap.

"I'll take care of Maria."

"You needn't worry yourself. I'll simply forbid her—"

"No!"

Olivia straightened, her hand fluttering to her chest. "Very well, Matthew."

"I'm sorry, Mother," Matt said, though he loathed himself for saying it. "Maria means well. She and I have been . . . friends"—why did the word now seem wholly inadequate—"since we were kids."

"She's not good enough for you."

"If anything, she's too good for me."

"Matthew, she's the daughter of a ranch hand. And she's—"

"Don't!" Again his voice was harsh.

"Now, Matthew," Olivia clucked, adjusting the lap quilt so that it covered his stockinged foot, "I'm only doing what I think best. You're hardly in a position to

82

support a wife." And she added ever so gently, "I know Maria's always talked about having . . . children."

For one cold instant Matt Jordan hated his mother. Hated her for voicing the one terror he worked hardest to ignore. Though he longed for it, he could never be intimate with Maria, never be intimate with any woman. Never had been. How could he subject a woman he loved to the horror of his maimed leg?

"Anyway," Olivia went on, oblivious to the fact that Matt was shaking, "I came in to tell you that I think it would be best if I talked to Logan alone first."

"No." Matt struggled to sit up straighter. In this, his mother would not defeat him.

"Just for a few minutes," Olivia assured him. "I want to find out why he's really here. That it's not to hurt you any more than he already has."

"No," Matt said again. "He came here to face me. I don't intend to disappoint him."

With obvious reluctance Olivia relented, and Matt didn't object when she helped him shave. His leg was throbbing now. Olivia brought him whiskey without his having to ask. He poured himself a drink. The fiery liquid slid down easily. Within minutes the pain grew dull.

"What's keeping Logan?" he asked. "Why hasn't he come to the house yet?"

"Maybe he's afraid," Olivia said, though clearly she didn't believe it. "After all, the man crippled you. It can't be easy for him to come here."

"We were boys," Matt said, staring at his hands. He didn't want to go through with this, didn't want to face Logan Blackstone ever again. But there was no help for it, no running away from it. Not now.

Olivia stepped behind his wheelchair and began

83

pushing it toward the outer room. "Yes," she said, "you were boys. And your father always said Logan Blackstone made a boy's mistake. But the biggest mistake he's ever made is coming back to the Circle J."

Logan could have curried a team of horses in the time he had taken to bed down the chestnut gelding from Robinson's Livery. He found himself questioning why he was indulging in delaying tactics. If he'd followed Cat into the house, he would have already endured his initial reunion with Matt Jordan.

But Cat herself had become an unforeseen deterrent to doing just that. Logan didn't want a bitter confrontation with Matt in front of the man's sister. It was obvious Cat didn't know the full truth of what had happened fifteen years ago. He didn't want her finding out in a shouting match.

Memories continued to nag him. Over and over he tried to marry his memory of a sweet, cherubic four-year-old, comforting him in the darkness of the Circle J barn to the denim-clad tomboy who'd attacked a drunken cowboy in Red Springs.

She had been a little girl with a mind of her own. Quite obviously she had grown into a woman with a mind of her own as well.

Try as he might to ignore it, he had been intensely aware of that woman for the entire journey out to the ranch. She was no pampered, perfumed debutante. She was a woman used to hard work and the satisfaction that went with it. Something about her tugged at him, fascinated him, challenged him.

He found her forthright and genuine and irresistibly appealing.

He had sensed her embarrassment at being on the receiving end of Chastity Vincent's sharp tongue. But she'd worked hard not to show it. For himself, it had been all he could do not to put the insensitive Miss Vincent in her place. But doing so would only have made things worse for Cat.

He finished currying the horse. What did any of it matter anyway? He would be gone in a few days. And Cat Jordan would once again be nothing more than a pleasant memory.

Logan gathered an armful of fresh hay and put it in the feed box for the gelding. He should go up to the house. It was late enough; Matt and Olivia might well have decided to wait until morning before they met with him. He raked a hand through dark, thick hair. Matt would wait as long as it took, but Logan had to wonder if Olivia would meet with him at all.

He thought again that this all might be a big mistake on his part. Perhaps he should have done as his father had suggested and handled everything through an intermediary.

But though the rift between the families ran long and deep, even Logan could see the sadness in his father's eyes when they'd received word of Hadley Jordan's death. If Jeremy Blackstone's own health wasn't sometimes fragile, Logan didn't doubt that his father would have accompanied him to Texas.

"I don't like the idea of your going alone," Jeremy Blackstone had said, his once-dusky hair now white as new-fallen snow.

"I have to. I think we both know that."

"You don't owe Matt Jordan anything."

"I owe him a chance to face me, just once, as a man."

The sound of the barn door creaking open brought

Logan snapping back to the present.

"Did you die in here or what?" Cat asked, striding over to him. "Mother and Matt are waiting for you at the house."

"With a Winchester?"

"Of course not!"

Logan found it difficult to take his eyes off her. The light of the lantern hanging on the stall post glinted like moonlight off her tawny gold hair. Freshly combed, it tumbled about her face in soft waves.

She was wearing the same denim pants, but she'd changed her shirt. This one was a soft muslin that buttoned up the front, and though it did little to flatter the soft curves of her breasts, he found the effect unnervingly pleasing.

To shift his mind from the direction in which it was headed, he gestured vaguely toward her shirtfront. "You, um, missed a button or something."

"Oh," Cat said, suddenly flustered. "Thanks." She stared down at her shirt, noting the off-line gaps and gathers, and felt like a first-class ninny. So much for her attempt to improve her appearance. She'd stopped short of putting on a dress, because she didn't want Logan Blackstone entertaining any absurd notions that she would have done such a thing for him. Yet she'd been positively possessed by the need to tidy herself up before she saw the man again.

And she'd certainly bowled him over with her efforts! His only comment was that she'd buttoned her shirt wrong. Now she faced the daunting task of rebuttoning it—daunting because she was wearing her gloves.

She didn't dare take them off. She'd become so self-conscious about her work-roughened hands that she'd

86

smeared one of her mother's softening potions onto them. She would rather die than let Logan see the green-fingered results.

"Isn't there an easier way to do that?" he asked, as the buttons continued to outduel her.

"I think I know how to dress myself, thank you."

She battled each mother-of-pearl circlet until the shirt was fully unbuttoned.

Logan cleared his throat self-consciously. "Do you always adjust your clothing in front of strange men?"

Cat gasped, her head jerking upward to catch Logan staring at her much too intently. She felt her cheeks heat. "I didn't think I had to worry about being ravished in my own barn," she snapped, hoping her tone masked her mortification. In the dim lantern light she hadn't really thought about his being able to see anything he shouldn't see. Besides, she was making certain the sides of her shirt stayed together. "I thought you were a gentleman. That maybe you'd turn your back!"

"Even a gentleman has his limits. Mine end when a lovely lady starts undressing herself in my presence."

"Undressing herself!" she choked. "I'm rebuttoning my shirt! How dare you . . ." She stopped dead. "Lovely lady?" Her eyes narrowed. "Are you making fun of me, mister?"

"Of course not," he said. "Why would you think such a thing?"

He seemed so genuinely disturbed by her question that she decided to believe him. But somehow that knowledge made her all the more flustered. She swore the infernal buttonholes were now leaping out of her way.

Grimacing, Logan stepped closer. "May I?"

She looked up, disconcerted to find his face almost

directly above her own. She didn't recall his seeming so tall before.

"I'll be the perfect gentleman," he vowed.

She let her gloved hands fall to her sides.

He seemed to take special care not to touch anything but the edges of the material—button to buttonhole. For herself, she seemed to have stopped breathing.

Her whole world narrowed down to his long fingers working the buttons of her shirt. By the time he reached the third one, she wasn't the only one who had stopped breathing.

He mastered the final button. Her gaze had never left his face. His gray eyes glittered with suppressed passion. His lips, bare inches from her own, looked so soft, inviting. She didn't move, didn't react, didn't even close her eyes, as his mouth descended on her own.

She tasted him, warm, honey sweet. Her eyes slid closed, her arms lifting of their own accord to circle the hard expanse of his back. She didn't know how long they stood there, his lips, ever gentle, exploring her own. She only knew that she could have stood there the rest of her life.

It was Logan who drew back.

Cat blinked, bringing a gloved hand to her lips. "Why did you do that?" she whispered.

"I don't know," he said, clearly as confused as she was. "Maybe it was a long overdue thank you."

"Thank you? For what?"

"For not hating me fifteen years ago."

"I was just a little girl."

"Meaning you've had time to reconsider?"

The sudden edge to his voice rang false. Cat had the distinct impression that Logan Blackstone would not be

88

angry to learn she shared her mother and brother's hatred of him. He would be hurt.

"No, I haven't reconsidered. I mean . . ." Good grief, what did she mean? She could scarcely think. Just being near the man was playing havoc with her senses. "Actually," she blurted, desperate to change the subject, "what I really want is to talk to you. About getting an extension on the loan until after the roundup this fall."

She'd said it all wrong. She knew it the instant she looked into his eyes.

"Is that what your little performance with the buttons was all about? Is that why you let me kiss you? To make me more amenable to your terms?"

"No! Oh, no, Logan . . . Mr. Blackstone, I . . ." She blushed furiously. "How could you even think such a thing?"

But he was no longer listening. "The kiss meant nothing. It was just an overreaction to a long day. I'd been thinking about a trusting little girl. I hadn't yet met the conniving woman."

"Conniving! Why you . . . you—"

"There won't be any extension, Miss Jordan," he said. "I came to finalize the paper work between our families. My father's bank will foreclose and I'll take over the ranch with the intention of selling it."

"You can't do that! You have to give me a chance." She caught his arm. "Please."

"Your father made a bargain."

"My father is dead!" She may not have been as diplomatic as she could have been in bringing up the extension, but at least she had brought it up. She had to make Logan listen. He couldn't take the Circle J away from her. "Pa was heading to Red Springs to send a wire to your father the day he died."

"My father would have turned him down."

Cat felt tears burning the backs of her eyes. But she wouldn't cry. She wouldn't give Logan Blackstone the satisfaction of seeing her cry. "Yes, I suppose he would have turned him down, wouldn't he? I always found it rather curious that the default date of the loan was in June. Ranches are notoriously short of cash during the summer months. My father had to have asked for a fall date."

"Your father agreed to the terms."

"And that means your father tried to steal the Circle J!"

A muscle jumped in Logan's jaw, his gray eyes now near black with anger. "My father loaned your father money when no one else would. He loaned it to him even though your family treated my family like they carried the plague."

"You mean treated *you* like you carried the plague!" she shouted.

He grabbed up the currycomb and raked it across the gelding's back.

"That's what you mean, isn't it, *Mister* Blackstone? Your problem is the way my family treated *you*. Well, it's just too bad if you got your feelings hurt! My brother lost his leg!"

"Don't tell me what your brother lost," Logan hissed. "Don't ever tell me that."

Cat took a step back, jolted by the despair she felt in him. Logan Blackstone was suffering more than hurt feelings. "Look," she said, "this is going all wrong. I didn't mean to ask you about the loan after you kissed me. I mean"—she blushed furiously—"you . . . you

90

took me by surprise . . . I . . . I don't get kissed real often. I . . . well, I mean, not lately . . . or . . ." Good grief, she didn't want him thinking she was a wallflower. "I . . . I'm sorry."

He balanced the currycomb on top of the stall door, but said nothing.

"Can we start over?" Cat asked.

"There won't be an extension."

"You're not being fair," she said, but she was no longer angry. This man was hurting as much or more than her brother. And all she could do was feel for them both.

"And how fair are you being?" he demanded. "Trading on your father's death and my *guilt*." He spoke the word as if it were an oath. "That's fair?"

"If you hear me out, that's what would be fair."

He couldn't argue with that. "All right."

"We can talk in the house," Cat said.

"So the three of you can gang up on me?"

"It'll be the other way around, I assure you."

He looked puzzled.

"My mother and my brother want nothing more to do with the Circle J."

"So that's why your father left controlling interest of the ranch to you."

"Exactly. Now can we go up to the house?"

"After we get one thing straight. I *am* sorry about the kiss."

"All right." She really didn't want to hear that he was sorry. She wasn't sorry at all.

"It won't happen again."

"I'm glad to hear it," she managed to get out, fighting off an oddly fierce disappointment. She hurried out of the barn ahead of him, but waited for him at the door of the house. "I think I should warn you about Matt."

Logan shrugged fatalistically. "He won't welcome me with open arms. What more is there to say?"

"His leg gives him a lot of pain."

Logan's eyes narrowed. "All this time?"

Cat nodded.

"Has he seen a doc—"

The word was cut off as the door swung inward, opened from the inside. Olivia stood just within, her fingers so tightly intertwined that her knuckles showed white. Her eyes were cold, glittering shards. But hate wasn't the overriding emotion in her brown eyes. It was fear.

Cat found herself reaching for her mother, wanting to take her somewhere safe, where she didn't have to face ugly memories from the past. But Olivia stepped around her to face Logan directly.

"You're not welcome in my house," Olivia said.

"The situation being what it is, Mrs. Jordan," Logan said quietly, "this house is technically no longer yours."

Cat couldn't blame Logan for answering her mother's bitterness in kind. Still, she found herself wishing that it didn't have to be so, that everything, somehow, could all miraculously be forgiven.

"Cordelia," Olivia said, "I would very much appreciate it if you would go to your room. Your brother and I would like to meet with Mr. Blackstone alone."

"Mother, you know I can't do that. I won't do that. You and Matt would write off the ranch in a minute."

"No," Olivia said quickly, "it isn't about that. I just think Matt and I should . . . be alone . . . for a few minutes."

"Your mother may be right," Logan said.

92

"I'm not leaving," Cat said.

Olivia seemed to draw inside herself. "Very well."

Cat knew how difficult this was for her mother. She'd always been so fiercely protective of Matt. And now, this one time, there was nothing she could do to prevent Matt's being hurt.

Cat wasn't helping matters by defying her mother's wishes, but it couldn't be helped. Cat had to be in on any discussions about the ranch.

She did stay back a little, as Logan and Olivia walked ahead of her into the front room.

Matt sat next to the horsehair settee in his wheelchair, clean-shaven, his hair combed. Though his color was pale, and Cat knew his leg was bothering him, his eyes remained steady. In all her imaginings this was not the way she had pictured this reunion.

It was calm. Too calm.

"Matt," Logan said, his voice flat.

"Logan."

Cat studied both men. There was something between them, palpable, hidden. And just as with her mother, Cat had the unmistakable impression that Matt was afraid.

Chapter Six

Cat had seen a prize fight once. Her father had taken her to one in Dodge City six years ago. Two men had squared off against each other in a roped-off ring, while the crowd made wagers on who would still be standing at the end.

Cat's stomach churned at the memory of bruised and bloodied faces, eyes swollen shut from the merciless pounding of bare-knuckled fists. By the fifth round both men were staggering, barely conscious, and Cat had begged her father to interfere, to stop them. But the men had chosen to fight, he'd said. No one would be satisfied, including the fighters, if the battle was called off.

And so the men had continued to pound on each other. Until in the ninth round, at the same instant, both men had collapsed.

There had been no winner that night, only two battered and beaten human beings.

Cat had much the same feeling as she watched Logan and Matt size each other up across the front room of the Circle J. They would draw no blood, but both men would emerge from this meeting bruised and battered.

And there would be no winner.

Logan, perhaps because he was the interloper here, appeared content to be on the defensive, waiting for Matt to strike the first blow. Matt did not disappoint him.

"So, Logan, old friend, you're back in Texas," he said, curling a fist into the quilt that covered his legs. "And how was your trip?"

"Just fine."

"Brought back fond memories, did it?" Matt yanked the quilt from his lap and flung it to the floor. "I know your visit has brought back a lot of memories for me." He patted the stump of his leg.

"I'll just bet it has," Logan said, looking Matt straight in the eye.

Though Cat didn't understand why, she knew Logan had just struck Matt a telling blow. Her brother's already pale features grew ashen, though he showed no signs of retreat.

Logan walked toward the fireplace. He seemed weary all at once, as though some part of him had hoped that past animosities would have been laid to rest. "It's been a long time, Matt."

"Not long enough."

"I never meant what happened."

"I don't want your apology," Matt hissed.

"I'm not apologizing. I did that fifteen years ago. And if you—"

"Your apologies meant nothing then," Olivia cut in, her hands knotted into fists. "And they mean even less now. We don't want you here. Just finish your business about the ranch and leave."

"It isn't that simple."

"It is that simple," Olivia insisted, sounding almost desperate. "There's nothing for you here. Nothing!"

Cat felt the tension in the room spiking to unbearable levels. "Please, Mother," she said quickly, "no one needs to be upset here. Mr. Blackstone agreed to hear me out about the extension. I—"

"No," Logan interrupted.

Cat looked at him. "What?"

"There won't be an extension." Logan looked from Matt to Olivia and back again, then pulled a folded packet of papers from the inside pocket of his coat.

"What are those?" Cat asked.

"Foreclosure papers."

"You can't." Her voice shook, and she hated herself for it.

"I made a mistake in coming back here," Logan said. "And the quickest way to rectify it is to file these papers, take the ranch into receivership, and sell it to the highest bidder."

"You said you'd hear me out."

"There's no point."

His voice was not unkind, and it gave Cat the tiniest glimmer of hope. It wasn't much, but it was enough.

"Maybe we can wait until morning to talk about this," she said. "It's so late. It's been a long day for all of us."

He seemed to waver for a moment; then, to her relief, he relented, shoving the papers back into his pocket. "In the morning then," he said. He gave a polite nod to Cat and Olivia. Ignoring Matt completely, he showed himself out of the house.

Cat hesitated, then started after him.

"Stay away from him, Cordelia," Olivia said. "Please."

"If I talked to him alone, maybe he'd listen. He's got to give me a chance. I owe it to Pa."

"You can't expect a favor from a Blackstone. I told you that."

"Pa got the loan from the Blackstones."

"Stay away from him!" her mother said again. "He's nothing but trouble for this family."

"Ma's right," Matt said. "You saw him. He didn't even apologize."

Cat felt an infinite sadness for her brother. And a sudden burning anger as well. She was tired and scared, and she had found Logan Blackstone to be no two-headed ogre with horns and a tail. "The day might well come, Matthew," she said softly, "when it's you who apologizes to him."

"How dare you, Cordelia!" Olivia snapped. "How dare you say such a thing to your brother! That man—"

"That man made a mistake, as you have both reminded me for fifteen years, when he was twelve years old. Have you ever considered what it would have been like if it had been the other way around? If Matt had made a mistake that cost Logan his leg?

"You would have hurt for Matt as well as Logan, wouldn't you, Mother? And, Matt, wouldn't you have wanted to be forgiven? To have an end to the hate?"

Matt wouldn't meet her eyes. Olivia hurried over to pick up the discarded quilt and tuck it back around his legs. "I want him off this ranch," Olivia said. "Whatever it takes, I want him gone."

"And I want to save my home." Cat headed toward the door.

"You can't trust him," Olivia called after her. "Please, Cordelia, he'll hurt you."

97

But Cat was gone. She hurried across the yard toward the barn. She found Logan inside.

"I hope you didn't come out here to try to change my mind," he said, arranging a pile of straw in an empty stall.

"I wouldn't dream of it," she said, though they both knew she was lying.

He picked up a horse blanket and tossed it atop the pile.

"What are you doing?"

"Making my bed."

"For heaven's sake," Cat exclaimed, "you don't have to sleep in the barn. You can sleep in the bunkhouse. We have a spare bunk or two."

"I'll be fine here."

Cat planted her hands on her hips. "You just want to make it easier for yourself, don't you?"

"I beg your pardon?"

"It might be more difficult to throw me out of my own home if you accept my hospitality."

"Maybe your hospitality is suspect."

"Not that again."

A breeze shifted the open front of his shirt, allowing her a brief glimpse of a hair-roughened chest. Quickly, he fastened one of the middle buttons. "Sorry. I wasn't expecting to entertain any more visitors tonight."

"Of course not," Cat said, suddenly acutely aware of being alone with this man—the enigmatic Logan Blackstone, who seemed at once compassionate and cold, empathetic and aloof.

He brushed his hands together, wiping off the remnants of straw clinging to his fingers. "Tell me something, as long as you're here, has your brother cursed my name daily for fifteen years?"

Cat sensed he was not as nonchalant as he pretended

while he awaited her answer. "Not every day," she said. "In fact, there were times when he even regaled me with tales of the trouble you two got into with my father. Like the time you both fell out of the hay loft, pretending to be eagles."

Logan smiled. "I'd forgotten that one."

"And the time Matt shot Pa's horse, the time you played coyotes and attacked the chicken coop, the time you snuck off to track a cougar . . ." She shook her head. "No, he hasn't always cursed your name. It's gotten bad the last few years, I think, because the leg hurts him so much. And because Ma . . ." She stopped.

"Won't let him be a man?" Logan finished.

"She's very protective of him," Cat said, not knowing why she felt the sudden need to defend her mother.

"It wasn't a judgment," Logan said. "Not of your mother or of Matt."

"Please don't pay too much attention to what he says. I don't think he hates you nearly as much as he hates himself."

"I guess after so much time I'd hoped he'd gotten past the bitterness."

"I haven't given up on him, if that makes you feel better."

Logan hunkered down to better straighten his bed of straw. Cat had the peculiar feeling that he was weighing his next words very carefully. "What do you actually remember about that time, Cat?"

"Not very much really," she admitted. "But sometimes, just out of reach, there are snatches of things." She shivered suddenly, though the night temperature was warm. "I know I must have been terribly frightened. There was a lot of shouting. My mother was . . ."

He stood. "Your mother was what?"

"She was so upset, over Matt's losing his leg."

Cat wasn't certain, but she could have sworn Logan let out a sigh of relief.

"I remember coming into the barn," she said, twirling a bit of straw between her gloved fingers, "and that you were crying. And I didn't want you to cry. You were my friend. And I knew, somehow I knew, you weren't crying because you were in trouble for what happened to Matt. You were crying because Matt was hurt." She looked at him. "And you loved him."

He turned his back to her, staking his hands on the top of the stall door. She watched the play of muscles under his shirt. Was he angry? Had she pressed too far into his pain? Had she misread it, then and now?

"You did care about him, didn't you?" she asked softly.

Logan let out a long, shuddering breath. "You'd better go back to the house."

"Logan, please . . ." She curved a hand over his shoulder. "I'd like to be one member of this family who doesn't cause you pain."

He whipped around. "Why? Why does that matter to you?"

"I . . . I don't know," she said. "I just think . . . well, I know a little about putting up a front with people." Good heavens, why did she say that? "I mean, well . . ." Oh, what did she mean? And who did she think she was, trying to figure out Logan Blackstone? She took a deep breath, forcing a too-bright smile. "It is late, isn't it? Ma's probably wondering what happened to me . . . I . . ." His eyes, dear God his eyes. There was so much pain in those eyes.

"I don't want to involve you in this," he said hoarsely. "You don't deserve to be hurt. You were only a child."

"Hurt by what?" she asked, bewildered, for he was clearly not referring to losing the ranch. "My mother said you would hurt me, Logan. Why would—"

"No!" He pressed his fingers to her lips. "I won't hurt you, and please don't ask."

She reached a hand toward him, a gesture of comfort, of kindness. And in the next instant she found herself swept into the awesome strength of his embrace.

His mouth came down on hers, possessive, devastating. This was not at all like the gentle kiss he'd given her earlier. "Corie, sweet, Corie . . ." He moaned low in his throat, his mouth trailing soft kisses across her cheeks, her forehead, her eyes.

She felt herself ignite, her body aflame with new and wondrous sensations. She traced a path upward across his shoulders and down, her gloves proving a frustrating barrier between his flesh and her own when she reached the open neck of his shirt.

"Logan," she murmured, fighting to maintain some tiny hold on reality, "Logan, why is this happening?"

But he gave her no time to answer, his mouth claiming hers once again. A fearsome heat fired every part of her just as she perceived the driving need in him, a longing she suddenly feared had nothing to do with her but with an aching emptiness born in this place long ago.

He was tired and vulnerable, and so was she.

He would use her tenderness, her caring, to assuage a soul-deep hurt.

And then *she* would be hurt.

And he would hate himself.

Because in spite of the onerous judgments of her

mother and brother, Logan Blackstone was an honorable man.

She pulled away, and he made no move to stop her. An indefinable, overwhelming sense of loss swept over her, as her body broke contact with his. She was not imagining the rigid way he held himself in check. He was feeling it too.

"I . . . I'd best go inside," she said, her voice a quavering mockery of itself. She backed toward the barn door. "You sure you'll be all right out here?"

"Fine," he said, that one word as bold a lie as she had ever heard.

She all but bolted outside then, though she forced herself to walk toward the house. She didn't want to be out of breath if her mother and brother were still up and about.

Thankfully, they were not. She didn't think she could abide another emotional confrontation tonight. Going straight to her room, Cat peeled off her clothes, then crossed to her wardrobe. Almost reverently, she lifted the ivory peignore from its hiding place. Slipping the delicate garment over her head, she reveled in the satiny feel of it against her bare flesh. Never had she been so vividly aware of its texture, its almost ethereal lightness. And for that she could thank Logan Blackstone.

Thank or curse?

She refused to consider the question. Collapsing into bed, she pulled the sheet up to her chin. She longed for sleep, but it eluded her, thoughts of this amazing day rippling seductively through her mind. All but forgotten was her altercation with Rafe Latigo. What she couldn't forget was her soul-searing reaction to Logan Blackstone.

Against her will, she tried to sort it out, to make sense

of what she was feeling toward this man she should by rights detest. After all, she had been instructed to loathe him for years. His mistake, no matter how unintentional, had maimed her brother for life. And, on top of it all, he had come here to take away the ranch she loved.

Yet there was about him an elusive spirit that intrigued and enticed her, a kinship that promised common ground as yet unsuspected. She knew instinctively that the Logan Blackstone who drew her into his arms tonight was not the Logan Blackstone he presented to the world. He was a man of passion and feelings not easily shared.

Nor could she be certain about why she had been the one to reach him. It could be as simple as fatigue from his long journey. Or as complicated as fifteen-year-old memories that swirled ever out of her reach.

But the fact remained, certain and unalterable, that she was drawn to Logan, a possibility so fanciful and remote that it had not even entered her mind this morning as she'd pondered the potential outcome of his visit.

Certainly the man was handsome. Undeniably so. And he very likely had beautiful ladies at his beck and call all over the East Coast. But it had been Cat Jordan whom he had pulled against him tonight, Cat Jordan who had experienced the wonder of his kiss.

Quickly the doubts set in. There were no East Coast beauties here to distract him. Not even Chastity Vincent. Cat was here, and all too shamelessly available, if he were to judge by her behavior tonight.

What if he was playing her for a fool? She could be little more than a diversion from the unpleasantness of her mother and brother. She could even be his revenge.

It was with doubts crowding in on her that she finally

103

fell asleep.

The next morning Cat took much longer than usual to dress. Refusing to examine her motives, she pulled on a dove gray riding skirt and the blouse Maria had given her for Christmas. Smiling giddily, she twirled across the room to pause in front of her mirror.

The smile faded. Had she really thought a skirt and blouse would transform her into Chastity Vincent? Cat's lightly tanned skin held none of the porcelain fragility that made grown men follow after Chastity like mewling pups. Her figure seemed almost boyishly slender when compared to the curvaceous Chastity's. And her hair, always wild and untamable, would never tolerate being molded into a regal crown of ringlets and curls. In the end Cat had to settle for catching it up in a ribbon at the base of her neck.

At least the greenish cast had disappeared from her hands. She wasn't certain, but her skin even seemed a little smoother than before. She would try the potion again tonight.

From her doorway she heard the unmistakable sounds of her mother slamming pans about in the kitchen. All the unease of last night threatened to crash in on her again. She was not going to start her morning with an argument. Without a backward glance, Cat crossed to her window and climbed out.

She started toward the barn, but stopped when she noticed Maria striding toward her.

"Cat, *mi amiga*," the girl chided with amused affection, "why are you not helping your mother prepare Mateo's breakfast?"

"You know I love cooking almost as much as my mother does," Cat said. "But I'm surprised at you. I thought you would be more upset about not cooking for

Matt anymore."

"I give your mother two more days, maybe three. Then I will be taking Mateo's breakfast to him once again."

Cat chuckled. "From the sounds I was hearing in the kitchen she may come out and get you today."

"I hope so. I miss Mateo, even though he is not always so happy to see me."

"That's because you remind him he's still alive," Cat said. "And that scares him to death."

"You think so?" Maria asked, her voice hopeful.

"Sometimes I think he's really tired of being an invalid. That maybe he's ready to do something about it." Cat squeezed her friend's hand. "You keep after him, you hear? You're the best thing that could ever happen to him."

"*Gracias, amiga.*" Maria looked toward the cookhouse. "You're coming for breakfast?"

"I decided eating with you and the hands would be easier on my digestion. I'll join you as soon as I fetch Mr. Blackstone."

Maria frowned. "Fetch him from where?"

"The barn." At Maria's continued puzzlement, Cat added, "He slept there."

Her friend had the good grace not to comment on the sleeping arrangements of a Circle J guest, though she couldn't resist a question. "How did Mateo take their meeting?"

"Not very well, I'm afraid."

"Señor Blackstone is very bad?"

"Señor Blackstone is most certainly *not* bad," Cat snapped.

"Ahhh," Maria said thoughtfully. "Now I understand."

"Understand what?" Cat asked warily.

105

"What it is that inspired Cat Jordan to dress in a skirt and blouse for the first time since Christmas."

"Never mind," Cat said, fuming when she felt her cheeks heat. "I'll be up in a few minutes." With that she headed for the barn, while Maria continued toward the cookhouse.

Cautiously, Cat nudged open the barn door. She didn't want to surprise Blackstone if he wasn't decent.

She spied him at once. Her heart thudded. He was shaving, or rather attempting to shave. Naked from the waist up, Logan was standing in front of a banged-up pie tin, squinting, trying to see his face reflected in its dull surface. Cat couldn't take her eyes off of him. For a supposed dandy, his upper body was all well-honed muscle.

"Are you going to stand there gawking all day," he called, not looking up, "or are you going to come in and say good morning?"

"I was not gawking," she lied, striding over to him. But she certainly wished her heart would stop pounding so crazily. "Did you sleep well?" she managed.

"Well enough," he said. His voice was clipped, though not rude. He was keeping his distance. Was it to avoid a repeat of what had happened last night? He turned, his gaze tracking her from head to toe. "I see you slept well too."

She felt her cheeks heat yet again. Blushing was becoming an all too common occurrence around this man. Was he wondering if she'd dressed this way to gain his notice? Disconcerted, she stammered, "I came to invite you to breakfast with me and the hands at the cookhouse. Maria makes a mean omelet."

He was using the shirt he'd worn yesterday to wipe the

excess shaving lather from his face. "Sounds good."

Cat shook her head. "Things are a little more primitive here in Texas than they are in Boston," she said, "but we do have towels up at the house."

He shrugged into a clean shirt, his gray eyes continuing to study her intently. "I'll remember that."

Suddenly nervous, she said quickly, "Let's hurry, shall we? I'm hungry."

"So am I."

She had the distinct impression he wasn't talking about food. But she allowed herself no time to dwell on it, hurrying out of the barn ahead of him. She led him to a squarish clapboard building a couple of hundred yards from the main house.

Inside the cookhouse four Circle J waddies milled about an eight-foot-long pine table, waiting for Maria to give the word breakfast was ready.

Cat brought Logan over for a round of quick introductions. First up was Jim Spence, a twentyish towhead with a peach-fuzz beard and an easy smile. He was jockeying for position at the head of the chow line with lanky Obidiah Johnson, a black man of indeterminate age, who was readily acknowledged by the Circle J crew as the best bronc buster in the state of Texas.

"You'd think neither one of them yahoos ever got a decent meal in their lives," Dusty Yates grumped to Cat, even as his gaze settled curiously on Logan. Dusty didn't object as head wrangler Esteban Hidalgo stepped in front of him in line.

"For once I will get my share of my daughter's buttermilk biscuits," Esteban said, unaware of the crackle of tension between Logan and Dusty. Cat had wanted to question Dusty about her father's death, but decided it would be wiser to wait until she had him alone.

"Maria and me got a deal on them biscuits, 'Steban," Dusty said, though his eyes never left Logan.

"You two remember each other?" Cat prodded.

Dusty didn't answer her directly, saying instead to Logan. "Been awhile, boy." His voice seemed wary, as though his reaction to Logan was dependent on Logan's reaction to him.

"That it has, Dusty," Logan said. For the briefest instant he hesitated, then proffered his hand.

Dusty accepted it, his wariness becoming a grudging respect. To Cat's disappointment they then went on to discuss the relative merits of marmalade and strawberry jam, as Maria ladled each of them a plateful of food.

Everyone took a place at the table, Maria sitting to Cat's left, Logan to her right. The ebony-haired girl smiled politely when Cat introduced her to Logan, but Cat sensed Maria's reluctance and suspected she was reserving her judgment because of Matt.

"Everything smells delicious, Maria," Logan said.

"*Gracias, señor,*" Maria replied softly.

As they ate, Cat was surprised at how easily Logan fit in with their trail-rough ranch hands, seeming to thoroughly enjoy their hair-raising anecdotes about life on the range.

"Handlin' that rattler was about the scariest thing I ever done," Obie said, finishing one particularly outrageous yarn.

"Almost as scary as Cat comin' in here this mornin' in a skirt," Dusty cracked. "I thought somebody musta died."

Cat threw a biscuit at him.

Dusty ducked, hooting loudly.

Cat dared a glance at Logan, wondering if he had attached any significance to Dusty's remark. Though he appeared disinterested, he seemed more engrossed in his meal than he had before.

"I brought Obie and Jim in from the range," Dusty went on, "'cause we got some horses to break today."

Cat gasped, delighted. She twisted on the bench seat to face Logan. "Would you like to watch them?" she asked.

"I'm afraid I won't be able to do that," he said, not meeting her eyes. "I'll be heading back to town as soon as I get all my papers signed."

She felt as though he'd punched her in the stomach. "What are you talking about?" she demanded. "You said we could talk."

"*You* said we could talk. I told you there's no point."

"Damn you!" she hissed, slamming to her feet. "That is not the impression I had last night when you—"

The rowdy chatter had ceased. All eyes watched Cat. Logan stood. "Thanks for the meal," he said. "It's been a pleasure." He started toward the door.

Cat pounded her fist on the table. "You can't do this. I won't let you!"

He opened the door. "I'll be leaving inside an hour," he said, and was gone.

Chapter Seven

Logan stalked into the barn and slammed open the rear stall door with such force that the chestnut gelding inside snorted and shied.

"Easy, boy," Logan said, holding up a hand to soothe the startled animal. "I didn't mean to take this out on you."

At any moment Logan expected Cat to come stomping in on his heels. He had left her confused and angry. And she had every right to be. He was pretty damned confused and angry himself.

He'd spent half the night tossing and turning on his makeshift bed, going over everything that had happened to him since he'd arrived in Red Springs yesterday. The stage robbery already seemed a distant memory. But what he couldn't get out of his head was what he felt for Corie. By rights, he told himself, he shouldn't feel anything at all, except perhaps gratitude for a child's long-ago kindness.

But it wasn't gratitude that had slammed into his vitals last night when he'd pulled her into his arms. It was lust, strong and fierce, tempered with a tenderness he hadn't even known he could feel.

He'd bedded his share of women in his life, wild oats sown in his youth. But over the past few years he'd indulged his carnal appetites only rarely, finding brief encounters shallow and unfulfilling. He had not met the woman who could tempt him to risk a more abiding commitment.

And then there was Corie. Cordelia. Cat. Even thinking of her now sent a pleasant heat sifting through his veins. His fascination with her defied the part of him that valued logic and order. But the fact remained—he wanted that woman.

He'd wanted her last night, when he'd sensed her compassion for his twisted relationship with her brother. And he'd wanted her this morning, when he'd turned to see her standing beside him so fresh and beautiful with her big green eyes and a smile that could stop the tides.

She'd looked so pretty, he'd almost told her so. But it would have opened new territory between them and he couldn't chance that. Yet perhaps she'd opened it herself. The teasing comments of Dusty Yates suggested Cat's being seen in a skirt and blouse was only slightly less rare than a July blizzard. Had her change in appearance been for his benefit?

The thought was bittersweet. What did it matter now? Logan strode over and hefted the gelding's harness from its peg on the wall.

Maybe if things were different . . .

But they weren't.

And they never would be. Not with so much history between their families. Better to hurt her this way than to make a mistake and risk an even bigger hurt should she learn the truth.

And the longer he stayed, the more likely he would be to let something slip.

He couldn't do that to her. Though he suspected she would deny it to the death, she was not nearly the tough-as-cowhide female she made herself out to be. Under that I-don't-give-a-damn exterior beat a very vulnerable heart.

He was not going to be the man to break it.

With each step she took Cat's temper slipped another notch. She had been nothing but patient with Logan Blackstone . . . diplomatic, considerate, demure—well, as demure as she ever got, she amended honestly. And for what? The bastard had obviously had his mind made up from the first minute. His behavior with her last night was probably just his idea of a Blackstone bonus.

Her pace slowed. No, that wasn't true. Logan had been as disconcerted as she was by that kiss. He had come to Texas to foreclose on Matt Jordan, not to start up a passing dalliance with the man's sister. He had enough problems with the Jordans without creating new ones.

Still, she'd believed him when he'd said he'd listen to her regarding the loan. His abrupt departure from the cookhouse had left her feeling bewildered, infuriated. Betrayed.

The sense of betrayal astonished her because it suggested a misplaced trust. Why should she have trusted Logan Blackstone? Yet she had. And he had failed her. His hatred for the Jordans had overcome his capacity to be fair.

Fair or not, she was going to confront him about the

extension. She had no choice. Beyond her ambivalent feelings about Blackstone was the incontrovertible fact that her home was at stake.

Cat was halfway to the barn when she heard a shuffling sound coming from somewhere behind her. She glanced back.

Matt.

Up and about on crutches for the first time in . . . She couldn't even remember when the last time was. He was moving with painful slowness toward the corrals, where soon Esteban and the others would be saddle-breaking new horses for the Circle J remuda.

Cat looked toward the barn, then looked back toward Matt. This could be her last chance to convince Blackstone that the Circle J should stay in Jordan hands. How better to stack the deck than to make one last effort to win her brother over to her side?

"Good morning!" she called.

Her shout startled him. His head jerked up, and he had to grab for a corral rail to keep from falling.

"Matt, I'm sorry," she said, hurrying over to him. "Are you all right?"

"Fine," he said, though he straightened with obvious difficulty. He was hurting, but for once he didn't acknowledge it. "I . . . you surprised me, that's all."

"What are you doing out here?"

"I can't walk around my own ranch?" he snapped. "Just because Pa left controlling interest to you, doesn't mean he left me out completely."

"I didn't mean it that way, and you know it," she said. "Now quit being so grouchy and answer my question. What are you doing out here?"

"I'm taking a damned walk."

Cat's lips thinned. "You can be so charming, you know that? I can see why Maria fell in love with you."

His eyes narrowed ominously. "Don't talk to me about Maria. I've had enough of your sisterly advice."

"I only give it to you because I love you," she said softly.

He sighed, his shoulders sagging, then hitched both crutches under his left arm and leaned back against the corral rail. "I know. I'm sorry. I just . . ." His gaze flicked about the ranchyard.

"It's finally hitting home, isn't it?"

"What is?"

"The fact that Logan Blackstone is going to take all of this away from us."

"It can't be helped."

"Yes, it can. Dammit, Matt, Pa only left the ranch to me because he . . ." She hesitated, groping for the right words.

"Because he figured I wouldn't be man enough to stand up to a Blackstone," Matt finished bitterly.

"This ranch belongs to both of us," she said. "I've never wanted it to be any other way. You must know that."

"We can't run it, Cat. My leg—"

"There's nothing wrong with your brain. You can give the orders. The men will listen to you."

He seemed to consider it, then shook his head. "The men feel sorry for me, they . . ." He didn't finish, saying instead, "It couldn't work."

But for the first time in a very long time Cat had seen a hint of the brother she had long believed Matt to be, a brother buried under a mountain of self-pity and the attentions of a mother who, out of guilt or love or both,

114

had smothered the spirit out of him. "We could, Matt! Don't you see? Together we could do anything. Logan couldn't stop us."

"Logan is foreclosing on the ranch."

"No! If we both talked to him, asked him—"

"I'll ask him to go to hell!"

"And wouldn't that be perfect!" she gritted out, slapping a hand against the rail in frustration. "That should convince him to give us the extension!" Then she quickly drew rein on her temper. Picking a fight with her brother would gain her nothing. "Matt," she said evenly, "can't you see? It's all of this past business between the two of you. He—"

"What did he say to you?" Matt cut in, catching her arm in a viselike grip. "What did he say?"

"Nothing specific," Cat said, her eyes narrowing suspiciously. "It's more of a feeling than anything else." She pried his hand away, rubbing the spot where his fingers had dug into her arm. "That hurt."

"I'm sorry."

His apology was as distracted as his actions. Cat was certain he didn't even realize how tightly he'd been squeezing her arm. "Matthew," she said slowly, "what do you know about all this that I don't?"

"Not a thing," he said, but he said it too quickly.

"Matt—"

"Drop it, Cat," he snapped, then added, "please."

His words were different from Logan's, but the request was the same. *Don't ask.* Frustration burned through Cat. What was this hidden something between her brother and Logan Blackstone? What else had happened that long-ago shadowy night? "Does this have to do with your accident?" she demanded. "It was an *accident*, wasn't it?" A sickening dread rippled through her. "My God, Logan didn't deliberately push you—"

"Drop it!" Matt shouted. "Dammit, Cat, I mean it!"

"I won't drop it, not if it has something to do with why you won't fight for this ranch."

"It has nothing to do with the ranch! Dammit, Cat, this is my home, too." He was shaking, whether from pain or anger or both, Cat couldn't have said. But when he spoke again, there was no emotion whatsoever evident in his voice. "Go ahead and ask Logan for the extension. I won't fight you on it anymore."

It was a small victory, and she took no pleasure in it. She had all but blackmailed him into coming over to her side. But for now she would live with it. It would gain her time at least. Besides, whatever lay between Matt and Logan was ultimately their business. All she wanted was the ranch. "You'll help me? You'll help me run the Circle J?"

"I'll help."

She threw her arms around him in a quick hug, then hurried toward the barn. Blackstone had gone back inside. She found him packing his shaving things into his valise.

"You can't leave," she said. "We have to talk."

He looked up, his face a mask of indifference. "I shouldn't have come out here in the first place. Everything could have been handled from town."

"Logan, please. Matt isn't going to fight me on the extension anymore. If that was your reason—"

"It wasn't." He hefted the valise, tucked his cane under his right arm, and stepped past her toward the door.

Cat stared after him. He was leaving. Just like that.

116

Matthew's capitulation had been for nothing. Cat saw everything she'd ever dreamed of slipping through her fingers. All because of this man, this man who had loosed undreamed-of emotions in her just last night. She raced after him and caught his arm.

"Please, Logan," she said, her heart thundering. "I'll do anything to save the ranch. Anything."

He turned slowly, his gaze trailing suggestively along the curves of her body, settling with insulting heat on the revealing bodice of her blouse. "Anything?"

She gasped. "I didn't mean it that way!"

"Didn't you?" For an unguarded instant something flashed in those gray eyes, but she was too upset to analyze it.

"How dare you!" she blustered.

"Why so angry?" he drawled. "I didn't say I'd turn you down."

She arced a hand toward his face, but he intercepted the blow, his wrist banding hers in a grip of iron. "You're despicable!" she cried.

"Then it's finally unanimous among the Jordans." He let go of her and started out the door.

This wasn't happening, Cat thought wildly. It couldn't end this way. "Logan, don't do this."

"Prolonging the process will just make it more difficult for everyone."

"More difficult for you," she said. "That's it, isn't it?"

He dropped the valise, turning fully to face her. "I don't want to hurt you, Cat."

"Then don't. Give me a chance to save my home."

"You're asking more than you know."

"Three months," she said. "Three months and we'll sell the fall herd. You'll have your money."

117

"It's not the mon—" He swallowed the rest, his jaw tightening. "I had it all planned, you know. I'd come back here, look your brother straight in the eye, tell him . . ."

"Tell him anything you like," Cat interrupted. "But tell me that I have the extension."

"You're a very stubborn woman."

"Does that mean yes?"

"That means I'm a fool not to climb in that buggy and get the hell out of here."

"At least it's not a no."

He shook his head. "I've had business dealings with the crowned heads of Europe, and none of them have given me as much trouble as you."

"I'll consider that a compliment." Stepping close to him, she smiled up into warm gray eyes. Her smile faded, when he stepped back.

"This is business," he said gruffly. "If I even consider this extension, that has to be clearly understood. Strictly business."

"Of course," she said, flustered. "I wouldn't have it any other way." Then why did it hurt to say that?

He left the valise where he'd dropped it, leaned his cane against the barn wall and moved out into the sunlight. "You'd be able to pay off the debt when the herd is sold?"

Cat's hopes had soared and fallen so often these past twenty-four hours, she barely registered their flickering to life once again. "I could pay it all, and half again more."

"That wouldn't be necessary."

"Yes. It would."

He stared at her, stared into green eyes, now blazing emerald bright. He needed to put an end to this, as much

118

for her sake as his own. She didn't know the true cost of maintaining a Jordan-Blackstone alliance. And he couldn't be the one to tell her.

So why didn't he say no? Why didn't he simply foreclose on the Circle J and head back to Boston?

She kept looking at him, her eyes wide, expectant. He couldn't find the words it would take to turn her down. Instead, he deflected them. He looked toward the ranchyard. "Weren't the men going to be breaking some horses this morning?"

"What does that have to do with the loan?"

"Maybe I should refresh my memory on how this ranch works on a day-to-day basis," he hedged. "It'll help me decide if I think you can pull it off."

"Oh, of course." She hurried past him. "Come on, I'll show you."

"I haven't said yes," he reminded her.

"But you will." She allowed a tentative smile. "You will." The man was as perplexing as ever, but she hadn't misjudged him after all. He was fair, and she would count on that. And though he frowned in consternation at her declaration, he made no attempt to discourage her, as they headed across the yard toward the swirling dust clouds the wranglers and their mounts were already stirring up in the main corral.

"Is that one of the horses they're breaking?" Logan asked, gesturing toward the blue-black roan pacing alone in a small pen away from the others.

Cat shook her head. "That's Blue Demon. He's thrown off every rider on the ranch at least twice. But Esteban's determined not to give up on him."

"Looks like he's got some Spanish blood."

"That's what Esteban thinks," Cat said, impressed by

119

Logan's savvy about horses. "He thinks Demon's bloodlines go all the way back to the conquistadors. He and Dusty both figure him for a good stud, if they can just convince him who's boss."

The stallion snorted and reared. "I think he already knows," Logan said.

Cat laughed. "You may be right. If no one can ride him, Esteban will probably let him loose on the range again."

They continued along to the holding pen where Esteban and the other wranglers had herded a half-dozen broomtails. The adjacent corral, connected by a common gate, was the largest on the ranch. It was in this enclosure that most of the horses were broken to saddle on the Circle J.

"Time to see some real cowboys at work," Cat said, waving to Dusty, who was working the new horses from the back of a wiry little bay mare. Cat urged Logan to follow her up to the best seat in the house—the uppermost rail of the corral.

"Real cowboys?" he questioned, balancing himself beside her. "You mean real men, right? Not bankers." He slapped a spot of dust from his jacket and adjusted his string tie.

"Can a banker sit a bucking horse?"

"Is that your criterion for manhood?"

"It's one of 'em," she said dryly, pleased when he smiled a little. "I bet you've never raised a callus in your life."

Impulsively, she grabbed his right hand. Her initial notion of poking fun at its softness ended with her awareness of the life pulsing beneath the layering of flesh. Was it her imagination or did his skin feel warmer

120

than her own? She had to steel herself to look disdainful. "Lily white. Good for adding up figures maybe . . ."

"Good for other things, too," he said, his voice husky.

She dropped the hand, forcing herself to sit at prim attention on the rail. "I wouldn't know about such things, sir."

"I'd be happy to teach you."

She cast him a sideways glance. "Is this the same man who said everything was to be strictly business between us?"

He scratched his chin thoughtfully. "I'd conduct lessons in only the most businesslike manner."

She smiled, blushing, amazed at the easy charm that seemed to come so naturally to Logan Blackstone. Maybe he wasn't above passing dalliances after all. She would have to be on her guard. A man of his sophistication could no doubt take his pleasure where he found it. But what would be no more than a pleasant diversion for him could never be so to her.

She paid exaggerated attention to young Jim Spence as he prepared to ride the first horse, a piebald mare. But she couldn't take her mind off Logan. As he had from the first, the man continued to baffle her. When not even aware of it, he could be friendly, even flirtatious, with her. But when something reminded him of why he'd returned to Texas in the first place, his demeanor almost by force of will would grow cold and distant.

Just sitting next to him like this had her pulses racing. Did he feel it too? Some indefinable, yet undeniable, kinship between them? She studied his handsome features covertly. She would have to be very, very careful. Yesterday it had been only an absurd joke, made to herself, that the last person on earth her mother would

121

want her to marry was a Blackstone. And while any consideration of marriage was still an absurdity, her own feelings of what she would think of such a proposition were being inexorably altered by the very presence of this puzzling, fascinating, vexating man named Logan Blackstone. Some inner void, some part of her life she hadn't even known was empty, was in serious danger of being filled by this man.

With a force of will, she fashioned an overbright smile when she noticed him watching her. Again she sensed regret in him. As though he fought some unknown inner battle every time he was with her. When his gaze grew more intense, she shifted her attention to the corral's interior.

"Get her, Jim!" she cheered. Dusty and Esteban had hazed the mare into a narrow chute so that Jim could settle himself on the horse's back before she was released into the corral.

Esteban threw open the chute. At first the mare just stood there, trembling. A nudge from Jim's bootheels convinced her to move out into the corral, but she made only a halfhearted attempt to buck Jim off, then spent three minutes galloping around the perimeter of the corral.

"Not much fight in this little lady," Jim said, looking thoroughly pleased with himself. He reined the mare over to the rail near Cat and dismounted. "Must be my natural charm with women."

The mare promptly nipped him in the behind.

"She just has subtler methods of handling men," Cat said, laughing.

Jim swatted playfully at the mare with his hat, then led her out of the corral.

"Looks like we've got another spectator," Logan said.

Cat followed his gaze to see Matt making his way toward them along the outside of the corral.

"He's been on those crutches all morning," Cat said, not liking at all the tight-lipped way her brother was holding himself. The pain was getting worse. She looked toward the house, expecting to see her mother come scurrying out with Matt's wheelchair. "Ma must not know Matt's out here." Cat herself wished fervently that he was not.

Logan leaned toward her. "Has he ever checked with a doctor about that pain?"

"Sanderson says it's nerve damage."

"Sanderson?" Logan's brow furrowed, as if trying to place the name. "Is he the same—"

"The one who amputated Matt's leg. Yes."

"Has he ever been to see anyone else?" Logan asked, then straightened as Matt reached them.

"Talking about me?" Matt asked.

Cat cringed at the belligerence in her brother's voice. He had promised to be on her side about the extension. Baiting Logan wasn't exactly her idea of living up to that agreement.

"Logan wanted to see the boys break some horses," Cat said, praying her voice sounded more nonchalant to her brother than it did to her. She was surprised when Matt struggled up onto the corral rail beside her. "Are you sure you should do that?" she asked.

An angry glare was his only response. Very pointedly he turned his attention to the corral. Cat was forced to do the same. She wasn't imagining the hostility crackling between the two men now sitting on either side of her.

Obidiah rode the next two horses. The third, a

cantankerous bay gelding, sent Obie flipping head over heels into the dirt. As the veteran wrangler tried to rise, his knee buckled.

"Tough one," Obie grudgingly admitted, limping over to the rail. "But I'd be on him again if not for this danged knee."

"Maybe Logan could give it a try," Matt said.

"Him?" Obie snorted, slapping his hat against his thigh. The other wranglers joined in with boisterous, though good-natured, guffaws.

"Five greenbacks say he'd hit the dirt before his butt hit the saddle," Dusty said.

"Maybe I could make it even more worth his while than that," Matt said.

"What did you have in mind?" Logan asked, his voice deceptively mild.

Cat glared at her brother. What was he up to? And why was she already certain she wasn't going to like it one damned bit?

"Does your asking mean you're game for a little bronc ride, Logan?" Matt smirked, listing so far forward that he almost toppled from the rail. Quickly Cat caught his shoulder, easing him back. It was then she noticed the scent of whiskey. She grimaced. The pain of using the crutches had been too much for him and he had gone back into the house for his third crutch. "Matt, please," she said. "You're drunk. Logan is no wrangler, and you know it."

"I can fight my own battles, Miss Jordan," Logan said, and Cat had to wonder if he'd reverted to addressing her formally because of her brother's presence or because she'd embarrassed him by trying to intercede with Matt on his behalf.

"One little ride," Matt taunted.

"And what would this ride cost me, if I didn't make it?"

Matt didn't blink an eye. "The Circle J."

"Matt," Cat hissed, "what are you talking about? Is this the *help* you promised me?"

"I believe I already have full control of this ranch," Logan said, ignoring her completely.

"But this would clear your conscience about it," Matt sneered. "We all know how seriously you take your moral obligations."

Cat felt the fury coming off Logan in waves. If she hadn't been sitting between them, she was certain Logan would have put his fist in Matt's face.

"Think about it," Matt continued. "The Circle J would be all yours to do with as you will. No more hassles from the Jordans." He looked meaningfully at Cat. "None of us."

"And that would clear my conscience, eh?" Logan said, his voice tight with suppressed violence. So much so that Cat was suddenly wildly afraid that these two men could actually be capable of killing each other.

"I fall off," Logan continued, "you get the ranch. Just like that."

"Oh, I wouldn't expect you to be that generous," Matt said, his words slurring. "You'd just give us the extension Cat wants."

Logan's head jerked toward her. The accusation was in his eyes. Had she and her brother concocted this whole performance? She longed to deny it, but she couldn't add to her brother's disgrace by taking Logan's side against him. Her insides knotted as Logan's gaze hardened with disgust.

125

"It sounds like I'm taking most of the risk," he said.

Cat couldn't believe he was actually considering this madness.

"Scared?" Matt taunted.

"Tell me where I can change my clothes," Logan said, jumping down from the corral rail. "This suit isn't exactly bronc-busting material."

"Help yourself to whatever you like," Matt said, gesturing drunkenly toward the house. "My room's the first one on the left."

Logan stalked away without a backward glance.

Instantly, Cat turned on her brother. "Are you out of your mind?" she demanded. "He trusted me. He was going to give me the extension. I know it."

"There's no trust between Jordans and Blackstones, Cat," Matt said, his eyelids drooping against the glare of the sun. "It's time you learned that little lesson the hard way."

"Have you even considered the half of what you've done?" she cried, outraged. "What if Logan makes the ride? He's not the complete dandy he looks. We could lose everything."

"Take it easy," Matt said, waving off Dusty who had started to haze the bay into the mounting chute. "Not that one," he said angrily. "Saddle up Blue Demon."

Chapter Eight

Cat shuddered, as she stared at Blue Demon. Teeth bared, ears flat against his head, the stallion reared again and again within the cramped confines of the holding chute, slamming body-long against the slatted sides. The pine splintered, cracked, threatening to give way altogether under the vicious onslaught of hooves and brute strength.

"Hold him in there!" Esteban shouted, cursing as Dusty's third attempt to get a saddle on the beast failed.

"It's like tryin' to saddle up the devil hisself!" Jim Spence groaned. For the fourth time he risked life and limb to retrieve the downed saddle from the bottom of the chute.

"We'll get him this time!" Dusty yelled.

"Blackstone better hurry," Cat heard Obie mutter, "or there won't be no corral left to ride this damned hoss in."

The whole time the men battled the stallion, Matt stood off, watching, a belligerent light in his deep brown eyes. Leaning against his crutches, he tipped a whiskey bottle to his lips and took a long pull.

Cat looked away, pity vying sharply with disgust.

On their fourth try with Blue Demon, the men succeeded.

"You really going to let Logan ride 'im, Cat?" Dusty asked, coming over to stand beside her at the rail. He was using the bandana he'd had tied around his neck to wipe the sweat dripping from his brow.

"I don't recall my having any say in the matter."

"Never known that to make no never mind with you before."

Cat picked at the rough-edged wood of the rail, not looking at him. "Do you think he could be hurt?"

"Ya mean more'n a twisted knee or a bump on his noggin?"

She nodded.

"Even Obie don't always have a choice how he parts company with a bronc. You know that as well as I do."

"Maybe Logan won't make the ride," Cat said hopefully. "Maybe he'll call the bet off."

"No," Dusty said. "He won't."

"How can you know?" she demanded, wondering at the fear that rippled through her at Dusty's quiet pronouncement. "You haven't seen him since he was twelve years old."

"Knowin' the boy he was, I'd 'uv made a wager of my own on the kinda man he'd be. And I'd have been right."

Cat glanced at Demon, now standing almost placidly in the loading chute, waiting. She glanced toward the house, from which Logan had not yet emerged. "Just what kind of a boy was he, Dusty?"

"That ain't my place to say."

"I think it is," Cat said. "You know Matt and mother's

128

opinion. I was only four years old then. I need to know from someone who was there. Someone who could be fair."

He stared at the ground. "If your pa never told ya, it ain't my place to say," he repeated stubbornly.

Cat sighed heavily. "I don't know how much more of this secrecy I can take." She turned toward him. "Sheriff Toby told me about your own secret, Dusty."

He looked uncomfortable.

"Why didn't you tell me?"

"He shouldn't 'uv said nothin'. I could be mistaken. I didn't want to worry you. And I sure don't want to upset your ma."

"I'm glad he told me. If Pa was murdered, then that means whoever killed him is still out there."

"Now don't you go gettin' any fool notions," Dusty said, scowling. "I been nosin' around here and there myself. If'n I find somethin', me and Toby will take care of it."

"He was my father, Dusty," Cat said. "I'll expect you to come to me."

"Right now what you gotta do is save the Circle J. That's what your pa woulda wanted."

"*I* already saved the Circle J!" Matt slurred, hobbling back over to where Cat and Dusty stood. "Logan's going to land on his head in five seconds flat."

Dusty shook his head sadly and headed back over with the other wranglers. Cat knew there was no getting through to Matt when he was this drunk, so she didn't even try. Instead, she glanced anxiously toward the house, praying Dusty was wrong, that Logan would not be foolhardy enough to come back out here. She'd barely finished the thought when the front door opened and

Logan stepped out.

Her heart turned over. He had scavenged a pair of Matt's scruffy denims and a white cotton shirt. If she had found him handsome before, she couldn't take her eyes off him now. As he walked he threaded a hand through dusty black hair to settle a battered Stetson atop his head. To complete the transformation he yanked a red bandana from his back pocket and knotted it around his neck. Citified, dandified Logan Blackstone looked every inch a lifelong cowboy.

Cat shook herself, aware that he'd seen her staring. She swallowed her embarrassment, unable to give in to such trivialities now. She had to make him listen. She hurried over to him. "You mustn't do this."

Blue Demon's shrill whinny split the air. Logan looked toward the corral and noticed the stallion for the first time. His eyes widened with what Cat at first labeled disbelief. Then he looked at her.

"I . . . didn't know," she said, barely able to think under the quiet loathing of that gaze. "Please, you don't have to go through with it."

"The wager stands." His voice was ice, his gaze tracked the rise and fall of her décolletage. "I must say," he went on with deceptive calm, "I admire your attention to detail, Miss Jordan. Every nuance of your little drama was carried out to perfection. I wondered why you seemed so . . . understanding in the barn last night. Now I know."

"Dammit, don't do this. Don't—"

"Spare me any more theatrics. I have a horse to ride." He allowed himself a sardonic smile. "And then you and your family can start packing to get the hell off *my* ranch."

130

He stepped around her. Cat couldn't believe the hurt that sliced through her. That he believed her capable of such deceit tore at her as nothing ever had. He had come back to Texas expecting to be treated badly by her mother and brother. But from her he had obviously expected, if not friendship, at least a peaceful neutrality. And after last night—much to his dismay to be sure—his expectations may well have taken a decidedly more intimate turn. Even had they not, he would never have expected overt enmity between them.

And now, thanks to her brother, Logan saw her as just one more Jordan who would stop at nothing to gain her way with a Blackstone.

She ran back to the corral.

Logan had climbed up the side of the chute and was straddling its width, positioning himself above the high-strung horse.

"Ride 'em, cowboy!" Matt shouted from where he'd again climbed to the top rail of the corral.

Logan ignored him. Twice he almost got aboard Demon, only to have the stallion buck upward, forcing him to scramble back topside.

"Hold him steady," Logan growled to Spence and Hidalgo. Then he shoved his hands into the gloves Dusty offered him.

"You sure you want to do this, *señor?*" Esteban asked.

Logan didn't answer.

Cat stalked over to her brother. His eyes were glazed. "You can stop this," she said.

"He agreed," Matt grumbled sullenly.

"Not to Demon."

"What do you care?" He sneered. "If Logan falls off, you get your extension. That's what you wanted,

131

isn't it?"

"Not this way." And it was true. As desperately as she wanted to save the ranch, she would rather give it over to a passing transient than win it like this.

"He owes me," Matt said.

"His life? He could break his fool neck. Is that what you want? Would that make you even?"

For an instant Cat thought she had gotten through to him, but then he very deliberately shifted his attention back to the center of the corral, shutting her out. He had laid his pride on the line—in front of Logan, in front of the men. He wasn't going to take the wager back.

Cat held her breath as Logan lowered himself onto Demon's back. He curled the reins around his right hand three times, then gave the nod to Esteban.

The chute flew open.

Cat's hands flew to her mouth. In an explosive burst of equine muscle Blue Demon reared and bucked all in one motion. Twisting, kicking, leaping, the stallion battled to rid itself of the man.

One second . . . two . . . three . . . Cat felt each drag by interminably, expecting any instant to see Logan catapulted through the air to land in a twisted heap in the dirt, or to be trampled by Demon's hooves.

Ten seconds . . . twenty . . . Still Logan hung on, his body whiplashed in grotesque rhythm with the stallion's.

"It's been long enough," Cat cried. To Dusty and Esteban, she shouted, "Get him off!"

The wranglers started toward their mounts.

"No!" Matt bellowed. "He rides him to a standstill or he loses the bet!" In that instant Demon slammed into the corral not eight feet from where Matt sat. The vibrations rocked through the wood. Matt, drunk and off

132

balance, made a feeble attempt to right himself, but caught only air.

Cat let out a shriek of horror, as he pitched forward, tumbling into the corral. Matt screamed in pain as he landed full force on his left side. He lay there, writhing, helpless.

In a heartbeat Cat scrambled between the railings, one eye still on the bucking stallion. She caught Matt under the shoulders and pulled with all her might. She couldn't budge him.

Blue Demon had seen these new intruders. Trumpeting a challenge, the stallion raced toward the fallen Matt. With a superhuman effort, Logan hauled back on the right rein, trying to turn the horse. The stallion tripped, crashing heavily to its left. Logan leaped aside, hitting the ground at a dead run. He reached Matt as the stallion regained its feet.

"Get out of here!" he shouted at Cat.

She dove back between the rails as Logan gripped Matt under the armpits and dragged him toward the loading chute.

Dusty and Esteban whipped the gate shut, as the stallion thundered by.

Cat had no time to feel any relief. Scurrying under the lowest rail, she rushed to her brother's side.

"Don't touch me," Matt gasped, his arms flailing as Logan fought to keep him still.

"You may have broken something," Logan gritted. "Don't move."

Matt ground his teeth together to keep from screaming. Then his whole body shuddered, his head lolling to one side.

"Matt!" Cat dropped to her knees beside her brother.

"My God, Matt." Wild-eyed, she whirled on Logan. "Is he dead? Please don't let him be dead."

Using a gentle pressure Logan lay his fingers alongside Matt's throat. "He's all right. He just passed out."

"We have to take him inside!" Cat cried.

Spence and Dusty lifted the unconscious Matt and began to carry him toward the house. Cat hurried ahead of them.

Aware that Logan followed, she dared a glance back. Her heart thudded.

He looked grim, dangerous. And she had to wonder who he loathed more—her brother or herself.

Chapter Nine

Cat banged open the door to the house, ahead of the wranglers carrying Matt. "Take him straight to his room. I'll get my mother." She wasn't looking forward to telling Olivia about Matt's injury, but there was no help for it. Cat started toward the kitchen, hoping to reassure her mother before she actually saw Matt.

But Olivia must have heard the commotion. She was already standing in the kitchen archway. For a frozen instant she stared at Cat, not comprehending. Then with a shriek of horror she was across the room.

Cat tried to intercept her, but Olivia shoved past her. She clutched at Matt's shirtfront with such violence that Jim Spence almost lost his grip on Matt's shoulders.

"Mama, please," Cat said, trying to pull her back.

"He's not moving!" Olivia cried. "My God, he's not moving." She clutched at Cat's arm. "Cordelia, please, he's not . . . he isn't . . ."

"He's unconscious," Cat said quickly, motioning for the men to go on ahead of her, "but he'll be all right." Briefly she told her mother what had happened, wanting to calm her as much as possible before her mother went to Matt's room. She would be no help to him if she was hysterical.

"We put 'im in bed," Dusty said, coming back up the hallway. "You need us for anything else, Cat?"

"No," Cat said. "Thanks. You can finish with the horses." She glanced behind Dusty and Spence, then back toward the living room, her heart sinking when Logan was nowhere in sight. "Dusty," she called, "did Mr. Blackstone leave?"

"No, ma'am," the foreman said. "He's in there with Matt."

Olivia gasped. Cat was on her mother's heels as they both bolted down the hall.

They found Matt, still unconscious, settled atop the bedcovers, Logan sitting beside him. Logan was just starting to unbutton Matt's shirt.

"Don't touch him!" Olivia cried, storming over to the bed. "You'll not harm him again."

"Get me some water," Logan said, not looking up. Cat watched as he applied pressure with his hands against Matt's rib cage.

Matt groaned, but did not wake up.

"Stop that!" Olivia cried, grabbing at Logan's arm.

Logan pulled his arm free and glanced up briefly, his face a mask of stony indifference. Though he looked at Olivia, he directed his anger toward Cat. "If your mother can't control herself, Miss Jordan, get her out of here."

Cat winced at the leashed fury she sensed in him. He was still livid over the bet. Yet there was no evidence of anything but calm detachment in the way he continued to work on her brother.

"Mama," Cat said, trying to guide Olivia toward a

136

chair at the back of the room. "I think it would be better if—"

Olivia pulled away. "I take care of Matthew," she said, an edge of hysteria creeping into her voice. "I always take care of Matthew." She walked around to the other side of the bed, lifting Matt's limp hand into her own. "I took care of him this morning, brought him his breakfast."

Cat could tell her mother was fighting back tears and, more than that, was battling a thoroughly unwarranted guilt. "Mother, Matt came outside of his own accord. He wanted to watch the men work the horses." She hadn't told her mother of Matt's outrageous wager with Logan.

"He told me he wanted to sleep," Olivia went on, as though Cat hadn't spoken. "He was cross . . . I mean, tired," she amended swiftly. "He needed more rest. I—" She looked helplessly at Cat. "I always take good care of him."

"Of course you do," Cat said, coming over to awkwardly put her arm around her mother's shoulders. Cat felt woefully inadequate in this unaccustomed role of comforting her mother.

"Is one of you going to get me that water?" Logan broke in tersely. "Or do I have to do it myself?"

Quickly Cat led Olivia to the chair in the far corner of the room and sat her down; then she went to Matt's dressing table and poured water from the pitcher into the tin basin alongside it. She brought the basin to Logan, setting it within easy reach on Matt's bedside table.

"I'll need clean cloths and some whiskey," Logan said.

Cat complied, then sat down on the opposite side of the bed to watch as Logan dipped one of the cloths into the water and smoothed it over Matt's forehead and face,

137

checking critically but not ungently for cuts and bruises.

"How is he?" she asked, unable to keep the tentative note out of her voice. She kept expecting Logan to snap her head off. Instead he continued his emotionless, methodical examination of Matt's injuries. And he didn't answer.

Matt groaned again and Cat prayed her brother remained unconscious until Logan had finished. If he should waken to find Logan tending to him . . . She didn't even want to finish the thought.

Cat glanced back at her mother, who was now being unnaturally quiet. Olivia sat, wringing her hands, her eyes shifting nervously from Logan to Matt and back again.

"How is he?" Cat asked again, the silence in the room beginning to unnerve her.

"I don't know yet," Logan allowed, wiping his hands on one of the towels. "I want you and your mother to leave for a few minutes."

"Why?" Cat blurted.

A muscle in Logan's jaw jumped, but he did not repeat his request.

"Mother," Cat said, turning to Olivia, "maybe you should have some broth ready when Matt wakes up."

Olivia stood at once. "Yes, yes, that would be good for him, wouldn't it?"

Cat nodded, relieved when her mother left the room. She looked at Logan. "I'm staying."

He didn't argue, speaking in that same toneless voice, "Do you have a knife?"

Her eyes widened, but she reached into the drawer beside Matt's bed and pulled out a small paring knife.

Logan cut at the bloodied pantleg of Matt's denims.

Only then did Cat realize his intent. "No," she said, catching his wrist. "You can't, you mustn't. Not his leg. He doesn't let anyone—"

"There's blood. I think he landed on it."

"If he wakes up . . ."

"It needs to be cleaned."

Cat felt herself trembling, tears hovering at the corners of her eyes. "My mother's the only one he's ever allowed to see it. And that was because he was a boy when it happened and he had no choice. I can't let you do this."

Logan sat back. "Fine," he said tightly. "Send for a doctor."

Cat closed her eyes. If she sent a rider to Red Springs immediately, it would be eight hours before Doc Sanderson could get here. And that was assuming he was in his office and not on call at some outlying ranch. "Matt would never forgive me," she whispered helplessly.

"It has to be done. If it gets infected . . ." He didn't need to finish.

She felt herself giving in, sensed that other options were closed to her. But she couldn't help pressing Logan further. "Are you . . . are you sure you know what you're doing?"

He hesitated, not seeming to want to justify himself to her.

"He's my brother," she said softly.

Logan let out a heavy sigh. "I went to Harvard Medical School for two years," he said. "I had to drop out when my father took ill."

She looked again at his hands, remembering their suppleness beneath her own rough palms. Long fingers, skilled fingers. The man had wanted to be a doctor. A doctor! Had his curiosity about Matt's pain been more than aging guilt?

"I also keep up with medical journals," Logan went on, "and I did work at hospitals when I was in Europe."

Logan was speaking matter-of-factly of how qualified he was to treat Matt, as though Matt were one of the hands. Surely he knew Matt would not even have allowed Logan into the room were he awake and aware. "He'll hate me," she murmured. "He'll hate me."

Logan sat quietly, saying nothing else. A minute passed, then two. Cat knew she had only one choice.

"All right," Cat said. "Do it."

Logan again began to cut away at the denim. Cat thought about leaving the room, feeling as if she were irretrievably violating Matt's privacy. But she didn't want to leave him alone with Logan. Not out of any fear of what Logan would do, but out of fear for her brother. If Matt awoke and tried to fight Logan, he could worsen his injuries.

Logan peeled back the material of the pantleg.

Cat stared at the maimed flesh that had for fifteen years tormented the brother she loved, and despised herself for wanting to turn away.

Logan's hands remained gentle, unhurried. Slowly he massaged the leg where it ended just above the knee. There was no revulsion in his gray eyes. "Hand me the whiskey."

She did so.

He poured a little on a clean cloth and began to dab at the nasty scrape that had caused most of the bleeding.

"Is it serious?" she asked.

"The cut is fairly superficial, but . . ." He continued to examine the limb.

"But what?"

"I can't be sure," he said slowly, "but I think there are bone spurs on the femur. The bone is longer than it should be for the amount of flesh."

Cat shuddered. She was not handling this conversation too well. "Um, is there . . . is there something that can be done about that?" she managed.

"Additional surgery might reduce the pain."

"Cut his leg again?" Cat knew she sounded as horrified as she felt, but she couldn't help it.

"The pain of the surgery would go away," Logan explained with a genuine patience that surprised her. "And then he'd have the real possibility, if not of being pain free, at least of having reduced it to more tolerable levels. He wouldn't have to rely on the whiskey and the laudanum quite so much."

"Do you think Doc Sanderson could do this operation?"

"I think Matt should have it done at a hospital. I know a fine surgeon in Philadelphia."

"Matt would never agree . . ."

Matt groaned, his head shifting from side to side. He inhaled sharply. He was feeling the pain now. He was waking up.

Cat smoothed the cool cloth over his forehead, while Logan continued to dress the leg. "It's all right, Matt," she soothed.

"Maria," he murmured, "Maria." Slowly, as though the effort itself were painful, he opened his eyes. Logan reached for the laudanum. Matt took two spoonfuls before realizing who'd given them to him. When he did, his whole body stiffened. Seemingly against his will, his gaze trailed downward. He looked at his leg. He looked at

Logan and Cat.

He began to shake uncontrollably.

Cat could feel his humiliation as fiercely as if it ripped through her own body. His eyes were overbright. "Get out!" he rasped. "Both of you! Get out!"

He yanked at the bedcovers, but Logan and Cat were sitting on them and the covers didn't budge.

"Get out!" he cried again. "Get out!"

"If you want me to send for Dusty and Esteban to sit on you while I finish dressing your leg, I will," Logan said, his voice so implacable, so merciless it made Cat wince.

"Matt, please," Cat said. "It's all right."

"Don't talk to me!" he shouted. "You let him do this. You let him see . . . you let him . . ." His voice broke.

Cat would never forget the look of betrayal in her brother's eyes. Tears tracked unheeded down her cheeks. "You were hurt," she said, her own voice breaking. "He helped you." But Matt wasn't hearing a word she said.

"Get away from me!" His arms flailed violently.

Logan pinned him down and Matt swore. His swearing became little more than an impotent whisper when he couldn't force Logan off of him. "The sooner you let me finish this the sooner I'll be out of here," Logan said.

Matt turned his head, but let his hands go limp. He shut his eyes tight, his body became rigid as Logan tied off the bandage on his leg.

Logan rose and Matt instantly drew the bedcovers up to his chin. He did not open his eyes. "Get out," he rasped again.

Cat started toward the door, expecting Logan to follow. Instead he said, "You go ahead, I'll be out in a minute."

She wanted to insist, but the look in Logan's eyes told

142

her he wasn't about to listen to anything she said. Her heart aching, she closed the door on her brother's fury.

"I'll never forgive you for this, Cat. Never," he called after her.

Logan stood at the foot of Matt's bed and waited. He wasn't looking forward to this, but it couldn't be helped. He and Matt had to have this out. It was why he had come back to Texas.

He admitted the timing wasn't the best. Matt was hardly in any condition for a confrontation. But maybe that would work to their advantage. Maybe the pain would make Matt honest.

Matt struggled to sit up, his lips white against the agonizing pain in his leg. He didn't waste any words. "Did you tell her?" he demanded.

"No."

"Are you going to?"

Logan didn't answer.

"Damn you."

"Damn me?" Logan hissed, his own temper snapping. Matt Jordan might not be ready for honesty, but he was going to get it anyway. "Yes, by all means, damn me. Again and always. Damned by you for fifteen years." He stepped back toward the bed. "But if you'll remember, I damned myself too."

"That's because it's your fault."

"My fault you're a drunk?"

"Get out of here."

"Not just yet. I think we both know this conversation is long overdue."

"You want them to know, don't you?" Matt said, his

143

voice rising. "You want mother and Cat to know what I did."

"I made you a promise. I've kept it for fifteen years."

Matt snorted contemptuously. "*Saint* Logan. Always the martyr. Always so damned honorable. You make me sick!"

"You make yourself sick." Logan paced over to the window, though he kept his attention on Matt. "Do you really think your mother would give a damn if she knew the whole of it? She'd hate me just the same. And Cat—" He paused, not certain where his thoughts were about Cat Jordan. "Cat wouldn't blame either one of us. She'd understand."

"Like I never did, right?" Matt grabbed up the whiskey bottle and took a long pull. "Well, I don't have to understand. I'm the one that lost my leg. That should pay me back. That should sure as hell pay me back." His voice shook.

"Dammit," Logan said. "You don't deserve this. Nobody does. It's the pain and the whiskey talking. I checked your leg. I think surgery might—"

"Who made you a doctor?" Matt yelled. "Sainted Doctor Logan Blackstone! God spare me!"

"If you'd listen—"

"I'll listen to nothing you have to say. Nothing!" He took another drink of the whiskey.

"Fine. You lay in that bed another fifteen years. See if I give a damn."

"I hate you! I hate your damned guts!"

"No more than you hate your own," Logan said coldly, starting toward the door. "I'll show myself out."

"And stay away from my sister!" Matt shouted. "I saw

144

the way you looked at her. You keep your filthy hands off her. She's young. She doesn't know any better."

"Whatever happens between Cat and me is our business." Logan said it, though he knew he dared let nothing happen between them. He told himself he wanted to goad Matt into an argument, to force him to fight back. But the anger coursing through Logan was genuine. His hands were balled into fists. He wanted nothing more than to knock some sense into Matt Jordan's stubborn head. And that wasn't fair. That wasn't fair at all.

Logan stood there, his hand on the doorknob. "I'm sorry, Matt. More than you know."

Matt swore viciously. "I'll just bet you are." He laughed without humor. "*Bet* you are. Get it? Bet! At least Cat got her extension. You can go back to Boston, back to your precious bank accounts. You can update your ledgers about your contribution to the Jordan charity case."

"It wasn't charity. It was business. And maybe it was friendship too."

Matt swore again. "The Blackstone version of friendship? Your being here to foreclose shows how much that's worth. As if you needed that loan money. What we owe can't be more than an ink blot on the Blackstone fortune."

"The loan was a debt of honor. Your father understood that. But I don't suppose you would."

Matt heaved the whiskey bottle at Logan. Logan sidestepped, the bottle crashing, splattering against the wall.

The door flew open, Cat rushing into the room. She

145

stared at Matt, who sat up in bed, trembling violently. Cat turned accusingly toward Logan. "What did you say to my brother?"

"Not nearly enough," Logan said, his voice edged with an acid bitterness. Then he stepped past her and was gone.

Chapter Ten

Logan stalked toward the front of the house, fighting to control his temper. Fifteen years. How had Matt held on to such hatred for fifteen years? More to the point, why?

Hadley's long-ago letter had hinted at unresolved bitterness. But to cling to it all these years just didn't make any sense. He paused, recalling something Cat had said. That there had been times Matt had regaled her with the adventures he'd had with Logan that summer. It wasn't much. But the fact that there had been interludes in Matt's bitterness—at least with Cat—gave Logan some hope.

So why Matt's burning hatred now? It couldn't just be the ongoing legacy of the accident.

Was it Olivia's doing? Certainly her smothering overprotection was part of it. But the Matt Jordan Logan had known could not have been made into a simpering invalid, even had he lost both legs, unless . . .

Unless it was the pain. The maddening, unending pain in Matt's leg.

Logan stood by the door, thoughtful. Could that be it?

Surely pain like that could drive anyone mad. Over time, ambition and independence and self-worth—all—would succumb to the overwhelming obsession of finding surcease from the pain. And it seemed obvious the only surcease Matt had yet been able to find was in a bottle.

But there could be another way. Logan's examination of Matt's leg had been proof of that. He had meant what he'd said to Cat. That additional surgery could help. He had seen it for himself, with crippled war veterans at hospitals in Boston. They would come into the hospital in agony from amputations botched years before in some makeshift field hospital during the War Between the States. Reconstructive surgery would often alleviate, even eliminate their pain.

Matt could benefit from the same technique. The only stumbling block was getting him to listen.

Logan glanced down the corridor toward Matt's room. Now that his temper had cooled, he considered going back and trying to reason with him. Instead of rehashing the past, they could look to the future. If Matt could foresee a life free of pain, maybe, just maybe he could let go of the bitterness that ate at his spirit like a cancer.

Logan took a step down the hallway, then stopped. What was he thinking? If Matt had been in no mood to listen before, he would be doubly reluctant now after the humiliation he'd suffered from having Logan tend his injuries.

Logan's only hope lay in convincing Cat. He had felt her agony in Matt's bedroom. Her decision to allow Logan to see Matt's leg had torn her apart. That she loved her brother, Logan had had no doubt, but seeing how deeply she empathized with what Matt was going through tugged at a part of him that had long ached for the same

148

kind of understanding. Matt wasn't the only one in pain.

Logan shook off the unwelcome self-pity. Still he was glad he could sort through some of the anger he'd been feeling toward Cat. For a time his cynicism had overshadowed his reason. Otherwise, he never could have believed—even for an instant—that Cat had been part of her brother's outrageous wager with Blue Demon.

In fact, she had done all she could to stop it—short of dressing down her brother in front of the Circle J crew. And that she couldn't do. Rather than blame her for that, Logan admired her loyalty.

That he could so easily exonerate Cat only unsettled him further. What was happening to him? Things were not going at all as he'd intended when first he'd told his father he would be traveling to Texas. He'd truly planned to do the Jordans a favor and foreclose quickly, quietly.

Then had come the thunderbolt from Cat; she didn't want him to foreclose. She wanted the chance that death had denied her father, a chance to keep her home alive. And every time Logan looked into those emerald eyes of hers, he felt his resolve to settle things quickly dissolve a little more.

Legally, he owed her nothing. But morally? Had Hadley been on his way to Red Springs to wire for more time when he'd died? Was his death somehow connected to that request? Logan hadn't wanted to say anything to Cat, but it was possible someone other than the Blackstones wanted the Circle J out of Jordan hands.

Who would benefit most by acquiring this ranch? If Logan went through with the extension, would such a move put Cat's life in danger?

These were things he had to discuss with her. When both of them could be calm and rational, when his blood didn't run hot just looking at her.

He swore inwardly. This wasn't getting any better. Perhaps he should just get away for a while. He would travel to Red Springs and finish the paperwork for the extension. He'd file all of the necessary papers with the town banker—what was his name?—Abner Vincent. Maybe it would be best if Cat dealt with Vincent from now on.

He was about to head outside when he was halted by Olivia's voice coming from somewhere behind him.

"How is my son?" she asked, a strange timidity in her tone.

Logan turned to see her peering anxiously at him from the kitchen.

"He'll be fine," Logan said.

Her hand fluttered to her chest, a shudder of relief coursing through her. "Thank God," she whispered.

Logan could tell she wanted nothing more than to flee down the hallway to her son's room. That she didn't, told him just how desperate she was. "How long are you going to make me suffer?" she asked finally.

"Suffer?" Logan questioned coldly. "You?"

"You're dragging this out as long as you can, aren't you?"

He didn't want this conversation. He didn't want it at all. "I came here to settle a debt."

"And we both know what that debt is, don't we?"

"Believe what you want, Olivia."

"Let the past die. Please."

"Like you have?" he gritted out. "Maybe if you'd done that fifteen years ago none of this—"

"I beg you!" Olivia cut in. "I can't bear it any longer.

150

You have to leave here. You have to leave at once. Please!"

The sound of footsteps in the hall made them both turn.

"What's going on here?" Cat demanded, crossing to her mother's side.

"It's nothing," Olivia assured her. "Nothing. How . . . how is your brother? I have some broth ready."

"He's awake." Cat never took her eyes from Logan.

Olivia hurried down the hallway, but not before she sent a pleading look back over her shoulder, directed at Logan.

Logan stiffened resolutely, wondering how much longer he was going to be able to deflect Cat's curiosity, wondering how much longer he even wanted to.

"First my brother, now my mother," Cat said, studying him with such fierce concentration Logan had the disturbing impression she was trying to read his mind. "I always thought they . . ." She hesitated, uncomfortable, he was certain, with what she had to say, but then saying it anyway. "I thought they hated you. But there's more to it than that, isn't there? They're afraid of you. Why?"

He shoved his hands into his pockets, musing about why the fates had made the most honest, open woman he'd ever met a member of a family who despised him. "I can't answer that."

"Can't or won't?"

"Take it any way you like."

"No! You have to tell me. Logan, please, this is my family we're talking about."

"I'm sorry." He frowned. How had *he* wound up

151

apologizing to *her*?

She moved closer to him, stopping bare inches away. He looked into those wide green eyes, surprised to find them brimming with sympathy.

"They've both hurt you," she said. "I know that."

"I cost Matt his leg." He hadn't meant to say the words. And he certainly hadn't meant them to be laced with such pain.

She extended a hand toward him, laying it against his chest. He told himself he should step back, leave. But he couldn't seem to summon the will to move.

"And that must have hurt *you* as much as it hurt Matt."

"No one ever considered how I felt," he said, knowing he was stepping on very dangerous ground, knowing how close he was coming to telling her everything.

"Make me understand, Logan. I want to understand."

With a groan he pulled her to him and kissed her hungrily, fiercely. His hands twined in the silky fullness of her hair. This was madness. She was Matt's sister. Nothing could ever come of it.

And yet just holding her, reveling in the fact that she kissed him back, felt so good, so right. He never wanted to let go.

"Corie," he rasped, raining kisses across her cheeks, her forehead, her neck. "Corie, I don't want to hurt you, too."

"You won't," she breathed. "You won't. Oh, Logan, I—"

"Cordelia!"

Cat jumped back.

Logan closed his eyes, swallowing a low curse. Why hadn't he heard Olivia coming back up the hallway? He looked at Cat, sickened by the stricken look in her eyes. The one thing he hadn't wanted to do was hurt her. Yet that was precisely what he'd done.

Stiff-backed, Olivia Jordan walked over to him. "I knew you came back to settle an old debt," she said. "But I never imagined just how far you'd go to settle it. To use my daughter . . . I guess I thought even a Blackstone wasn't capable of that."

"I told you before, Olivia," Logan said, "believe what you want to believe." He longed to ease the guilt and confusion he saw in Cat. But he couldn't do it with Olivia there.

"What does my mother mean, use me?" Cat demanded shakily. "Is that what you were doing?"

"No," Logan said.

"Liar!" Olivia shouted.

"I'd better go," he said.

"Logan, please," Cat said, catching his arm. "I need to know."

"We'll talk later."

"Stay away from her," Olivia hissed, yanking Cat's hand free of his arm. "Go back to Boston where you belong."

He kept his eyes on Cat. "We'll talk later," he said again. He didn't care what Olivia read into those words, he just didn't want Cat to believe him capable of using her. He wasn't sure he'd gotten the message through. In fact, he could have sworn she was regarding him with a rising suspicion. But there was little he could do about it now.

He only knew his departure from Texas had just been indefinitely delayed. He could live with Matt Jordan's hate. And Olivia's. But he knew, suddenly and irrevocably, that Cat's hatred he could never abide.

He would talk to Cat, explain to her that it was never his intention to involve her in this Jordan-Blackstone miasma of hate. He would convince her of that, even if it meant betraying a fifteen-year-old promise. Even if it meant telling Cat the truth.

Chapter Eleven

For long minutes after Logan left the house, Cat remained in front of the fireplace, trembling. She had come out of Matt's room expecting to face Logan's wrath about the bet. Instead she'd found him arguing with her mother. And it had been her own temper that had flared. When her mother had hurried to check on Matt, Cat had demanded that Logan tell her what was going on. As before, he had refused. And as before, she had sensed *his* pain.

And somehow she had wound up in his arms. The wonder of his kiss had left her shaken, bewildered. To have her mother walk in on them had only doubled her confusion.

Even after Logan had left, Olivia hadn't moved from where she stood in the hallway. Nor had she said another word. Somehow her silence was more condemning than any tirade could have been.

Using her. Olivia had accused Logan of using Cat. He had denied it. And Cat had ached to believe him. But underneath all of this bitterness lay a veiled something she couldn't begin to understand, because no one would tell her the full truth of it. And so the doubts remained.

If her mother was so certain Logan could use her—for vengeance, to settle an old debt, or simply out of Blackstone cruelty—then how could Cat entirely dismiss the notion? Her mother knew the whole of what had gone on fifteen years ago. Cat did not. Olivia would know how strong Logan's motivation could be. She would know if Logan had reason enough to use her daughter.

No! Cat denied it with an inner fury that astonished her. Her mother might have known Logan, the boy. But she did not know Logan, the man. Logan Blackstone would not use Cat Jordan.

Cat bit her lip, fighting back tears. Please God, he wouldn't, couldn't.

He had promised they would talk later. But when was later? Cat knew he was getting ready to head for Red Springs. Once there, she feared he might change his mind about setting things straight between them, that he might take the next stage back to Boston.

Cat couldn't let that happen. She turned to her mother. "I'm going to talk to him."

Olivia's eyes blazed. "No. I forbid it."

"I'm sorry, Mother. I don't want to hurt you. But I have to hear him out. I have to."

"Cordelia, you don't understand."

"Then tell me!" Cat cried. "For the love of heaven, Mama, make me understand. Tell me the truth."

Olivia twisted her hands in the folds of her skirts. "I can't."

"You *won't*. Just like Logan won't. And Matt won't." Cat dug her fingernails into the palms of her hands in frustration. "It isn't fair. Not to any of you. And

156

certainly not to me."

"Then let it go, Cordelia."

"I wish I could. Believe me, I wish I could. But there's something, something I can't even begin to explain. When I'm with Logan . . ." She paused, groping for the right words, realizing there were no right words—not to her mother, not about Logan Blackstone. So she chose the words most right for herself. "I think I'm falling in love with him, Mama."

Olivia gasped, her eyes wide, despairing. "Cordelia, I beg you, as your mother, please, *please*, stay away from that man."

"Why? Tell me why, and maybe I would. Maybe I could, if I knew why he upsets you so much."

Tears rimmed Olivia's eyes. "I can't." She shook her head, murmuring over and over. "I can't."

"And I can't stop myself from feeling the way I do. Any more than he can."

Olivia's head jerked up. "No! He's using you. He wants revenge, he wants . . . oh, what's the use. You're stubborn, like your father. You'll do what you want. And you'll learn the hard way like—" She sighed. "Go then. Just go. Break your own heart. I can't stop you."

Cat started toward the door, then stopped. "I . . . I need to see Matt first."

"Leave your brother out of it. He's been hurt enough today." Olivia turned and walked down the hall. She did not look back.

Cat felt as if her mother had closed a door. She sensed it wide and solid between them. She longed to tell Olivia that it didn't have to be this way. That the kiss with Logan had been a mistake. That it would never happen again.

But she couldn't say it. Because it wasn't true. She had

157

seen the look in Logan's eyes when he'd told her they would talk later. Logan was not using her. At least not the way her mother meant it. He was not manipulating her for some vengeful hidden motive. If anything, he was more disturbed by the attraction between them than Cat was.

And that was what her mother refused to see, refused to believe. In Olivia's eyes, Logan was the villain. Black and white, no middle ground. And as long as she felt that way, Cat and her mother could never reach any kind of understanding about Logan Blackstone.

Stiffening her spine, Cat headed down the corridor toward her brother's room. Matt hadn't accepted her apology for having Logan tend to his injuries. Nor did she expect him to now. But she intended to give Matt fair warning that she was going to have this out with Logan. If she couldn't get the truth from her brother or mother, she would try her best to get it from Logan Blackstone. Maybe an ultimatum would force Matt to tell her his side of the story.

Inside Matt's room, Olivia was already scurrying about, fluffing up his pillows, getting him a book to read. She reached to pour him a glass of whiskey. "I should never have left you alone with Logan," she said. "I'm so sorry, Matthew dear."

Matt downed the drink, saying nothing. His glare settled on Cat. "I don't want you in here," he said.

"Perhaps you'd best leave, Cordelia," Olivia said.

"Logan took care of your injuries, Matt," Cat said evenly. "Better than Mother or I could."

"Don't defend him to me," Matt said.

"I don't need to defend him. You know it's the truth."

"Get out."

158

"I intend to," Cat said. "But I wanted to let you know I'm going to get to the bottom of this. I'm going to get Logan to tell me the truth."

"You know the truth," Matt shouted. "Anything he'd tell you would be a lie."

"I guess I'll have to judge that for myself."

Cat turned to leave. As she did, she noticed Logan's city clothes draped over a straight-backed chair in the near corner. In the aftermath of Matt's being hurt, Logan had probably forgotten them. She gathered them up. They would provide a buffer, an excuse to begin a new conversation.

She looked at her mother, at Matt; hoping for a word, a gesture that told her they understood. Neither spoke. Cat left the room.

As Cat headed outside she wished fervently that she could remember that long-ago summer. Then no one would be betraying any secrets. She would simply remember. And she could draw her own conclusions.

That she might not draw them in accordance with her mother's and brother's interpretation of what had happened had already occurred to her. And she wasn't sure she was ready to face that eventuality. But she would worry about that if and when she had to.

She passed the corral. The men had finished up with the horses and headed out to the range. As she walked, she almost stumbled over a small stone, nearly losing her grip on Logan's clothes. She had to snatch at the jacket to keep it from hitting the ground. As she did so, something fluttered out of one of its pockets.

Cat picked up the crumpled paper, frowning. It was an old letter, addressed to *Master Logan Blackstone*. Her heartbeat quickened as she recognized the handwriting.

This letter had been written by her father.

She glanced behind her, wary all at once, as though fearful of being observed. Though she loathed herself for doing so, she opened the letter. She read it quickly, two sentences especially seeming to leap out at her: ". . . I never asked for, nor even expected you to keep silent about what happened. . . . Just know that I don't hold you to blame for any of it and never will."

Her father didn't blame Logan. At all.

How could that be? Cat wondered. Each time Cat had asked him about what had happened that summer, her father had kept stubbornly silent. Why? Never once had Hadley Jordan defended Logan to Matt or her mother. If Hadley thought Logan innocent of any wrongdoing, why had he never once spoken out in Logan's behalf?

Cat curled the letter into her fist, more questions assailing her. The first and foremost being: why had Logan brought this letter with him: Did he intend to show it to Matt? Her mother? Had he already done so? What impact would such a letter have on them?

One powerful enough for Cat to be fairly certain neither one of them had yet seen it. They would not have been able to hide their reactions to such a devastating blow. For a blow it would be. To discover that Hadley had been paying mere lip service to their bitterness all these years would likely only serve to infuriate her mother, but it would crush Matt.

In that instant Cat thought about destroying the letter. Even if Logan had no intention of showing it to Matt, the fact that it existed left open the possibility of her brother coming across it by accident, as she had done.

But her conscience was already jabbing at her for reading the letter. Destroying it was out of the question.

Reluctantly, she refolded the paper and started to shove it back into the pocket of the jacket. Then she hesitated. To put it back was to lie—to Logan. Muttering about the perversities of conscience, she stuffed the letter into her own pocket.

She found him in the barn collecting his shaving things and packing them into his valise. "I have to talk to you," she said.

He shut the valise and straightened. "I hope your mother wasn't too rough on you," he said, his voice husky.

She frowned, confused, then realized he was referring to her being caught kissing him. She blushed furiously. "She, uh, didn't say too much more about it actually."

He seemed ready to challenge the point, then decided to let it drop. He hefted the valise. "I'd best be going."

"I didn't want you to forget these," she said, handing him his clothes.

"No," Logan said. "We wouldn't want me to have any excuse to come back."

She frowned. "What do you mean? You have to come back. In the house you said—"

"I said too much," he interrupted. "It's just best for everyone if I go."

"No, you can't," she stammered, then took a step back, flustered. "I mean, we have to talk about other things too. Like the ranch, the extension."

"You and your brother won the extension." There was just the faintest sarcasm in his voice.

"You have to know I had nothing to do with that bet."

"I do know, but you have it anyway."

She swallowed hard, then said, "I can't accept it."

"I beg your pardon?"

"You heard me. I can't accept the extension. Matt manipulated the bet. It wasn't fair."

"You mean that, don't you?"

"I do."

The left side of his mouth ticked upward in a thoughtful, if lopsided, grin. "The extension is yours, Cat Jordan," he said. "A business transaction between you and me. If you can pay off the note this fall after you sell your herd, the ranch is yours."

She resisted the urge to fling her arms around his neck, certain that he would set her away from him. Whatever emotions had been loosed in him, he was now holding them in tight check. She said simply, "Thank you."

He walked over to the near stall and collected the gelding's harness. "There is something I need to ask you." He seemed nervous all at once, ill at ease.

She waited, her heart thudding. Perhaps she'd misjudged his reluctance. Maybe he wasn't trying to keep his distance. Maybe he did want to kiss her, maybe he wanted even more. His next words drove the thought from her mind.

Logan began slowly. "I keep thinking about something the sheriff said. About his uncertainty regarding your father's death." He settled the harness onto the gelding's back, arranging the traces as methodically as he was now choosing his words.

"What about it?" Cat asked, not sure she wanted to know where this was leading.

"I want to give you your chance to save the ranch, Cat. But I don't want that chance to mean I'm putting your life at risk."

"What are you talking about?"

"Your father's death may well have been a tragic

accident. But if it wasn't . . ."

"Then Barney Jackson had friends who are going to pay for their revenge," Cat said.

"Or maybe Barney Jackson didn't have anything to do with it."

"What do you mean?"

"I mean maybe someone wanted the Circle J to go under."

Cat stared at him. "But why?" She paced to the other end of the barn and back, then answered her own question. "Because someone else wants the ranch." Why hadn't she thought of it before.

"The same thought occurred to me," Logan said. "Can you think of anyone who wants the Circle J?"

"You mean someone who would murder to get it? No. No one. The people around here are our friends. They would never . . ." She stopped, a most unwelcome suspicion forming in her mind. She dismissed it at once.

"Tell me," Logan prompted.

"A lot of people would like this ranch," she hedged. "We have good grazing, good water."

"Who?" Logan persisted.

"Ryan Fielding made Pa more than one offer," Cat said. "But Ryan would never—"

"Fielding?"

"He owns the Rocking R to the north." She picked up a piece of straw, running it nervously through her fingers. "Ryan may be a strutting peacock—obnoxious, boring and thoroughly irritating—but he would never stoop to murder."

"Are you sure of that?"

"Of course I'm sure." She said it, but in the saying the seed of doubt was planted. She stalked toward the door.

"I don't want to talk about this anymore."

"I'm sorry. I had to bring it up. I couldn't put your life in danger with this extension."

She stared past the ranchyard to the rolling plains beyond, the patches of green somehow more vibrant against the stark blue of the sky. "This ranch is my life, Logan. It's worth the risk. It's worth any risk."

"I doubt your father would have agreed."

"My father and I could both be mule stubborn, and we didn't see eye to eye on everything, but he would have given his life for this land. He'd expect no less from me."

"Your father would not expect you to live out his life. He'd want you to live your own."

The words were spoken with such vehemence that Cat looked up sharply. She had the distinct impression Logan was no longer talking about Hadley Jordan. She crossed back over to him. "I'm sorry," she said softly.

He went back to straightening the harness with a vengeance. "For what?"

"That your father did . . . does expect you to live out his life. That he fought you so hard about being a doctor that you"—she stumbled over the words—"gave it up for a while."

"You mean quit."

When she tried to protest, he held up a hand. "It's all right. It's nothing I haven't said to myself."

"I'm sorry. I had no right."

He ambled over to the first stall and sat down on the hay bale abutting one of the sides. When he spoke, his voice was strangely toneless, as though the words were a litany he'd repeated to himself countless times before.

"My mother suffered several miscarriages and still-births before I was born. Various doctors prescribed

164

different regimens. None worked. My father got disgusted and sent them all away. My mother was desperate for a child. She went into a deep melancholy. It was so bad that my father even sent for more doctors. Nothing worked.

"My mother grew more and more depressed. She convinced herself she wasn't a real woman." Logan's eyes grew pained. "She sent my father away. I know it was the worst time of his life, even though he never really spoke of it. Eventually they reconciled. But my father never forgave the doctors, not even a year later, when I was born."

"How sad for both of them," Cat said, "but how wonderful that they had you."

Something unreadable skimmed through his eyes, but he said only, "Medicine's come a long way, especially since the war."

"If being a doctor is what you really want, you should do it."

"I intend to, but first I have to put my father's affairs in order." He looked away. "He's dying. That's why I quit medical school. That's why I almost didn't come here."

"Oh, Logan, I'm so sorry."

"He's had a good life. And he's not in pain. He may have another year or two."

"Will he be angry about the extension?"

"No, I don't think so. He was very close to your father. I don't think he ever quite got over the rift." Logan stood abruptly. "I'd best finish hitching up the buggy."

Mention of the rift sparked a renewed twinge of Cat's conscience. She hated to spoil the mood, but she had no choice. Reaching into her pocket, she pulled out the

165

letter. She held it out to him. "This fell out of your jacket when I was bringing it from the house."

He stared at it, his jaw tightening. "You read it." It was not a question.

"Yes." Mortified, she hurried on. "I saw my father's handwriting. I had no right, I know. But I'm not sorry I did. The rift wasn't your making. It was Matt's. And my mother's. Wasn't it?" She caught his arm. "Wasn't it?"

"I made a promise fifteen years ago."

"My father never asked for your silence."

"I made the promise to Matt."

She gasped. "Matt? You've kept a promise to Matt?"

"I've never broken it. Never thought about breaking it."

"Until today?"

He nodded.

"Because of me?" she all but whispered.

He nodded again. "If I truly thought it could make things right, maybe I would." He was wrestling with his own conscience. His promise, even made to his own detriment, was his word of honor.

"You don't have to tell me," she said suddenly, though she longed to know. "I said it before, Logan. I don't want to add to your pain."

He trailed the backs of his fingers across her cheek, then twined a stray tendril of hair behind her ear. "I don't know what it is about you. I'm not even sure I want to know. Another time, another place . . . maybe you and I could have . . ." He shook his head. "Never mind."

She caught his hand before he could pull away and curved her fingers around his. "It doesn't make any sense, does it?" she murmured, bringing his hand to her lips. "I teased you about these hands by the corral. I said

166

they were good for adding up figures." She kissed each fingertip. "You said they were good for other things too. That you could teach me those things."

"I . . . I don't think that would be a very good idea." He was trying very hard to keep his mind on what she was saying, not what she was doing. But more and more what she was saying only fueled the fire of what she was doing. This wasn't right. It would only complicate an already enormously complicated situation. But his body didn't seem to care. Nor did his heart.

She was in his arms, her hands threading through his hair, her lips claiming his mouth. Her whole body burned with the need to touch and be touched by this man. "Logan, please . . ."

He groaned low in his throat, his hands tracking the curves of her body. "We can't, we can't." He said the words, but his body betrayed them. She could feel his arousal, hard against her thigh and she gloried in the knowledge that he wanted her.

Gloried in it and feared it. She had never been with a man before, not this way. And to be with a man as practiced and bold as Logan Blackstone . . . God, what if he found her wanting?

But then it didn't matter. Nothing mattered, as the practiced, bold Logan Blackstone guided her down to the soft layering of clean straw scattered across the stall floor.

His hands cupped her breasts, teasing the sensitive nipples beneath the thin fabric of her blouse. She moaned against him, white heat igniting in every pore of her being. She wanted him, she would have him. Here. Now.

She fumbled with the buckle of his belt, tore at the

buttons of his shirt. Her hands skated featherlight across the broad expanse of his chest.

"Corie, sweet Corie . . ." Logan's body was on fire. He burned with need for this woman. Yet somewhere, somewhere, a niggling voice of reason screamed to be heard.

Corie will be hurt. Corie will be crushingly hurt. The words thrummed through his mind over and over, words his body battled to deny.

She will be hurt. And I will be the one to hurt her.

He pulled back, his breathing ragged, harsh. "No." He said the word aloud, once, twice. And then he was pushing to his feet, cursing; cursing the day he'd ever been foolish enough to think he could come back to Texas, to think he could lay old ghosts to rest.

All he had done was conjure up new ones.

He looked into Cat's eyes, wide, passionate. She wanted him.

To take her was to hurt her.

To reject her was to hurt her.

He swore, stalking away, hearing her muffled sobs, feeling each tear like a lance through his heart.

Chapter Twelve

The sound of hoofbeats out in the yard sent Cat bolting to her feet. Swiping at her tears, she fought to straighten her clothing, even as she dared a covert glance at Logan. Why had he stopped? Why? He hadn't heard the hoofbeats. He'd stopped before . . .

She had no time to consider it. The horses had been reined to a halt somewhere nearby. She stepped toward the door, jerking back when Logan reached toward her. But he only tugged free a few bits of straw clinging to her hair. She couldn't even look him in the face.

Never in her life had she felt as out of control as she did right now, and yet there was absolutely nothing she could do about it. She wanted to collapse onto the ground and sob her heart out. She wanted to fly at Logan and strike him. She wanted to die.

She was at war with herself. Her heart, her body, her mind. She was shaking so badly she could barely walk. And yet she had to walk. She had to talk; she had to force herself to act as though absolutely nothing were wrong.

Because she was not going to let Logan know the depth

of the hurt he had just inflicted on her. Her pride was all she had left.

She blinked savagely, swiping again at the tears that rimmed her eyes.

"Cat . . ."

The one word from him did it. The word laced with agonized sympathy and regret. Cat felt her whole body stiffen. She turned toward him, a coldness such as she'd never known stealing through her very soul. The coldness must have shown in her eyes, because he took a step back, his own eyes widening with concern and a sadness that only solidified her resolve.

Stalking to the door, Cat looked outside. Two riders had dismounted and were striding toward the house. Cat's shout halted them. They turned and headed toward the barn. Cat grimaced. Perfect! Ryan Fielding and Rafe Latigo.

She stepped outside. She dared a quick glance back at Logan, for just an instant her façade crumbling as she saw how utterly calm and detached he now looked, as though he hadn't a care in the world.

She bit the inside of her lip, the pain making her focus on the task at hand—making certain Ryan and Latigo suspected nothing.

As the two men approached, Logan stepped close to her, speaking only loudly enough for her to hear. "I'm sorry."

She wanted to scream. She was standing here, hanging on to the last shred of her self-control and the man was apologizing for something she couldn't begin to acknowledge, not with Ryan and Latigo present.

"I'm so very sorry, too, Mr. Blackstone," she said loudly, primly, all the while smiling at Ryan, whose face now broke into a reciprocal grin.

"Sorry for what?" Ryan asked, coming up to give her a swift hug.

Latigo stood to one side, regarding her sullenly, but Cat ignored him.

Cat gave Ryan her most radiant smile. "I was just telling Mr. Blackstone how sorry I was that he couldn't remain in Texas any longer. It's just been so very delightful for the two of us to reminisce about his previous visit to the Circle J, when he was just a boy."

The smile remained on Ryan's lips, but his gaze grew curious, whether about Cat's subject matter or her uncharacteristic effusiveness, she couldn't have said. But she wasn't about to drop the act for even a second. If she did, she would fall apart.

"So you're Logan Blackstone," Ryan said, extending his right hand toward Logan.

"I am," Logan said, accepting the handshake.

"You may recall we met in town yesterday," Ryan went on. "A most unfortunate incident."

"Most unfortunate." Logan eyed Latigo with open contempt.

Cat couldn't get over how composed Logan was, how totally unaffected. With her, it was all an act. With Logan . . . Was this the behavior her mother had suspected him capable of when she had warned her that Logan could break her heart?

"An incident that will not be repeated," Ryan continued, and Cat had to force herself to pay attention to the man. For all of her determination not to let Logan perceive how much he had hurt her, she was having an extremely difficult time concentrating on anything but the pain she was feeling.

171

"In any event," Ryan said, directing his attention to Cat, "I didn't stop by to discuss my foreman's inability to hold his liquor."

It was then Cat's gaze picked up the six-gun he wore strapped to his right thigh. She had never seen Ryan wearing a gun before. "What's happened?"

"We had a few head rustled last night. I wanted to let you know. I'm warning the other ranchers as well."

"Thank you," Cat said and meant it. She was grateful for the warning and maybe, perversely, grateful for the rustlers. It would give her something to worry about besides Logan Blackstone.

"I'm sure," Ryan went on, "that Latigo and my men will track down the culprits. But just in case I'm along when that happens," he patted the six-gun, "I want to be able to do my part in meting out the appropriate justice."

"You take them to the sheriff, Ryan Fielding!" Cat said. "You've got no right—"

"Now, Cat, just because you don't have a stomach for justice, doesn't mean—"

"Lynching a man isn't justice," she snapped.

Ryan chuckled, looking at Logan. "Women! What are you going to do with them, eh?"

Cat's lips pursed with fury. At least Logan had the good sense not to respond.

"I thank you for the warning, Ryan," she managed. "Now if you don't mind, I've got a lot of work to do around here."

"That's what I like about you, Cat," Ryan said. "Always neighborly to a fault."

She stomped her foot. "I am damned neighborly," she said. "But I don't have to stand here and be patronized on my own ranch."

Ryan's eyes brimmed with a hurt look that was so patently phony Cat almost laughed out loud.

"Now, now, Cat," he said, "you and I have been friends a long time. I know how difficult things have been for you lately. That's another reason I stopped by."

Cat felt her suspicions rising. "What are you talking about?"

"I found out why Mr. Blackstone has come calling on you."

"That's none of your business!"

"Isn't it?" He shook his head sadly. "Your father was a very dear friend of mine. He would never have wanted you or your brother or your lovely mother to have to go through such stressful times."

"I said it's none of your business, Ryan."

Ryan directed his attention to Logan. "Perhaps if I could have a moment of your time alone, Mr. Blackstone?"

"If you're going to talk about the Circle J," Cat said, "you're going to talk about it to my face."

"My dear," Ryan said, affecting the tone of an adult placating a mulish child. "I know your father left you a majority share in the ranch, but Mr. Blackstone and I are going to be discussing finances here. Very boring for the ladies."

"I think we've been over this before, Ryan. I'm not a lady."

Logan swallowed an amused snort, for which Cat sent him a killing glare.

"Time and again I've offered my help," Ryan said, making a helpless gesture at Logan. "But she won't listen. What can I do?"

"Your idea of help is to buy my ranch. Well, it isn't,

173

wasn't, and never will be for sale!"

"I beg to differ, Cat dear, but it's my understanding that it is. If Mr. Blackstone is here to foreclose, then it's only good business for me to assure him that he need look no further than yours truly for a suitable buyer."

Cat swore, enjoying the shocked expression in Ryan's green eyes. "Rustlers be damned," she said. "You came here to be the first buzzard in line to steal the Circle J."

"It would hardly be theft."

"It won't be anything," she said. "Because Logan granted me an extension on the loan."

"He what?"

"An extension. When I sell the herd this fall, I'll pay off the loan and keep the Circle J. So you can just forget about expanding the Rocking R at my expense."

"That was never my intention and you know it," he chided. He was trying hard not to show it, but he was clearly outraged about the extension. Still he hardly missed a beat as he came over and gave her a friendly hug. "I'm so happy for you, sweetheart. I was so worried that we might not be neighbors anymore. You know how openly encouraging your parents always were about my calling on you."

Marry me, marry the Circle J, Cat thought furiously. The man was so transparent he might as well be a windowpane.

She resisted the urge to jerk away from him, as he gave her another healthy squeeze. She dared a look at Logan, wanting—hoping?—to find just a hint of disapproval—jealousy!—in those gray eyes. But he was coolly indifferent.

Ryan brushed her cheek with his lips. "Well, now that that's all but settled, why don't you come with me to the

174

dance tonight in Red Springs and we'll celebrate."

Cat almost choked. Ryan had never asked her to a dance before in her life. A picnic or two, yes, where he could pile on the false flattery and tell her what a grand ranch a combined Rocking R and Circle J would be. But a dance? Where he would have to be seen in public as the escort to the notoriously unladylike Cat Jordan? Never.

"I know it may still be too soon after Hadley's death. But I just can't seem to get you out of my mind."

Especially now that I have that extension, Cat thought acidly. "I'm so sorry, Ryan," she soothed, trying to affect a similar mock sympathy, "but Mr. Blackstone is my guest, at least for the rest of today. I wouldn't feel right deserting him."

She hated using Logan as an excuse, but his presence seemed the most expedient reason for turning Ryan down.

"Don't deprive yourself of Mr. Fielding's company on my account," Logan said, his voice dripping with sarcasm. "I have an engagement of my own this evening, remember?"

She gave him a blank look.

"I'm dining with Chastity Vincent."

Cat felt as though he'd slapped her. Of course she had been there when Chastity had asked him to dinner yesterday. But Cat had completely forgotten. Obviously Logan hadn't.

Ryan was regarding Logan with a new intensity. "You know Chastity Vincent, Mr. Blackstone?"

"Briefly," he allowed. "We met on the stage. And the lady was gracious enough to extend an invitation to dinner with her family tonight."

"Ah, yes, I heard about your bravado on the stage line,

but I didn't realize you'd also been offered a reward for your services."

Logan's gaze darkened ominously, so much so that Ryan hastened to add, "I meant nothing untoward, Mr. Blackstone, I assure you. It's just that Chastity, too, has been a dear friend of mine for a long time."

"In other words Ryan wishes Chastity had been my father's daughter instead of me," Cat said, noting with infinite satisfaction the horror that came into Ryan's eyes at her so bluntly stating the truth.

"Tut-tut, Cat dear," Ryan said, chuckling. "I forgot what a marvelous sense of humor you have."

"I'm so glad you think so," she said, batting her eyelashes at him in perfect Chastity fashion.

Ryan bussed Cat on the cheek. "I guess I'd best be going. You're sure you won't change your mind about the dance?"

"It's been a long day," she said, suddenly infinitely weary.

He nodded, obviously not pleased. And just as obviously concerned about Logan's upcoming dinner with Chastity. Again he pressed Logan for assurances that there was nothing more than dinner involved.

Cat started to stalk away in disgust, when Latigo, who had been loitering near the corrals, moved quickly to block her path. "Maybe you'd like to go to the dance with me," he said, his smirking leer making her skin crawl.

"Get out of my way," she ground out.

"Don't think I've forgotten what happened in town yesterday, little miss," he growled. "Some day me and you will dance, and there ain't gonna be no one around to cut in. If you get what I mean."

Cat straightened. "Get off my ranch. And don't come

176

back. Your boss is welcome. But I never want to see your face here again."

"We'll dance, missy," he said again. "We'll dance long and slow, all night long. You think about that."

"Latigo!" Ryan called. "Come on! We're leaving."

There was no hint in Ryan's manner that he was at all aware of Latigo's insulting behavior. He tipped his hat to Cat.

"My congratulations again," he said, "on your good fortune to have such an understanding banker as Mr. Blackstone."

Cat kept her frozen smile in place. Had there been some double meaning in that remark? Had Logan and Ryan talked about something other than Logan's outing with the Vincents tonight? She waited until Ryan and Latigo had ridden out of the yard; then she turned on Logan.

"What did you say to him?" she demanded.

He started back toward the barn without answering.

She caught up with him and grabbed his arm. "Answer me."

"I don't know what you're talking about."

She swore.

"You're very good at that," he said, obviously disapproving.

"Ladies in Boston don't talk that way, huh?"

"No *lady*," he emphasized the word, "I've ever met talked that way."

She swore again.

He stomped into the barn.

Cat stomped after him. He wasn't going to deflect her anger about what had happened before Ryan's ill-timed arrival by chastising her choice of colorful language.

But Logan seemed just as determined to avoid the entire issue. He threw his valise into the buggy and climbed inside, gigging the horse forward. Cat had to leap at the gelding's bridle and yank the horse to a halt.

Logan swore.

Cat gave him a smug look.

He tied off the reins on the brake handle and climbed back down. "Are you trying to get yourself killed?"

"I'm trying to talk to you."

"We have nothing to say."

"Nothing?" she asked steadily, though her eyes stung.

"Nothing except . . . I'm sorry."

That wasn't what she wanted to hear. "Sorry for what?"

"For a lot of things."

"Don't bother."

He gripped her arms and pulled her to him. "Damn you, you don't know what—" He bit off the words and Cat shoved away from him.

"Do you know how infuriating that is?" she demanded. "Every time you're about to say something to me, you stop yourself. You want to say it, Logan. You want to tell me, to explain all of this pain between our families. I know it. But you won't. Because of some stupid promise you made my brother. My brother, who hates your guts!" She took a deep breath, feeling the tears again burning her eyes, but she refused to shed them. "That's what stopped you in the barn, isn't it? That's what's stopping you now. Stopping you from . . ." She swallowed the words—*loving me.*

It was all so crazy, so confused. She didn't know what

to think any more about anything.

"I have to go," he said hoarsely. "I don't belong here. I never did. I never can." He climbed into the buggy and slapped the horse into a trot. This time Cat did not interfere.

Cat watched him drive off, feeling a sense of loss such as she'd never known. It wasn't right. It wasn't fair. Why wouldn't he talk to her?

His promise. His blasted promise to Matt! What could he have promised that would stand in the way of his caring for her? Damn, how had her whole life turned upside down in a day?

She thought about him having dinner tonight with Chastity Vincent and it was only more salt on an open wound. Chastity would maneuver him into taking her to that dance, too.

Cat let out a shuddery sigh. She'd gotten what she wanted, hadn't she? The extension was all that mattered. At least it was all that had mattered before she'd met Logan Blackstone. Now . . . She didn't want to think about now.

She wandered back into the barn and looked forlornly at the scattered hay in the near stall, remembering. With an anguished cry she turned away. It was then she noticed Logan's cane leaning against the barn wall.

He wasn't that far away yet, she could ride after him.

Or send one of the hands.

Or mail it to him.

She picked up the cane, caressing the gold lion's head, thinking of passion and promises, thinking of how she'd never given up on anything in her life that she felt was worth fighting for. Until now.

179

She gripped the cane fiercely. No! She hadn't given up, wouldn't give up. There was one other way to get the cane back to Logan Blackstone. Once she was certain he'd had enough time to get to town and sit down to dinner with dear Chastity.

Cat tucked the cane under her arm and headed toward the corral to saddle Nugget.

Chapter Thirteen

Cat reined Nugget to a halt, wondering what had become of her rekindled determination to face down Logan Blackstone about passion and promises. She'd been riding for over an hour now, deliberately keeping Nugget's pace slow, taking back trails, not chancing overtaking Logan's buggy.

How could she be prepared to face him in Red Springs, if she couldn't even face him alone in open country? She lifted her Stetson, raking her sweat-dampened hair away from her forehead. The heat was doing nothing for her self-confidence. By the time she reached town she'd look like she'd ridden drag for a week. Her clothes clung cloyingly to her slender frame.

She supposed she could visit Maude Dancey's boardinghouse and take a hot bath. Maybe a trip to Isabelle Harkins's dress shop wouldn't be a bad idea either. After all, she reminded herself grimly, she was going to be facing Logan on Chastity Vincent's home ground. In a contest of femininity and grace, Cat couldn't imagine too many red-blooded males glancing twice at the competition while in Chastity's company.

Cat cursed under her breath. She had come on this ride because she'd decided she was no quitter. Now here she was hardly an hour from the ranch, and offering up all kinds of excuses to quit all over again.

Well, she wasn't going to do it! Logan wasn't a man to be fooled by an empty-headed ninny like Chastity. He'd simply been too much of a gentleman to turn down her simpering dinner invitation in front of witnesses, that's all. If Logan had a fault, it was his inability to be rude to the right people at the right time.

Cat grinned ruefully. Maybe she could give him a few pointers.

Besides, there was more to all of this than Chastity. Logan was dealing with old ghosts, old ghosts conjured up by his reunion with Matt and Olivia. Logan had to have time to work things through, if not with Cat's family, then with himself.

Cat would give him the time he needed, and would hope he could put the ghosts to rest once and for all. Her concern was that he stay in Texas to do it. If he returned to Boston, she feared he would never come back.

"You can't leave me," she murmured. "Not this way." She eyed Logan's cane, where it rested beside her Spencer in her saddle boot. She would hand it to him tonight in town, maybe at the dance. Maybe when she walked right up to him and asked him to dance with her.

Cat felt her face heat. Who was she kidding? She didn't even know how to dance! Maybe she'd best take this man-chasing business one step at a time.

Man chasing? She grimaced. Was that what she was doing? A slow smile spread across her face.

Damned right!

She nudged Nugget forward with her knees, settling the mare into a ground-eating trot. Sage, blue grama, mesquite, and cedar all went by in a blur.

Man chasing! Cat Jordan was chasing the man she loved. And she was lost in the incredible wonder of it. She was in love with Logan Blackstone!

It was that simple and that complicated. The man who had so long been villified by her mother and brother, the man who, for whatever reason, was trying desperately to detach himself from his feelings for her—that was the man she loved.

And somehow she was going to convince him that he loved her back. Because somehow, some way, Cat Jordan always got what she wanted.

Cat guided Nugget over to a stand of cottonwoods that flanked a wide stream that was actually a meandering branch of the Brazos. Dismounting, she stretched happily. She was being too fanciful, she knew. But she couldn't seem to help herself. After all, she'd never been in love before.

She tried to imagine Logan at her side running the Circle J. Her mood darkened a little. Being in love might not be enough.

She tramped down the grass in front of a massive tree and sat down. Leaning against the rough bark, she tried to decide exactly when in the last twenty-four hours she'd actually lost her mind.

What did she think she was doing? She might be in love, but how was she going to make Logan fall in love with her? With Cat Jordan who had never felt adequate as a woman, who hid ivory peignoirs under her longjohns lest her mother discover that she had a remotely feminine thought.

183

Or even her father.

Cat frowned. Where had that thought come from? Hadley Jordan had always been there for her, loving her, sharing his life with her. Teaching her to ride herd, brand calves, drink beer . . . He'd been so proud of her. She'd done everything he'd wanted, always.

She tensed. No. She had wanted it too. She'd lived her life the way she chose. She still did. Just exactly the way she wanted.

Then why did thinking about it jar memories of her father tying ribbons in her hair the summer Logan came to visit. After that summer, there'd been no more ribbons.

Cat slapped the ground hard. She was being absurd. Matt's accident had nothing to do with hair ribbons. Neither did being in love with Logan. Then why all these renewed doubts about herself as a woman?

She threaded her fingers through sweat-dampened curls. For weeks after Matt's surgery her father had stayed at his bedside, encouraging him, trying to get him to believe that all wasn't lost. But Olivia's influence had been at work, too. And slowly it had won out. Matt had given up, had allowed himself to be a cripple in every sense of the word.

And on Cat's fifth birthday her father had taken her out and shown her how to fire a rifle, how to track a rabbit, how to flush a stray steer. And he had taken the ribbons out of her hair.

He had begun replacing his son.

Cat trembled. It was her insecurity about Logan that was making her think this way. Logan and this place. Her father had first brought her to this spot when she was seven years old, to fish. They had spent whole days here,

184

talking, laughing.

Cat arced a small stone toward the stream and watched the ripples circle out from where the rock broke the surface. Such a long time ago. She stared up through weaving branches, seeing only patches of blue sky. She could almost feel the tug of the fishing line, almost hear her father's voice. . . .

"I think I got one, Pa." Cat giggled, tugging on her line.

"Don't yank him!" Hadley Jordan cautioned. "Just play him easy." The big, broad-shouldered man ambled over and hunkered down beside her. "Looks like a big one. And just in time for supper too."

It was her first day fishing. Spring rains had swollen the stream to the edges of its banks. After days of pestering, her father had finally relented and brought her out here.

She had been certain fishing was some mysterious activity that boys liked to keep all to themselves, just so they didn't have to share the fun. At least that was the impression she'd got from that smart aleck Eddie Mapes.

Every time Eddie bothered to show up for school, he made sure to tell all the girls that fish were slimy, scary monsters that liked to eat people, especially little girls. Whenever a boy told Cat a girl would be afraid of something, Cat was the first one to leap in and grab for that something.

Fishing had to be fun. Cat wanted some of that fun. Mostly because it seemed like nothing had been very much fun for a long time. Ever since Matt had gotten hurt. Maybe if she went fishing, she could make Pa laugh again. And she could laugh too.

And she was laughing, she was laughing so hard tears were streaming down her cheeks, as she tugged on the line with the jumping fish. She worked it for over three minutes, then finally managed to haul it up on the grass-choked bank. The shiny gray body flopped and jumped, avoiding her every attempt to corral it.

Her father grabbed it instead, and freed it from the hook. Cat stared fascinated as the fish's mouth opened and closed, its gills working desperately on either side of its body.

And suddenly she burst into tears. "Throw him back in, Papa!" she shrieked. "Throw him back in the water. Or he'll die!"

Her father had tossed the fish into the bucket of water they'd brought along to keep their day's catch fresh until it could be cleaned. "That's our supper," he said, not ungently.

"I don't want to kill him."

"That's the way of things. Big fish eat little fish. People eat big fish."

"You wouldn't want anybody eatin' us, would ya, Pa?"

Hadley Jordan frowned in consternation. "Sometimes you could be a little less smart, you know that."

"I still don't want the fish to die, Papa."

"So I throw the fish back. And what do we eat for dinner?"

"Beefsteak!"

Hadley chuckled. "And where do we get beefsteak?"

Her face scrunched up in thought. "From the cows," she said. "They make it."

The look on Hadley's face suggested he was about to be

in big trouble, finding himself with a daughter who would never eat again. But he was straightforward and honest. As he always was. "God gave us these creatures to serve us. As long as we don't abuse that gift, we'll always have enough to eat. And there'll always be plenty of fish still to swim."

"So we only catch what we need to eat, Pa?"

"Right."

"And the fish don't mind?"

He rolled his eyes. "Maybe the fish was about to get ate up by a bigger fish, or maybe he heard how the creek all but dries up in the summer, and he figured this was a better way out."

She bobbed her blond curls in agreement. "All right, Pa. If you say so."

They caught several more fish that day. And when suppertime came, Cat decided the fish had indeed come to a good end. Back at the ranch Maria Hidalgo's mother dipped them in batter and fried them to perfection. In fact, eating itself had become a pure delight since the Hidalgo family had come to work on the Circle J three months before.

No one made fried tortillas like Elena Hidalgo. And having a permanent new friend like Maria was like having a sister. Even Cat's mother had not objected. Giving up the cooking she loathed allowed her extra time for the special tutoring she gave Matt. Hadley had tried to insist that Matt attend school in a wheelchair, but Olivia had become so upset he'd soon abandoned the idea.

Cat worried about Matt. She worried about him a lot. He'd been a pretty good big brother until he'd gotten hurt three years ago. Now he never laughed anymore. Never had any fun.

"Pa," she said, as she sat fishing the next day, "can we bring Matt with us tomorrow?"

Her father had been baiting a hook. He stilled. "I wish we could, honey."

"So why can't we?"

"I don't think your mama would like the idea too much."

"We could fix up some blankets in the back of the wagon," she said, getting more and more excited by the idea. "Matt would be real comfortable. And when he's fishin' he could be sittin' down, just like you and me. He'd like it, Pa. I know he would. He never has any fun all stuck up in his room all the time."

Hadley tossed in his own line. "Matt's in a lot of pain, sweetheart."

"He wouldn't have to think about the hurt in his leg if he was fishin'. He could think about catchin' fish."

"Your mama still wouldn't like it. She doesn't like to let Matt out of her sight."

"Then Mama could come with us!"

Hadley shook his head. "Your mother? Fishing? That would be worth seein' all by itself."

"What, Papa?"

"Nothing." He looked thoughtful though, and Cat knew Matt would be coming with them soon.

Over Olivia's vehement objections Cat and her father had packed Matt in the back of the buckboard the very next day. It was soon apparent Olivia wasn't the only one objecting.

"I don't want to go fishing," Matt said tightly, as Cat settled into the back of the buckboard beside him.

"Sure you do, Matt," Cat said. "It's fun!"

He didn't say another word all the way to the creek.

188

Once there, her father helped him over to the water's edge, where Matt lay on the grass, his mood dark, sullen. Cat baited his hooks for him, helped him all she could, and still he did nothing but complain and say he wanted to go home. At fifteen his complexion was unnaturally pale, his body thin, weak.

Suddenly he had a bite on his line.

"Matt!" Cat squealed, "you've got a fish!"

Matt sat up and pulled hard on the line. The fish broke loose.

"Aw, don't worry, Matt," Cat said, "that happens sometimes. You'll get another one."

He rubbed a hand on his left thigh, grimacing.

"Does your leg hurt, Matt?"

"Of course, it hurts," Matt gritted out. "It always hurts."

"You don't have to snap at your sister," Hadley said, striding over to sit on Matt's opposite side.

"I don't know why you both can't figure it out. I can't do what other people do. I'm a cripple!"

"No, you're not, Matt," Cat said with all the innocence of a seven-year-old. "I saw a man in town last week. He didn't have a leg either. I was being impolite, Pa said, because I was staring at him. So I apologized. But the man said it was all right. He came right over and told me all about how he lost it in the war. But he wasn't mad at anybody. He had a peg leg. He said the onliest thing he had to worry about was termites!"

Matt only scowled.

Cat sighed. Even she had laughed when the man had told her that one. She felt bad. She had hoped fishing would help Matt laugh, like it had helped her.

Matt's line dipped again. This time Matt played the fish

189

right and landed it.

"It's a whopper!" Cat cried. "The biggest one I ever saw!"

"Really?" Matt beamed.

"The biggest!"

"He sure is," Hadley said. "Must be eight pounds."

"Probably lived a long tough life to get this big," Matt mused. He freed the hook from the fish's mouth and tossed it back into the creek.

"What did you do that for?" Cat asked. "It's okay if we eat 'em. Pa said so."

"Not that one, little sister. That one deserved to die like he lived."

Cat thought about it a minute. Then she grinned. "It made you happy catchin' him though, didn't it?"

Matt smiled. "Yeah, it did."

He lay back and after a while his leg didn't seem to bother him nearly as much. For a while he even fell asleep.

"See, Pa," Cat said, "I told you Matt would like fishing."

Her father's brown eyes seemed troubled and faraway when he looked at Matt. "I wish it could be like this for him more often."

"It will," Cat said. "You'll see. Even when you have to work on the ranch, Matt can bring me fishing. And once he feels better, I'll bet he'll even get on a horse again."

"You've got it all planned out, don't you, little Cat?"

"Yep! You'll see, he'll be my big brother again."

Her father turned away abruptly, working overhard at untangling a snarled line. Cat was never sure, but she thought she heard him say, "Maybe he could be my son again too."

When Matt woke up, he was still feeling more free and comfortable than he had for three years.

"Where's Pa?" he asked, looking around.

"He went for a walk. He likes to do that. It helps him think, he says. Are you gonna come fishin' again sometime, Matt?"

"I just might," he said.

"Then I can make new mem-ries."

"New what?"

"New mem-ries," she repeated. "You know, like when you 'member something fun that you did when you were a kid. Like I 'member when you used to chase me all over to make me stay out of your room."

"You were a pest that's why. You still are." But he was grinning.

"I'm not a pest."

"All right, you're a kid sister. Same thing."

"See? That's my mem-ries. You used to call me that all the time. But I haven't got any new mem-ries for almost three years."

Matt tugged at a piece of grass. "It's been rough on you, too, hasn't it?"

She patted his arm. "I love you, Matt."

He sucked in a deep breath. "How'd I ever get stuck with a silly kid like you for a sister?"

Her lower lip trembled.

Matt reached out and grabbed her to him. "I'm sorry, Cat. I was just teasin'. I wouldn't have any other sister in the whole world, but you."

"None?"

"Not a one."

"Tell me a story, Matt. You haven't told me a story in such a long time."

191

Matt scratched his head, thinking. "A story, huh? How about the time me, you, and Logan went huntin' Injuns."

She giggled, delighted. She liked to talk about Logan, though she would never have dared bring up the subject herself. But since Matt had done so, it had to be all right. "You and Logan were the cowboys and I had to be the Indian because you wanted me to do all the cookin'."

"You were the squaw."

"Logan said I was the Indian princess."

"That's 'cause he never had any brothers and sisters pestering him all the time back home."

"I liked Logan. He gave me flowers when Buttons died."

"That dumb old pup."

"He wasn't dumb!"

But Matt wasn't listening. "I remember the time me and Logan went flyin' out of the hayloft, pretending to be eagles. I about broke my neck when I missed the haystack."

"You should've known you couldn't fly without feathers."

He laughed. "We went huntin' a lot too."

"Did you hunt bears and buffalo?"

"Yep. We even tracked a cougar once that was bringin' down yearlings."

Cat's eyes widened with awe. "Did you catch him?"

Matt wasn't smiling anymore. He looked away. "No."

"Did you even see him?"

"No." He began fussing with his fishing line.

"Well, what happened with the cougar," Cat persisted.

"Nothing. Just shut up about it, will ya? There you go bein' a pest again."

"I was not." She was getting mad though. And that

felt kind of good. For too long she'd felt too sorry for Matt ever to be mad at him. She was about to tell him so when her father came back from his walk. "Hey, Pa," Cat called, "Matt was tellin' me about the time him and Logan—"

"Shut up, Cat!" Matt hissed. "I mean it. Shut up!"

Cat shrank away from the wild look in her brother's eyes.

Matt had all but leaped toward her, and he cried out now as the movement brought a slicing pain to his leg. He moaned, writhing in agony.

Hadley hurried to his side. "Easy, son," he soothed. "Just take it easy now. Stay still."

But the pain didn't subside and they wound up taking Matt home. Olivia was furious.

"I should never have listened to you, Hadley," she said. "I should never have allowed you to take him." She hurried after them, as Hadley carried Matt down the hall to his room.

"We asked you to go with us, Mama," Cat said.

"Don't you sass me, young lady," Olivia said. Then she turned to Hadley, "Don't think I'll ever forget this. I know what you were trying to do. I know."

Her father said nothing, merely settled Matt on his bed, then turned and stalked from the house. He didn't come back for quite a while, missing supper completely. Cat found him in the barn well past dusk, when she went out to pet her pony.

He had looked sadder, more defeated than Cat had ever seen him.

"Me and Matt were talking about Logan when Matt got upset, Pa. It's my fault."

"No, it isn't your fault. It's . . ." He shook his head.

193

"It's nobody's fault."

"Did you like Logan, Pa?"

"He was a good boy."

"And it's Logan's fault Matt lost his leg?"

"Isn't it past your bedtime?"

"Logan was nice to me. Matt said it was because he didn't have any brothers and sisters to be pests on him at home. But I don't care. I liked him."

"Then you go right on liking him."

"He was sad that night."

Her father stilled. "What night?"

"That night when the doctor came to cut off Matt's leg. I found Logan crying. He was so sad. I wanted to give him a hug."

"You were in the barn?"

She didn't notice the agitation in her father's face. "I wanted to pet Princess. I couldn't sleep. I was so sad for Matt. But Mama wouldn't let me in to see him."

"What else did you see in the barn?"

"I don't know." She shrugged. "It was dark and spooky."

He relaxed. "I think you'd best go on in the house and get to bed, young lady."

"Are you coming in? Elena saved you some supper."

"I'll be in in a little while."

She gave him a kiss on his cheek. "I love you, Papa."

His big arms swept around her and he crushed her to him. He smelled of sweat and leather and sagebrush. "I love you, too, baby. I love you too."

"Do you think Matt loves us, Pa?"

"I know he does."

"Will his leg ever not hurt him?"

"I don't know, sweetheart. I don't know."

194

She wasn't used to her father's saying he didn't know something. He was supposed to know everything. She was a little afraid as she walked back toward the house.

Cat stood up, shaking off the memories as surely as she shook off the dust that had settled on her skirt. Her earlier determined mood had now been tempered by melancholy. But she wasn't going to let it deter her. She was on her way to Red Springs to see Logan, maybe even to admit she was in love with the man. And, amazingly, just thinking of him gave her spirits a lift.

Mounting Nugget, she rode out. She would have to stop at Isabelle's dress shop for sure now. She wasn't going to go up against Chastity without having every possible weapon at her disposal.

She didn't even notice the trail she'd been taking until it was too late. She reined Nugget up sharply. Just ahead lay the prairie-dog town where her father had died. A sense of foreboding skittered through her. She had to resist the sudden impulse to turn and spur Nugget back to the ranch at a dead run.

Instead she gigged the mare forward at a walk and when she reached the dog town, she dismounted and led the horse through on foot.

In spite of herself Cat found herself smiling at the busy little creatures. Her father had brought her here often. Other ranchers might have poisoned the furry beasts or shot them. But this colony was out of the way and her father always held they had a right to be about their business as long as they weren't a danger to his livestock. As with the fish, her father never took anything from the land that couldn't be put back.

That her father would have galloped through here didn't make any sense. Unless . . .

Unless he was being pursued. Cat felt herself shaking. She didn't want to think about this, didn't want to consider the alternatives to an accidental fall. Maybe something had startled Buck, her father's favorite gray stallion. Maybe he'd been unable to slow the horse until it was too late.

She stepped carefully, watching the more curious animals peek out of their burrows, scolding her for her intrusion into their domain.

Nowhere was there any evidence that a human being had ever crossed here, let alone died here. Cat did find the bones of a horse. Buck. Picked clean by scavengers. The stallion had broken its right foreleg in the fall. Her father had flown over Buck's head . . . landed hard.

It was an accident. It had to be an accident.

Cat shuddered. She had to get out of here.

She tugged on Nugget's reins, leading the horse through the dog town at a faster pace than was wise. But she wanted to hurry now. She wanted to get to Red Springs. She wanted to see Logan, make sense of her world again.

More than that she wanted to get away from this place where her father had died, and where she now had the unmistakable impression she was being watched.

Chapter Fourteen

Logan hadn't yet decided if coming to Texas had been a complete mistake, but as he walked toward Abner Vincent's house, there was no doubt that accepting Chastity's dinner invitation had been one. He was not looking forward to an evening of inane social chatter. He had too much on his mind. If he was lucky, he could excuse himself after dinner and head for the hotel.

What he had yet to decide was whether or not he would be on tomorrow's stage out of town. The thought brought with it an image of Cat as she had been in his arms this afternoon in the Circle J barn. She would have let him make love to her. Just knowing that sent a fearsome heat to his loins. God, how he had wanted her. He couldn't remember ever wanting a woman that much.

And yet, if he'd indulged himself, allowed his passion to rule his reason, he wouldn't have been able to look at himself in a mirror. Because Cat Jordan didn't deserve to be victim to transitory lust. Not that that was what he felt, but it was all it would seem. Because he could never stay in Texas.

That he was attracted to her wasn't in the least surprising. She was a lovely woman, in spite of her continued attempts to conceal the fact with ill-suited clothes and trail dust.

But his attraction to her ran far deeper than physical beauty. It was her spirit that drew him, like a blind man to the light.

And she was light in the darkness that had been his soul too long. But that was danger. To her. To him. If she had been anyone else but a Jordan, he would not have stopped this afternoon in the barn.

His hand clenched automatically in a familiar gesture of frustration. Instead of closing over the shaft of his cane, his fingers curled tightly into his palm. He'd realized soon after he'd left the ranch that he'd forgotten the cane. But he wasn't going back to retrieve it. He would hire a rider to fetch the cane in the morning.

He paused, lifting the Stetson he wore to run his hand through damp tousled hair. If he looked as disgusting as he felt, Chastity Vincent would likely renege on her invitation to dinner. The thought brought a smile to his lips, but propriety sent him toward a sign he saw sitting in the window of the boardinghouse across the street.

Hot Baths—75 cents.

Even Chastity deserved a passably clean guest for company. He was still wearing Matt's clothes.

Hefting his valise, he went inside the boardinghouse and within half an hour he'd settled himself into an intoxicatingly hot tub. A shave and a change of clothes worked further wonders, and he was on his way to the Vincents' with time to spare.

He considered how much more pleasant the evening ahead would have been if he'd been getting ready to

198

escort Cat Jordan to that dance Ryan Fielding had mentioned. Logan admitted he'd been pleased when Cat had turned the man down, a fact that had only added to the muddle of feelings he'd experienced ever since he'd laid eyes on her yesterday.

He didn't want Cordelia Jordan with any other man but himself, yet he was the one man on earth who could never have her.

Such thoughts only made him consider again the irony of his return to Texas. Of course it had been to settle things with Matt. But had some part of him, deep in his vitals, known the woman Corie would have become?

She had been an open and honest child. And incredibly giving for one so young. He had adored her from the first. It was hard even now to admit it, but he had had almost as much fun with her antics that summer as he'd had with Matt's. He had dubbed her an unofficial cousin. And he had loved her with the same childish innocence that she had loved him.

And then, back home in Boston, he had put her out of his mind. He'd thought of her only rarely over the years, mildly curious about what she might look like, who she'd married, whether or not she'd had any children. And always with such musings had come the vague hope that she hadn't found anyone she'd deemed good enough to be her husband.

The woman, Cat, had grown shy, just a little. Open about her opinions still, but not as much with her feelings. Life had taught her, as it had taught him, that open feelings often meant open wounds.

With a resigned sigh, Logan shook off the reflective mood. It was time to end this romantic nonsense. Cat was a rancher. He was a banker, who intended one day to

199

be a doctor. There could be no common ground between them, no future together no matter what their feelings, feelings that would die a natural death when he returned home.

Determined now, he checked into the hotel. Just knowing this was where he would spend the night seemed to seal his decision to leave Texas in the morning. Leave Cat. Depositing his valise in his room, he headed back outside. He couldn't put it off any longer. It was time for dinner with Chastity Vincent.

According to the hotel clerk, the Vincents lived on Third Street. Logan had no difficulty finding it. A sturdy two-story brick building on a corner parcel, the house overshadowed the other homes along the block, most made of wood or adobe. Rose bushes lined the fieldstone walkway leading to the door.

Logan knocked and the door swung inward. A portly, bespectacled man in his fifties greeted him effusively. "Do come in, Mr. Blackstone," he said, proffering his hand. "I've been so looking forward to meeting you."

Logan acknowledged the handshake, looking past Vincent to the parlor directly off the entryway. A Queen Anne loveseat of rose velvet sat against one wall, flanked by matching chairs. Cut yellow roses adorned the leaded crystal vase atop a Chippendale table. The table itself occupied center stage in front of a massive bay window that looked out over the street.

"Please sit down, Mr. Blackstone," Vincent said, gesturing toward one of the chairs in the parlor. "We do want our guest of honor to be comfortable."

Logan took a step, then stopped, wondering about the wisdom of crossing the lush Aubusson carpet wearing dusty boots.

"Don't give it a thought," Abner Vincent said, seeming to read his mind. "The maid will clean up in the morning."

Logan walked over to the chair, but remained standing.

"I must thank you again, Mr. Blackstone," Vincent went on, "as Chastity has already done, I'm sure, for your bravery with those brigands at the relay station. It still frightens me to think what might have become of my beloved daughter if you hadn't been there. A person isn't safe anymore. I don't know what this country is coming to."

"At least the men responsible are in jail."

Vincent looked disgruntled. "I take it you haven't heard?"

"Heard what?"

"Those two desperadoes escaped the deputy who was escorting them to the county seat this afternoon."

Logan swallowed a curse. "Was the deputy hurt?"

"No, thank heaven. But now those men won't be getting the punishment they so richly deserve."

To Logan's mind Yerby and Doakes's escape seemed a fitting ending to a daylong list of irritations. He just hoped the two outlaws had the good sense to leave the territory.

"But enough of this unpleasantness," Vincent went on. "Please, sit down, Mr. Blackstone."

"Logan will do," Logan said. "And I'd rather stand."

"Do call me Abner." Vincent opened the humidor on the table. "Cigar?"

"I don't smoke."

Vincent pulled out a long stogie, running his fingers down the length of it, then biting off one end. He put the cigar in his mouth and lit it.

Logan grimaced inwardly. He detested cigar smoke. The only saving grace of this evening—a potentially good home-cooked meal—had just been effectively thwarted.

"Where is Chastity?" Logan asked, more out of politeness than interest.

"Patience, my boy," Abner beamed.

Logan coughed into his hand. This night was going to be even longer than he'd thought. Leona wasn't the only matchmaker in the family. "Actually, Abner," he said, deciding business might be a safer subject, "I was hoping for a moment or two of your time to discuss a financial matter."

"By all means," Abner said, his eyes lighting with keen interest. "What is it?"

Logan didn't say, because at that moment Chastity swept into the room. She was wearing a lime green silk gown with an even more daring neckline than the outrageous dress she'd worn on the stage.

"Logan," she purred, curtsying sweetly and offering him her hand. "I had no idea you'd arrived." She looked petulantly at her father as Logan bestowed a polite kiss on the back of her hand. "Daddy, you naughty boy, you should have told me he was here."

"A lady should always make a grand entrance," Logan said. "Especially one so lovely." He was getting a free meal, after all, he thought without the slightest trace of conscience. The girl was hopelessly infatuated with herself anyway. His opinion one way or the other wasn't going to make a whit of difference. And he did need Abner's help with the papers on the Jordan extension.

She giggled merrily. "I told Daddy you were such a gentleman. He was so looking forward to meeting you. Of course he's thanked you for—"

"Done," Logan interrupted. If he was thanked one more time, he wasn't going to be responsible for his actions.

Chastity opened a gaily decorated fan and fluttered it coquettishly in front of her bosom. "Oh, Logan," she sighed. "I'm just so delighted to see you again. I can't tell you how happy I am that you could have dinner in our humble home."

"It's very lovely," he said.

"Do sit down. I'll get you some lemonade. I made it fresh all by myself."

"Perhaps Mr. Blackstone would like something a little more substantial, my dear," Abner chuckled.

"Oh, of course! If you would be so kind, Papa. I don't know the first thing about preparing spirits."

Abner crossed to the decanter on the mahogany table in the far corner of the room and poured Logan a brandy.

"Perhaps you should help your mother in the kitchen, dear," Abner suggested.

Chastity stamped her foot impatiently. "Now, Daddy, it's not my fault the cook got sick. Mama said I should come out and entertain our guest."

"Just make sure everything's running smoothly, won't you, dear? I have a business matter to discuss with Logan. It'll only take a moment."

"I'm sorry, Daddy. Of course." She turned back to Logan. "Now don't you go away."

"Not a chance," Logan said, adding churlishly to himself, *unfortunately*.

"She can be so impetuous," Abner said, after Chastity left the room. "Do forgive her."

"Of course. She's very young."

"Oh, no, she's nineteen. Quite the right age, don't

203

you think?"

Logan was not going to answer that one. "Maybe we should take care of that financial matter . . ."

"Forgive me. Please, just tell me what I can do for you, and then consider it done."

"I have papers for the Circle J I'd like to have processed."

"Of course," Abner said. "It's so sad, isn't it? They've had such an unfortunate run of luck. And now to lose their home. Well, I'm sure a buyer can be found quickly. It is a fine ranch, if not the most profitable."

"Actually, I've given Cat . . . Miss Jordan . . . an extension."

Vincent choked on his brandy. "Dear me," he said. "I hesitate to say so, Logan, but I do believe you'll be throwing good money after bad."

"I don't recall asking your opinion."

"Of course not," the man demurred. "I didn't mean to speak out of turn. Do forgive me. It's just that as a financial expert in my own right, I find it difficult to hold my tongue when I see someone making a most unwise decision regarding investment capital."

"It is, I seem to recall, Mr. Vincent, my money."

"Of course. And if anyone knows how to handle money it would be a Blackstone. I've . . . heard of your father. By reputation of course."

"My father's been in banking many years. He finds it quite to his liking."

"Do I detect a note of disapproval in your tone, Mr. Blackstone? Perhaps you're not as drawn by the wheelings and dealings of the financial world."

"Perhaps not," Logan allowed, wondering why he did so. He supposed he was tired, and more tired still of attending to business matters he found wearisome. Seeing to Matt's injury this afternoon had triggered again the burning desire he had long held in check—the need to be a doctor.

"I'll see to the papers, of course," Abner said.

"Thank you," Logan said, distracted. It was most certainly a day for regrets.

"I hope Daddy isn't boring you too much with talk about silly old money," Chastity said, flouncing back into the room. "Mama said supper wouldn't be ready for another twenty minutes. Would you care for a walk, Logan?"

"I'd be delighted," Logan said, eager to escape the room now stinking of cigar smoke, "if it's all right with your father."

"Oh, you young people run along, run along," Abner said, opening the door for them. "We'll be right here when you get back."

Chastity immediately entwined her arm with Logan's, as they headed for the main street of Red Springs. "Wasn't that ever so clever of me?" she asked coyly.

"Excuse me?"

"Suggesting we take this little walk together." She gave Logan a smile that seemed suddenly much beyond her nineteen years. "Now we're all alone."

"It has cooled off a bit, a nice time for a walk." He decided the weather would be a good topic right about now.

"The heat is perfectly dreadful and you know it," she said, pouting. "Just like this town. Dreadful, dreadful, dreadful. But Papa insisted he wanted to start his own bank."

"Was he a banker before?"

"Papa's always been very clever about money." The smile was back, "just like I'm clever about men." She batted her eyelashes at him. "You do find me beautiful, don't you, Logan?"

"You are an attractive woman," he admitted. "Just how long have you and your family lived in Red Springs?"

"A couple of years." She sighed, obviously wishing he'd lingered longer on the subject of her beauty. "We came here from Atlanta. Now there's a city!"

"Is that where your family is from originally?" He asked the question though he couldn't possibly care less about the answer. The girl had all the depth of a rain puddle.

"By way of Baltimore," she told him. "We've lived in several places actually, though this is by far the most primitive. Father has assured Mother and me that it's only temporary. In a few more months we'll be moving back east, maybe to New York. I can't wait. The opera, the symphony, the stores. Father has even mentioned Boston as a possibility. Wouldn't that be lovely? We might be neighbors."

"Lovely."

They were passing a cul de sac on the main street, when Chastity startled him by grabbing his hand and pulling him into the small alleyway. "I do so like you, Logan," she breathed. "I so admired your courage when you saved my life."

"I think we'd better head back to—"

She threw herself at him, literally, her arms locking around his neck with more force than he would have thought her capable of. The scent of her jasmine perfume filled his nostrils. Her breasts pressed suggestively against his chest.

"Logan, I want you," she whispered urgently. "There's a room in the back of Papa's bank, with blankets and brandy and everything we need."

He caught her arms and tried to set her away from him, but she resisted and he didn't want to hurt her.

"Kiss me, Logan, kiss me, please."

She was a beautiful woman. Perhaps one of the most beautiful women he had ever seen. Ebony hair, crystal blue eyes. Ivory skin. Lovely. Exquisite. Yet looking at her, all he could see was wind-tumbled blond hair and spitfire green eyes.

"Chastity, this is not a good idea."

She kissed him, full on the mouth.

He caught her wrists and pried her loose, taking a step back. He was about to give her a piece of his mind when he noticed her gaze looking past him toward the boardwalk. He didn't want to, but he turned around anyway.

Cat stood there, hands on her hips, a searing disgust firing her green eyes. "Taking a tour of the town, Mr. Blackstone?" she inquired acidly. "Or maybe a private tour of one of the more interesting attractions."

He groaned inwardly, then wondered perhaps if the fates had done them both a favor. He settled his arm around Chastity's waist and guided her toward Cat. "Miss Vincent is a most proficient guide."

"I'll just bet," Cat said, turning on her heel and stalking back up the street.

"Such a hoyden," Chastity clucked.

Logan jerked his arm free of her with suppressed violence. He felt like something that belonged under a rock. *It's for the best,* he kept telling himself. If Cat hated

207

him, it would spare both of them this constant battle to stay clear of one another.

Still he looked for her as he walked Chastity back to the house. But she was nowhere in sight.

As Logan opened the door, Chastity caught his wrist. "I meant what I said about that room. I want you, Logan." There was no mistaking her intention. Logan wondered wearily if Abner Vincent was aware of how dangerously close he was to becoming a grandfather every time he let his daughter out of the house.

His preoccupation with Cat made dinner even more of an ordeal. When it was finished, he rose, fully intending to head for his hotel for the night.

"You can't retire already," Chastity chided. "I won't hear of it. You simply must escort me to the dance."

"Dance?"

"It's a monthly affair in the town hall," Leona explained. "Chastity has so been looking forward to it."

"Ryan Fielding would have asked me, of course," Chastity said. "But he's been too busy worrying about silly old rustlers or some such nonsense."

"It's been a very long day for me, Chastity," Logan said, hoping for a gracious exit. He had the disconcerting feeling that the only dance Chastity had in mind was going to be in that room she'd been talking about.

"Please do take her to the dance," Vincent put in. "As a favor to me. I could start work on those financial papers and bring them by your hotel in the morning."

"I couldn't ask you to work on a Saturday evening."

"I don't mind. I don't mind at all."

"I have to send a telegram," Logan said, now looking for any excuse.

"The telegraph office is closed on Saturday evening.

208

But if the message isn't confidential, I could pass it along to the clerk and he could send it as a favor to me."

"I suppose that would be fine," Logan said, acknowledging defeat. He wrote out the message, addressed to his father, regarding his progress on the Jordan situation, keeping strictly to business. He then headed out the door with a thoroughly delighted Chastity ensconced on his arm.

He paid little attention to her chatter this time as they walked toward the town hall. Again and again he thought of Cat, wondering if she'd returned home safely, wondering why she'd come to town at all.

Had it been to see him? Did she fight as fiercely against this attraction between them as he did? Or did she seek it out, as he wished to God he was free to do?

At the town hall, he nodded politely again and again as Chastity took him around the room and introduced him to people whose names he forgot almost before he heard them. He was being an idiot to stay here with this silly girl-woman. Yet he supposed he deserved it, as fitting punishment for his unforgivable behavior with Cat.

"You must dance with me, Logan," Chastity purred, as the music started. "You must dance with me for at least the first two dances. And then we can make a discreet exit to your hotel room now that I know you have one."

His temper snapped. He caught her wrist, his face bare inches from hers. For appearance's sake he kept a tightly controlled smile on his face, but his voice was harsh. "I appreciate the fact that you're a spoiled young brat," he said. "But I will not be led around by the nose by anyone for any reason. You are not going to my hotel room with me tonight or any other night. I do not make love to children. Do I make myself clear?"

She nodded, her eyes wide.

"Now," he said evenly, "I will have that dance with you, so that you are not embarrassed in front of your friends. And then I will take my leave. And you will not see me again."

Her body trembled against his as they danced, and he experienced an odd feeling that he had not so much frightened her as enraged her. The silly chit needed more of the fear of God in her. Heaven knew what kind of men she invited back to that room of hers.

When the dance ended and he started to leave, Chastity's arm was still linked in his. He supposed he should be gentleman enough to take her home.

He had just placed his arm around her when Cat Jordan swept into the room.

Chapter Fifteen

Clinging to the last vestiges of her pride, Cat had staggered away from the soul-searing discovery of Logan in Chastity Vincent's arms. She'd made it as far as Maude's boardinghouse before she'd burst into tears.

"Cat, dear, what is it?" Maude asked, hurrying from behind the small desk in the hall to Cat's side. "Tell Maudie what's wrong."

"Nothing," Cat lied, swiping viciously at the tears that streaked her dust-grimed face. "I'm fine. I . . . I just got some dust in my eyes."

Maude clucked sympathetically. "That's happened to me more times than I care to count." She put her arm around Cat's shoulders. "Rowdy cowpunchers! They think they own the streets. Tearing up and down on those horses like to kick up a dust storm all by themselves. Fools have no respect for a lady on the boardwalk."

"I'll be fine, Maude," Cat said, trying hard to hold her emotions in check. "Honestly. I . . . I think I got most of the dust out."

"Well, let's make sure, shall we? You come on over

here and sit down." Maude guided Cat over to a well-worn ladder-back chair near her desk. "I'll make us a spot of tea and you can clean up a bit and we'll have a nice visit. It's been a long time since we really talked, hasn't it?"

Cat nodded, drying the last of her tears with the handkerchief Maude handed her. "Thanks, Maude. I'm all right. Really."

When she tried to rise, Maude immediately put her hands on Cat's shoulders and sat her back down. "You're having that tea, young lady. And I won't have any argument about it."

"What I really need, Maude, is a bath."

"Tea first, then a bath." Maude bustled over with a china teapot and two mismatched cups. "Never did get used to that godawful coffee the mister used to drink."

Cat took a polite sip from the cup Maude handed her, though she'd never gotten used to sissified herbs. Maude also had a habit of pouring honey into her teapot by the dipperful. Cat held her breath and swallowed quickly as she forced down a second sip.

"Delicious, isn't it?" Maude prompted.

Cat nodded vigorously and prayed she didn't throw up. At least Maude's horrific tea was taking her mind off Logan for the moment.

"Now what brings you to Maudie's?" Maude asked, finishing off her first cup of tea and pouring a second.

"The bath, actually," Cat said.

Maude looked disappointed, and Cat hastened to add, "I mean, I knew I'd need one when I got to town today, and I figured it would be the perfect excuse to stop by and see you. I never did like the way the hotel provides their baths." Cat made a face.

Maude looked properly mollified. "I know what you mean. Sandpaper towels, tepid water, and peeping-tom hotel clerks, it's a positive disgrace." She set her empty cup on the desktop. "But you still haven't told me why you're in town. I haven't seen much of you at all since your dear pa passed on."

"There's a lot to keep me busy now, Maude."

"How's Matt?"

"He's fine," Cat said, "so's Ma."

Maude looked dubious, but didn't press the issue. "So will you and your family be movin' to town soon, after the ranch is sold?"

Cat sighed. "Does everyone think we're selling?"

"It's the talk all over town."

"Well, it's not going to happen. Pa left the ranch to me, and I'm not going to lose it."

"I wish you'd tell that to Chastity Vincent." Maude sniffed.

Cat stiffened. "Chastity?" She closed her eyes, remembering again the girl's full lips on Logan's mouth. For an instant Cat couldn't seem to breathe.

"Dear me," Maude said. "I shouldn't have said anything. I didn't mean to upset you."

"No, no, Maude, don't be silly. I'm fine. Please, what did Chastity have to say?"

"The little trollop," Maude sniffed. "God forgive me," she added parenthetically. "She's been telling anyone who'll listen that her father is the world's smartest banker for not loanin' you folks money last fall. If you ask me, her father should take that little tart—God forgive me—over his knee and teach her some manners!"

"I think it's too late," Cat muttered. She stood, not wanting to talk about Chastity anymore. "Do you think I

213

could have that bath?"

"Of course, dear. Right away." The plump, cheery-faced woman led Cat to the back room where three wooden tubs were partitioned off from one another. "It's all right," Maude assured Cat, "I don't have any gentlemen back here right now." She gave Cat a mischievous wink. "You'd know if I did, because I'd be back here looking for an excuse to dump more hot water in their tubs."

"Maude!" Cat gasped. "You're outrageous!"

"You take what you can get when you've been a widow for over six years," Maude said, her giggle sounding more like that of a schoolgirl than a forty-eight-year-old woman. "Now you just go behind that screen there and get yourself undressed, and I'll fetch the water for you."

"Thanks, Maude." Cat couldn't wait to begin scrubbing the day's deposit of dirt and grime. She only wished she could scrub away the cutting image of Logan kissing Chastity as well.

Maude served up the hot water in short order and Cat immersed herself in the luxury of it. But even the cleansing water could not cleanse away her hurt. How could Logan have done such a thing?

Chastity is a most proficient guide, he'd mocked.

To her bedroom! Cat thought furiously.

She slapped at the water. God, how had she been such a fool? She had actually been coming to town to tell the man she loved him, that she knew he'd just been holding himself back because of his scruples about Matt and her mother.

Scruples! Bah! Logan didn't know the meaning of the word.

"Had a handsome stranger in here earlier tonight,"

214

Maude said, coming in with another bucket of steaming water. "As soon as I seen him, I thought he'd sure make a good catch for a purty thing like Cat Jordan."

"I'm not looking to catch anybody, Maude."

"Bosh and nonsense, girl! You told me once, you didn't want to be no sashaying flirt to attract a man. That if he didn't like you the way you were, the hell with him. And I said, good for you!"

"And I still say that," Cat put in stubbornly.

"Let me finish, will you?" Maude chided, handing Cat a towel as she did so. "You remind me so much of myself when I was your age. That's about the time I met my first husband, Frank."

The boardinghouse mistress crossed over to a small bureau and pulled out a dressing gown for Cat to slip into. "I thought I was the most independent woman there ever was, and Frank, why he was proud of the way I could think for myself. Said he was sick to death of helpless females."

"What does that have to do with handsome strangers?"

Maude's eyes clouded in fond remembrance. "Frank and me were happier than two people have a right bein'. And the point is that there *is* a man out there for a woman like you. And it could well be that stranger, a Mr. Blackstone he said his name was."

Cat nearly fell out of the tub.

"Here, here," Maude said, reaching for her. "Be careful now, the floor must be slippery."

Cat straightened, hoping Maude didn't notice how all the blood had drained from her face.

"Anyway," Maude went on, "there was just something about him that put me in mind of you. It was so odd."

Cat clutched the dressing gown tight around her, sinking down to sit on the edge of the tub. She wasn't sure her knees were going to continue supporting her.

"He was truly the handsomest man I have seen in a long time. And so polite and . . . and kind of"—Maude groped for the right word—"lost."

"Lost?" Cat murmured.

"Not lost like he didn't know where he was, but lost like he didn't even know he was lost."

"I think you're bein' fanciful, Maude," Cat managed. "The man only took a bath here, didn't he?"

"He surely did," Maude giggled, completely unaware of Cat's turmoil. "And I added plenty of buckets of hot water, if you know what I mean!"

Cat choked so hard, she had to scurry out to the front room and drink down some of Maude's tea. Then she choked some more.

"Are you all right, dear?" Maude asked, patting Cat sharply on the back. "My goodness but you seem to have two left feet this evening."

"It has been that kind of a day." Cat went back to the bathing room to fetch her clothes, hoping Maude had exhausted the subject of a certain handsome stranger. "I do hate to put these things back on," she mused aloud. "I didn't have the presence of mind to bring a change of clothes with me."

"Never you mind about that. You're not through visitin' with me yet, young lady."

"I really do have to get going, Maude." Where, Cat hadn't yet decided.

"Sit," Maude said.

Cat sat.

"Now," Maude continued, "you may not believe this,

but I have known ever since you came through my door that the hand of providence is at work here tonight."

"I beg your pardon, Maude?"

"Think about it, dear. Mr. Blackstone comes in—an incredibly handsome prince charming if ever there was one."

Cat wasn't certain she was yet going to be able to keep down Maude's tea.

"And who do I think of right away but you! Now you haven't been to visit for weeks. But who comes through my door not an hour later? You! It's fate, I tell you."

"It's bad timing," Cat said dryly.

"I'll bet Mr. Blackstone found out about the dance tonight," Maude said, "and he likely considers it the perfect way to get to know new people on his travels."

Cat wasn't going to like where this was heading. She wasn't going to like it one bit.

"You're going to that dance," Maude stated.

"I'm not."

"Yes, you are."

"I don't have anything to wear."

"Yes, you do."

Cat sat dumbfounded as Maude ducked into another room. When she came back she was carrying the loveliest dress Cat had ever seen.

"Pure silk," Maude said, running her fingers caressingly over the exquisite, pale rose-colored garment. "And such simple lines it's never gone out of style. Please, try it on. You're about the same size I was back then."

Reluctantly, Cat did so. It truly was exquisite. Cat had never worn anything so pretty in all her life. But Maude refused to let Cat see herself in a mirror. "First, I have to do your hair. I want you to see the whole affect."

217

"Maude, this is all crazy."

"Hush, now. Humor an old widow woman."

"You're not old."

"Then humor a middle-aged widow woman."

Grumbling to herself, Cat sat down and let Maude fuss with her hair. In half an hour Maude had transformed the tumbled locks into a crown of soft curls.

"Now, the mirror," Maude said, nodding her approval. Her soft brown eyes brimmed with tears as she surveyed her handiwork. "Oh, my, my," she breathed. "I never did that dress justice. I surely never did."

Cat stood in front of the full-length mirror in Maude's private room and stared. She couldn't believe she was looking at her own reflection.

"You are so beautiful, my dear," Maude said.

"Cinderella for certain," Cat said, shaking her head with something akin to wonder.

"And I'm your fairy godmother."

Cat gave Maude a fierce hug. "That you are, and I thank you."

"Oh, I was happy to do it, sweetheart," Maude said, dismissing Cat's gratitude with a wave of her hand. "You've always been a special favorite of mine. Doin' me favors and such. And you keep Sheriff Toby guessin' about me too."

"You two should get married."

"I might let him do that one of these days."

Cat giggled, then caught her breath. "Oh, Maude, do I really dare go out in this? Everyone will laugh at me."

"Ain't a man alive would look at you and laugh. Not in that dress. Now be off with you. The dance started twenty minutes ago." Maude shooed her out the door.

Cat's heart thudded wildly on her walk toward the

town hall. Twice she got admiring whistles, and it was all she could do not to bolt for Nugget and head for home.

At the town hall she stood outside the door fidgeting for some minutes, trying to work up the courage to go inside. What if Logan was in there with Chastity?

What if he wasn't?

More to the point, why did she care? Hadn't he proved beyond a doubt today that he'd just been using her? That she was convenient? As soon as he got back to town he got back to Chastity.

The last thought decided her. She'd show him! Jutting her chin defiantly she opened the door and stepped into the room.

Nearly three dozen people milled about in the large open area that on other nights served as a community meeting place. A small band composed of local musicians was tuning up in the far corner. But Cat's eyes went past them all, seeking out Logan.

She found him.

His arm, as before, was firmly twined around Chastity's waist. But this time Cat didn't let it throw her.

He hadn't yet noticed her. But she knew it the instant he did. It was in his eyes. Not the astonishment she had expected, because she could fix herself up to look passably female. But a glowing warmth, as though he'd known it all along. And then, just that quickly, his gaze registered no reaction at all, as though a shutter had been drawn. He turned back to Chastity.

Shaking, trying hard not to, Cat made her way over to the buffet table. In the fifteen-foot distance she traveled, three men approached her, each from a different direction, each asking her to dance. Cat blushed, feeling giddy, happy, in spite of Logan Blackstone. Still she very graciously turned each man down.

One of them proved more persistent and brought her a glass of punch. She accepted it, but again declined the man's invitation to dance. There was one little detail neither Cat nor Maude had remembered to take into account for this evening's Cinderella performance. Cat couldn't dance.

She sipped the sweet liquid slowly, glad when the small band started playing, returning most of the people to the dance floor. Even so, her courage was slipping away at an alarming rate. She shouldn't have come. She shouldn't be here. She was only making herself more miserable.

Who was she fooling anyway? Logan didn't care. He was with Chastity. Whatever Cat had read in his eyes when she'd come through the door, her appearance here had ultimately meant nothing to him. If anything, he was angry. He probably thought she was following him around like some love-struck puppy.

Well, she was lovestruck. She wasn't going to deceive herself on that account. But she would get over it. He would be going back to Boston. And she would use her memories of him as an object lesson on just how foolish the human heart could be.

"You look beautiful." His voice, deep, sensual, was coming from directly behind her. She gripped the cup she was holding more tightly, lest it drop from her trembling hand. Her breathing seemed constricted all at once. She did not turn around.

"Thank you," she managed, praying her voice sounded nonchalant.

"I didn't expect to see you here." He was beside her now, ladling punch. Two cups. One for him, one for—

"Cat, dear," Chastity said ever so sweetly, insinuating

220

herself between Logan and Cat, "I do believe this is the first time in my life I've ever seen you in a dress. It took me a full minute to realize who you were."

"At least you figured it out," Cat said, smiling just as sweetly. "I've known you for years, and I still don't know who you are."

Chastity's lips pursed with outrage. She turned to Logan. "Be a dear and get my shawl for me, will you? You did say we were leaving."

He hesitated briefly, then moved away.

"He's taking me back to his hotel room," Chastity said, her voice smug. "So you can rid yourself of any notions you may have had in trying to wrest him away from me." Chastity's smirk grew cruel. "It's too bad, too. You wasted a perfectly good bath."

Cat was careful to let no reaction show in her face. Logan was taking this woman to his hotel room? Cat was not naïve. She knew precisely what Chastity was implying. And the thought was like a knife to her heart.

Logan came back, slipping Chastity's shawl across the ebony-haired woman's bare shoulders.

"You two have a wonderful time," Cat said, vowing inwardly to show not the slightest hint of the pain she was feeling. "In all my life I've seldom seen two people better suited to one another."

Logan bid her an oddly subdued good-night.

"Yes, it is a good night." She held her head proudly, as she watched him guide Chastity to the door. They paused there, and for just an instant Cat's hopes flickered. But then Logan opened the door and they were gone.

Cat told herself to leave, go home. But she couldn't move. She felt ill. Logan was going to be making love to that woman. Whispering sweet words, holding her, kissing her . . .

Cat stomped over to the punch bowl, ladled herself another full glass and drank it where she stood. She then repeated the procedure.

Two more men came up and asked her to dance. She declined as gracefully as she could manage.

"You're breaking a lot of hearts here tonight," a husky voice said, his breath warm against the back of her neck.

"You . . . you left," she said stupidly.

"I'm back."

Cat glanced about, hating herself for doing so. "Chastity took ill?"

"I took her home, or at least I started to. She decided—"

"I don't much care what she decided," Cat cut in. "If she preferred someone else's company, that's your problem. If she dropped dead, that's your problem. If she took wing and flew back to her cave, that's still your problem."

To her complete amazement and total fury, he laughed.

"You are one helluva woman."

"Get out of my sight!"

"I should, I know."

"But you can't seem to help yourself, right? Maybe if you ever get to be a doctor, you can find a suitable cure for your disease."

"Maybe."

"You're despicable!"

"I know that too."

Cat slammed her punch glass onto the tabletop. "You don't even care that you used me, do you? And you had the gall to turn right around and use Chastity."

222

"I did not use Chastity, at least not any more than she used me."

"Oh, spare me."

"I'm trying to. Believe me, I'm trying to." His gray eyes were serious now, though he was still trying to shutter away whatever it was he was feeling.

"You want me to hate you, don't you?" she said, the words more of a statement than a question.

"It would be infinitely easier on both of us."

She didn't even realize how rigidly she'd been holding herself until she let out a long, slow breath. "That doesn't make one iota's worth of sense."

"It does to me."

"Do you know how much it hurt me to see you kissing her in a public alley?"

"I have a pretty good idea."

"Then why did you do it?"

"I wanted to put an end to whatever this is between us."

She stared at his eyes and knew that he was telling the truth, knew that he was losing the same battle she was. "She kissed you, and then you saw me and decided not to stop her."

"Something like that."

"That was awful of you."

"I know. I'm sorry. And I tell you here and now, I wish to God I had the courage to let you keep on believing the worst of me. But I don't." He rubbed a hand across the back of his neck in self-disgust. "I had to come back. I had to at least try to explain it to you. And that you so easily understand proves that I was right to use Chastity to make you hate me."

"Why, Logan? Why?" How could breaking her heart

be for her own good?

"Because I'm only going to hurt you more. Don't you see that? It's inevitable. If not today or tomorrow, then the next day or the next . . . if . . ."

"If I would ever be foolish enough to fall in love with you?"

He didn't answer.

She placed her hands on either side of his face. "It may already be too late, Logan," she said softly. "It may already be too late."

He closed his eyes and she sensed his regret, but she was certain she sensed joy in him, too. And she clung to that, for she had never felt so exposed, so vulnerable. One word, one look—and he could destroy her.

When he opened his eyes, his gaze was warm, kind. Not quite what she would have wanted, but more than she'd dared hope for. She knew he battled the demons of their families' pasts. He would not easily exorcise them. But tonight, tonight, she assured herself fiercely, they would start.

"Dance with me," he said, his voice deep, sensual.

She bit her lip and shook her head.

"Please?"

She shook her head again.

He actually looked hurt. "I can't dance," she said quickly. "I don't know how."

His smile nearly melted her heart. He held out his arms and she went into them. He led effortlessly and she followed. In minutes she was gliding across the dance floor as though dance had been invented especially for her.

"Oh, Logan," she murmured, "what are we going to do?"

ACCEPT YOUR **FREE GIFT** AND EXPERIENCE MORE OF THE PASSION AND ADVENTURE YOU LIKE IN A HISTORICAL ROMANCE

Zebra Romances are the finest novels of their kind and are written with the adult woman in mind. All of our books are written by authors who really know how to weave tales of romantic adventure in the historical settings you love.

Because our readers tell us these books sell out very fast in the stores, Zebra has made arrangements for you to receive at home the four newest titles published each month. You'll never miss a title and home delivery is so convenient. With your first shipment we'll even send you a FREE Zebra Historical Romance as our gift just for trying our home subscription service. No obligation.

BIG SAVINGS AND **FREE** HOME DELIVERY

Each month, the Zebra Home Subscription Service will send you the four newest titles as soon as they are published. (We ship these books to our subscribers even before we send them to the stores.) You may preview them *Free* for 10 days. If you like them as much as we think you will, you'll pay just $3.50 each and *save $1.80 each month* off the cover price. *AND you'll also get FREE HOME DELIVERY.* There is never a charge for shipping, handling or postage and there is no minimum you must buy. If you decide not to keep any shipment, simply return it within 10 days, no questions asked, and owe nothing.

GET FREE GIFT

MAIL IN THE COUPON BELOW TODAY

To get your Free ZEBRA HISTORICAL ROMANCE fill out the coupon below and send it in today. As soon as we receive the coupon, we'll send your first month's books to preview Free for 10 days along with your FREE NOVEL.

FREE BOOK CERTIFICATE

ZEBRA HOME SUBSCRIPTION SERVICE, INC.

YES! Please start my subscription to Zebra Historical Romances and send me my free Zebra Novel along with my first month's Romances. I understand that I may preview these four new Zebra Historical Romances Free for 10 days. If I'm not satisfied with them I may return the four books within 10 days and owe nothing. Otherwise I will pay just $3.50 each; a total of $14.00 (a $15.80 value—I save $1.80). Then each month I will receive the 4 newest titles as soon as they come off the press for the same 10 day Free preview and low price. I may return any shipment and I may cancel this arrangement at any time. There is no minimum number of books to buy and there are no shipping, handling or postage charges. Regardless of what I do, the FREE book is mine to keep.

Name _____
(Please Print)

Address _____ Apt. # _____

City _____ State _____ Zip _____

Telephone ( ) _____

Signature _____
(if under 18, parent or guardian must sign)

12-88

Terms and offer subject to change without notice.

"Shhh." He pressed his fingers to her lips. "Just dance with me, Corie. Just dance."

And they did.

The dance went on and on, and she didn't question him again. She just danced.

And they drank punch and they laughed and they danced some more. This night, this night with Logan, she danced.

"Oh, my," she breathed, leaning hard against him at the end of a particularly energetic piece. "I think I may have to sleep for a week."

"You're having fun?" he asked.

"You doubt it?" she demanded incredulously. "Oh, Logan, I have never been so happy, so—" The words froze on her lips.

The main door had swept open, and Cat had looked up to see Chastity Vincent stalk back into the room. Cat thought with a modicum of satisfaction that the girl looked mad enough to kill somebody.

"I'd better handle this," Logan said.

As he headed toward Chastity, Cat felt a hand lock onto her arm and squeeze it none too gently. She turned to encounter a thoroughly irate Ryan Fielding.

"I thought you were too busy to come to the dance with me," he gritted out.

Cat hadn't seen him come in. In spite of the fact that she owed him no explanation, she found herself feeling sorry for him. She hadn't meant to slight him.

"I'm sorry, Ryan. I told you I had a guest. And I also told you I didn't want to go to the dance. Both of those things were true at the time."

"You certainly seem to have changed your mind." His gaze raked her from head to toe. "Not to mention your clothes."

"Mr. Blackstone forgot his cane at the ranch, you see. And I brought it into town, because I thought . . . well, actually I ended up leaving it in my rifle scabbard now that I think about it. And . . ." She frowned bemusedly, as the room seemed to tip ever so slightly. "Do you think there's something in the punch, Ryan?"

"Allow me to refill your glass, my dear."

Cat looked past him to see Latigo lurking in the shadows. "Why is that beast here?" she demanded. "I am sick of seeing that man everywhere I look. I think you should fire him."

"I think you have enough on your hands running the Circle J right now," Ryan said tightly. "I hardly think you need concern yourself with the Rocking R."

Latigo stepped closer. "Want to dance with me, missy?" He smirked. "I promised you one, remember?" His arm jerked up, jostling the punch glass Ryan was handing to Cat and nearly upsetting it.

Cat grimaced, then took a quick sip from the overfull glass. Whatever was in the punch it was much too good. She really should stop drinking it.

She was about to set the glass down, when Chastity stormed up to her.

"Logan called me a spoiled brat!" Chastity said angrily. "I've never been so humiliated in my life. And it's all because of you!"

"Ryan," Cat said, "maybe you should take her—"

"Leave me be!" Chastity hissed, her venom still directed at Cat. "I'm supposed to be the belle of the ball in this crummy little town. You had no right."

The girl was drunk. Cat wished fervently Ryan would take her out of the town hall before she embarrassed herself beyond redemption. But no one moved.

"I just wanted you to know that I hate you," Chastity finished, slapping Cat's punch glass so that this time it did spill. "You spoil my night, I spoil yours."

Cat stared in horror at the spreading red stain on Maude's lovely dress.

Chastity cackled. "As if wearing a dress can hide what you are. Or what you aren't. Do you think your silks and satins fooled anybody here tonight? They were all laughing at you. Every one of them." Her voice grew more high-pitched, evil. "I heard them whispering, I heard them. 'Did you see poor, pathetic Cat Jordan,' they said, 'pretending she's a woman?'" Chastity lunged at Cat and grabbed a handful of her dress front, ripping savagely. "It isn't a costume ball, Cordelia. You were supposed to come as you are!"

Cat clutched the torn front of her dress, feeling hot tears stinging her eyes, suddenly aware that everyone in the room was staring at her. Worse, she saw Logan striding toward her, and she was certain she saw raw pity in his eyes. He must have heard every word.

The clock had surely struck midnight. She just hadn't been paying attention. Cinderella had to go home.

With a sob Cat bolted past them all, running, running as she never had. She didn't stop, not even when she heard Logan calling her name.

Ryan Fielding hadn't minded Chastity Vincent's little scene with Cat in the least. His only regret was that he had not been able to reach Cat in time to prevent her from running out. He would have liked to offer his sympathy in her time of need.

227

His smile was not pleasant. He had to face getting Chastity home. She had most certainly outlived her usefulness for the night. For one thing, she'd been too drunk to really appreciate his attentions in the storeroom at the back of her father's bank. He'd run into her an hour ago, as Logan Blackstone had been escorting her home.

She'd been livid. When she'd stopped to tell Ryan her troubles, Blackstone had merely tipped his hat and bid her good night.

"I can't believe he actually prefers that tomboy over me," Chastity had fumed. "How dare he insult me like that? After all I've offered him."

"Your storeroom bordello?" Ryan had mocked.

"You've never complained about the times you spent there."

"And I don't now. But what is all this about Blackstone and Cat Jordan? The man is only here to do some paperwork on the loan her father had with the Blackstone bank."

"He has more in mind than paperwork with that bitch," Chastity said. "Much more."

Ryan was not pleased.

"Why do you care?" Chastity demanded. "What is any of this to you?"

"You know I wouldn't take kindly to any competition for Cat's favors."

"You mean for her ranch."

"Same thing."

"Well, I've never been so humiliated in my life. I want Logan Blackstone to pay for what he's done. I want him to pay dearly."

That part had pleased Ryan very much. He had agreed

to escort Chastity back to the dance to find out for himself just how much competition Blackstone might offer to Ryan's quest to acquire the Circle J. Finding Cat and Blackstone dancing so intimately had soured his mood considerably.

"We can be of mutual benefit to one another," he'd purred in Chastity's ear. "You get what you want. I get what I want."

"And what is it I want?"

"Revenge. Against a certain Boston banker. A very wealthy Boston banker."

"And you get Cat's ranch."

"Precisely." Perhaps she wasn't as drunk as he'd thought.

"Even if you have to marry Cat Jordan to get it?"

"She can be my wife. But that hardly means she'll be the only woman in my bed."

"And how do we go about getting what we want, Ryan darling?" Chastity had asked, twining one arm around his neck, while her other hand roamed lewdly over other parts of his body.

"Why don't we go to your little room and discuss the possibilities . . . privately."

She'd smiled a wicked smile as he led her from the room.

Chapter Sixteen

Sobbing, Cat stumbled into Robinson's Livery, moving blindly along the barn wall until she slammed into a spare wheel the hostler had leaned against a support stud. She cried out, rubbing her knee, then huddled quickly into the deeper shadows lest anyone hear her and come to investigate. Thankfully, no one did.

Still she waited, trembling, gulping in air as she sought to catch her breath. She had run the entire distance from the town hall. It was late and she'd seen no one. Most of the people still up and about were either at the dance or in the saloons at the opposite end of the street. But she would take no chances.

Her stomach churned and she had to fight the overwhelming urge to be sick.

Deliberately, she straightened. Taking long, slow breaths she forced herself to listen, to take stock of where she was.

She heard the soft scuffing of a horse in one of the stalls somewhere to her left. As she dared walk forward, Nugget whinnied a greeting from the near stall on her right. Cat didn't stop. Instead she hobbled toward the back of the barn.

Once there, she scrambled up the ladder that led to the hayloft. Here at least she wouldn't have to worry about anyone finding her. She didn't explore the thought too deeply, telling herself she simply needed to be alone.

In the near pitch blackness of the loft she flung herself down on a mound of fresh hay and sobbed brokenly. How had everything turned out so badly? She would never be able to show her face in town again.

Worse, Logan had heard every vicious word Chastity Vincent had uttered. He knew now what Cat had tried so pathetically to hide. That she was no lady of the world. Cat Jordan was a cowgirl, more at home on a horse than she would ever be at a soiree.

She pulled her hankie from where she'd tucked it between her breasts and blew her nose. Her heart hurt, her eyes hurt, and now her nose did too, from all the crying she'd been doing over the past twenty-four hours. Likely there hadn't been such a waterworks display since the flash flood on the Brazos a few years back.

The last thought at least brought a ghost of a smile to her lips.

But when she touched her dress front and felt again the jagged rip Chastity had torn in Maude's treasured gown, Cat began crying anew. What was she going to tell her friend about the dress? What was—

She stilled suddenly, cocking an ear toward the edge of the loft. Had she heard someone moving around down below? Or had it been just the echoes of her own sniveling.

Sniveling! That was the word all right. How had she ever let a spoiled viper like Chastity Vincent ruin what had become the most wondrous evening of her life?

A hinge creaked.

There was no denying it this time. Someone had opened and closed the barn door. She sat there, listening. Footfalls padded across the straw-strewn floor.

Dear heaven, had Latigo followed her? Was he coming to make good on his vile threat? She held her breath. She had no weapon, nothing. Very slowly she moved toward the loft's edge. From where she sat hints of moonlight filtered through haphazard cracks in the barn's four walls, offering only the vaguest suggestion of light.

A shadowed figure appeared at the top of the ladder. "Lose your way home?"

Startled, Cat leaped back. "Logan Blackstone!" she gasped, "what are you trying to do? Scare me half to death?"

"I'm sorry," he said, climbing up the ladder's final two rungs. "I wasn't expecting you to be peeking over the side."

Her heart still hammering inside her chest, she managed to squeak out, "Go away."

"No."

"Please." She was in no mood for company, not even Logan's. Maybe especially not Logan's.

"I'm not leaving." To prove it he felt his way toward her and plopped down on the hay beside her. "It's dark up here."

"Did you come up here to tell me that?"

"Hardly." He crawled past her to the wall and ran his hand along the wood until he found the four-foot-square doorway that facilitated hauling hay bales up from the street. With a hard jerk he freed the latch and let the door swing inward.

A cool night breeze immediately lifted several stray tendrils of Cat's once carefully styled hair. She drew in a deep, cleansing lungful of air.

"Feel better?" he asked.

"No." She wasn't going to make this easy for him. She was too miserable. Her hands shook as she fumbled with the tattered remnants of her dress front.

"Here, take this." He shrugged out of his jacket and settled it gently around her shoulders.

"Thank you."

"You're welcome." He again settled down beside her. "Now do you want to tell me what you're doing cowering in a hayloft?"

"I'm not cowering!" she snapped.

"What would you call it?"

"I'm . . ." She bit her lip, scouring her brain for any excuse that sounded better than cowering. "I'm thinking," she pronounced finally.

"I see," he said, though she was sure he didn't. He reached a hand toward her, then seemed to think better of it and let it drop back to his side. "Well, with all this thinking, are you all right?"

"I'm fine. Though I'd be much better if you'd go away."

"If I really thought that, I'd leave." His gaze held hers, until she shifted uncomfortably and looked away. "Why did you come up here, Cat?"

"The clock struck midnight," she whispered sadly. "It was time to go home."

He frowned and took out his watch. "It's only eleven."

"Cinderella's midnight," she said. "I lost the glass slipper."

233

"Oh," he said, understanding. "I guess I'm not a very good Prince Charming. I didn't find it either."

She gave him a wan smile, not caring if the love she felt for him showed clearly in her eyes. "You were the most charming of princes tonight, Logan Blackstone."

It was his turn to look away. She sighed, disappointed to see that he was still trying to keep an emotional distance between them. Didn't he know it was a losing battle, lost almost from the moment they'd met yesterday in the street.

"I'm amazed you could think so," he said, "after what I did to you earlier with Chastity."

"We went through all that," Cat said. "I was thinking of the dance. I've never had such a night." She lay down next to him, resting her chin on her hands. "It was wonderful."

"I'm glad you liked it." He was having trouble concentrating. She had absolutely no notion of the havoc she was wreaking on his self-control. He should move, sit up, do something, anything. But he only continued to lie there, watching her, wanting her with every fiber of his being.

He could make love to her. She was vulnerable, hurting, and—for better or worse—half in love with him. In fact, he was more than half in love with her.

Just pull her into your arms, Logan, his body urged. *Make love to her. She'll feel better, you'll see. Just make love to her.*

He swore inwardly. Perfect! Make her feel better by taking her innocence. Some Prince Charming.

"Maybe we should go to the hotel," he said, barely recognizing his own voice. His body was winning the war with his conscience. He wanted this woman. He wanted her, here, now. To hell with secrets. To hell with Matt and Olivia Jordan.

He stood abruptly, straightened too quickly and slammed his head into a rafter. "Son-of-a—" He practically bit off his tongue trying to bite off the curse.

She was on her feet beside him at once. "Are you all right? Is it bleeding?"

"I'm fine," he muttered, rubbing the rising knot on his skull. When she tried to touch it, he jerked away savagely.

"It is bleeding, isn't it?" she cried. "That's why you won't let me see it."

"It's fine," he said again, "just don't . . . touch me. All right?"

She took a step back. "I'm sorry."

Now he'd hurt her feelings again. Damn it to hell! "I'm the one who's sorry. I didn't mean to snap at you. I just . . ." He sagged wearily to his knees.

She sat down, saying nothing.

"I said I was sorry."

"I believe you."

He shook his head. In coming to Texas, he had lost his mind. That was the only explanation that made any sense at all to him anymore. "Let me take you to the hotel. Please."

"I don't have any money for a room."

"I'll pay for it."

"I owe you enough already."

He swore and this time he didn't apologize.

"It's kind of nice to know you're not always a perfect gentleman," she said.

"What's that supposed to mean?"

She hesitated, then said, "I mean I'm glad your

235

gentleman's cloak slips a bit every once in a while. It makes it a little easier to face not being a perfect gentleman's idea of a lady."

"The next time I see Chastity Vincent," Logan growled, "I'm going to wring her neck."

"You'd better not," Cat said.

"Why not?"

"Because she's not worth hanging for."

He had to chuckle. "You've got a point there."

She lay back down on the small hay mound. "This is better than a hotel. I can sleep here tonight."

"I'm not going to leave you alone in this hayloft."

There was the briefest silence before her softly spoken, "Then stay."

His heartbeat quickened. He tried to distract himself, think of something innocuous to say, but it didn't work. He stared at her, outlined in moonlight and felt the heat in his blood spread to his loins.

"I can't stay," he managed to get out. "You know I can't."

She met his eyes. "You can."

"Damn." He sank down beside her. "You don't know what you're saying. You drank too much punch."

"It doesn't matter how much punch I drank. I know exactly what I'm saying." She knew he was fighting his conscience, knew he was afraid of hurting her. But the only hurt she couldn't bear right now, would be the hurt of his leaving.

She studied his face in the moon-touched shadows. Strong, handsome, and more open than he would like to believe. Most people would read arrogance into those sharply carved features, but Cat had learned quickly to watch his eyes. She had yet to see arrogance in those eyes. And she had seen more gentleness in him than in any man she'd ever met.

She knew exactly what she was saying.

"I love you, Logan."

He pulled her to him and kissed her, the warmest, sweetest kiss she had ever known. She could feel the touch of his lips flow inward to every part of her. She felt this man touch her soul.

"I love you, Cat."

His eyes never left her face. She saw his fierce joy, tried not to see his sadness.

But the sadness was there, and she knew why. Her fantasy that he would stay in Texas was just that. Fantasy. Even if the bitterness between their families was resolved, Logan Blackstone was no rancher.

No more than she was Cinderella.

She loved him, but there could be no fairy tale ending. Love was not enough.

But for tonight she would make it enough. For tonight it would be enough for both of them.

"Love me, Logan. Love me now."

She felt the hold he'd had on himself give way. With a groan he gathered her to him, murmuring her name. She surrendered hungrily, eagerly, as his hands sought the fastenings of her dress.

"Corie, Corie, you're so beautiful. I want you so badly. So badly."

Tears stung her eyes. Tears of wonder and delight. She felt the trembling in his hands and realized the depth of his passion, the passion he felt for her. Cat Jordan. And no one else.

His ardor fired a boldness in her such as she'd never known. It was suddenly vitally important that she please him as much as he pleased her. Even though she knew nothing of a man's needs, for Logan she found the courage to learn.

And learn she did.

He sucked in his breath as she undid the buttons of his shirt, arching his head back as her mouth nipped a path from his neck to his navel. She loved him with every part of her—her hands, her body, her mouth. Each time he shuddered, gasped, she would repeat and enhance whatever she'd discovered that pleased him.

And he did the same and more for her.

And when she couldn't bear to be separate from him for even another heartbeat, he rose above her and thrust himself inside her. He made their two bodies one. She experienced the essence of his maleness, even as she fully realized the unlimited power of his gentleness.

He made certain she reached the spiraling light first before he cried her name and followed her into sweet, sweet madness.

Long afterward Cat lay, drowsy, content to be nestled in Logan's arms. Blissfully tired, she resisted sleep. Dawn would come soon enough. She wanted the rest of this night with Logan. Trailing a finger through the dusting of hair across his chest, she traced feathery circles around his nipples until he shifted his head to nip playfully at her ear.

"Have mercy, woman," he said. "I am, after all, only one man. Besotted with you though I may be, my body can only do so much."

"Perhaps I should call down to the street for volunteers," she teased. "Now that I know that such

238

magic exists, once is definitely not enough."

"Don't you dare," he growled, though he was chuckling when he said it, and she liked the rumbling sound it made in his chest.

"Oh, Logan," she murmured happily, "I could lie here with you forever." She wished the words back as she felt him stiffen slightly. He was thinking that there was no forever, there wasn't even tomorrow. She spoke quickly, hoping to recapture the mood, "Do you remember Buttons, Logan?"

He relaxed. "A little gray bundle of fluff with white feet."

She was ridiculously pleased that he recalled the mongrel pup that had captured her heart when she was four years old. "When the cow kicked him, and he died, Pa was just going to throw him out on the range. But you wouldn't let him."

"I just told you I'd bury him for you."

"You did more than that. You arranged for a proper funeral."

"I wore knickers as I recall. I'd brought them along from home."

Cat giggled, remembering. "Matt laughed so hard he was sick." She sobered. "You dug the hole out by the creek and you gave me flowers to put on the grave. You even got out a Bible and said words over Buttons just like he was a person. I loved you for that."

He kissed the top of her head. "You were so sad. I remember your eyes. You looked up at me like I could help. You made me feel important."

"You were important. You were my knight in shining armor."

"I don't know how shiny the armor was, but I liked the

way you depended on me. It was nice."

"I don't know what I would have done if you hadn't been there. Pa didn't understand and Matt thought the whole thing was a foolish waste of time."

Logan picked up a piece of hay and chewed absently on one end of it. "Matt cried later, you know. Out behind the barn. He liked Buttons too."

"He did?" Cat pondered this bit of insight into a brother who so often scoffed at her for being too sentimental. "Why, that charlatan! He always called me the world's biggest baby for caring about my pets."

"Matt was never very good at showing his feelings."

"That's the truth. I've been trying for years to get him to admit that he wants to be part of running the ranch again."

"Maybe he'll come around now that . . . Never mind."

"Now that my father's dead?"

"I didn't mean to suggest a connection."

"I've thought about it myself. It's like Matt had himself set in a pattern of being helpless. He didn't know how to get out of it. And my father . . . my father sort of gave up on Matt over the years."

"That must have hit Matt pretty hard."

"He never showed it if it did."

"No, he wouldn't."

Cat propped herself up on one elbow. "How can you have known him for one summer, and know him better than I do?"

"We shared a lot that summer."

She was surprised at how matter-of-factly he said it, expecting any moment for him to shut the door on the subject. But he surprised her further by continuing.

"My father sent me here, hoping to make a man of me. My mother did a lot of the same things to me that Olivia does to Matt. She'd waited so long for a child—gone through hell to have one—that she was terrified to let me out of her sight."

"But she let you come here a whole summer?"

"It was one of the few times my father went against her wishes. And he only did it because he knew it would be best for me. My mother was certain I'd be scalped by Indians."

"She may not have been far wrong," Cat said. "My mother told me Matt was born right after an Indian raid the first year they were in Texas."

"It must have been hard for her."

"She and your mother were good friends once."

"Mother never talked about it much."

"All I know is that my pa loved my mother enough to stay in Boston running a shipping business he despised, until she finally agreed to marry him. Only he didn't tell her that once they got married, they would be going west to start a whole new life.

"I don't think Ma ever got over it."

Logan sat up and shifted over to the loft opening, staring out at the empty street.

Cat snuggled up beside him. She brushed at the hair that tumbled across his forehead. "Your hair has always done this," she said. "It's what I remembered most about you." Her breathing quickened. "It's what I remember about that night."

"What night?"

She hesitated. To talk about it would very likely spoil what time they had left together. And yet perhaps in their newfound intimacy, he would be more willing to share his pain about that tragic time. "The night the doctor came to . . . amputate Matt's leg."

He was instantly wary, and her hope dimmed. "I don't want to talk about that." His voice was terse.

"I know you don't. I just wish I could sort it all through in my own mind."

"What is there to sort through?"

"Shadows."

"What?"

"I have this dream sometimes. At least I started having it after Pa died. You're in the dream and Matt. I remember going to the barn. It was dark, and there was a storm coming."

Logan was staring out into the night, but she knew he was seeing everything as she described it.

"I found you. You were crying and I wanted you to feel better. I tried to give you a hug. And that's when the shadows came in. There was shouting, a lot of shouting."

"You heard the words?" He was rigid as stone.

"No. I can never quite make them out."

The tension drained out of him.

"Dammit, Logan!" She caught his arm, forcing him to face her. "What *are* those words? Matt wasn't there. Those words can't be part of your promise to Matt."

"I can't tell you."

"But you want to, don't you?"

He shook his head, as though the gesture would make his denial more convincing. It didn't. He did want to tell her. He was tired of carrying the burden of those words alone. But for whatever reason, he remained silent.

"It's all right," she told him. "Someday I'll remember on my own. I know it."

His words chilled her. "I hope to God you don't."

"Why? What could be so awful?"

"People would be hurt, Corie. People . . ."

When he stopped himself, she guessed he'd already said too much. The anguish in his eyes tore at her heart. She threw her arms around him. "I'm sorry, Logan. Forgive me. I shouldn't have asked."

"Corie, sweet Corie." His hands were like firebrands, igniting flame wherever they touched.

She moaned against him, her mouth finding his. They came together quickly, hungrily, each trying to squeeze a lifetime of loving into this one night.

But it wasn't enough, would never be enough. This time she couldn't stay her tears, and she wept against his chest. "I'm going to miss you so much," she whimpered.

"No," he said fiercely, "you're not."

She frowned, confused, and then he said the words that turned her world upside down. "Corie, come to Boston with me. Be my wife."

Chapter Seventeen

Cat lay stunned, speechless. Logan had asked her to be his wife! Her heart soared with happiness. It took every bit of willpower she possessed to keep from flinging herself into his arms and crying, "Yes! Yes!" Of course she would be his wife! She wanted nothing more in the world than to be his wife!

"You belong with me," he said. And she thought she'd never heard words that sounded so right.

So much so, that for a moment she believed him. She believed that that was all there was to it, that all she had to do was say yes. Yes to the passion in his eyes, warm and real and alive.

But she didn't say it.

What was wrong with her? Wasn't this exactly what she had wanted? To be a permanent part of his life?

But in her fantasy it was Logan who became part of her life, not she who became part of his. "I'd be as at home in Boston as a steer at a quilting bee."

"That isn't true."

"It is, and you know it."

It was there, as real an obstacle as a stone wall. And it was she who built it. She loved him. But she couldn't imagine leaving her home, leaving the Circle J for a world about which she knew nothing. Except that she would never fit in.

Moreover, to leave was to betray her father's memory. She pulled back, wincing as Logan's eyes narrowed.

"So, you don't love me quite as much as you thought, eh?" he said, and the renewed bitterness in his voice hurt more than she could have thought possible. For this time it was not Matt or her mother who'd put it there. She herself had hurt him.

"Logan, you don't understand."

"I understand too well," he said, grabbing at his clothes.

"Logan, please, don't do this."

"Don't do what? Leave? What would you have me do? Stay and make love to you again?" He swore softly. "You'll have to forgive me. I'm not used to being a concubine."

Her eyes widened with fury. "How dare you!"

"How dare I?" he snarled. "Who's been used more here tonight, Miss Jordan?"

"That's not fair! You asked me to go to Boston to be your wife. You know I can't leave here. I have the ranch. I can't abandon it."

"Can't or won't?"

"It's my home."

"It isn't mine."

She sagged back miserably. "Logan, what are we doing? How can we spoil what we had this way?"

He paused in the midst of shoving his arms into his shirt. "Forgive me," he sneered. "I should be more polite. I don't know what's the matter with me. I ask a woman to be my wife, a woman who claims to love me, and she turns me down flat. I don't know why I'd be angry about that."

"Logan, I do love you!"

"Don't say it," he hissed. "Don't say it again. You don't know the meaning of the word."

"Logan, please . . ." She had to get through to him. This wasn't about the two of them. It was the ranch, couldn't he see that? "You knew we could never be together. You knew it when you came up here tonight."

He finished buttoning his shirt. Embarrassed now that he should be dressed when she wasn't, Cat quickly pulled on her own clothing.

He started toward the loft's edge. Cat caught him. "Please, we can't let the night end like this. We have to talk."

"There's nothing to say."

"There is. There has to be. I love you." She barreled on even in the face of his contempt. "I know you don't want to hear it. But it's the truth."

"Then come with me to Boston."

"We have to slow down," she pleaded, desperate for him to understand. "We need to be realistic. We've only known each other a day."

"I've always known you."

His words startled her, because she had so often felt the same way. But more than that, she was struck by the intensity with which he spoke them. Was she being a complete fool? How could she think about the ranch in the face of the love she felt for this man, the love he felt for her?

"No," she said, trying as much to convince herself as

him. "This is crazy. We're two people who were naturally drawn to one another, and now—"

"Now you're admitting this whole night was a mistake." He stood, being careful not to straighten to his full height. "I knew it was a mistake even before I came up here. I guess I just didn't realize how big a mistake it would be."

"I'll never regret this night, Logan."

"That makes one of us." He pulled on his jacket. "I wish to God I'd never come back to Texas."

She stood, reaching a hand toward him. When he stiffened, she let it fall back to her side. "I do love you. And I never wanted to hurt you."

"Thank you very much. That makes it all better."

Her lower lip trembled. She'd been trying so hard not to cry. But she couldn't seem to help herself. His muttered curse didn't help any. She sank to her knees, weeping. "Please don't hate me."

He went to one knee beside her, but did not touch her. "I don't hate you. Maybe I hate myself for letting this happen. I should have realized that first and foremost you're a Jordan and I'm a Blackstone. That's a lot like oil and water."

"No. It doesn't have to be. You could stay here."

"Be a rancher? I could just see Matt and Olivia welcoming me to the family fold."

"If they don't want to stay, they could move to town. It's what my mother wants anyway. Then you and I could—"

"I intend to be a doctor, Cat. To do that I have to go back to school, back to Boston."

"Then you could come back."

"And what happens in the meantime? You run the

247

ranch by yourself until I finish school?"

"Then you admit you like the ranch. You like being part of it." It gave her a flicker of hope at least.

"I do like it. Just like I did that summer fifteen years ago. But I don't fit in, not really. It's your life, not mine. I'm a city boy, born and bred. It's where I feel most at home. I'm sorry. But that's the truth."

She sat back, staring at her hands. It was there, unbreachable. Their two different worlds. And though he might, if he chose, fit into hers, she could never fit into his. She was a rancher's daughter, not a society belle. But if she were to confess her fears to him, he would wear her down, convince her she was being foolish, that nothing mattered but that he loved her.

But it would matter. For the rest of his life it would matter. She couldn't embarrass him like that.

"Can we . . . can we put all this aside for now?" she asked, not wanting to think anymore, only wanting to take what was left of this night for the two of them.

"For now?"

"It's still . . . still four hours until dawn."

This time he swore savagely. "I don't believe it. Two hours ago I compromised the virtue of a virgin. And now . . . what have these two hours made of you, madam?"

Her whole body burned with humiliation. She tried to tell herself that he was just trying to hurt her back. But she had never been with a man before. Maybe she had gone too far. Maybe the things she had done to please him had, in fact, repulsed him. She had overheard the wranglers speak of it once. Men expected one thing from a practiced woman, quite another from a wife.

"I . . . I only thought to make you happy," she said,

mortified. She couldn't look him in the face. "I'm sorry if I didn't do it right. I never felt that way before. I"—her voice broke—"I thought you liked it."

"Jesus," he said softly, pulling her against him. "I'm sorry. I didn't mean it." He sighed. "Maybe I did. No one's ever made me feel that way. And the thought that I'll never feel that way again . . ."

"You're going to leave in the morning, aren't you?" she asked softly.

"Yes."

"Can we have these next four hours? Can we have 'til dawn, Logan?" She held her emotions in tight check, fully expecting him to hurt her again. Instead, his voice was subdued, defeated.

"I think we've done each other enough harm."

"Please? You want it too, I know you do."

He tried to resist, to refuse to let her further ensnare his heart. But he could no more stop loving her now than he could stop the sun from rising. He had come to Texas to confront his past, confront Matt.

And instead he had found what had eluded him all of his life. Because what he'd sought hadn't been in Boston or Europe or anywhere but here. It was Corie.

And though it tore at his heart, he didn't stop her when she began unbuttoning his shirt. Her touch on his flesh was such bittersweet agony that it was all he could do not to weep. How could he bear to leave here without her, even when he knew she was right. She wouldn't be happy in Boston. And he could never stay here. Even starting their own ranch would be a compromise. It was the Circle J that fired Cat's life's blood.

And then he wasn't thinking of anything but being part of her, letting her be part of him. They didn't even finish

249

undressing. He was hard and ready in seconds, pressing her down into the soft hay. He was not gentle this time, but she didn't seem to care. She shared his desperation. But while he accepted her passion, even a degree of her caring, he did not accept that she loved him.

If she loved him, she would come with him. But that did not alter the fact that he loved her. And in the loving, he took them both where neither could journey alone.

Then, exhausted, they slept.

He woke a short time later, disturbed by a sound out of sync with the night sounds of the livery. He lay still for a moment, trying to sort it out in his passion-sated mind, then rose and moved stealthily to the loft's edge. Nothing seemed out of the ordinary in the moon-shadowed darkness. But still he watched.

"What is it?" Cat whispered, awakening to his movements.

Her initial fear that he'd been leaving subsided, to be replaced by a vague uneasiness. Something was wrong. She crept close to him. "Logan, what—"

She smelled it first. Smoke! "Logan, the barn's on fire!"

He grabbed her wrist. "Out the loft window."

"No! The horses!" She pulled away and scrambled for the ladder.

Logan quickly followed.

She could see flames now, rising in the far corner of the barn. She raced to the nearest stall and opened the door. The horse inside stood there, trembling.

"We'll have to blindfold them!" Logan shouted. He grabbed a saddle blanket and moved past her to hold it over the gelding's eyes. "Open the main door!"

Cat hurriedly did so, the rush of air sending flames

250

shooting rafter high.

Logan slapped the gelding on its haunches, sending it thundering up the street.

Cat was already back inside, struggling with the latch on Nugget's stall. It stuck fast. The smoke was so thick now that she couldn't see. Her eyes teared, stung. Coughing, choking, she doubled over, still trying to free the latch.

The mare reared, neighing shrilly.

"Easy, girl!" Cat shouted. "Easy." The latch broke free. Cat swung open the door, but the terrified mare tried to back further into the stall. Cat caught Nugget's halter and pulled hard. The mare balked and reared again.

"Cat!" Logan shouted. "Cat, let her go!"

"No!"

The rafters burned overhead, the loft where they'd made love now a blazing inferno. A thunderous crack split the smoke-choked air, a rafter splitting free.

Cat screamed, instinctively jumping back. The rafter crashed to the floor just inches behind the terrified mare. Nugget bolted forward, knocking Cat off her feet. Cat tried to rise, but she could barely move. She couldn't breathe at all.

Her lungs screamed for air. She groped blindly, but she no longer knew the way to the door.

She heard Logan shouting, cursing, then everything went dark.

Chapter Eighteen

Cat wondered if she was dead, then decided against it. Surely, someone who was dead couldn't feel this kind of pain. Everything hurt. It hurt to move, it hurt to breathe.

Breathe . . . breathe . . . Someone was telling her to breathe. *In and out . . . deep breaths . . . that's a good girl . . . breathe. . . .*

She must be alive then. Dead people didn't breathe. She drew in more air and felt a searing pain in her lungs. She struggled, coughing, choking. A pair of hands held her down. She fought them, but they held her down anyway, gently, firmly.

"Easy, Cat," the voice said. "Take it easy." Something cool and wet touched her lips. "Drink this. That's it. That's a good girl."

Water. She didn't realize water could taste so good. She drank deeply even though her throat ached abominably. Where had all this pain come from? What had she done to herself? Again, she tried to rise. Again, the hands held her down.

"Lie still," the voice said. "You've got to lie still."

Maybe if I open my eyes, she thought. Maybe that will help.

She tried, but the light hurt them. Whatever this place was, it was very bright.

"Draw the curtains," the voice said.

Things grew darker then, and it didn't hurt quite so badly when she tried to open her eyes. She blinked once, twice, and felt tears streaming down her cheeks. Yet she didn't feel as though she were crying.

She raised a hand to her face. It was hot and dry. Her skin felt tight, almost as though she were dehydrated. As though she were . . . burned.

The fire! It all came back to her in a rush. Dear God, the fire. Logan! Where was Logan?

She sat bolt upright, the hands not reacting quickly enough to stop her this time, though the voice remained soothing. She blinked again and again, trying to focus, but she saw nothing. Was she blind? Where was Logan?

She screamed his name.

"I'm here," the voice said, calm, gentle. Logan. He had been there all along.

"The fire!" She was trembling, terrified.

"It's all right. Everything's all right."

"The horses?"

"They're fine."

She clutched at his arm. "My eyes . . ."

"Your eyes are fine. They're just irritated by the smoke." He smoothed a cool cloth over her forehead. "Now lie back. You have to rest."

"Poor thing." Another voice. Feminine. And altogether insincere. Chastity Vincent.

Cat lifted her hand, drawing the cloth along her face and away from her eyes. Very slowly, she tried again to

253

focus. It hurt, but she could see vague images now.

"You're in Abner Vincent's house," Logan said, sensing her distress at hearing Chastity's voice.

Of all the places for him to bring her . . . "I want to go home," Cat said.

"You're not going anywhere," Logan said. "Not until I say so."

Other things came back to her then, things that brought a different kind of pain. "The stage," she murmured. "You were going to catch the stage." He was going away, leaving her. She had turned down his marriage proposal. She tried to remember why she had done something so stupid, but it hurt too much to think.

"There'll be another stage."

"Of course," she said. Her head continued to throb, but she ignored it. She needed to get her wits about her. She and Logan had to talk. He couldn't leave until they talked. She remembered it all now. Their lovemaking, his proposal, the fire . . .

"Are you all right?" she asked.

"Just fine."

There was an edge to his voice that hadn't been there earlier when he'd been telling her to lie still.

"Why did you bring me here?" Her eyes were painful slits as her gaze trailed to Chastity. The girl had been uncharacteristically silent since her condescending "poor thing." But her silence hadn't been inspired by any sense of concern for Cat, false or otherwise. Cat watched the girl's face, those blue eyes, sly, cunning. The look in them disappeared the instant Logan turned toward her.

"Is there anything I can get the poor thing, Logan?" Chastity asked.

"Some lemonade, if you have it," he said.

"Of course." The girl left immediately.

"How helpful of her," Cat said through clenched teeth.

"Don't worry, she's been looking daggers at me too."

"Why on earth did you bring me here?" Cat repeated. "I'd rather be lying in a mud hole in the street, than—"

"Abner insisted," Logan cut in.

As though speaking his name had the power to make him appear, Abner Vincent strode into the room, a cigar jutting from one corner of his mouth. "How are you feeling, my dear?" the man asked, his own eyes alive with feigned concern. At least Chastity came by it honestly, Cat thought grimly.

"I've felt better," Cat said.

"And you will again, I'm sure," Abner said, puffing deeply on the stogie.

Cat instantly began to choke.

"Could you take that into another room, Vincent," Logan gritted.

"What? Oh, yes, of course. How inconsiderate of me." He cast a baleful look at Cat as he exited the room.

Something important hovered on the edge of Cat's mind, but just as she was about to grasp it, it slipped away. She tried to concentrate. She had to remember. Remember what?

"Do you feel sick, nauseous?" Logan was asking.

She shook herself. "You should have taken me to Maude's," she said. "I don't want to be here."

"I don't blame you," Logan admitted. "But I had some papers to pick up from Abner. And I wasn't about to leave you in any mud hole. So this seemed as good a place as any."

255

He helped her take another sip of water. She tried and failed to meet his gaze. He cleared his throat self-consciously. "I want you to breathe for me," he said.

"What?"

"Deep breaths. I want to listen to your lungs." He picked up a stethoscope.

Her eyes widened and she winced, as the movement caused them pain. "Where did you get that thing?"

"Dr. Sanderson's office."

"Where's Sanderson?"

"On a call. A pregnancy. The Wilkinson ranch, I believe someone said."

Cat nodded. "It's about fifty miles south. Should be number six for Mrs. Wilkinson."

"Now will you breathe for me?"

He put the ends of the stethoscope into his ears and placed the circular tip against her back. "Now."

She breathed and immediately broke into a fit of coughing. Logan brought her another glass of water. She drank it down quickly, then held out the empty glass to him. He set it aside and again took up the stethoscope.

Her eyes watered, her throat hurt, her heart pounded. "I don't want to breathe," she rasped.

"I can understand why, but do it anyway."

He moved the stethoscope around on her back, pausing several times, each time asking her to breathe. It was then she realized how professionally he was behaving. Detached. As though she were a stranger. A patient.

"Logan," she began, then stopped. She wanted, needed, to talk to him about last night, but she didn't know how. "The fire didn't spread, did it?"

"No, thank God," he said. "There wasn't much of a

256

breeze, and the barn was freestanding. A bucket brigade finally managed to put it out just after dawn. That was about five hours ago."

"Five hours?" Cat gasped. "I've been here that long?"

"Longer. It's nearly noon."

No wonder the light from the window had hurt her eyes.

A sudden knock on the door brought Chastity back to answer it. "Why, Ryan, what a surprise," the girl purred. "I had no idea you were still in town."

"I came by to check on your houseguest."

"Do come in." Chastity stepped to one side, allowing Ryan entry into the parlor.

Cat noted the soot and grime on his clothes. He must have been part of the bucket brigade.

"How are you feeling, Cat?" Ryan asked. At least his concern seemed remotely genuine.

"Just fine," Cat managed. "Thanks to Logan."

"Yes, quite the hero," Ryan said with just the merest suggestion of a smirk. "He's making quite a habit of saving the fair maidens of Red Springs." Ryan peered closely at Cat. "It really is remarkable that he happened along when he did, isn't it?"

"I was fetching my cane," Logan put in, hefting the gold-handled walking stick from beside the settee.

Cat blinked. When had he . . . ?

"Ah, yes. Cat mentioned bringing it to town for you."

"Ryan, dear," Chastity said, "let's you and I go have a little lemonade, shall we?"

Cat guessed she wasn't going to be getting any.

"It sounds wonderful," Ryan said, then looked again at Cat. "That is, if you don't need me for anything, my dear."

"I'm fine, Ryan."

"See how resilient she is," Chastity said. "It's just amazing. She'll be out brandin' cows again in no time. She won't even have to change her clothes." Chastity looped her arm in Ryan's and preemptorily led him from the room.

It was only then Cat noticed that she was no longer wearing Maude's torn gown. She was dressed in a plain blue cotton shirt and denims. "My clothes," she murmured, looking at Logan.

"The dress was unsalvageable. Maude brought these things over for you, while you were still asleep."

"Was she . . . upset about the dress?"

"She only cared that you were all right."

Cat gripped her shirtfront self-consciously. "Who . . . uh, who . . . ?"

"Maude changed your clothes for you."

"Oh," Cat said in a small voice. That would only have been proper, of course, but still it somehow served to put even more distance between herself and Logan. Each minute that passed made the time they shared seem more a dream than reality. "Are you sure you're all right?" she asked. "The smoke, the fire didn't—"

"No *physical* damage," he said, his eyes hard.

She looked away. "Logan, I . . ."

"Don't bother. We said it all last night."

"No, we didn't. I—"

Another knock sounded at the door. Cat cursed under her breath. When none of the Vincents seemed to have heard it, Logan responded. Toby Fletcher wasted no time on amenities, striding at once toward Cat.

"How are you feeling?" he asked.

"A little worse for wear, but I'll be all right."

"I'm sorry I didn't have time to come before now, but I had to make sure the fire was completely out, check the damage, that sort of thing." He was obviously nervous, agitated. He looked again and again at Logan, finally saying, "Can I see you alone a minute?"

"What's going on?" Cat demanded.

But the two men ignored her. Logan and Toby moved over by the window, speaking in tones too low for her to hear. As they talked, Logan glanced at her once, his gray eyes unreadable.

When they finished, Logan crossed over to her. "If you're feeling up to it, I'll ride out to the ranch with you."

She frowned. "Why would you do that? I thought you wanted to be on the next stage."

"There's been a change of plans. I'm staying."

Her heart did a somersault in her chest. She wanted to throw her arms around him, but the look in his eyes gave her no cause for rejoicing. "What is it?" she asked. "What's wrong?"

Toby stepped over to her, clutching his Stetson in front of him, his hands knotted on the brim. "The fire was no accident, Cat. Someone tried to kill you."

Chapter Nineteen

Matt Jordan burrowed deeper under his blankets, pretending he didn't hear Maria's gentle knock on his bedroom door. Maybe, if she thought he was still asleep, she would go away.

He should have known better.

The door swung open. He listened, unmoving, as she came into the room. He could hear the clink of dishes and flatware. She was bringing him his breakfast. And he wished to God she wasn't.

"Good morning, Mateo," the girl called, either not believing his pretense to be asleep, or deciding it was time to wake him.

He didn't respond. He didn't dare. After the dream he'd had last night, he was afraid to even look at her, lest the depths of his need for her show in his eyes.

In his dream she had come to his bed, naked, eager. She had not turned away in revulsion when she'd seen his leg for the first time. Neither had the leg pained him, as he had dared make love to her.

Unconsciously, he shifted, his loins tightening. The

leg throbbed less than usual this morning, and he had to wonder if he could credit the dream as therapy.

"Come on, Mateo," Maria chided. "I know you are awake. Quit pretending to be such a sleepyhead."

Groggily, he opened his eyes. "What are you doing here? Where's my mother?" He hadn't meant the edge to creep into his voice, but just looking at her was conjuring all too vivid memories of his erotic dream.

Her hair tumbled around her shoulders in soft, ebony waves, her coppery skin was scrubbed fresh and clean, and as always her dark eyes were alive with a vitality and warmth that drew his starving soul like a beggar to a banquet.

"Your *madre* has given up her new position as cook," Maria answered merrily, setting the food tray on the table beside his bed. "I think it is none too soon. You won't be losing weight anymore, now that you will be fed my good meals again."

"Are you saying my mother can't cook?"

"I'm saying, even your *madre* says she can't cook."

Matt smiled in spite of himself, then instantly regretted it. It would take a blind man not to see that she had developed some kind of infatuation for him. But she was young, impressionable. She hadn't had any experience with men. Her interest in him would fade soon enough, once a good-looking young caballero came calling on her.

He'd already heard talk among the wranglers that young Jim Spence hung around Maria like a mewling pup. And Jim Spence wasn't a cripple.

"Come, Mateo," Maria said. "Sit up. Eat. You will feel better."

"I'm not hungry."

261

"Your leg still bothers you? Señora Olivia was quite concerned about the fall you took yesterday." Maria's face darkened, her voice carrying an unaccustomed anger. "She would not allow me to come and see you."

"It's all right, Maria. I slept most of the day anyway."

"Next time I will go through the window. Like Cat."

Matt scowled. "I'm not sure I like the idea of your following in Cat's footsteps." Thinking about his sister, though, prodded his conscience. "Have you seen her yet this morning? I need to talk to her." He'd given her a pretty rough time yesterday. He wanted to apologize.

"Cat followed Señor Blackstone to town yesterday afternoon."

A muscle in Matt's jaw jumped.

Maria hurried on to explain. "She said he forgot his cane. It was a beautiful cane. She didn't want him leaving without it."

"Leaving?"

"She said he is planning to go back to Boston."

"What?" The news struck Matt like a blow. And the fact that it did stunned him. Logan's leaving Texas was precisely what he wanted, wasn't it? Then why did the thought leave him with a foul taste in his mouth?

Because absolutely nothing had been resolved. One way or the other. "Was Cat certain Logan was leaving? It doesn't sound like something he'd do."

"She seemed very certain. That was why she was so sad."

"Sad? Sad!" Matt's temper flared anew. "What the hell does that mean?"

"Please, Mateo, you are going to upset yourself. I think you should eat your breakfast while it's still hot."

"Never mind my breakfast." Matt's eyes narrowed

with suspicion. "Why would my sister give a damn that Logan Blackstone is heading for home? Especially after she got the extension she wanted."

Maria wouldn't look at him.

"Maria, answer me."

"Cat . . . did not feel your wager . . . was fair," she stammered.

He ignored that. "You're avoiding the question, Maria. Why?"

"Mateo, please. Your sister is my best friend."

"She's my sister!" he exploded. "I love her. I don't want to see her get hurt."

"She is a grown woman. Just as I am a grown woman. She has a mind of her own."

"She's interested in Blackstone as a man? Is that what you're trying so hard *not* to tell me?"

Maria didn't answer.

"Son of a bitch! How could she be so stupid?" He pushed himself up. He would find her, talk some sense into her. "Where is she?"

"I . . . haven't seen her this morning."

"She didn't come home last night?" Matt slapped a hand against the mattress. "Is that it? She didn't come home?"

"She could have stayed with friends. It may have been late when Señor Blackstone left on the stage."

"You don't believe that for a minute, do you?"

Maria straightened. "It is not my place to spy on your sister, Mateo. I do not know where she is. But wherever it is, I am sure it is a place of her own choosing."

"Is that so?"

"It is." Maria slammed a chair up to his bedside. "Now you are going to eat your breakfast."

263

"No, I'm not. I'm going after my sister."

"You hurt your leg yesterday," she said reasonably. "A trip to town would not be a very good idea."

He sagged back. She was right. He wouldn't make it halfway, even in a buggy, without being in agony.

"Mateo, please, Cat is a very sensible woman."

"Since when?"

Maria tried hard not to smile.

The tension went out of Matt. "You win, Maria. For now." He shook his head. "But I fully intend to have a serious talk with that sister of mine when she gets home."

"I would like to see that."

"I'll just bet you would."

Maria's smile tugged at his heart. He forced his attention to his breakfast tray, watching as she poured him a steaming cup of fresh coffee. "Just the way you like it," she said, handing him the cup.

He took a sip. She'd made it with an egg, keeping the grounds to a minimum. "You spoil me, Maria."

"I try, Mateo." She blushed prettily and he closed his eyes against a rush of pain in his leg.

"Mateo?" she asked anxiously, touching his arm.

"I'm fine," he said, though he could feel the sweat breaking out on his forehead. "Just give me a minute."

"Do you want your medicine?"

"No." He refused to be dependent on the laudanum, at least not in front of Maria. Besides, it wasn't yesterday's fall that had aggravated the pain. It was his desire, his passion for this woman. He had to get her out of here. "I . . . I'm not hungry, Maria," he said. "I think I should get a little more sleep."

"Please, Mateo, do not put lies between us. We have

always been able to talk to one another. Even when your leg bothers you."

That was before I fell in love with you, he thought despairingly. "I think my mother is right, Maria," he said, not looking at her. "Maybe it is for the best if you don't bring me my meals anymore."

"I have done something wrong?"

"You've done nothing wrong, Maria. I just don't think it's a very good idea, that's all."

"It *is* your leg, isn't it?"

"Please, go."

Instead she moved from the chair to the edge of his bed. He closed his eyes. "Maria, go."

"Cat told me how upset you were that she let Señor Blackstone tend to your injury."

"I don't want to talk about this." The problem was his leg, but not in the way she was thinking.

"What Señor Blackstone did was necessary," Maria went on. "Cat told me he went to a school for doctors. I am sure if he did this, he already knows more than Dr. Sanderson."

"Logan had no right to touch me," Matt said. "Cat had no right to let him."

"Would you rather they let your leg get infected? Is that what you want? Then they might . . ." Maria flushed.

"Then what?" he asked with a bitter irony. "They might have to cut it off!"

"Please, Mateo, I did not mean—"

"I know. I'm sorry. I don't mean to take my temper out on you."

"I don't mind."

"You should mind. You should stay the hell away from

me, Maria. I'm no good for you."

"Mateo, I love you."

"No. You can't."

"I do."

He turned away, forcing his attention to his breakfast. "Flapjacks and strawberry preserves," he said, his eyes burning with unshed tears. "It smells wonderful." He picked up the knife, his hand trembling. He dropped it and it clattered to the floor. Maria stooped quickly to retrieve it.

"I'd like to eat alone, Maria," he said, his voice shaking.

"No." She used the fork to snare a bit of flapjack, then held it to his mouth.

"I can feed myself."

"I know." Her voice was so soft, so sensual, it was all he could do not to shove the tray to the floor and take her in his arms. She held the morsel of food enticingly, inches from his lips. He opened his mouth. The fork clicked against his teeth.

He chewed slowly, then swallowed, never taking his eyes from her face. "You're so beautiful, Maria." The words came out before he could stop them. He looked away. "You'd better go."

She slid her hand over his. "I play no games, Mateo. One day I came into your room and I was no longer a little girl. When I looked at you I saw a man. Please believe me. I love you, Mateo."

"You deserve a whole man. Someone who can give you some kind of life, a home, a . . . ." He didn't finish. How could he add . . . a family?

"You are a whole man, Mateo. You have just lost faith in yourself. Let me help you find it." She leaned toward

266

him, feathering his cheek with a shy kiss.

Heat fired in his blood, an aching need tore at his soul. He kissed her back.

Fumbling, tentative, he threaded his fingers through her hair. She smelled so sweet, so good. He felt the thickening in his loins. "Maria, we can't. Please . . ." He pulled away. "It can never be, Maria."

Her eyes were downcast. "You do not care for me in that way?"

More than you can ever know, he thought hopelessly. "No," he said. "I don't."

She looked up at him. "You are not a very good liar, Mateo."

"I don't know what good it does for you to ask a question if you're not going to believe the answer."

"Tell me you want me to go, and I'll go."

His whole body ached with what it cost him not to pull her into his arms. He had to put a stop to this once and for all, for both their sakes.

"Maria, please, you have to understand," he began hoarsely. "I've spent the better part of my life in this house, in a wheelchair. I . . . I've never even been with . . . I mean, I . . ."

He expected to see pity when he looked at her, or embarrassment. Instead, if anything, he watched her love for him intensify before his eyes.

"We would teach each other, Mateo," she said, ever so softly, her palm caressing his cheek.

With a groan he dragged her against him, his breathing ragged. Emotions so long dammed inside him burst forth in a fevered torment. His tongue teased her lips until she opened her mouth to his loving.

"My God, Maria," he moaned. "I want—"

The door slammed open.

"Maria!" Olivia cried.

Maria scrambled to her feet, her cheeks flaming.

Olivia marched into the room, her features tight with controlled anger. "I wondered how it could take so long to bring in a breakfast tray," she said. "I can see now that I can allow you to cook, but I will bring Matthew his meals."

"No, *señora*, I—"

"I want you out of this room, Maria," Olivia said. "I want you out of this house. I'll be out to talk to your father later."

"*Señora*, please . . ."

Maria looked beseechingly at Matt, and he knew she wanted him to defend her, to stand up to his mother. But in the space of time since his mother had entered the room, he had realized how close he had come to making a serious mistake. He had to end it. For both of them. Maria was wrong. He was no man for her. He was no man at all. "You'd better go, Maria," he said.

Tears rimming her dark eyes, she fled.

"I'm sorry, Matthew," Olivia said, coming over at once to finish cutting up his flapjacks. "I warned her. Now I'll have to talk to Esteban."

"You say nothing to Esteban," Matt said. "Nothing, do you hear me?" He caught his mother's hand. "And put down that goddamn knife. I can cut my own flapjacks."

"Now, Matthew," Olivia soothed. "I know you're still out of sorts over yesterday."

"I'm out of sorts over your behavior with Maria," Matt gritted out. "And you had best put an end to it."

"It's that Logan Blackstone," his mother said, angrily

268

shaking her head. "He's the one who's got you all upset. Thank God that man is leaving."

"He should have stayed."

Olivia stood stock-still. "I beg your pardon?"

"You heard me. It settled nothing for him to come here for a day and then leave."

"There's nothing to settle," Olivia insisted, a strange nervousness threading through her voice.

"We both know there is."

Olivia sank onto the chair beside the bed. "What do you mean, Matthew?"

"I mean Logan deserved better than he got."

"He deserves nothing. How can you say that?"

"The same way I always say it. I hate him to his face, but here alone in this bed, with this stinking leg for company, I know who deserves what."

"You . . . you've been under a terrible strain since he arrived. You need rest." Olivia put another blanket on top of the sheet that covered him.

Matt threw it off. "For God's sake, Mother, it's ninety degrees outside."

Olivia backed away, her agitation mounting. "I'm going out to talk to Esteban," she said, as though speaking to herself. "You're too upset to realize what that girl is trying to do."

"You will not interfere between Maria and me," Matt said. "She is my business. Mine."

"But dearest, she'll only hurt you, reject you. Maria is a spirited young girl. She'll require a great deal of . . . attention from a husband."

"Get out, Mother."

"Matthew, I don't mean to upset you."

"Get out!"

With a look of half-pity, half-hurt, Olivia hurried from the room.

After letting out a savage curse Matt heaved his breakfast tray onto the floor. Then he reached for the medicine best suited to his affliction. With a searing self-loathing, he raised the whiskey bottle to his lips.

Chapter Twenty

Nugget chafed at the bit, eager to run, but Cat held the mare to a canter. The palomino seemed none the worse for its brush with death in the livery the past night. Cat wished she could say the same for herself. She had scars that would last a lifetime. Scars that had nothing to do with physical injuries, nothing to do with the fire.

She dared a covert glance at her riding companion. Logan rode astride a chestnut gelding he'd hired from the livery. He was never farther than six feet from her, but he might as well have been six miles away. He kept his attention on the trail they rode, his every sense alert as though any second he expected an ambush.

What he would do if one happened she had no idea—he carried no weapon other than his swordstick—but she was certainly not about to ask him.

They'd spoken not so much as a word since they'd left Red Springs nearly four hours ago. He seemed determined to remain as aloof as he'd been when he'd examined her after the fire.

They hadn't even talked of Toby's suspicions, but the

mere fact that Logan was here and not on his way to Boston attested to the fact that he had not taken them lightly. He'd felt obliged to escort Cat home, though he hadn't felt obliged to like it.

They had made love last night, shared an intimacy of body and spirit of which dreams were made. And in the throes of that intimacy he had dared risk even more. He had dared ask her to be his wife.

And she had turned him down.

Her reasons made no difference—the ranch, her insecurities. No matter what excuses she gave, she had rejected him. And he wasn't a man to take such a rejection lightly.

If only he knew how fiercely she suffered as well. She had said no to the man with whom she wanted to spend the rest of her life. And no matter how she rationalized that decision—to him, to herself—her heart remained unconvinced. And she feared it always would.

With a quiet oath she reined Nugget to a halt, mopping the sweat from her brow with her bandana. Logan pulled up, waiting. His gaze, constantly moving, never once flicked to her.

Dismounting, Cat led the mare over to a small grove of willows that lined the bank of a narrow creek bed. She expected Logan to object, then realized wearily that to do so would require him to speak to her. Grabbing her canteen, she tromped over to one of the trees, brushed aside its ground-sweeping branches and sank down in its shade.

Tugging the cork free from the canteen, she took a long drink. They were only a short distance from the ranch now, and there were things that had to be said. Whether he wanted to hear them or not, whether she wanted to say them or not. She began slowly. "I want to thank you for riding out with me. I know you'd rather have been on that four o'clock stage."

"I couldn't let you ride home alone."

"Toby could've come with me."

"He needs to do a little more investigating into the fire."

"He won't find anything," she said stubbornly. "No one tried to kill me."

"I'm not taking any chances."

Her lips thinned, but she didn't argue the point further. "We're almost home," she said. "I can make it the rest of the way alone."

"I'm going with you."

"I don't want you missing any more stages on my account." The lie almost stuck in her throat.

"I won't be going home for a while. I thought I made that clear." She took a perverse satisfaction in the growing tension in his voice. Why should he be calm when she was so upset?

"I thought you only meant to see me home."

"Then board the next stage while someone may still be trying to kill you? How gallant of me."

"I never asked you to be gallant!" Blast the man! His damned manners could be so infuriating.

"I'm not going home," he said quietly, "until I'm sure you're safe."

Her shoulders sagged. "Logan . . ." His leaving today would have been difficult enough to handle, but for him to stay some indeterminate length of time—days, weeks, months—and then leave her? How could she bear it?

She looked at him, hopelessness tearing through her. And she knew then that it didn't make any difference when he left. Today or next year he would still break her heart. She might as well take what sweet pleasure she could in being with him—no matter how uncomfortable they made each other. "What am I supposed to tell my mother and Matt about your coming back? They . . . may well have thought they'd seen the last of you."

"Tell them you've hired an extra hand for the fall roundup."

She smiled wanly. "I'll tell them you're keeping an eye on your investment. But, please," she cautioned, "don't tell them what Toby said. I don't want to worry them over what may be nothing."

He started to object, then thought better of it. "Agreed." He hadn't let go of the gelding's reins. "We'd better keep going."

"There's something else."

"What?"

"Us."

"There is no us. You made that clear."

"But there could be, for a little while at least."

His gaze seared her and her heartbeat quickened. "I want you," he said. "Day and night, every minute I want you. I won't lie and say I don't. But it can never be again. I won't do that to you. Or me."

"Why? When we both want it?"

"For one thing, you could get pregnant."

She blushed furiously. She hadn't even considered the possibility. Logan's child. Her child. The mere thought brought tears of happiness to her eyes—along with the incontrovertible knowledge that if she were pregnant, he could never leave her.

But to trap him? How could she love him and even consider such a despicable act?

She knew the answer. She couldn't. Because to trap him would mean to sacrifice her own honor. Above all else, Logan valued honor. A marriage without it would be no marriage at all.

She watched forlornly as he remounted and waited for her to do the same. He'd told her he wanted her, but how easily he seemed to hold his passion in check.

"Stay close to me," he said, scanning the road ahead as they moved out.

"You don't really think there's someone out there pointing a gun at me, do you?" she asked, not sure which subject was more distressing—Logan or killers.

"I know there's no sense taking chances."

She shivered. She hadn't really let herself think about being a target. To do so was to do more than admit a danger to her own life. It was to give credence to the possibility that her father had been murdered, that now his killer stalked Hadley Jordan's daughter. "Killing me doesn't make sense."

"We talked about who might want the ranch. You're the principal owner now. And maybe the killer knows how quickly your mother and brother would sell if . . ."

"If anything happened to me?"

"Nothing's going to happen," he said, and she experienced a surge of pleasure at how fiercely protective he sounded. She wondered if he was even aware of it.

"You can't watch me every minute."

"I'll tell Dusty and the others to keep an eye out for you."

The thought rankled, but she supposed it couldn't be helped. A thought that disturbed her more, as they rode into the Circle J ranchyard, was how she was going to break the news to her mother and Matt that Logan

275

Blackstone was now working for the Circle J.

"Maybe I'd better go in alone," she said, tying off Nugget at the hitching post in front of the house.

"It'll be easier if your mother takes it out on me," he said, falling in step beside her.

Cat didn't say so, but she was grateful. They walked into the front room to find her mother in tears on the settee. Cat rushed over to her. "Mother, what is it?"

"Nothing. I'm fine, Cordelia." Olivia looked past Cat to see Logan. The sadness in her eyes became a kind of wistful resignation, like that of a condemned prisoner accepting the news that a request for a pardon had been refused.

"Logan is staying until the herd is sold," Cat said, prepared for any reaction but the one she got. None.

"I'll sleep in the bunkhouse, Olivia," Logan said. "We won't have to see each other."

Cat knew Logan offered the words as reassurance and was again grateful. But her mother didn't even seem to hear him. Logan looked at Cat. "Maybe I'd better go see about that bunk," he said.

Cat nodded, watching him go, then peered anxiously at her mother. "Ma, please," she said, sitting beside her on the settee, "what's happened?"

"Matthew hates me." Tears tracked slowly down Olivia's pale cheeks.

"That's absurd!" Cat cried.

Olivia shook her head sadly. "I tried so hard to be the best mother I could be. I tried so hard."

"You wait here," Cat said, gently squeezing her mother's hand. "I'll be right back. You hear?"

Her mother only stared.

Cat hurried down the hallway to Matt's room. He was

drunk, groggy. Cat sat beside him on the bed and shook his shoulder, trying to rouse him.

"Maria," he mumbled, "Maria . . . love . . . can't . . ."

"Matt," Cat said. "Matt, it's Cat. Please wake up."

"Ma's right," he choked out, his bloodshot eyes overbright. "Never work. Never."

"Matt, please . . ."

He blinked, trying to focus. "Cat?"

"Yes." She caught his hand. "Matt, what happened?"

"I'm tired, Cat. I'm so tired of being nothing."

Cat's eyes burned. "Oh, Matt, you're not nothing."

"I can't . . . Ma's right. I . . ."

"You can do anything you want," Cat said fiercely. "Let Maria help you. She loves you."

"Love." He gave a bitter laugh. "I want to love her. I want to."

"Then do it. Dammit, Matt, do it."

"Ma said—"

"Never mind what Ma said. Just do it!"

His eyes grew dull. He reached for the whiskey, but didn't pick it up, instead curling his hand into his fist. "I love her, Cat. I love her so much."

Cat smoothed her brother's hair away from his forehead. "Then that's all that matters, that's all that matters in the world."

He closed his eyes then and fell asleep. Cat rose, wondering why the words seemed hollow before she realized how bad she was at taking her own advice. Feeling thoroughly miserable, Cat headed out to the Hidalgo house. Maria answered Cat's sharp knock, alarm showing in her brown eyes. "What is it, *amiga?*" the girl demanded. "Mateo . . . ?"

"Is drunk as usual," Cat said. "But it's my mother that worries me more. What's been going on around here?"

"You'd better sit. We can talk." The girl led Cat into the small kitchen and sat her down at a squarish pine table. "Drink this." She poured Cat a cup of freshly made coffee, then poured one for herself.

Maria seated herself in the chair opposite Cat's. Sparing herself no small share of blame, Maria told Cat what had happened that morning in Matt's bedroom.

"The world is going mad," Cat muttered, when Maria had finished. At Maria's hurt look, Cat hastened to add, "I only mean that nothing is simple anymore, not since Pa died."

"Nor since Señor Blackstone's arrival."

Because the time seemed right for baring one's soul, Cat took a deep breath and told her friend what had happened in Robinson's Livery.

"Ah, *mi amiga,* no wonder you think the world has gone mad. But at least you have shared yourself with this man you love. I fear Mateo and I will never . . ." She dropped her gaze, shaking her head sadly.

"Matt's been fighting back, but it's hard for him. Hard to change fifteen years of dependency. But he *is* trying. And I think it's because of you. He loves you, Maria. But he doesn't think he has much of a life to offer you."

"He is so wrong."

"Then you keep after him."

Maria's eyes lit up. "I will."

Cat finished her coffee and started to rise. "I'd better get back to the house. Make sure Ma's all right."

"Maybe, too, you should take your own advice."

Cat sank back down, wondering if Maria had taken up mind reading. "What do you mean?" she asked, pretending not to understand.

"You should keep after Señor Blackstone."

Cat fingered the rim of the empty coffee cup. "I'm the one who turned him down, remember?"

"A foolish mistake. But easily fixed. Just tell him you changed your mind."

Cat shoved the coffee cup away from her. "I can't live in Boston. This is my home."

"You can live anywhere."

"And betray my father?"

"Your father would not wish you misery."

Cat didn't know why she continued to argue against what she wanted most in the world—Logan. But she couldn't seem to help herself. "My father left this ranch to me because he trusted me to build it up in his memory."

"He left the ranch to you because he loved you. But he did not tie it around your neck. He did not know you would fall in love with Señor Blackstone." Maria's eyes brimmed with sympathy. "Do you not see it, *mi amiga*, it is not Señor Blackstone or Boston you fear, it is reliving the mistake of your parents."

"What are you talking about?"

"Think!" Maria said. "Does the tale not sound familiar? A woman marries a man and then is forced to follow him to a place she fears, a place she hates."

For a full minute Cat said nothing. Then slowly she shook her head. "You're wrong, Maria. This is not the same at all. My parents' marriage has nothing to do with my feelings for Logan."

"You fear Boston, as your mother feared Texas. She married your father and wound up living a life she despised."

279

"It's not the same," Cat insisted.

"No," Maria agreed, "it isn't. But your mind thinks it is. You think your love for Señor Blackstone will die if you live in a place not of your own choosing."

"That's not true," Cat said stubbornly. "But, you have to admit, it *did* happen to my parents."

Maria looked infinitely sad. "Your mother's love for your father did not die in Texas, *amiga*. It never existed."

Cat leaped to her feet. "That's a lie!"

Maria flushed in the face of Cat's fury, but she did not stop. "Mateo and I spoke of it once, right after your father died. He told me he truly believes your mother married your father for reasons other than love. He would hear them arguing about it."

"I won't listen to this!" Cat started for the door.

"Hear me out and I won't speak of it again."

Cat stopped, but she didn't turn around. Maria's voice was gentle, loving.

"Your mother, Mateo said, married your father . . . for his money. Money he did not use for fancy living in Boston, as your mother expected. But money he used to build a cattle ranch in Texas."

Cat was shaking. "That's not true. None of it. How dare Matt say such a thing."

"I did not tell you this to hurt you, Cat. I love you like a sister. I say it only so you will see what you have with Señor Blackstone is different. Your mother wanted a life of comfort in Boston. Your father may have once loved her, but even so he wanted her to be different than who she was."

"Lies!" Cat bolted for the door.

Maria intercepted her. "I would not hurt you for the world. You know that."

Cat closed her eyes. "It's all lies," she repeated, her voice breaking.

Maria held out her arms and Cat went into them. She sobbed quietly for long minutes. Finally, she straightened. "I'd better go."

Maria didn't stop her this time. Cat needed time to think. Outside, Cat saw Logan coming out of the barn not a hundred feet away. She spun abruptly and headed in the opposite direction, grateful when he didn't follow. She only stopped running when she reached her father's grave. Sinking to her knees, Cat tried desperately to calm herself.

"Maria's wrong, Pa," she said aloud. "She has to be. You and Ma loved each other. And you and Ma have nothing to do with Logan and me."

Then why did it all make perfect sense?

If love had indeed been the missing ingredient in her parents' marriage, it would explain so much.

And it would offer much, too. Because love was not missing in what she had with Logan.

Sitting here, gazing out at the grass-studded plains that were her home, a thousand unwelcome memories crowded through her mind, memories of unresolved shouting matches, whole evenings of cold silences, months of mutually welcome separation because of the demands of the ranch.

Her parents had made each other miserable for years. But the question she couldn't answer was had it always been so?

What if Matt and Maria were wrong? Maria had only come to the Circle J years after Matt's accident. And Matt—could a brother so bitterly fought over by his mother and father truly have objective hindsight about his parents' relationship?

Even Cat had clung to the notion that her parents were separately troubled, not that their marriage was in trouble.

And yet in Maria's words had been a powerful truth, one Cat had fought hard not to recognize—the real reason she had turned Logan down. That it was not necessarily about Boston or the ranch at all. It was about fear. Fear that the very thing she wanted most—to be with Logan no matter what their differences—would inevitably destroy them. As it had destroyed her parents.

Unless she faced that fear, and soon, she would never know, because her future would be decided for her. Logan would go back to Boston, and she would lose him forever.

Chapter Twenty-One

In her life Cat had never shied away from a challenge—until now. In her years on a cattle ranch she had battled drought, tick fever, dust storms, and flash floods. She had defeated them all. But now, facing a challenge of the heart, she found herself up against an altogether more insidious enemy—self-doubt.

Four weeks had passed since she'd made love to Logan, four weeks since the barn fire, four weeks since her revealing talk with Maria, and not once in those four weeks had Cat found the courage to approach Logan about anything more compelling than which saddle he should use when he was practicing cutting steers from the herd.

Of course, the man was being no help at all. He was so remote and distant she wondered if she might have unknowingly contracted some sort of plague.

She was grateful for the distraction of the roundup. For one thing, being on the range with the crew made her feel safe, even against imagined enemies. The only drawback was that the presence of Dusty and the boys apparently absolved Logan of his feeling of personal responsibility for her. He didn't hover quite so nearby when she was with the crew.

At least during those brief respites she was spared his seemingly perpetual scowling. She hadn't seen a smile on the man's face since . . . She blushed, recalling only too vividly where she'd been and what she'd been doing when last she'd seen him smile. Bleakly, she wondered if she would ever see that smile again.

"Yes, you will, Cat Jordan," she muttered aloud, letting Nugget do most of the work of cutting a maverick from the herd. The experienced mare won the battle of wits with the wily longhorn, maneuvering the heifer into Jim Spence's waiting rope. The wranglers were using this last day before the trail drive to brand a few unmarked cattle.

Cat didn't even look back once Spence had the heifer down. She hadn't seen Logan for a couple of hours now and she was inordinately curious about what he was up to.

He was usually right there with the crew, lending a hand wherever they needed it most. The men had been more than patient with him, teaching him the rudiments of herd-handling skills that it took months, even years, to perfect. To Logan's credit he was holding his own. And the men openly complimented his hard work.

Tomorrow joint crews from the Circle J, Rocking R, and four other ranches would band together for the drive north. Ryan had been in camp more than once to remind everyone to be on the alert for rustlers. He wouldn't be accompanying the herd—owners often didn't—but he wanted everyone to be wary. Cat would be going along. In fact, she was looking forward to it, looking forward to six weeks with Logan when neither one of them had to look over their shoulders for possible killers.

Ryan's admonition about rustlers had prompted her to take precautions, though. This morning she had strapped on the six-gun holstered to her thigh. She didn't like wearing the gun, but she would take no chances. She'd come too far to lose the battle for the ranch now. The market was good. With the four thousand head of Circle J beef she would be able to pay off the Blackstone loan.

And then he would be gone. Death threats or not, he couldn't stay in Texas forever on the chance that someday someone might try to harm her. Not unless she gave him a reason to stay. Or worked up her courage to go.

Cat crested a rise and spotted Logan about a hundred yards to the north near an arroyo studded with a half-dozen twisted clumps of mesquite. He was on foot, carrying a lariat.

Cat dismounted and watched, fascinated, as Logan stalked toward the largest mesquite bush. He let the rope fly and she jumped, startled, when a steer bolted from the scrub brush. She only started breathing again when she saw that his toss had fallen short of its mark. Was the man out of his mind?

She swung into the saddle and thundered toward him, intercepting him as he was making his way back to his gelding. "What the hell were you doing?" she shouted, as she leaped from the saddle and rushed up to him. "You could have been killed!"

"Just practicin' my ropin', ma'am," he drawled in an infuriating mockery of a Texas accent. He wasn't looking at her.

"You don't rope a steer on foot! What were you

285

thinking of?"

"Impressin' the boss?" he asked, sounding as though he'd just decided it was as good a reason as any.

She was in the midst of continuing her tirade when her mind clicked and made sense of what he had just said. "You did that on purpose?" she accused. "Because you knew I was watching you?" For the first time she noticed just a hint of a teasing warmth in those gray eyes. Had he deliberately left the herd, hoping she would come looking for him?

"I was just going to throw the rope at a tree stump," he continued in the same lazy drawl, "until I saw you come over the ridge. That was about the same time I noticed the steer."

She put her hands on her hips. "Logan Blackstone, that was about the stupidest thing I ever saw."

"I missed."

"Exactly. You don't know the half of roping yet. You could have accidentally hooked one of those horns!"

"All in a day's work, ma'am. I must say I'm lookin' forward to the drive tomorrow. Or should I say, tah-*mahrah*?"

"You can say whatever the hell you like," she said, "just don't pull a fool stunt like that again."

"You'd hate to lose one of your best drovers, right?"

"I'd hate to lose you," she said honestly, gaining a measure of satisfaction from seeing the smug look in his eyes vanish. The aloofness that replaced it for once seemed forced.

"I'd best be getting back to the herd," he said.

She walked over to a small boulder and sat down. She held her breath as she waited to see if he would make good on his word and leave. Instead he re-coiled the lariat and strode over to stand beside her.

It was then he noticed the gun. "What the hell is that?" he exploded, yanking the six-gun from her holster.

"A Colt .45," she said reasonably. "Now would you mind giving it back to me?"

"I mind very much. You shouldn't be wearing something like this. For God's sake, you could get yourself killed."

"I'm perfectly capable of handling a firearm." She was furious that he could think her capable of toting around a weapon she didn't know how to use.

"I'm not letting you wear this thing." He started toward his horse.

She caught up with him, grabbing his arm. "You give me back my gun. Now."

"No."

She took a step back, momentarily undone by what she saw in his eyes. It was fear. Fear of what, she couldn't have said. She supposed it was some primal male fear for her safety, a thought which only rekindled her fury.

"Give me my gun," she said again.

"No."

"Fine. I'll just go back to camp and get another one. The chuck wagon carries a few extras."

With a curse he shoved the gun toward her, butt first. As she reached for it, she heard the rattle, the deadly warning rattle of a snake. She stood stock-still, sensing the diamondback behind her near the rock.

"Shoot it, Logan. Hurry."

"Stand still. It'll go away on its own."

The rattling continued, intensified.

"Logan, please . . ." Cat felt sweat break out on her

forehead. The snake must have been coming out to sun itself on the boulder. Her movements had startled it.

She moved her head slightly, saw the rattler coiled to strike barely three feet from where she stood. Terrified, she leaped toward Logan, grabbing the gun as the snake struck. It missed her by inches. As it coiled to strike again, she fired. She didn't miss. But her knees buckled.

Logan caught her in his arms. "Are you all right? It didn't strike you, did it?" He was running his hands along the denim above her boots.

"I'm fine." She pulled away, her voice shaking. "No thanks to you."

He looked away quickly, and she didn't see what was in his eyes. "I'm not any better at shooting than I am at roping," he said, the lightness in his voice forced, stiff.

Cat headed for her horse. "I'd better get going. I'll see you back at camp."

He nodded, but still didn't look at her.

She rode off, more angry with herself than with Logan. He'd said it himself. He was a lousy shot. So why did it gnaw at her that he hadn't even tried? The snake had only missed her by inches.

Back in camp she tried in vain to shake off a vaguely unsettled feeling. She succeeded only when she saw her mother, Matt, and Maria drive up. To say the least, she was surprised to see them. Her astonishment grew when she noticed it was Matt, not Maria, guiding the buckboard's team of matched bays.

"Come to see us off?" she asked, hurrying over as Matt pulled the team to a halt.

"That we did," Matt said, holding Maria's hand as the girl jumped to the ground. Maria retrieved his crutches from the wagon bed and handed them to him. Matt hopped down gingerly, settling the crutches under his arms.

He turned then and held up his hand to Olivia, but she sat on the wagon seat and stared straight ahead, ignoring the gesture.

Cat's heart sank. She had hoped that in a month's time her mother would have gotten used to the idea of Matt trying to fend for himself, of his increasingly loving attention to Maria.

"No change?" Cat asked, looking from Matt to Maria.

Matt shook his head. "She gets mad as blazes every once in a while, but only at Maria. When I try to get her to argue it out with me, she just tells me she knows what's best. I've been gettin' out to the cookhouse for breakfast. Ma doesn't care for that at all."

"It's been a hard summer for her," Cat said, feeling awkward talking about her mother as though she weren't even there. "The one reason she's had for living all these years is taking care of you."

"That was as much my fault as hers," Matt said, surprising Cat with how matter-of-factly he accepted part of the blame. "It's still hard sometimes, when the leg acts up." He balanced himself on the crutches and put his arm around Maria's shoulders. "I've only made it this far, because Maria's so patient. I'd have knocked me out a long time ago if I were her."

Maria smiled. "He does not know that he is using up all of my patience, and one day there will be none left. And then . . . and then Mateo will see that his sweet little Maria can have the temper of a dust devil."

Cat laughed. "Come on over here you two and have some coffee." She tried again to entice her mother to join them, but Olivia offered only a stoic shake of her head.

Cat passed out the cups, then poured the coffee, nearly dropping the pot when Matt said, "I came out here to tell you I wanted to go along on the drive."

Cat swallowed an instinctive no, and managed to croak out, "You have been making progress, haven't you?"

Matt's request proved too much for Olivia. She started to climb down from the wagon seat. Cat moved to assist her, but she was too late. Olivia marched over to the campfire. "You cannot go, Matthew," she said. "I absolutely forbid it. You'll kill yourself. Your leg—"

"Would hurt like hell," Matt agreed. "I know, Mother. That's why I'm not going. But I want to go, and next year I will."

"Next year?" Olivia said. "There can't be a next year. This ranch is finished. This cattle drive is a fool's mission. Rustlers, thieves, and a Blackstone on the other end with his hand out."

"The ranch will make it, Ma," Cat put in. "And Matt and I will run it. We'll make Pa proud."

"Your father's dead!" Olivia hissed. "Just like you'll be dead, and Matt, if you don't give up this godforsaken land." Her face crumpled, but she didn't cry. Instead she turned, her shoulders stooped, and walked back to the wagon.

"Let her go," Matt said, when Cat again started toward her. "You can't talk to her. She won't listen, no more than I did up until a month ago. That last drunk made me take a hard look at myself."

"It's good to have my brother back," Cat said. "Real good, Matt." She gave him a swift hug. When he stiffened slightly, she thought perhaps her display of sisterly affection had embarrassed him, until she followed the direction of his gaze.

290

Logan had returned to camp and dismounted. He strode to the campfire and poured himself a cup of coffee. "You look good, Matt," he said, as though they always exchanged innocuous greetings.

"Thanks." Matt's voice was tense, but at least he wasn't belligerent. He finished his coffee and tossed the cup by the fire. He shifted uncomfortably on the crutches, using both of them now, as Maria surreptitiously put her arm around his waist to help support him. His leg was hurting, but his pride would not allow him to sit down with Logan there.

She was grateful when he said, "I guess I'd better be getting back home."

Logan came around the fire and stopped directly in front of Matt. He wasted no words. "I meant it when I said new surgery could help the leg."

The truce vanished. Matt's lips thinned. "You've done damn well enough for my leg, Blackstone."

"There's a doctor in Philadelphia."

"No." Matt tried to turn toward the wagon, but the movement hurt and he had to pause to catch his breath.

"Matt, at least think about it," Logan said.

For the briefest time Matt hesitated, and Cat hoped the leg was not throbbing too much for him to hear what Logan had to say. Then, amazingly, Matt asked, "How much more would they have to cut?"

"Hardly anything, most likely," Logan said. "They'd probably cut the nerves, remove the bone spurs, then reshape the stump so that you might even be able to tolerate a peg leg."

Matt eyed Logan levelly, and though there was something hidden, unreadable in his gaze, for the first time he warily accepted that Logan bore him no malice.

291

"I'll think about it," he said.

"Good," Logan replied, the look in his eyes just as unreadable.

As Matt and Maria climbed back into the wagon, Cat tromped over to the chuck wagon. She came back carrying an extra six-gun. She looked at Logan. "Since you seem to be in a more reasonable frame of mind than when you tried to rope that steer this morning, I thought maybe you'd like to start giving yourself a few lessons with this." She held the Colt out to him.

He looked bored. "If I wanted a gun, I'd have one." He headed back toward his mount.

"If I live to be ninety, I will never figure out that man," Cat grumbled, shoving the extra gun in the waistband of her pants.

"Leave him be," Matt said. "He can't turn into a cowboy overnight."

Cat stared at her brother. "And I can make it to a hundred," she said, "and never figure *you* out."

Matt picked up the reins. "See you in six weeks, sis."

"With a ranch to run!"

He smiled and gigged the bays into a trot. Maria waved good-bye. Beside them, Olivia sat, unmoving.

It was late evening before Cat saw Logan again. As he'd been this morning, he was away from the herd, this time sitting on a tree stump burned out by some long-ago prairie fire. She rode up and dismounted.

"Something wrong?" she asked.

"No." He didn't even have the courtesy to turn around.

"Change your mind about going along on the drive?"

"No."

"You're riding drag tomorrow, you know."

"I know." It was where the least experienced hands rode.

Her lips thinned. Maybe she'd have to live to be two hundred to figure out this man. "Something *is* wrong," she said.

"I just felt like being alone."

"Oh." Now she felt like an intruder. "I'm sorry. I'll go."

"No. Stay," he said, then added, "please."

She hunkered down beside the tree stump. "I'm sorry I gave you a hard time about the snake. The danged thing just scared me, that's all."

"Forget it."

"And I want to thank you for talking to Matt. I think he really will consider the operation."

"I hope so."

"Do you hate me so much?" she asked, unable to stand this stilted formality between them one more second.

He looked at her, clearly astonished. "What are you talking about? Why would I hate you?"

"It's my fault you stayed in Texas when you wanted to leave. My fault you're even on this blasted cattle drive. I know these things can't be easy for you. And to complicate it all is how I feel about you." She was babbling, but she couldn't seem to stop herself. Now that she was saying these things, she wanted to say it all, everything she'd kept bottled up inside since that night in the barn.

"I've tried, Logan," she said, her eyes filling with tears, "I've tried hard not to care. To tell myself that it's for the best, that we don't belong together, but I can't . . .

293

Logan, I can't . . ."

He leaned toward her and cupped her face with his hands, then he closed his eyes and let her go.

"What was that for?" she asked softly.

"I just felt" he said haltingly, "like I had to touch you, just touch you, or I was going to die."

Her heart leaped at the searing passion threading his words, passion restrained by a precariously fragile leash.

Of their own accord her arms curved around his neck and she drew his mouth to hers. He groaned, sliding off the tree stump. With an explosive oath he bore her down to the carpet of soft grass.

"I want you," he breathed. "Sweet Jesus, I want you so much." His body was on fire, his passion banked far too long. He was rapidly losing the ability to think clearly, to think at all. All he wanted in the world was to make her his one more time. Just one time. That was all. Just once.

"Love me, Logan," she pleaded. "I want you too. I want you. Oh, Logan, take me. Take me now!"

His hands were fevered. He unbuttoned her shirt, his mouth seeking the warm, tender flesh of her breasts. She arched back, moaning, gasping, her hands flying out to hold him to his erotic task. He teased her nipples into twin peaks of desire, his own need spiraling out of control.

With a cry—part profanity, part prayer—he drove himself inside her. His body quivered, trembled, exulted in being part of her again. He closed his eyes, lost in the exquisite torment of possessing her, letting her possess him. Her hips moved rhythmically in time with his own, the tension in them both building, until neither could bear it a heartbeat longer. And then they shuddered, collapsed, rejoiced in this primal celebration of their love.

For long minutes neither moved, neither wanting to break the spell.

"Why did we waste so much time?" Cat murmured.

He didn't answer. He only held her closer, the tensions of the past month, for the moment at least, at bay.

But they would be back. This space of time was illusion, he knew. Reality would intrude soon enough. Reality with its questions, decisions, regrets.

Already Logan could feel the elusive peacefulness he found only in her arms slipping away. His gray eyes were haunted, ancient ghosts closing in on him, pieces of the past coming inexorably together. The day's events had driven the point home hard and fast. Cat would know the truth soon. He couldn't stop it. And then she would wish him out of her life forever.

Chapter Twenty-Two

Matt struggled to get into his wheelchair. He'd been overdoing it lately, he knew. But today his leg would just have to put up with a little more abuse than usual. Maria had invited him to lunch at her house. With her father gone on roundup and Olivia asleep, Matt was looking forward to an afternoon alone with her.

He wheeled the chair toward the door to his room, pausing briefly in front of the mirror. "Is that really you, Matt Jordan?" he asked the image peering back at him. Gone was the sallow color he had long called his own. Gone, too, were the dark circles that had undercut his eyes for years. Only rarely now were his nights interrupted by pain.

Not that the pain was gone. Far from it. But he no longer allowed it full reign over his life. And for that, and so much more, he had to credit the lovely woman toward whose house he now headed.

Though she assured him he'd done it all by himself.

Wheeling the chair toward her doorstep, he took a moment to rake his dusty blond hair away from his face.

He wished now he'd thought to comb it. When he reached Maria's door, he stopped. He told himself he was here for lunch, and a chance to talk with this woman he now fully admitted he loved. But the heat in his blood said otherwise.

Fear had long kept his passion in check. But Maria, with her gentle loving, broke through the barriers more and more every day.

Somehow he knew that after today there would be no more barriers between them.

The thought almost made him turn and go back. It was as if he could feel the fear in him digging in for one last desperate battle.

Maria was so special. What if he ruined it for her? He'd never been with a woman. A woman as sweet, as innocent as Maria deserved a man who knew how to please her, how to . . .

The door swung inward. "I did not hear you knock, Mateo." Maria's soft voice.

"I . . . just got here," he said, swallowing hard.

"Come in, Mateo," she said. "I have been waiting."

Inside, his nervousness mounted. She brought him the crutches he had left yesterday, when he'd come for supper. He thanked her, using them to maneuver himself to the worn horsehair settee in the small living area off the kitchen.

"Would you like a drink, Mateo? My father has some whiskey put away."

He blinked, startled. Maria had never offered him liquor before. "No," he said. "Thank you."

She came over to sit next to him on the settee.

"I'm hungry," he lied, feigning enthusiasm for the meal ahead. "Maybe we should eat." He sniffed the air.

"Something sure smells good. Chicken?"

She nodded, but she didn't move from the settee. "I am not hungry for food just now, Mateo. The chicken will not be ready for more than an hour."

"Did I come too early?" he asked, stammering, he thought, like a fool.

"You are right on time," she assured him. Her hand touched his shoulder. "Right on time, Mateo."

He was trembling. *I can't do this. I can't.*

"Maria," his voice was tormented. "I should go. I'll come back when lunch is ready. I—"

"I love you, Mateo."

He shut his eyes as a fierce pain shot through his leg. But some part of him knew it wasn't the leg at all. Not this time. It was fear, sharp and lethal. Poised to destroy every inch of progress he had made.

"I have to go, Maria. I have to." He couldn't let her see his leg. He couldn't make love to her. He couldn't, couldn't, couldn't . . .

She stood and held out her hand. For what seemed an eternity he only stared at it. Slowly, so slowly, he raised his own hand to link it with hers. She helped him up, helped him to her bedroom. Inside the warm, cozy little room he stood with his back against the wall.

Maria crossed to her bed and sat down. She raised her dark eyes toward him, her gaze so full of love and trust it made his heart ache to look at her.

"Come, Mateo," she beckoned, holding her arms out to him, "let us share our love."

"I . . . Maria, I can't. I'm sorry."

She stood, never taking her eyes from his face, and slowly lifted her blouse over her head.

298

He let out a strangled gasp. Her breasts were naked, lovely. Perfect. Perfect for his hands to touch, to love. He moved across the room, his crutches thudding to the floor beside her bed. He sank down next to her, his arms locked rigidly at his sides.

"I love you, Maria," he said. "I love you."

"I love you more than my life, Mateo." She touched her breasts, circling the nipples with the tips of her fingers. "They have waited so long for your touch."

With a groan he reached for her, murmuring over and over, "Maria, you *are* my life."

He kissed her, and felt his head pound, his blood catch fire. And then he pulled back, his hand tracing the soft curve of her jaw. "I'm afraid, Maria," he whispered. "I shouldn't say it, I know."

"I am afraid, too, Mateo." She stroked her fingers through the hair that fell boyishly across his forehead. "I am afraid I will not please you."

To allay her fears, he forgot his own. Tenderly, he undressed her further, until she lay naked beneath his gaze. "You're beautiful, Maria. So beautiful."

Her smile was radiant. "And now I want to see you, all of you, Mateo. To love you as you have loved me."

She unbuttoned his shirt, easing it away from his shoulders, and they lay back, her mouth trailing a path of fire all across his chest. He sucked in his breath as she kneaded the bulge that strained to be free of the denims he wore.

"I want to see you, Mateo," she breathed. "I want to feel your bigness inside me."

He cried out, his passion flaring past the bonds of reason. "Yes, Maria," he said. "Yes."

But when she reached to unbutton his fly, to have him lie there as naked as she, he froze. "Maria . . . I . . . wait."

"It is all right, Mateo. I love you. All of you."

All that he was, all that he could ever be, he put on the line at that moment. Unmoving, he allowed her to ease his trousers past his hips. He watched her eyes when she saw his leg for the first time. He wept unashamedly when, ever so gently, she kissed him there.

There was no pity, no revulsion in her dark eyes, only love, love for him.

For the first time in fifteen years he felt no pain. He eased her onto her back and rose above her. With a fierce primitive joy he drove himself inside her, linking his body, his soul to this woman he loved.

Together they rode the crest to oblivion.

Much later, Matt woke and kissed the woman sleeping so peacefully beside him. "I love you," he whispered.

She moaned sleepily, but did not awaken. His heart quickened when she instinctively cuddled closer.

He wanted to take her again, make love to her. But his leg throbbed miserably and he had to bow to common sense. He would be back tomorrow. It would be best if he got back to the house before his mother came looking for him.

Not that she would. Olivia seemed to have accepted his visits to Maria's. Matt only wished his mother would accept Maria as well.

But there had been no progress on that account. Maria told him it was his mother's way of trying to hang onto him, to keep him helpless, dependent. Matt only hoped that one day his mother would give in, just a little. He was certain if she allowed herself to know Maria, she couldn't help but love her.

He swung toward the house on the crutches, feeling more at peace with himself and the world than he ever had in his life. Even before he'd lost his leg. Then he'd had to battle constantly for his father's approval. And it had seemed never to come easily.

When Cat got back, he would be a full partner with her, help her run the ranch. Relearn skills he'd long since allowed to lie fallow. He would have the operation Logan had mentioned.

He paused, leaning against the rear door of the house. The operation frightened him. He harbored no illusions about it. But if it would give him a chance to burn these crutches, burn the wheelchair, he would do it. He would do anything to be the best husband he could be to Maria Hidalgo.

Maybe someday he could even buy out Cat. He knew she loved the place, but he had also seen the way she looked at Logan Blackstone. Maria, too, had been less than subtle in her hints about Cat and Logan.

He didn't have the energy right now to sort through how he felt about his sister marrying Logan. Maybe he wouldn't mind. Maybe it was time the truth all came out anyway. He was tired of hiding his part in it, maybe even tired of shoving so much of the blame on Logan.

Maria had taught him a lot about being responsible for his own life. She had given it back to him.

He was letting go of the past and it felt good, damned good. He opened the back door quietly. He didn't want to disturb his mother if she was still asleep. He was in no mood for an argument. He felt too damned good to fight

301

with anybody.

He stepped into the small alcove that served as a pantry for extra supplies, then eased the door closed behind him. He stood stock-still, listening. At first, he heard nothing. But something wasn't right.

Moving with extreme care, so as not to make a sound, he crept forward. Voices. Voices coming from the main room. He wondered why he didn't just call out. So a neighbor had dropped by, or a drifter looking for work. It wasn't so unusual. But he didn't call out. He edged forward, straining his ears to hear what was being said.

"You're sure Matt's still with the Hidalgo girl?"

Matt frowned. Ryan Fielding's voice.

"I'm sure," Olivia told him. "Now go on with the plan. I want to know every detail. I want to be certain in my own mind that nothing can go wrong."

Matt hugged the wall, his heart hammering. The tone of their voices said it all. Something was very wrong. Very wrong indeed. His blood ran cold as he continued to listen.

"Timing is going to be everything," Ryan said, the scraping of his boots telling Matt that he was near the fireplace. "We get the money after the herd is sold, but before Cat gives it to Blackstone. Then the Circle J debt can't be paid off."

Matt fought back a fearsome rage. Fielding was planning to rob Cat of the herd receipts and his mother was giving the man her blessing!

"No one must be hurt," Olivia was saying. "You promised, no one would be hurt. Not even Blackstone."

"No one," Ryan assured her. "I've hired men I can trust."

Sweet Jesus! Matt seethed. Fielding was talking about

302

hiring thieves as though it were no different from hiring a line rider. And his mother! Until now, he'd never realized the depths of her hatred for the Circle J.

Slowly, he edged his way back to the rear door. He dared not confront them. They would make sure he stayed put, that he warned no one. He had to get to town. Alert the law. Toby could send a telegram to Abilene to warn Cat and Logan.

Outside, Matt looked toward Maria's and decided not to involve her. It would be dangerous if she knew anything. It was going to be difficult enough for him to look his mother in the face from now on. He couldn't let on that he knew, not even after he returned from town.

If the plan were set in motion as he'd heard it, there was a good chance of its being successfully foiled. If Fielding found out Matt knew, the Rocking R rancher would amend the plan any way he chose and Matt would have no way of warning Cat and Logan of Fielding's new strategy.

With great difficulty Matt saddled a black gelding. Sucking in a lungful of air, he hauled himself into the saddle, trying to ignore the steady thrumming of pain now beating through his leg.

In the future he would have to remember not to make love and then go horseback riding afterward. The thought brought a slow smile to his face. God, how he loved Maria. He couldn't help thinking how proud of him she would be if she knew what he was doing right now.

He nudged the horse forward, careful to keep it to a walk until he was well out of the yard. More than once he looked back to assure himself he had not accidentally alerted Fielding.

Damn the rancher anyway! Matt couldn't believe he

would stoop to such treachery to gain the Circle J. Fielding had always professed such friendship for Hadley Jordan. And Matt hadn't missed the man's occasional overtures to his sister either. All, no doubt, part of the snake's plan to ultimately have the Circle J for himself.

Three miles into the ride, Matt had to rein in. His leg was white heat. Sweat dripped from every pore of his body. He thought of Cat falling victim to Fielding's scheme and forced the gelding forward.

He cried out, rubbing his thigh. Damn, not now. Not now. He fumbled in his saddlebags looking for something with which he could write a note, in case he passed out. Then if someone found him—pray God, not Fielding— the message would be taken to Toby Fletcher.

He found no paper, no pencil. He licked his lips, tasting the sweat. His vision blurred. He had to keep riding. He had to warn Cat.

A rabbit darted out of the brush. The gelding shied. Matt tried to right himself in the saddle, but failed. He felt himself falling, felt the ground slam up to meet him.

A bolt of agony such as he'd never known tore through his leg. He heard himself screaming and then he heard nothing at all.

Chapter Twenty-Three

Shadows. Voices. Voices, screaming. This time Cat was determined not to shy away from them. This time she would approach the shadows, find out at last who they were.

She was in the barn, looking for her pony, when she saw the boy sobbing. She approached him shyly and patted his arm. He tried to smile, using his shirtsleeve to swipe at his tears. The tears embarrassed him. Boys weren't supposed to cry.

"You should be in bed," the boy told her. "Your mama and papa wouldn't want to find you out here in the barn this time of night."

She dragged over an old apple crate and sat down beside him. "Matt's in the house crying. Mama was crying too. I saw her. And I think even Papa wanted to cry, 'cept he said big men don't."

"You'd better go," the boy said. "I don't want to get you in any trouble. I've caused enough trouble with what I did to Matt."

"I won't get in trouble," she assured him. "I always

sneak out to pet Princess when I can't sleep. And tonight I sure couldn't sleep. Everybody's so sad." She looked at him earnestly, eager to help make things right if she could. "Logan," she asked quietly, "what did you and Matt do to be in so much trouble?"

He didn't answer. She wondered if he might have, though, if it hadn't been for the barn door creaking open at that moment, its hinges protesting loudly. Cat heard a voice, but she couldn't tell who was speaking. The voice seemed muffled somehow. Indistinct.

Muffled by sobbing?

"Your fault. Your fault."

"Who is it?" she whispered to Logan.

The boy rose and shoved Cat behind him. Protectively, she thought. Like a bold knight in the tales he'd told her this summer.

A knight in shining armor.

"Go!" the boy said. "Go, before they catch you here with me. They won't want you with me."

"Why? You're Matt's friend. Matt needs you. Come to the house and make Matt stop crying."

"Go!"

He pushed her out the side door into the darkness. The door slammed shut behind her. She shivered. It was cold out. Above her in the night sky a big silver moon scudded behind gray clouds.

Cat sneaked back to the door and listened, cowering in the darkness. Shadows hovered everywhere. Shadows huge in the flickering lantern light.

"Your fault. Your fault."

Cat squinted. Papa! It was Papa! She would go to him. He would help Logan. He would make Logan stop crying. And then Logan could make Matt stop crying. She opened the door a little wider.

Then stopped.

Papa looked big, scary. She'd never been afraid of her papa before. She crouched low. Maybe Logan was right. Maybe Papa wouldn't want her out here tonight. Maybe Papa had best not see her.

Papa grabbed Logan—shouting, shouting.

"No, Papa," Cat whimpered. "Don't be mad at Logan. He's my friend." But she didn't say it loud enough for him to hear.

Another shadow hovered close.

Screaming.

Papa raised his hand, curled it into a fist. Such terrible screaming. The other shadow was screaming.

Who was it? Who was it? Why couldn't she see who it was? Why couldn't she make out the words? Closer . . . closer . . .

Cat sat bolt upright, trembling, struggling to pull free of the arms that held her, sought to comfort her.

"It's all right," Logan soothed. "It's all right. It was just a dream."

She stilled, trying to remember, trying desperately to remember. . . . But the dream images receded.

She began to tremble again. Concern edged sharply into Logan's voice as he asked, "Are you all right?"

"Fine," she managed.

"I've been trying to wake you for over a minute," he said. "You were having some kind of nightmare."

She looked around, taking in the sheltering circle of rocks where she and Logan had bedded down. They were a day out of Abilene and Cat had convinced him that they deserved to spend their last night on the trail together, alone and uninterrupted by bawling beasts.

He'd made only a token objection to missing his turn riding night herd. Their stolen moments of passion had been few and far between these past five weeks.

But not last night. Last night had been magic.

Magic because each had sought to give the other memories to last a lifetime. Because in Abilene the herd would be sold, the debt would be paid, and there would be no more nights of magic.

In all these weeks Logan had not repeated his proposal of marriage. And try as she might to convince herself, Cat had not found the courage to tell him she had reconsidered, that maybe they could take the best parts of their separate worlds and make a life together.

Instead, she worried that he regretted proposing at all. She feared if she told him she was willing to take the chance, he would tell her *he* had changed *his* mind. Maybe love wasn't enough, after all. Maybe it never could be.

Annoyed at her sudden melancholy, Cat climbed abruptly to her feet. Running a hand through sleep-tumbled hair, she told herself she was just overreacting to the nightmare. She picked up her blankets, shaking out the bits of grass that clung to them in the fresh dew of early morning. "I imagine the men have already started driving the herd the last few miles to the stockyards," she said, trying hard to sound animated.

Logan stepped close to her, catching her hands, preventing her from continuing to fuss with her blankets. "What was the dream about, Cat?"

She stared at the hands cocooning her own. "I really should have brought my mother's softening potions along," she said. "My hands are like cowhide again."

He brought them to his lips, giving each a tender kiss. "I find them quite satisfactory," he murmured. "They each seem to know precisely where to touch me, when to touch me. . . ."

Her heart thudded at the sudden huskiness in his voice, and for the briefest moment she allowed herself to believe that he, too, had been thinking about Abilene, about trail's end. And about what it meant to each of them—their future together.

Instead he straightened, as though catching himself treading too close to a subject he'd planned to avoid. Again he pressed her, "What was the dream about, Cat?"

She swiped at an errant tear. There was no sense spoiling last night for both of them by letting him see how miserable she was. "It was about that night in the barn when I found you crying."

He didn't look surprised. She had likely only confirmed what he'd already suspected.

Would he talk about it? If she asked, would he at last tell her what had happened? So many times these past weeks she had been all but positive that he'd wanted to tell her, to get it over with, to unburden himself of memories carried alone too long.

But he never did.

"I remember more of the dream than I usually do," Cat said, watching him closely. "I remember seeing my father grab you, shout at you."

Logan trod over to pick up his own bedroll. "We agreed that you wouldn't ask me about that night."

"No, we agreed that I wouldn't ask you to break your promise to Matt. Matt isn't in the dream. I never see Matt. I know he's in the house, but I don't see him."

She finished rolling up her blankets and crossed over to him. "It isn't your promise to Matt that keeps you from telling me, is it?"

309

He didn't answer.

"Blast it all! I wish I could just remember for myself. It's there, I can *feel* it—but I can't remember."

"Maybe you're not supposed to remember. Maybe it's your mind's way of protecting you."

"Protecting *me?*" she asked incredulously. "What is that supposed to mean? I've always thought this is between you and my family. Now you're suggesting *I* need to be protected?"

"No, that isn't what I meant. Not exactly anyway." His lips thinned with self-disgust. "I'm sorry. I shouldn't have said what I did." He looked at her imploringly. "Don't ask me about that night. Don't ask me."

But she would not be dissuaded. "What can be so horrible that you can't tell me? My father was angry, but Matt was about to have his leg amputated. Of course he would be angry, angry at the whole world." She shut her eyes tight, searching her brain for the images that danced enticingly out of reach. "Why can't I remember who the other shadow was? How many other people could it be? One of the hands? My mother?"

Logan gripped her arms. "I hope you never remember. Do you hear me? Never."

She saw the torment in his face and it tore at her heart. "Whatever it is," she murmured, "I can't believe that it's worth your hurting like this. If you tell me, we can put an end to it."

"I wish to God it was that simple." He turned away and busied himself breaking camp, and nothing she said would induce him to speak of it again. They mounted and rode out in silence. They caught up with the herd just before noon.

Cat reined in on a bluff above the trail, while Logan

310

rode on ahead. She stared out over the dust-choked sea of beef, and for the first time in her life felt trapped by it, trapped by expectations she had long claimed as her own. She had wanted the Circle J to be one of the most successful cattle operations in the whole of Texas. But now, facing the prospect of losing the man she loved because of that ranch, some part of her questioned whose expectations they had been after all. Hers or her father's?

Was the idea of giving up the ranch becoming more acceptable now, because it was the only way she could have Logan? Or would she have reached this point anyway—a point where she had to make hard choices, but choices that were indeed her own?

She lifted her Stetson, using her bandana to mop at the sweat on her brow. She was almost glad Logan had ridden ahead. The way her thoughts and emotions were roiling around on top of one another, she was liable to say—do—something that would ruin everything. She couldn't just blurt out that she wanted to marry the man.

"I may not be a society belle," she muttered, "but I know a thing or two about subtlety." Or at least she had learned a thing or two lately.

She had rejected his proposal and his pride had been stung. He'd accepted her decision, and perhaps had even grown grateful for it. But he'd also accepted her passion these past weeks. Had he accepted it by assuring himself it was only temporary, a product of proximity? Or did he hope that it heralded what had actually happened—that she could no longer imagine her life without him.

Even if the latter were true, Cat knew it would be up to her to make him see it. The reality that she may have only a few more hours to do so stiffened her resolve.

She would have to make certain Logan stayed the night

in Abilene. Even though she would have the cattle receipts to pay off the Blackstone note by late this afternoon, she would avoid making it official until morning.

Besides, after long weeks of eating dust Logan would want a bath and a good night's sleep in a real bed. Without the distraction of the herd maybe, just maybe, they could talk. The thought of his leaving, being gone from her life forever, was the compelling jolt she needed to tell him the truth about how she felt.

Three hours later she rode into the bustling cattle town, ignoring much of the activity that in years past she'd found wholly captivating. Even at four in the afternoon the saloons were raucous dens of iniquity. She went directly to the stockyards. She expected to find Logan there, and when she did not, she went to the purchasing agent and sold off her share of the herd.

When the man laid out thousands of dollars from the company safe to pay for the sale, Cat blanched. She hadn't thought about being paid in cash. Acting as though it were the most normal thing in the world for her to be carrying so much money, she stuffed the packets of greenbacks into her saddlebags and headed for the hotel.

Again and again she found herself looking over her shoulder. Though they'd encountered no rustlers on the trail, she had never quite been able to shake the feeling of being followed. One night she'd shared her anxieties with Logan, expecting him to dismiss them, tell her she was being foolish. Instead he had expressed the same fear. And now the feeling was back full force.

"Stop it!" she muttered aloud. If someone hadn't had her pegged as a target before, they would soon by the way she was behaving.

Still she felt infinitely safer when she reached the hotel and found Logan in the lobby. "I lost track of you," he said, striding up to her. "Where did you go?"

"To the stockyards, where else?" Irrationally, her nervousness turned to annoyance that he hadn't been able to read her mind.

Logan gripped her arm, propelling her toward the far corner of the room. "You're not going to tell me you're carrying the herd money in those saddlebags."

"I am."

He swore. "I can't believe you'd take a chance like that." He paced across the lobby and back, trying hard to control his temper. "You could've at least taken Dusty or Esteban with you," he ground out, "if you didn't want me along."

She blinked in astonishment. "Not want you there? I couldn't find you. I just wanted to get the paperwork out of the way. Don't worry, I didn't lose your money."

"I wasn't worried about the money."

"You weren't?" She smiled hopefully.

He pulled her toward the registration desk. "I've signed us in for tonight. Two rooms. Is that all right?"

"Fine," she said, her lips thinning. He had every intention of spending the night in Abilene—he just wasn't planning to spend it with her! Well, that's what he thought!

He lifted the saddlebags from her shoulder. "These," he said, "are going in the hotel safe. Right now."

"All right," she said. "But I still have to count out the money I owe you."

"Later."

Upstairs, he escorted her into her room first. She laid a second set of saddlebags on the bed. She was looking

313

forward to a bath and clean clothes.

"I want you to get cleaned up," he said. "I'm taking you to dinner."

"You are?" She couldn't help the surge of hope that swept through her. Perhaps propriety had forced him to sign for two rooms.

"I am." He started toward the door.

She bit her lip. "I don't have anything to wear."

He dug into the pocket of the denims that now looked as natural on him as a cloudless Texas sky, and handed her five twenty-dollar gold pieces. "Buy whatever you like."

She bristled. "I'm not going to owe you even more money."

He gave her a thunderous look. "Consider it a gift."

"It's not my birthday," she countered stubbornly, and wondered if she'd lost her mind. Why was she baiting him when she wanted nothing more than to pull him into the next room and draw him down onto her bed?

"I'll be back in two hours," he said. "Be ready." With that he stomped out of the room.

Cat stood for a long minute, staring at the closed door. Had Logan planned all along to make their time in Abilene special? And if so, why? Was it his way of saying a fond good-bye, or did he hope, too, as she did, that somehow the night would bring with it a way to bridge their differences, a way to form a new alliance from their love?

"Well, whatever *his* intentions," she said aloud, "I know what my intentions are." She headed for the mirror above the water basin. "That man is not walking out of my life tonight. Not without a fight!"

That decided, she felt giddy, light-headed, better than

314

she had in months. Gripping the money Logan had given her, she marched downstairs, where she ordered a bath to be drawn and ready for her when she returned within the hour. Then she went shopping.

She returned with several bundles, happily depositing them on the bed. She had taken longer than she'd planned, but the lime green silk gown seemed well worth it. The bathwater felt tepid as she stepped into the wooden tub. Even so it was heavenly. She was patting her refreshed body down with a towel, when she heard the knock on the door.

"Who is it?" she called.

"Your escort for the evening, madam," Logan returned dryly.

Cat considered pulling on the cotton dressing gown she'd pulled from her saddlebags, then decided against it. Gripping the towel more tightly around her, she marched to the door and flung it open.

Logan's eyes grew wide. He stepped quickly through the door and closed it behind him. "Anyone could be walking by in the hall," he groused, making what seemed a monumental effort to avoid looking at her.

"It wasn't anyone," she said reasonably. "It was you."

"You're supposed to be ready." She suspected his sudden tenseness had nothing at all to do with her tardiness and everything to do with the towel she just couldn't seem to manage to keep in place against her breasts.

"Isn't a proper lady supposed to keep a gentleman waiting?"

"I wouldn't know," he said, still not looking at her. "I haven't been with a proper lady for quite some time."

At her outraged gasp, he relaxed a little. With a sly grin

he said, "I assure you, madam, never in my life has a proper lady beckoned me into her hotel room wearing only a towel."

She tried to stay angry, but couldn't. "I'm sorry." She laughed. "Shopping took longer than I thought it would. I don't do it that often."

"And where are the fruits of this shopping expedition?"

She really did want him to see the dress. Scooting behind the privacy screen, Cat emerged a short time later, grumbling fiercely. "I'll never be a lady," she said, groping at the back of the dress. "All these danged hooks and eyes are impossible!"

"Allow me," Logan said.

She turned her back and permitted him to work the fastenings, noting that he took his time, noting also that she trembled when his fingers made contact with her bare flesh. When he'd finished, she turned slowly, watching his gaze trail approvingly over the lime green silk. "I think this neckline would make even Chastity Vincent blush," Cat said, fluttering her hand self-consciously over the deep-cut front of the gown.

"Nothing would make Chastity blush," Logan said. "And never in my life have I seen a more beautiful woman than the one I'm looking at right now."

She bit back tears. "Thank you, kind sir," she managed.

He held out his arm. "And now, Miss Jordan, shall we begin our night to remember?"

The next three hours were like a dream. He took her to the restaurant in the hotel, where they both ate too much prime rib, sweet corn, and apple cobbler. And afterward they went for a moonlight stroll along one of Abilene's

316

less traveled streets.

They said little, but the looks they exchanged spoke volumes. Cat had never felt more special, more loved. Only when they returned to the hotel did a subtle nervousness intrude. Cat sensed Logan's reluctance outside her room.

"I guess I'll say good night," he said.

"Good night?" she echoed. Surely, he wasn't serious. But the look in his eyes told her he was. She drew in a deep breath and gathered her courage. "Come inside a minute?"

"I don't think that would be a very good idea."

"Please?"

"No."

"You don't want to?"

"More than anything."

She pushed the door open. "Then come in."

"Last night was difficult enough," he said quietly. "I won't make it impossible. I'm going home tomorrow. We both know that. You said it yourself the day after the fire—take what time we had together. We did." His eyes grew hard. "But no more. I'm not going to hurt either one of us anymore."

He turned and headed across the hall to his room. Cat felt her cheeks burn with humiliation. How could he end it? How could he just walk away from her like that?

Because their future together was up to her, that's why. She had known it was ever since she'd rejected his proposal. He wasn't going to make it easy for her. He wasn't going to ask again.

Then she would ask! She would lay her pride on the line and risk rejection just as he had done.

She looked at the door to his room, her heart

317

pounding. If she was going over there, she would need some kind of buffer. Quickly she hurried down to the lobby and had the startled clerk retrieve her saddlebags from the safe.

Back upstairs, she pounded on the door to Logan's room. He threw open the door, his gaze raking her angrily. But in that instant, she knew his anger was a defense. He did want her. Badly. And tonight she was not above using his passion against him. There was too much at stake not to.

"What the hell do you think you're doing?" he demanded.

"Paying a debt." She stomped into his room.

"I told you it isn't safe for you to be carrying that money around."

She tossed the saddlebags onto his bed. "And I told you I pay my debts."

"Fine. Pay me and then"—he stiffened perceptibly—"you'll have to leave."

"Of course," she replied innocently. "What else would I be doing?"

She grabbed up the saddlebags and stepped behind his dressing screen. "I'll count it out back here."

If he thought her actions peculiar, he said nothing. Cat flipped open the saddlebags and extracted the little extra something she'd packed when she'd left home five weeks ago. Before her courage fled, she quickly donned the ivory peignoir. Then she stepped from behind the screen.

Logan sucked in his breath, his gray eyes dark with what it cost him to remain on the opposite side of the room. Feigning complete indifference to whatever he chose to do, Cat gathered up the saddlebags and stepped back over to the bed. "Now let me see," she said, pulling

318

out several packets of money. "If I counted this right . . ." She leaned forward, allowing the fullness of her breasts to spill against the filmy material of the peignoir.

"Damn you," he murmured. "What do you think I'm made of?"

"Flesh and blood, I hope," she breathed, her indifference crumbling in the face of the undisguised longing she saw in his eyes. "Because I want you, Logan. I want you so much."

He was across the room in two strides, pulling her fiercely against him. "Damn you," he murmured over and over, even as he rained kisses across her cheeks, her chin, her neck.

"I love you, Logan. I love you."

They tumbled onto the bed, clothes flying everywhere. He had no patience for preliminaries; that whole evening he'd been in near constant arousal at just being with her. When he thrust himself inside her he thought he would fly apart from the sweet ecstasy of it, and groaned when she locked her legs around him, driving him deeper into her welcoming folds.

It was madness, sheer madness to give himself up to loving her one last night. But he couldn't help it, couldn't stop it. He loved her. Loved her. He cried her name as together they found the sweet, sweet light of paradise.

Much later, with Cat snuggled securely in his arms, he noticed the saddlebags lying forgotten on the room's floral carpet. "I'd better take the money down to the safe," he said.

Her arms tightened around his chest. "Don't leave me."

Smiling, he kissed the top of her head. "I'm not going

to have this money up here all night."

Cat pouted as he climbed out of bed and shoved his legs into his trousers.

Tell him, her mind pleaded, *tell him you've changed your mind, that you want to go with him, that you'll give up the ranch for him.* . . .

"Logan, I—"

The door crashed open. Cat stared in horror as three masked men stormed into the room.

Chapter Twenty=Four

Cat couldn't move. She sat on the bed, clutching the bedcovers against her and stared at the gun in the first outlaw's hand. And then she couldn't see him, because Logan shifted so he was between her and the gunman. The other two masked men had their six-guns drawn as well. All three revolvers were now taking dead aim on Logan.

"Don't shoot!" Cat shrieked, half sobbing.

"Nobody moves, nobody gets hurt," the bullishly built second outlaw said.

All three men wore ordinary trail clothes, their gunnysack masks making it impossible to tell even the color of their hair. Yet there was something familiar about the first one, the apparent leader. His clothes were nondescript, but Cat watched the way he carried himself, the way he swaggered about the room. When he spoke, it was in a raspy whisper, as though perhaps his normal speaking voice would be recognized.

"Get them hands up," the outlaw hissed to Logan.

Logan raised his hands. Barefoot, he was clad only in

his denims and an unbuttoned shirt. Cat bit her lip. She was still naked beneath the bedcovers.

"Now isn't this a purty scene," the outlaw said, coming closer to the bed. "Real purty."

"Stay away from her," Logan said, his voice deadly calm and somehow menacing, even though he was facing three loaded guns.

"And what are you going to do, if I don't?" the man sneered.

"Kill you," Logan said.

For an instant the outlaw leader hesitated, then Cat watched the gunnysack puff out where the man's mouth would be as he blew out a derisive snort. He levered back the hammer of his Colt. "Why don't we just see you do that?"

"No!" Cat cried. "Please."

The man lowered the hammer, but his next words made it clear his actions had nothing to do with Cat's plea. "We don't really want any loud noises, do we? But I'll tell you what we do want." He looked around the room and spied the saddlebags on the floor. "That better be what I think it is." He ambled over to the leather pouches.

Cat knew—*knew*—she had seen that walk before . . . *heard* it. . . .

The spurs! The spurs on his boots jangled as he moved, big Mexican spurs with vicious rowels.

Latigo.

"Rafe Latigo." She hadn't meant to say the name aloud. The man's head jerked up, his eyes narrowing ominously.

"So, little Miss Wildcat," he said, "you know who I am."

Cat felt tears sting her eyes, and wondered if she had just condemned Logan and herself to death.

"I told you we'd dance one day, missy," the man said, striding back over to the bed. "But I was hopin' to surprise you once I got you out of town."

"She's not going anywhere with you," Logan said.

"Maybe you haven't got it figured out," Latigo growled. "I'm the one with the gun." He signaled the other two men to keep their guns pointed at Cat; then he approached Logan. "I got a score to settle with you, too, mister. Maybe it's about time I got started."

With a lightning motion he slashed his gun at Logan's head. Logan staggered back, blood streaming from the jagged gash the gun barrel opened in his cheek.

"Logan!" Cat instinctively reached toward him, though she didn't loosen her grip on the bedcovers.

He held up a restraining hand. "I'm all right," he said, though it was obvious he wasn't. He used his shirtsleeve to swipe at the blood.

"Keep an eye on her," Latigo warned his two companions.

"Where's she gonna go buck naked?" the thickly built one leered.

"I know where I wanna go," the scrawnier one said, making an obscene gesture with his crotch.

Cat shrunk back, more terrified than she had ever been. Her eyes darted toward Logan's cane propped in the far corner of the room—out of reach and woefully outmatched against three guns. She cursed silently, wishing she and Logan had been in her room instead. She had her Colt in the other saddlebags.

"Get dressed," Latigo told her, though he didn't look at her.

Her heart thundering, Cat clambered out of the bed, all the while maintaining a death grip on the blankets. Never taking her eyes from the two nearest outlaws, she backed across the room and ducked behind the dressing screen. That Latigo had told her to dress surprised her, but she harbored no illusions that the man was acting out of concern for her feelings. Nor did she have any illusions that her humiliation at the hands of these men was at an end.

Because she had nothing else, she was forced to dress in the green silk. Her cheeks burned as she imagined these men gawking at the gown's revealing bodice. She had worn the dress for Logan. Now she wished she'd stayed in her trail garb. Struggling, she fastened the hooks herself. She would rather die than have these men touch her.

Taking a deep breath to steady her nerves, she stepped from behind the screen. The outlaws hooted lewdly. Cat looked only at Logan.

His eyes were glazed with fury, and she feared he would do something reckless. She'd barely thought it before he launched himself at Latigo. The outlaw fell back, spewing curses.

Logan connected solidly with Latigo's jaw, then doubled him over with a blow to his midsection. Latigo groaned and was seeking to straighten when Logan brought his fist down on the back of the outlaw's neck.

It had all happened so fast, the other two outlaws barely had time to react. Cat bolted for Logan's swordstick, deciding the weapon was better than none at all. But she was too late. The thickset outlaw blocked her path and leveled his gun at her face.

"You'd best back off, mister," the man snarled at

Logan. "Or you ain't gonna have nothin' worth fightin' for."

Logan raised up, releasing his hold on Latigo's shirtfront. The Rocking R foreman sagged back to the floor. Logan's own shoulders slumped as he realized his defeat.

Latigo struggled to sit up, blood leaking from his split lips. He pushed himself to a standing position and lurched toward Logan. "I'll kill you, you bastard."

Logan didn't move. He couldn't. Cat closed her eyes. It was because of her that he could no longer defend himself. If he did, they would kill her.

Tears streaming down her cheeks, she watched as Latigo shoved Logan toward the ladder-back chair abutting the wall. Using the rope the scrawny one tossed him, Latigo quickly secured Logan to the chair.

"Now I pay you back, bastard," Latigo hissed. "Now I kill you."

Latigo hit Logan once, twice. Each time Logan's head whipsawed back and snapped forward. He didn't make a sound. The only emotion Cat could read in his eyes besides hate for Latigo was a quiet despair when he looked at her, because he couldn't help her.

When Latigo drew his fist back in a full arc, Cat started to scream.

Latigo whirled. "One more sound," he said, "and I slit his throat. You understand?"

She covered her mouth with her hand, not trusting herself to keep silent any other way. Latigo hit Logan again. And again.

Logan's lips were cracked and bleeding, his left eye was beginning to swell. *Stop it, stop it,* her mind shouted, though not a word passed her lips. Even a whispered plea

325

for mercy could prod Latigo into making good on his threat of murder.

But as Latigo continued to brutalize Logan, Cat realized with a dawning horror that Logan might well die from the beating itself. His head already lolled listlessly from side to side as Latigo pummeled him. Cat feared he was unconscious.

She sank to her knees. "Please," she whispered. "I beg you. Stop."

Latigo paused, one fist still upraised. "You beg me?" he taunted, clearly interested in this Cat Jordan he had never seen before. "What's it worth to you for me to let him live?"

"Anything," she murmured. "Anything."

Latigo gripped a handful of Logan's hair, peering closely at him. He let go in disgust, Logan's head snapping back, then sagging forward, unmoving. "Let me get this straight," he said, taking a step toward Cat, "I let him live, and you'll walk out of this hotel with us, no screaming?"

She swallowed the bile that rose in her throat. "Yes."

"One word," Latigo repeated, "and one of us comes back and finishes him off. Understood?"

She nodded. "I promise."

Latigo took the bandana from around his neck and stuffed it in Logan's mouth; then he took a second bandana and tied it off as a gag.

"Let's go have that dance, shall we, missy?" Latigo said, smirking. He gestured toward the door.

"I love you, Logan," Cat said, taking one last look at his bruised and bloodied face. She said it again, even knowing he couldn't hear her.

"You love him, eh?" Latigo mocked. "I'll just bet you loved him real good in that bed tonight. Well, we'll see who's the better man, missy. We'll just see, won't we?" He shoved her toward the door.

He opened it first and checked the hall to make sure no one was about, then he led Cat and the others down the back stairs. Everything in her wanted to scream, but she knew with a chilling certainty that Latigo would make good on his promise to kill Logan, even if he had to do it with his last breath.

She knew with the same chilling certainty that these men would have their way with her tonight. And then they would kill her. Her only solace was that she had saved Logan.

Latigo led them to four horses tied off behind the hotel. They had planned all along to take her with them. The thought made her stomach churn. Latigo tied her wrists, then had her mount a roan gelding. He then secured a lead rope to the gelding's neck and dallied his end of the rope around his saddle horn.

The four of them headed silently out of town. They'd ridden only a short distance past Abilene's outer limits when Latigo reined in. The others did the same. He shifted in the saddle, pointing to his smaller *compadre*. "Go back and finish him off."

"No!" Cat jerked the gelding's reins hard, trying to unseat Latigo, to free the dallied rope. But he was too fast. He cuffed her on the side of the head with his fist, holding fast to the lead rope. "You said you'd let him live!" she screamed.

"I lied."

The gaunt outlaw rode out, heading back to Abilene at

327

a gallop.

Latigo's laughter seemed to echo from everywhere, the trees, the rocks, the smothering darkness. Cat felt her world shattering, collapsing. When the outlaw returned, it would be because Logan was dead.

Chapter Twenty-Five

Logan fought his way back to consciousness. His body fought him, sought to slip back into the pain-free world, but he wouldn't let it. Cat needed him. That was the reality that drove him past the agony, the throbbing agony that sluiced through every fiber of his being.

He tried and failed to open his eyes. His left eye felt thick, swollen. He tried harder to open the right, feeling his lashes tug free of the congealed blood that had trailed down from his forehead. He blinked, once, twice, trying to shift his head to scan the room.

His pain-fogged brain tried to sort out where he was, what had happened. The only clear thought he had was of Cat, that she was in desperate danger and he had to save her from it. He couldn't even remember what the danger was.

He tried to call out to her and almost choked. He couldn't move, he couldn't speak. Forcing himself to be still, he fought to think, to reason. The pain. What had caused the pain?

Latigo.

Latigo had beaten the hell out of him.

Latigo had Cat.

It all slammed back in one horrifying instant. Like a madman, Logan fought to free himself from the ropes that bound him, but they held tight. Again he forced himself to be calm. Slowly, rationally he assessed his circumstances. Slowly, rationally, he studied the room. It was then he noticed the shaving razor lying on the washstand next to the dressing screen.

Hunched, bound, he managed to maneuver himself and the chair across the room. Turning his back to the washstand, he felt for the razor and worked it laboriously across the blood-slickened ropes that bound his wrists.

Minutes ticked by. Twice he thought he was going to pass out. Once he thought he did. But he held onto the razor. Finally, his right hand jerked free. Yanking off the rest of his bindings, he leaned against the washstand and scooped handfuls of water onto his face.

Refusing to accept what he already knew to be true, Logan stumbled into the next room. He called Cat's name, his heart thudding, desperate for her to be there, to answer him.

She didn't.

The silence lashed him.

They had her. Three outlaws had the woman he loved. Logan staggered to the window, relieved at least to see that it was still night. Maybe they hadn't been gone all that long. Maybe if he could catch up with them quickly, he could keep them from . . .

His mind wouldn't complete the thought.

He would find her. He had to find her. They would kill

330

her when they finished with her. He started for the door, then straightened, half sobbing with frustration when he realized he didn't even know what direction they'd taken.

South, his mind reasoned. Latigo would go south, back to the Rocking R. It was a faint hope, but it was all he had.

Realizing he was still barefoot, he stumbled back to the bed and sat down. Allowing his head to sag forward so that he didn't pass out, he managed to pull on his boots.

Should he take the time to alert the law? No. Such a delay could cost Cat her life.

Wiping the last of the seeping blood from the cuts on his face, Logan grabbed up his cane and started toward the door. There he stopped, listening.

Had he heard something in the hall? The question was answered for him when the doorknob started to turn. He ducked behind the door and silently drew the sword from the cane.

A gun barrel poked into the room, gripped in the fist of one of the masked outlaws. Logan waited. The man had to be fully inside the room or he could bolt back into the hallway.

Logan didn't even breathe as the outlaw stepped toward the room's center, eying the empty chair to which Logan had been tied. He appeared nervous, uncertain. Suddenly the outlaw stiffened, started to turn.

Logan heaved himself against the door, his weight slamming it, body-long, against the outlaw. The man yelped in surprise, tumbling to the floor.

Logan slashed his sword across the intruder's gun hand. The Colt spun away.

"Don't kill me, mister!" the masked man pleaded,

331

throwing his hands over his masked face. "Latigo made me come back. Please, don't kill me."

Logan jerked the man's mask off. Doakes. The thief from the Henderson relay station. Logan gripped the man's shirtfront, his words coming through gritted teeth. "Where did Latigo take her? Where?"

The man trembled uncontrollably, but didn't answer. Logan shoved the sword point against his throat. "I'm not asking again."

"I'll show ya," he stammered. "I'll take ya there. Just don't kill me."

Logan shoved the outlaw ahead of him, down the back stairs of the hotel. He tied Doakes to his gelding, then led the horse through back alleys to the livery, where he quickly saddled his own horse.

Minutes later they rode out, Logan keeping Doakes's horse tethered to his own. It was all Logan could do to stay in the saddle. His head pounded in time to the gelding's hoofbeats. Thoughts of Cat and of what Latigo could be doing to her were all that kept him going.

When they were within a half-mile of the place Doakes was leading him, Logan pulled them both off the main road and dismounted. He didn't want to chance the horses giving them away.

At least the wind was in his favor, the breeze coming up from the south. He cocked an ear, listening, straining to hear anything, anything at all to tell him where Cat was.

"Any warning from you," Logan said to Doakes, "and you won't live to hear them say thank you."

"I won't say nothin'. Just don't kill me."

Logan tied and gagged Doakes, slipped the man's saddlebags from the gelding, then went back to his own horse and retrieved his cane. For several seconds he stood staring at the rifle in the saddle boot. Then he pulled it free and started south on foot, praying his long-ago adeptness at playing Comanche with Matt would stand him in good stead on this night. He didn't dare snap so much as a twig.

Memories swirled around him as he moved stealthily through the brush. Memories of the day he'd tracked that cougar with Matt. He paused, shaking. That was the last thing he needed to think about now. He couldn't think of anything but Cat.

He heard them then. They weren't even attempting to be quiet. It was obvious the only company they were expecting tonight was Doakes. On his belly now, Logan crawled as close to the camp as he dared. He had to gauge their positions, know what he was up against.

Latigo and Yerby were swapping a whiskey bottle, taking pulls on it in front of a campfire. Cat sat huddled between them. Though he couldn't tell at this distance, Logan was certain they had her tied.

When Latigo leaned over and planted a kiss on Cat's mouth, it was all Logan could do not to hurl himself across the fire and tear the man's heart out. He didn't just want to kill Latigo, he wanted to destroy him.

But he had to wait for the best chance. If he was caught, the outlaws would kill them both.

Slowly, he brought the rifle to bear. A cold sweat broke out on his forehead, the salt stinging still-fresh wounds. His vision blurred. He lowered the rifle, trembling—with rage . . . and something else. He had told Cat the truth. He was a lousy shot. He couldn't risk it. Couldn't or wouldn't? The trembling didn't stop.

333

Gripping the rifle in one hand the cane in the other, he crept closer to the fire.

Cat couldn't cry anymore. Crying wasn't going to save Logan. And it certainly wasn't going to save her. She had to get away. Logan would be all right. She'd already told herself that again and again. He would escape Doakes, come to her rescue. And she had to be alert when he found her.

She looked at Latigo with a quiet loathing. When he leaned close to her, the stink of whiskey on his breath almost made her gag. When he dared kiss her, she did gag.

The flames of the campfire leaped in his dark eyes, yellow light looking out from the black abyss of his soul. "I think it's about time for that dance I promised you, missy," he said. "I think it's just about time for that dance."

"Try it and I'll kill you," she spat out.

"And just how are you gonna do that?" he said, his words slurring. "I made sure those ropes were good and tight."

"A man like you would have to tie a woman." She sneered. "You couldn't get one any other way."

Yerby laughed.

Latigo slapped her, hard. "We'll see if I need to tie a woman. We'll see, missy." Frenzied, furious, he yanked on the ropes that bound her, the hemp burning into her flesh.

When the ropes fell away, Cat tried to rise. Latigo slammed a fist into her face. Bright lights exploded in Cat's head. She tasted the salty sweetness of her own blood. Terrified, she shook off the unconsciousness threatening to engulf her. If she passed out, she knew she would never wake up again.

She kicked and clawed, battling with every ounce of her strength, but Latigo was bigger, stronger. He drove her down, heaving his body atop hers, his hands pawing at her body, tearing at her dress.

Yerby stepped close. "Don't take it all, boss," he whined. "I want me some."

"She's mine until I say different," Latigo snarled. "You try to make somethin' of it and I'll kill you."

Yerby took a step back. Then everything seemed to happen at once. A shadow leaped out of the darkness. For a terrified heartbeat Cat thought it was Doakes returning, but the fire glinted off tempered steel. Logan's sword flashed through the night.

Yerby dragged his gun free of its holster, but Logan drove the sword into the man's chest before he could fire. Yerby slumped forward, dead.

Swearing savagely, Latigo rolled onto his back, dragging Cat atop him. In the same motion he pulled a six-inch knife from his boot.

"Come near me and I cut her," Latigo said.

"Let her go," Logan said. "This is between you and me."

Latigo snorted. "With that rifle in your hands? And that pig sticker? No thanks."

Logan dropped the weapons. "You and me, Latigo," he said.

Cat felt Latigo tense, then tighten his grip on the knife. "You'd just pick 'em up again," he said, his voice betraying his fear.

Latigo forced Cat to her feet. She could feel the knife blade press against her throat, his arm in a chokehold around her neck. She could scarcely breathe as he kept her in front of him and backed toward his horse. "You and me will have it out one day, mister," he said. "But it'll be on my terms. My say so."

Catching up the gelding's reins, Latigo shoved Cat away and vaulted into the saddle, then raked the gelding with his spurs. The horse leaped forward at a gallop.

Cat scrambled toward Logan. "Shoot him!" she screamed. "For God's sake, shoot him. He has the money!"

Logan picked up the rifle and brought it to bear, taking dead aim on the outlaw's back. But he didn't fire. Cat reached him, jerked the rifle away and took aim herself, but by then it was too late. Latigo had disappeared into the darkness.

"Why didn't you shoot him?" She was shaking, teetering on the edge of hysteria. "He took the money. The money for the ranch."

"It doesn't matter," he said, his voice strangely toneless. "You're safe."

"Safe!" Her voice was shrill. "The man tried to rape me! For God's sake, Logan. You could have shot him. Why didn't you? Why?" She wanted Latigo back there; she wanted Latigo dead.

"I'm sorry."

"Sorry! Sorry? He was going to kill me!"

"I'm sorry." He sank to his knees, and only then did Cat see the agony in him.

She forgot her anger, her fear, forgot everything but Logan. Rushing over to him, she dropped down beside

336

him. "Logan, my God, what is it?"

But he wasn't looking at her, he was staring off into nowhere. His voice was strangled. "Fifteen years ago I swore I would never fire a gun again in my life." He looked at her then, his eyes begging her to forgive him even before he said the words, "Fifteen years ago I shot your brother."

Chapter Twenty-Six

Cat huddled in front of the fire, staring across the flames at Logan as though she'd never seen him before. And perhaps, this Logan she hadn't. He was shaking, sick. His eyes were full of the past. A fifteen-year-old wound, festered and swollen, had tonight burst open.

"What do you mean you shot Matt?" she asked in a voice she didn't recognize as her own. She stepped around the fire to him. Automatically, she brought up the rifle. She doubted Latigo would be back. He had the money. He wouldn't stop riding until he hit Mexico. But she would be ready, just in case.

"It was . . . an accident," Logan said, his voice quavering. He sounded, heartbreakingly, like a boy, a twelve-year-old boy. "An accident. I didn't mean it. He knows I didn't. . . ." He swiped angrily at tears ages old. "I . . . swore I would never tell. I didn't mean to tell." He looked at her. "I didn't mean to tell. Never. Never."

She pulled him close, holding him, rocking him. She wanted to see to the cuts and bruises from Latigo's beating, but right then she sensed his physical injuries didn't matter. His pain went far deeper than any black eye. "Logan, it's all right. It's all right." Dear Lord, it had to be all right. Shot Matt? He couldn't have.

The shadows hovered near, but she wasn't dreaming. And for once she pushed them away. She couldn't— wouldn't—remember. Not now. Not when Logan needed her so badly.

"Tell me," she whispered. She wanted him free of this haunting memory. Whatever it was, she would make it better for him.

She cradled him against her, hearing the words, seeing the images through his eyes, feeling the horror as though she had lived it herself. . . .

Logan flexed the muscles of his forearm, grinning. Not bad for a twelve-year-old who three months ago could barely lift a ten-pound sack of cornmeal. He'd just tossed his seventh forty-pound sack of grain onto the growing pile of bags in the barn.

He paused to glower good-naturedly at the sandy-haired youth next to him. Matt had spent an inordinate amount of time unhitching the buckboard team and was only now coming back to help with offloading the grain. "Don't think I don't know what you're doing, Matt," Logan said. "Just because I'm not weak anymore you expect me to do all the hard work."

"I'm just doin' you a favor," Matt said, grinning. "I'm lettin' you keep those new muscles of yours a little while longer. When you go back to Boston next month, the most you'll be lifting is school books."

"I'm not going back to school," Logan pronounced. "I'm going to be like you. A rancher."

"You can't ranch in Boston," Matt scoffed. "All they've got are banks and wharfs."

"That's wharves."

"It's still stinkin' fish."

"I like lobster myself. And shrimp. You should try shrimp, Matt. Real tasty."

"I like beef."

"It does grow on you," Logan admitted, heaving another grain sack onto the double-column stack he was making in the corner of the barn. He'd developed quite a taste for beefsteak since he'd arrived in Texas almost three months ago. But it would be more than beef he would miss when he went back to Boston. Matt had opened new worlds for him here—teaching him about life outdoors, teaching him even more about friendship. Having been privately tutored, Logan had rarely had the opportunity to meet anyone his own age.

He finished shifting the last sack as a blond-haired bundle of unrestrained energy barreled up to him. The tiny girl pounced on the nearest pile, nearly toppling his morning's efforts.

"Get lost, Corie," Matt groused, grabbing her about the waist and setting her on her feet. "You're going to get yourself hurt and then Ma's going to yell at me."

Corie straightened indignantly, drawing up to her full three-and-a-half-foot height. "I can play in the barn if I want to."

"Not now you can't," Matt said. "This is boys' stuff. So get lost."

"I don't want to get lost, Matt. If I do I won't be able to find you."

Matt rolled his eyes. "You are so dumb, Corie. How'd I ever get such a dumb sister?"

Logan watched Corie's lower lip jut out in a fearsome pout. "Matt Jordan, you're mean! I'm going to tell Mama, if you don't stop it this minute."

"Tell her what you want. Mama's always babyin' you. Funny you can even feed yourself." He yanked at her hair ribbons, undoing one carefully tied yellow bow. "You've even got Pa puttin' these sissy things in your hair."

Corie drew her foot back and booted Matt in the shin.

"Yoww! Why you little—" Matt made a lunge for her and missed.

Logan caught Matt's shirtsleeve. "Leave her be," he said. "She's just a little girl. She doesn't know any better."

"Yeah, Matt," Corie pouted. "I don't know any better."

"She knows just fine," Matt grumbled. "Ma spoils her rotten. Anything she wants she gets."

"Mothers probably like to do that to little girls," Logan said. "Get 'em dressed up and such. Give 'em dolls."

"Baby stuff," Matt said.

"I am not a baby!" Corie shrieked.

"Hush, now," Logan said, putting his finger to his lips. "You don't want to give away our secret location to the Indians do you?"

Corie's eyes widened. "Injuns, Log'n?"

"Yeah," Matt said, "and they love to scalp little blond-headed girls!"

Corie shrieked again.

Logan hunkered down and put an arm around her, though he felt awkward doing so. "I'm not going to let any Indian scalp you," he assured her. "If one even tries it he'll have to answer to me."

341

Corie smiled a little. "Thanks, Log'n."

He didn't know why Matt had to be so mean to her. She was a cute little thing. And nice as anything too, if you treated her nice. He supposed there was some secret rule about being a brother that caused Matt to be so ornery to Corie. But he wouldn't have been that way with her.

"I wish you were my brother instead of Matt," she said with a shy smile. "Matt doesn't like me."

"Sure he does. He's just teasin'."

She was unconvinced. "Would you be my brother, Log'n? Would you?"

"If you want."

She smiled. "Can I tell you a secret, Log'n?"

"Sure, what is it?"

She leaned close and whispered in his ear. "I love you, Logan."

He blushed furiously. "I'm real glad, Corie."

"Do you want to play with my doll?"

"I'd better not. Matt would start teasin' me, too."

"I s'pose." She started off toward the house, then turned back to gaze at him with those trusting green eyes. "Do you think Buttons is in heaven, Logan?"

"I know he is. He's in heaven chasin' butterflies."

She sighed happily. "I sure do love you, Logan. You can come back and be my brother every summer."

"Thanks, Corie. I'd like that a lot."

She left then, and Logan returned his attention to the grain sacks, adjusting them squarely against the barn wall. Could visits to the Circle J really become a summer tradition? Matt had mentioned the possibility more than once, but Hadley had seemed less than enthusiastic. Logan knew the elder Jordan worried about Matt's increasingly reckless behavior, and wondered openly if

342

Logan's presence exacerbated Matt's need to show off.

Logan sighed and headed for the back of the barn. He would see if Matt wanted to go out for a ride now that their chores were done for the day. He hadn't taken two steps when a black-caped figure leaped from a shadowed stall, an unearthly noise issuing from its throat.

"Blast it all, Matt!" Logan hissed, his heart thudding. "Why do you do things like that?"

But Matt was on the floor, curled into a ball, laughing hysterically. "I got you! I got you!"

Logan shook his head. "You're not funny."

"Can't you take a joke? I thought I taught you better than that."

"Scaring people isn't funny," Logan said, hands on his hips.

"Yes, it is!" Matt said. "You should have seen your face!"

Logan grimaced, but quickly forgave his friend. They spent the rest of the afternoon roughhousing in the barn, though both barely missed breaking their necks when they soared out the loft window and misjudged their haystack landings.

"Must be dinner time," Logan said, brushing the dirt from his trousers. "We'd best go in. Your ma gets awful mad when we're late."

Matt caught Logan's arm. "Wait. I need to talk to you about somethin' first."

Logan didn't miss the sly look in his friend's eyes. He had a feeling he wasn't going to like what he was about to hear. Matt didn't disappoint him.

"Tomorrow," Matt whispered conspiratorially, "we're going after that cougar Pa was talkin' about at breakfast."

"Are you out of your mind?"

343

"Keep your voice down!" Matt cautioned, looking around quickly lest anyone be near enough to overhear. Satisfied no one was about he pulled Logan into the nearest stall and again spoke in low tones. "That cougar's killed three of Pa's best yearlin's. You and me are going to catch it and kill it and nail its hide to the barn door!"

"Your pa would have our hides on the barn door if we even tried it," Logan said. "You seen how mad your pa was when you killed his mare last week. He said no more huntin' for either one of us."

"That was before the cougar got the third yearlin' last night."

"That doesn't matter a whit and you know it. It was your lyin' that made him so mad!"

"Don't talk about that," Matt warned. "You said you wouldn't."

Logan scuffed at the hay strewn about the dirt floor. "I'm sorry. But it's like *my* pa says, anybody can make a mistake. What counts is the guts to own up to it. You didn't own up to it."

"What counts with my pa is killin' that cougar. And we're gonna do it."

A shadow appeared in the large entryway. Startled, both boys looked guiltily toward the bow-legged cowboy walking toward them.

"What mischief are you two cookin' up now?" Dusty asked.

"Nothin'," Matt lied, though he didn't look the wrangler in the eye.

Logan grimaced. Matt lied too darned easy sometimes. It was a bad habit, one that was going to get him in real trouble some day.

"You listen to me," Dusty said, "I know you too well,

344

Matt Jordan. I watched your eyes light up when your pa was talkin' about that cougar at breakfast. If you have one ounce of sense in that head of yours you won't even think about trackin' that cat. You hear?"

"Pa tol' me not to go huntin', Dusty," Matt said with such an air of feigned innocence that it was all Logan could do not to choke.

"I know what he told you," Dusty said, obviously not falling for Matt's act. "Now I'm tellin' you. If I even think you're gonna do it, I'm goin' straight to your pa, and I won't feel a lick o' guilt when he takes a strap to your backside." He shifted his Stetson back, scratching his head and eying Matt critically. "You give me your word you won't do it, and we won't say anything more about it."

Matt didn't even hesitate. "I give you my word, Dusty," he said solemnly, holding his right hand in the air.

"That's more like it." Dusty tousled Matt's hair and headed back out of the barn.

"Thank heaven," Logan said.

"What for?" Matt asked.

"We're not goin' after the cougar."

"Who said we're not?"

"*You* just said. You gave Dusty your word."

"I want that horse my pa promised me," Matt said. "If that means I have to say somethin' to Dusty to keep him off'n our butts, then I will. Tomorrow, Logan, we're going after that cat. And when I kill it, Pa'll be too happy to be mad at me."

"We can't." Logan wasn't just thinking of Matt's having given his word. He was thinking about future summers on the Circle J. If anything went wrong on their cougar hunt, Logan was certain Hadley would forbid him to return to Texas—not to punish Logan, but to punish Matt.

"You don't want to see me ridin' that danged pony again next summer, do you?" Matt asked dejectedly.

And just that suddenly Logan saw killing the cougar as a way of assuring his return. Hadley would be pleased to have the big cat dead. All Logan had to do was make certain nothing went wrong. Surely if he were extra careful, he could keep his friend out of trouble. "All right," Logan said. "We'll do it."

The next morning they told everyone they were going out riding, looking for arrowheads.

"Be careful," Hadley warned, as the boys mounted their ponies. "Stay clear of the ridge. Dusty saw sign of that cat up there yesterday."

"We will, Pa," Matt said.

They rode out, deliberately heading in the direction opposite the ridge, but soon circled back. By noon they were both on foot, casting about for cougar tracks.

They paused at the base of the ridge. Logan peered upward, shading his eyes against the blinding sun high in the sky. Wind-twisted cedars bristled all along a narrow series of switchbacks that led to the ridge top. The boulder-strewn summit would be unreachable on horse-back.

"I bet he's hidin' out in them rocks," Matt said, tying off Jingles to a clump of scrub brush.

"We're going to climb up there?" Logan asked incredulously.

"How else are we going to catch him?"

"We could wait here. Hope he comes down to stalk the herd."

"I ain't waitin'," Matt said. "I want that cougar pelt on

346

my bedroom wall. And I want it now."

From somewhere above them the cougar screamed, the sound sending an eerie chill up Logan's spine. "I think he heard you."

"Get your gun ready."

Logan checked the Spencer. The carbine held six shots, but somehow he doubted he'd have time for more than one. His heart was pounding, sweat beading on his forehead. He had a terrible feeling about this. But he couldn't tell Matt. Matt would just call him a baby, tell him he was no better to have along than Corie.

"Let's go," Matt said, his whole face alive with excitement. Reluctantly, Logan followed as Matt started up the slope.

Again the cat screamed. Logan took long deep breaths, telling himself everything was going to be all right.

"Dusty told me once he heard about a cougar that killed three men," Matt said, as they clambered up the narrow animal path.

"At the same time?"

"Yep."

Logan swallowed. "Maybe we'd best go back."

"Don't tell me you're scared!" Matt howled.

"Of course I'm scared," Logan blurted. "And if you had a lick o' sense you'd be scared too."

Matt only laughed. "Know what that ol' cougar did to those men after he killed 'em? He ate 'em!"

Logan felt the blood draining from his face.

"Dusty even said one old trapper got his leg chewed off by a mountain lion whilst he was still alive!"

"Stop it!" Logan hissed. "You're just sayin' that! You want me to be scared. You want the cougar all to yourself."

"We should separate now," Matt said, stopping at a

point where the trail forked to the left and right. "Come at him from both sides."

"I think we should stay together."

"This'll give us a better chance at him."

Matt circled away. Logan's skin crawled as he heard the cougar screaming from the rocks above them.

He crept forward, every sense alert.

A noise in the brush to his left startled him. He brought the Spencer to his shoulder, his heart threatening to explode in his chest.

With a spine-shilling screech Matt leaped from behind the bush, his arms raised, his hands curved downward like mock claws.

Something, Logan would never know what, something prevented him from squeezing the trigger. His arms jerked, the barrel of the gun slamming downward. "Gawd damn you, Matt!" he screamed. "I almost killed you!"

Matt only laughed. "Come on!" he called, waving Logan forward. "Let's get that cat!"

Logan saw it then, perched atop a boulder barely a dozen feet from where they stood. Matt stopped dead, his rifle clattering to the dirt. He stood, transfixed, his throat making strange, gasping sounds.

Desperately, Logan brought his carbine up. His foot skidded on a pebble. He tumbled backward, landing on his butt in the dirt, the shot firing wildly into the air. The cat sprang. Matt screamed, his arms instinctively curving over his head. From the ground Logan cocked the Spencer and fired again.

Matt kept on screaming as the cat raced off into the brush.

Logan scrambled forward on his knees. Matt's hands were wrapped around his leg, blood seeping through his fingers at a terrifying rate.

"Oh, God, Matt, I'm sorry!" He tried to pry his friends fingers from the wound, but Matt wouldn't let go."

"I'll go get your pa," Logan shouted.

"No!" Matt grabbed Logan's arm. "No! Help me up. The cougar could come back. Help me!"

Logan hooked an arm around Matt and half dragged, half carried his friend back down the trail. When they reached the horses, Matt collapsed. Quickly, Logan tore at Matt's pantleg and checked the ugly hole his bullet had made just below Matt's knee.

"It went clean through," Matt said, almost wonderingly. "It ain't so bad. It just stung a bit for a minute or two."

"I'm so sorry, Matt. I'm so sorry. I didn't mean it."

"I know you didn't." He said the words through clenched teeth. Logan could tell Matt was trying hard not to cry. "You can't tell anybody I was scared," Matt said. "Promise you won't say nothin' about me bein' scared. Promise."

"I won't say anything. I was scared to death myself. Damn, Matt, I'm sorry." He hurried over to the saddlebags and retrieved a spare bandana. With trembling fingers he wrapped it tightly around Matt's wound. Still the blood seeped through. "I've got to get your pa!"

"No!" Matt's face was ashen, but determined. "You can't bring him here. You can't tell him what happened."

"How can we not tell him?" Logan demanded. "I shot you!"

"Just shut up a minute. Let me think."

Logan got his canteen and poured water on Matt's wound. He pulled the bandana from around his neck and added it to the bandage. At last the blood flow seemed to stop.

"There," Matt said. "It'll be all right. It'll be fine. You'll see." He bit his lip. "I got it! We'll tell Pa I fell. So if I limp, he won't think anything of it."

"No, Matt, no more schemin'. We've got to tell him the truth. You need a doctor."

Tears glittered in Matt's eyes. "If we tell Pa, I won't get that horse 'til I'm twenty-seven. You can't tell, Logan. Promise me you won't tell. Promise me."

Matt's grip on Logan's arm was so tight, Logan could feel his hand tingle and grow cold from lack of circulation. "Your pa won't be mad at you," he reasoned desperately. "It's my fault. I shot you."

"We were huntin' that cougar. Why else would we have our guns out? Pa will know. Logan, please, please, if you're my friend, you won't tell. You won't tell."

Logan shuddered. "All right. I won't tell."

"You promise? You swear on a stack of Bibles?"

"I promise."

"No matter what my pa says, no matter what he asks you?"

"I said I promise!" Logan gritted. "I'll never tell anyone. Ever."

Matt relaxed a little then. "You'll have to sneak into the house and get me a clean pair of britches."

Logan's shoulders sagged. This was getting worse by the minute. They were never going to pull it off. But there was no going back on his word.

Near dusk, they returned to the ranch and made it into the barn undetected. Logan went through Matt's window into the house and brought them back both a change of clothes. Logan's own shirt and trousers were smeared with Matt's blood. He would have to wash them out later.

As carefully as he knew how, Logan tied off Matt's wound with two clean bandanas. "It looks bad, Matt," he said, hoping his friend would change his mind about hiding the injury.

He didn't.

For the next three days Logan and Matt stayed close to home. Whenever no adults were around, Logan did his best to do Matt's share of the chores. Matt hobbled painfully when they were alone, but somehow managed to hide even a limp when anyone came around.

Logan had to admire Matt's courage. But each day Logan's fears grew. Matt seemed more and more pale under his deep tan.

On the afternoon of the third day Logan was cleaning out the stalls in the barn, when Matt sagged to the floor beside him.

"Matt!" Logan felt his friend's forehead. He was burning up.

"I'm okay," Matt said, his voice weak, faraway.

"No, you're not."

"Are you playing cowboys and Indians?" Corie asked, sauntering into the barn.

"No," Matt said. "Just go away, Corie."

"You've been telling me to go away all the time," she said, pouting. "Even you, Logan."

"We don't have time to play right now," Logan said. "Matt and I have chores to finish up." He wanted Corie out of there. He wanted to check Matt's leg again.

"I could help," Corie said. "Mama said to come out and play. Just tell me how to help."

Matt sucked in a deep breath, trembling violently.

Logan whirled on Corie. "Get out of here! Now!"

Her eyes went wide with hurt. Without another word

she turned and ran from the barn.

Logan helped Matt ease off his trousers. The injured boy sat rigidly still, his hands balled into white-knuckled fists, while Logan gently eased the bandana away from the wound. Congealed blood came away with it and a vile-smelling pus. "Oh, God, Matt," Logan murmured. "I'm getting a doctor."

"You promised."

"I didn't promise I'd let you die!"

Hadley Jordan's voice carried to them from outside the barn. "What the hell are you two up to, scaring Corie half to death. I ought to . . ." He halted in the barn door, his gaze locking on where Logan's hands rested on Matt's leg.

"We were playing," Matt said, words rushing out of him in an explosive rush. "It was three days ago. Logan pushed me. He didn't mean to, but I fell on the pitchfork. Logan didn't want to get in trouble. He was afraid you'd send him home. He asked me not to say anything. Don't get mad, Pa. Don't keep me from getting my horse. Logan made me promise. Logan made me."

Hadley knelt down in front of his son, his face growing gray as he studied the wound. Without a word he scooped Matt into his arms and carried him to the house. Olivia saw them, followed them to Matt's room.

"What happened?" she asked.

"An accident," Hadley said. "I'm going for the doctor."

Olivia's hand flew to her mouth when she saw Matt's leg. "What happened?" she asked again, more shrilly.

"Logan," Matt gasped. "It was Logan, Ma. He pushed me. He pushed me."

Olivia looked at Logan, confused, frightened. She smoothed damp hair away from Matt's forehead. Matt lapsed into delirium soon after. Logan hovered nearby, wide-eyed, terrified, silent, until at last Olivia said, "I think you'd better go outside."

Then he fled.

Hours later the doctor came. Logan crept back into the kitchen, listening. Sanderson had Olivia and Hadley sit down. He spoke to them in hushed tones. Olivia screamed then, a horrible keening sound, before she stood and flew at Logan in a rage.

"How could you have done such a thing?" she shrieked. "Why didn't you tell us? Matthew is going to lose his leg! Do you hear me? He's going to lose his leg because of you. He's going to be a cripple because of you!"

"I . . . I'm sorry." Logan felt tears scalding his cheeks. "I'm sorry."

Olivia arced her hand back and slapped Logan hard across the cheek. She would have hit him again if Hadley hadn't intervened.

"Leave him be," he said. "What's done is done."

"He crippled Matthew. Elizabeth Blackstone's brat crippled my son!"

Corie came in then, carrying her doll clutched tightly to her chest. "Why is Log'n crying? Why is Matt sick?" Her green eyes were wide with fear, but she came over to Logan's side, gazing up trustingly at her mother. "Can you make it better, Ma?" she asked.

"No, Cordelia," Olivia said. "Nothing can make it better. Not anymore." She hurried from the room.

"Papa?" Corie said tentatively.

"It's all right, sweetheart," Hadley said, ruffling her hair. "It'll be fine." He, too, headed toward Matt's room.

"Don't cry, Logan," Corie said. "I don't want you to cry."

"I'm all right, Corie," he said, though his voice shook. He straightened, swiping at his eyes. His gaze trailed toward Matt's room.

"Why is everyone so sad?" Corie asked forlornly.

"Matt's real sick, Corie. Real sick."

"Is he going to die?"

"No!" he snapped, then added more gently, "Of course not. But he's going to be sick a long time."

Logan didn't want to, but he headed down the corridor to Matt's room. He stood outside, watching. The doctor hovered over the bed, while Olivia and Hadley stood on opposite sides of the room—Hadley stoic, watchful; Olivia close to hysteria.

The doctor looked at them, shaking his head. "I'm sorry. There's just no other way to save his life."

Olivia came over and sat on the bed, taking Matt's hand in hers. "My poor baby. My poor sweet baby." She turned on Hadley. "You were always making him be such a man. He tried to be so tough, so strong, and see what it's gotten him. See what you've done!"

"What's . . . happening?" Matt asked, his voice all but inaudible.

"Be still, boy," Hadley said. "It has to be. The leg's festered. There's no other way."

He looked at his mother. "Mama . . . ?"

Olivia sobbed quietly.

"I have to take the leg, son," the doctor said. "You'll die if I don't."

"Cut it off?" Matt's whole body began to shake.

Logan would never forget the screams that followed. He bolted for the door, sobbing. He didn't stop running

354

until he reached the barn. Inside, he fell to his knees sobbing, sobbing.

In the darkness, in his agony, he stopped crying only once—when he raised his hand to God and swore he would never fire a gun again as long as he lived.

Logan pulled away from Cat, and Cat instantly missed his warmth. He rose and stalked away from the fire. Cat followed. "Logan . . . ?" To ask how he was feeling seemed utterly inadequate.

"I promised," he said wearily. "I promised I'd never say a word."

"It wasn't your fault. None of it. You should never have had to make that promise."

"But I did."

Cat felt her eyes burn with unshed tears. Logan Blackstone had given his word, and now his sense of honor damned him for breaking it. She stepped up to him, wrapped her arms around him from behind.

He stiffened. She closed her eyes and hugged him tighter. She knew he wasn't rejecting her. It was only that his pain was so fresh, so raw. And his guilt too. And she had seen it in him when he'd refused to shoot Latigo. And now, when it was the last emotion he should feel, he felt it anyway—for exposing a fifteen-year-old secret made to a friend who'd had no right to ask for his silence.

She relaxed her hold on him slightly, resting her head on the broad expanse of his back. "You thought I would hate you, didn't you? That I wouldn't understand."

"I shot your brother."

"By accident. And if you hadn't shot when you did, that cougar might well have killed him, killed you both."

355

"Matt didn't see it that way."

"Matt's own foolishness cost him his leg, not you. He knew better than to track that cat."

"I should've stopped him."

"How? Tied him to a tree? Even if you'd told my father what he'd planned to do, Matt would have found a way to do it anyway. It was the way he was." She turned Logan to face her, reaching a hand up to feather it along his jaw. "How could he ever have blamed you?"

"I went in to see him a couple of days after the operation. He was so bitter, so angry. It was almost like he believed the pitchfork story. He hated me. We had been best friends, and he hated me. That hurt. God, that hurt. I was glad I was leaving that day. I ran outside to where your father had the buckboard ready to take me to the stage station."

"Pa knew, didn't he?"

"On the way to the stage he told me he knew it was no pitchfork wound in Matt's leg. He said he'd talked to Dusty, and together they'd pieced together what had likely happened." He looked at Cat. "Your father waited for me to confirm what he said, but I never did. He never asked me straight out, he just knew."

He pulled away from her then and went to put out the campfire. "We'll take Yerby's body and Doakes back to the law in Abilene, send a telegram to Fletcher about Latigo."

"You think he'll go back to Red Springs?"

"I know he will. He wasn't acting on his own."

She gasped. "Ryan? You think Ryan was behind this? No," she shook her head, "I can't believe he'd want the Circle J badly enough to kill for it."

"Who else would send Latigo here?"

356

"Latigo could have just . . . just decided . . ." But she didn't believe it. Not for a minute. Her thoughts took the inevitable next step. "Do you think Ryan had my father killed?"

"I'm afraid that's a very real possibility."

A searing rage shot through her. "I'll see him hanged. If he killed my father, I swear I'll see Ryan Fielding at the end of a rope!"

"I'll drag him up to the gallows myself," Logan promised, "but right now we have to concentrate on getting word to Fletcher."

"Are you going to tell Toby to arrest Ryan?"

"No. We've got no proof, not without Latigo. I'll fill Fletcher in, but the most we can ask for is that he keep an eye on the Rocking R, watch for Latigo."

"Latigo's got the money. Why won't he just head for Mexico?"

Logan managed a slight smile. "He'll head back to Fielding. Latigo doesn't have the money."

Her eyes widened. "He what?"

Logan walked to the tree near which Latigo's horse had been tethered. He bent to retrieve the saddlebags on the ground behind it. "I traded Doakes's saddlebags for Latigo's. Maybe he'll be halfway to Mexico before he notices, but when he does he'll head for Fielding. He'll want some compensation for all his trouble."

A single tear tracked down her cheek. "You saved the ranch. You saved the Circle J."

"Even if he'd taken the money, the ranch would be yours. Latigo stole the money from me, not you."

When she started to protest, he held up his hand. "Don't."

Cat had no strength to argue. She clutched the

357

saddlebags to her, but the feeling of elation she might have expected was not there. Instead she felt strangely bereft. The Circle J was hers. Logan had just provided her with an iron-clad reason to stay in Texas.

Stay in Texas, while he went back to Boston. Because there wasn't a doubt in her mind that that was what he intended to do once all this business with Latigo and Fielding was resolved.

He'd never repeated his offer that she come with him. And tonight, when he'd shared the most painful memories of his life with her, it was as though in the sharing he'd built an impassable wall between them.

It was there. Unsettled. Logan had told her all of what had happened that fateful summer night right up until he'd run out to the barn. But there he'd stopped, leaving out the shadows, the screaming.

He knew what she couldn't remember. And something of what he knew formed the brick and mortar of that wall.

But she felt no urgency to know. Not anymore. And somehow, in some way, she would convince him of that. For now she would give him the time and emotional distance he seemed to need. She could afford to now. Because ironically, thanks to Rafe Latigo, Logan was coming back to the Circle J.

In Abilene, things were settled quickly. They started for Texas the next morning. Logan rode stiffly because of his injuries, but he didn't spare himself the pace. At night they would lie down together, even share a blanket for warmth, but there was no intimacy.

And every night the dream would come. She could feel the shadows hovering, crowding in on her. Suffocating. But never did she see the face or recognize the muffled voice of the second figure.

Logan would wake her, comfort her, and grow more and more remote. She hated the dream, despised it, because it put the lie to her thinking that what had happened that night no longer mattered.

When they finally reached the Circle J ranchyard a week of hard riding later, they were physically and emotionally exhausted. "We'll change horses and head for town," Logan said, dismounting and falling into step beside her.

Cat nodded, trudging wearily toward the door to the house. "I'll tell Matt and my mother what's happened first."

Maria met them at the door. Cat's dulled senses took a moment to register her friend's swollen, puffy eyes. And then it struck her—Maria had been crying. Cat's gaze swept past Maria to her mother. Olivia was sitting on the settee, her body rocking, her face haunted.

Cat's breath snagged in her throat. "Matt," she murmured. "What's happened to Matt?"

Maria's voice broke. "He's dying."

Chapter Twenty-Seven

Cat stood at the foot of Matt's bed and stared at her brother's sallow features, the uneven rise and fall of his chest. He'd shown not the slightest signs of consciousness since she'd arrived home yesterday afternoon. According to Maria, he'd been much the same for over two weeks, ever since Toby Fletcher had found him unconscious on the road to Red Springs.

During those two weeks, Doc Sanderson had come out to the ranch only once. He'd left, shaking his head, saying nothing could be done.

It was then Maria and Olivia had formed a grudging alliance, evident even now as both women sat quietly in chairs on opposite sides of Matt's bed. They had taken turns easing broth down his throat, bathing his fevered body, exercising his limbs.

And somehow they had kept him alive. Yet even their fearsome determination seemed doomed now to fall short. Despite their heroic efforts, Matt had daily grown weaker.

Cat let out a shuddering breath. What in the world had

possessed her brother to try to make such a trip on horseback? And why hadn't he at least told Maria where he was going? As Cat understood it, Toby's finding him had been only the purest chance. Though the sheriff had been vague with Olivia, Cat suspected the lawman had been prowling about near the prairie dog town looking for more clues about Hadley Jordan's death.

If Matt had lain in the broiling sun much longer, Cat would have returned home to find a second grave under the cottonwoods near the creek.

When she couldn't stand another minute of listening to Matt's labored breathing, she went out to the kitchen and poured herself a cup of reheated coffee. She sank into the slat-back chair beside the table and discovered she was too weary even to cry.

"Logan, where are you?" she murmured aloud, listening vainly for the sound of his horse pulling up in the yard. His presence alone would have brought her some comfort. But after a quick visit to Matt's bedside yesterday, Logan had decided to continue on to Red Springs. He'd said he wanted to talk to Fletcher about Latigo.

As much as Cat wanted the outlaw found, wanted him hanged if he had anything to do with her father's death, right now all she could think about was Matt. Her terror that he would die seemed to magnify in the kitchen's oppressive silence. That his death would leave an aching void in her life was a given. But to imagine all the things she would never have a chance to say to him was an agony beyond bearing.

"No change?" The male voice came from the archway.

Cat jumped startled, looking up to see Logan striding toward her. "I . . . didn't hear you ride up."

"I went straight to the barn," he said, tugging off his gloves and tossing them on the table. "I pushed the gelding pretty hard. I wanted to rub him down, give him some oats."

"Matt's the same," she said, answering Logan's initial question. She couldn't believe how good it felt just to see him. Trail-dusted Levi's hung low on his lean hips. His once-white chambray shirt clung, skin-tight, to his sweat-drenched upper body. As she watched he used the red bandana knotted at his throat to swipe at the grime on his neck. He looked for all the world as though he'd ridden drag for a week. Yet he looked achingly appealing too. Instantly, she forced her thoughts elsewhere. "What did Toby have to say about Latigo?"

"He's had someone watching the Rocking R ever since he got our telegram, but so far nothing." Logan walked to the stove and poured himself a cup of coffee.

"The stuff's undrinkable," she said. "I should make some fresh."

He took a sip and shrugged. "I've had worse."

"Maybe Latigo won't come back," Cat said, though she didn't believe it. "If he does, he knows you and I could send him to jail."

"He'll be back." Logan came over to the table and sat in the chair opposite her. "He'll be back for that very reason. We can identify him."

Cat's hands twisted nervously around her coffee cup. "I haven't told Mother or Maria about any of this. They're both so worried about Matt . . ." She let her voice trail off.

Logan nodded his understanding.

Cat let out a tiny sigh of relief, yet her brow furrowed as she studied Logan's face. She hadn't noticed it when he'd first come in, but the finely chiseled lines seemed more sharply drawn than usual. He looked haggard with fatigue, fatigue not born of hard riding. She'd been so absorbed in her own reactions to Matt's condition that she hadn't even considered Logan's.

"Are you all right?" she asked softly.

He frowned, puzzled.

"About Matt."

"I don't know what you mean," he hedged.

"Yes, you do. You're terrified he'll"—the word caught in her throat—"he'll die. That you won't be able to put the past to rest between you."

"He won't die."

Cat felt a flicker of hope at how fiercely he said the words. She stood to pour herself another cup of coffee and noticed the black bag on the floor by Logan's chair. It was her turn to frown.

"Sanderson's," Logan said.

"He gave it to you?" she asked doubtfully.

"Let's say I borrowed it, when I found out he'd gone to St. Louis for some kind of family gathering."

"But why would you . . . ?" Her eyes widened, a trickle of apprehension tracking along her spine. "Logan, you can't."

But he ignored her. Scraping his chair back, he rose and headed for Matt's room. Cat followed, her pulses thrumming anxiously.

They found Maria bathing Matt's face with a cool, damp cloth. "If you'll permit me, Maria," Logan said, "I'd like to take a look at Matt."

"Of course, señor." Maria dropped the cloth in the basin and moved to stand beside Cat.

Logan rolled up his sleeves and quickly washed his

hands, then took Maria's place at Matt's side.

"I won't allow this," Olivia said, leaning forward in her chair on the bed's opposite side. When Logan reached to unbutton Matt's nightshirt, Olivia caught his wrist. "You're not to touch him. I won't let you touch him."

"Yes, you will," Logan said, his voice grim, hard. From where she stood, Cat couldn't see his eyes, but she was certain they matched his tone, because though her mother continued to regard Logan sullenly, her hand fell away.

Using a stethoscope and some other medical tools from Sanderson's bag, Logan spent the next several minutes checking Matt's vital signs. When he'd finished, he wrung out the washcloth and used it to wipe the perspiration beading across Matt's face and upper chest. "You and I have some unfinished business, Matt," Logan said quietly. "You'd best not be planning to die on me."

Matt moaned, his head shifting from side to side. But he did not wake up. Logan slipped the bedcovers down and examined Matt's leg.

Maria stepped closer, tears trailing down her cheeks. "It is very bad, isn't it, *señor?*"

"I won't lie to you, any of you," he said. "Gangrene's set in."

"Can you help him?" Cat heard herself ask.

"I don't know."

"But you're going to try." It was not a question.

Logan smoothed the covers back under Matt's chin. "I'll need boiling water for the instruments and a lot of clean strips of cloth for bandages."

"You're going to cut off more of his leg, aren't you?" Cat murmured.

364

"If I don't, he'll die."

Whatever control Olivia had had on her emotions snapped. "No!" she cried. "No! You'll get no chance to finish what you started fifteen years ago."

Logan's own temper broke. He stood, glaring at Olivia, something unreadable, but altogether chilling, in those gray eyes. When he spoke, it was through gritted teeth. "I would love to finish what was started here fifteen years ago, Olivia. Don't tempt me, or I'll do it right here and now."

Olivia paled. She slumped in her chair, her hand fluttering to her chest. For an instant Cat feared her mother was going to faint. Her bravado had vanished, as though it had never been. When she spoke again her voice was no more than a pathetic whimper. "Don't hurt him," she said. "Please, just don't hurt him."

Cat felt an aching surge of pity for her mother. She took a step toward her, but Maria put a hand on her arm, stopping her. "Let me, *amiga*." Cat could only stare as Maria hurried around the bed to Olivia's side. Gently, she urged Olivia to stand. "Come, *señora*," she said. "Señor Blackstone will do all he can to save Mateo. And we must do all we can to help him." She led Olivia toward the door. "We will boil the water, gather the bandages."

"He's my son," Olivia said, her voice shaking. "He's my son. I've always taken good care of him."

"Of course you have, *señora*," Maria said. "Mateo knows how much you love him." At the doorway, Maria paused, looking back to give Cat a reassuring smile. Cat tried to smile back, but failed.

When they'd gone, Cat turned to Logan. She longed to ask him what had just happened between him and her mother, but she knew he'd tell her nothing. Instead she said, "However this turns out with Matt, I know you'll have done everything you could."

He stepped over to the window. With his back to her he said, "Thank you."

"It's me who should thank you, Logan," she said softly, coming to stand behind him. "For everything."

He straightened. "There's no need." He turned to face her, his manner brusque, efficient. "We have a lot of work ahead of us. I'm going to need your help with Matt."

She frowned. Now what had she done? Or was it that her nearness reminded him of what still lay unsettled between them?

He stepped around her and went back to the bed, where he made an exaggerated display of again checking Matt's temperature, his pulse.

"Logan, please."

"I'm about to perform surgery on your brother," he said tightly. "Surgery I'm not even sure I'm competent to perform. I don't think this is the time or place to be discussing anything else."

He was right and she knew it. The last thing she wanted to do now was upset him.

Logan reached into the medical bag and drew out a small brown bottle. Cat read the label—CHLOROFORM. "This is in case he starts to wake up," he said, handing it to her. "I'll show you how to drip this onto a cloth above his face."

She nodded. "Fine." Matt was their only concern right now. Everything else could wait.

Maria bustled in then, carrying an armload of clean towels and bandages.

Logan indicated where he wanted her to set them.

"Did you get my mother to lie down?" Cat asked.

Maria nodded. "Lie down, *sí*. But she is so tired, she cannot sleep."

Logan brought over a bottle of laudanum. "Put a teaspoon of this in a glass of milk and get her to drink it," he said.

"*Gracias, señor.*"

"You'd best get some rest yourself, Maria," Logan said. "This is going to take awhile."

"I trust you, *señor*," Maria said. "Mateo's life is in good hands." She stepped over to the bed and bent low to brush a feather-light kiss across Matt's forehead, trail a gentle caress along his cheek. "*Te amo, Mateo,*" she whispered. "*Te amo.*" Blinking back tears, she left the room.

Logan went to Matt's wardrobe and peeled off the trail-worn shirt he was wearing in favor of one of Matt's. Shrugging into the fresh shirt, he crossed to the basin, replenished it with clean water, and again washed his hands. "I want you to wash yours, too," he said, holding the soap out to Cat.

Quickly, she did as he asked, watching while he readied the instruments, the towels, the bandages. Everything was going to be all right, she told herself. Logan would pull Matt through. And she would do whatever she could to help. Gripping the bottle of chloroform and a cloth, she stepped around the bed to come even with Matt's head.

"Ready?" Logan asked.

She nodded.

Logan loosed the bedcovers, exposing only the bandaged stump of Matt's leg. Gently he removed the bandages.

Cat's stomach lurched. The entire end of Matt's leg was a putrid, festering sore. Instinctively, she backed away, feeling her whole body break out in a cold sweat. She dropped the cloth. "I'm sorry. I can't do this."

Logan was beside her in an instant, guiding her to the chair in the far corner of the room. "It's all right," he said. "Take a few deep breaths. It'll pass."

"I'm sorry, Logan. I'm so sorry." She leaned her head into her hands, willing herself not to be sick.

"Take deep breaths," Logan said. "Deep breaths. That's it. You'll be fine."

"I won't be fine." She looked at him helplessly. "I can't do this. I can't help you cut my brother's leg."

Logan's gaze hardened. "You will help me, because there's no one else who can. Maria's too much in love with him, and your mother would be no help at all."

Her body trembled. "What help am I? I can't even look at his leg without being sick."

"Then don't look. I need you to handle the chloroform, to hand me the instruments." He caught her arm and gently, but firmly, led her back to the bed. "It isn't just me who needs you," he said. "It's your brother."

She looked at Matt's still, pale features and felt a fierce flush of shame. "I'm sorry," she said. "Just tell me what to do."

He handed her a clean cloth for the chloroform, then went back to his scrutiny of Matt's leg. The obvious faith he had in her buoyed her confidence. Their personal difficulties were not forgotten, but for now they were unimportant. What mattered was Matt.

For the next two hours Cat did exactly as Logan told her—measuring out the chloroform, handing him scalpels, sutures, even mopping the sweat from his brow.

And as she grew accustomed to the sight of the wound, she even found herself watching the surgery. Logan worked skillfully, expertly, seemingly unaffected by the knowledge that a man's life depended on the skill in his hands.

But when he'd finished, when he sagged back to look at the freshly bandaged limb, Cat knew differently. For the first time Cat saw the uncertainty, the fear in Logan's eyes. Considering Matt's condition, this would have been a difficult operation for any doctor. But Logan Blackstone was operating on Matt Jordan. Logan had put far more than his medical skills on the line. He had put his own future on the line.

"He's going to be fine, isn't he?" Cat asked quickly, wishing her voice didn't shake so.

"We'll just have to wait and see."

"No one could have done better, Logan."

"Who are you trying to convince?" he asked, the tiniest thread of sarcasm weaving into his voice. "Me? Or you?"

Cat wrung her hands together, but didn't answer. Deciding it was best to leave him alone for a while, she went out to tell her mother and Maria that the surgery was over. She found Maria keeping herself busy in the kitchen.

"Tell me the truth, *amiga*," Maria said, her dark eyes luminous in the lantern light. "Do you think Mateo will live?"

Until that instant, Cat had had her doubts. But a fierce certainty swept through her in the face of Maria's courage and love. "I know he will," Cat said. "I know it."

Maria flung herself into Cat's arms and wept brokenly, tears of relief, joy. Long minutes later she stepped back, dabbing at her tears with the hem of her apron. "Your mother is sleeping," she said. "I gave her the medicine as Señor Logan instructed." She gave Cat a watery smile. "How long will it be before Mateo awakens?"

"I don't know. Logan says we have to wait and see. It's up to Matt now."

"*Sí*, and God."

"I've been praying a lot, too," Cat said.

"Mateo deserves another chance at life, Cat. He has come so far." She gestured toward the stove. "I've made fresh coffee and quesadillas. You and Logan must eat."

"*Gracias.* I'll get him."

"I'll go with you. I must see Mateo for myself."

Cat found Logan slumped forward in the chair beside Matt's bed, asleep. Her mouth curved upward in a tender smile. Gently, she shook his shoulder.

His head jerked up. He blinked, and for an unguarded instant Cat felt her blood heat under the warmth of his gaze. Then he seemed to catch himself, realize where he was. The warmth vanished as he rose to his feet. "I guess I dozed off."

"Maria's made us something to eat."

"I can't leave Matt."

"Please," Maria put in, "let me stay with him. I promise I will call you if he wakes."

Logan hesitated, then nodded. "All right. But not just if he wakes. Call me if there's any change at all. Good or bad, understand?"

"*Sí, señor.*"

In the kitchen Cat ladled herself and Logan each a generous helping of Maria's quesadillas. But though the spicy beef-filled tortillas melted in her mouth, Cat found it impossible to eat more than a few bites. She was still on edge from the ordeal of Matt's operation.

Logan, too, pushed his food around on his plate, saying nothing. Finally he gave up, excused himself and headed outside. Cat considered letting him go. They were both exhausted. But maybe if he were tired, he would also be vulnerable. Heaven knew, she was. They had to talk. She intended to close the distance he'd forced between them ever since he'd told her the truth about Matt.

She found him alone in the dark of the bunkhouse. The other wranglers hadn't yet returned from Abilene. Cat had told them to take their time; she didn't expect them before the end of next week. In the dim moonlight sifting through a flyspecked window she could see Logan lying on his back on one of the bunks, one arm flung wearily over his eyes. He did not remove it, though he had to have heard the door open, heard her come inside.

She crossed to the small square pine table beside the bunk, fumbled for the match box that was ever present on its surface, then lit the table's only adornment—a kerosene lantern.

"I'm not in the mood for company," he said, no particular emotion evident in his voice.

"I need to talk to you."

"I don't want to talk."

She ignored that, sitting beside him on the bunk. "You saved my brother's life."

"I did what I had to do."

She grimaced. He was determined to make this as difficult as possible. When her hip brushed against his leg, he immediately shifted closer to the wall. "Don't."

"Don't what?"

She was too tired to consider caution, too tired to be anything but honest. "Don't pull away from me."

371

"Cat, I . . ." He shook his head. "Never mind."

"Please."

"Please what?"

"Please talk to me."

"It's no good, Cat. I'm tired of hurting—hurting you, hurting me."

"Then don't talk about hurting. Talk about loving." Her right hand caressed his denim-clad thigh. "We haven't made love since Abilene."

He caught her wrist. "And we're not going to now."

She didn't struggle, merely waiting, and he let her go. "I miss touching you." Her hand skated past the quiescent bulge at the apex of his legs. She smiled when she felt it stir to life.

This time he made no move to restrain her. "I'm not staying in Texas," he said a little desperately. "We both know that."

"You're here now. And I love you."

"If you love me, you'd . . ." He stopped, clamping his jaw shut, arching his head back when her hand grew bolder, tugging free the buttons of his Levi's, sliding under the rough material to fondle him, stroke him. A strangled moan escaped his throat. "Damn you."

The chains binding his control snapped free. He sat up, reached for her, his hands rough, clumsy, as they sought to work the buttons of her shirt. When the tiny circlets refused to cooperate, he gripped either side of her shirt and tore it open, a half-dozen buttons skittering across the wood floor.

"Damn you, Corie," he murmured over and over, even as his mouth rained kisses over her fevered body, even as her lips drove him to madness. She was only making their inevitable parting more painful. Couldn't she see that?

Reason vanished as passion ruled them both.

She straddled his hips, lowering her silken folds onto the throbbing core of him. And when she began to move nothing mattered but that they share the sweet ecstasy of their joining. He matched her movements with his own, his lust, his love for her spiraling outward until they both touched the veiling mists of paradise.

Afterwards, Cat snuggled into the crook of Logan's arm. Very deliberately, he pulled away. She winced.

He had been able to lower the wall between them while they made love, but now it was in place again—high, impenetrable, grounded in a long-ago night of shadows and in her own fear-inspired rejection of his proposal.

"You're sorry we made love, aren't you?" she asked sadly.

He was staring at the ceiling. "I told you—I'm tired of hurting. It shouldn't have happened."

"But it doesn't have to hurt anymore," she whispered urgently. "Don't you see that? It only hurts because we thought it had to end."

"And it doesn't?"

She propped herself up on one elbow, feathering her fingertips across his chest. "If I thought that, I wouldn't have come out here tonight."

"And if I thought there was a chance for us, any chance at all . . ." He blew out a long, weary breath. "There are too many bad feelings between our families, Cat. And even if we could overcome it all, you made your feelings clear when I asked you to marry me. This is your home. It isn't mine."

Her heart thudded. She would never have a better

opening, a better time to let him know how much her feelings had changed since that night in the barn. "Ask me again," she murmured. "Just ask."

He looked at her, his gaze an odd mix of tenderness and defeat and said the single word that broke her heart. "No."

She lay there, her hand frozen above his chest, feeling as though her body had turned to stone, but somehow she managed not to let the devastation she felt show on her face. "I see," she managed, her voice a croaking mockery of itself. "Well, I'm glad that's finally settled." She stood, forcing what she knew must be a pathetic excuse for a smile, but needing it to salvage some tiny scrap of pride.

"I hope we can still be friends," he said, and the utter sincerity of his tone made her want to ram her fist into his face.

"Yes, of course," she said. "Friends." She backed toward the door. "Thank you again for what you did for Matt. Thank you so much."

"Let me know if he wakes up."

"I will. I surely will." Fighting back the hellish pain that threatened to engulf her, Cat spun toward the open door and fled into the night.

Chapter Twenty-Eight

Logan blew out the lantern and lay back down on the bunk, allowing the darkness to envelop him once again. The darkness that matched his mood. He had hurt Cat badly, he knew. But it was for her own good. She didn't know what she was asking. He had been a fool to propose to her in the first place. There was simply too much bad blood between their families. He had come to realize these past weeks that he wouldn't just be asking her to give up Texas, he would be asking her to give up her family. Matt and Olivia would never forgive her for marrying a Blackstone.

That Cat had apparently reconsidered the idea of marriage to him tore at his heart as nothing ever had. And he couldn't help thinking that maybe the distance to Boston could make an estrangement from her family easier to bear.

But such thoughts were selfish. His act had ripped this family apart fifteen years ago. Cat's being a child had spared her the brunt of that, and he wasn't about to subject her to such agony now.

He let out a shuddering breath, his eyes burning as he looked into a future without her, and for the first time in his life he wished to God he wasn't Logan Blackstone.

Cat lay in bed, trembling. Over and over she relived what had happened in the bunkhouse with Logan. She had gone there to talk things out with him and, she admitted it, to seduce him. It had not been in her mind to ask him to repeat his offer of marriage, but when the opportunity had presented itself she had dared risk it.

And he had refused.

He had made love to her, but he no longer wanted her as his wife.

"Damn you, Logan," she muttered, wiping at tear-swollen eyes. "Damn your city-born hide." Levering herself to a sitting position, she focused on nothing in particular in the gloomy darkness of her bedroom. What had she expected anyway? Logan had been reluctant to continue the intimacy between them ever since she had rejected his first proposal.

He'd said he had been trying to spare her more hurt, trying to spare himself too. But she hadn't let him. In Abilene he'd tried to end their relationship with a pleasant evening. There, too, she had used his passion against him.

Again and again she had been the aggressor. She had not wanted to give him up. And yet she had never taken the final step, never told him she would give up the ranch for him, never risked learning his reaction. Until tonight.

And she knew why. Because some part of her had known what his answer would be.

What she didn't know was why, *why* had he said no?

The man could not make love to her like that and not love her. Battered as she was, she couldn't believe that.

With a despairing sign she forced herself out of bed and crossed to her washstand. Lighting a candle, she stared at the pathetic creature revealed by her mirror. Was this the same Cat Jordan who had spent a lifetime telling herself that she didn't want—didn't *need*—a man in her life?

She managed a rueful smile. What pitiful self-delusion! It wasn't that she didn't want a man, it was that she'd never thought she could have one. Not a man to want her for herself. Though her mother had constantly manuevered her toward marriage, it was always with the message that she had to "play the game," that she had to pretend to be something she wasn't in order to win a man's heart.

"Because I wasn't good enough to win him on my own, right, Mother?" Cat said aloud. "No man would want Cat Jordan."

And then Logan Blackstone had come back into her life. A more inauspicious reunion she couldn't imagine. There she'd been in trail-dusty denims, standing in the middle of a Red Springs street and taking on a drunk Rafe Latigo. Logan had stepped in to help, but he'd not judged her, not tried to change her. In fact—and obviously against his will—he had been attracted to her.

He had made love to her in a hayloft, and asked her to be his wife. No where in his proposal had he made conditions—that she would have to wear fancy dresses and give tea parties. He'd just said "I love you." And *she* hadn't believed in herself enough to believe *him*.

She could see now that her turning him down had been due to far more than avoiding the mistakes of her parents' marriage. It had also been a reaction to feeling inadequate as a woman, a *lady*. But somehow over these past weeks—thanks to Logan Blackstone—she had gotten past all that. Logan had made her feel every bit a lady, even as, in his loving, he'd left her free to be herself.

As she stood there in the graying light of dawn, Cat felt the self-pity drain out of her, felt her anger stir. Anger at herself, at her mother, her brother, and most certainly anger at Logan Blackstone. She'd be damned if he was going to get away with turning a goose into a swan and then abandoning her!

He may have fooled her for a little while, may even still be fooling himself—but he didn't want her out of his life. The man was just being his infuriatingly noble self. He couldn't expect a Jordan to marry a Blackstone.

Well, she would just see about that!

She took a step toward her door, then stopped. Maybe she should let him stew for a while, let him think that she was going to go along with his self-sacrifice, write herself out of his life. Perhaps if she wasn't the aggressor any more, he would think she really could live without him. And maybe he wouldn't like it one bit!

Feeling a surge of self-confidence that a few months ago would have been totally foreign to her, Cat pulled on a skirt and blouse, and decided it was time to sit with Matt for a while.

Her courage almost left her as she entered Matt's room to find Logan sitting in a chair at Matt's bedside. He was checking the bandages and did not at first look up. When he did, the haggard look on his face sent her hopes soaring. Evidently he had passed the night as miserably as she had.

"How is he?" she asked, feigning an aloofness she

didn't feel.

"His color's a little better."

Gray eyes searched her face, as though seeking signs of distress. Though her heart thudded against her ribs, Cat schooled her features to look impassive. "Where's Maria?"

"She was exhausted. I made her leave, get some sleep."

"My mother's still asleep, too."

"The laudanum might keep her out for a while longer."

Cat felt as though she were making polite conversation with a stranger, but she was certain now that this was the only way to get him to make the next move. *If that truly was what he wanted to do . . .* Angrily, she shoved away the self-doubt.

"Is there anything I can do to help?" she asked.

"Not really, I—"

Matt groaned, his head twisting from side to side. Cat rushed over to the bed, all thoughts of her problems with Logan vanishing. "Is he waking up?"

Gently, Logan shook Matt's shoulder and called his name. Matt's eyes opened briefly, though they seemed not to focus. When they started to close again, Logan caught Matt's chin and turned his head toward him, this time calling his name more urgently.

Matt's lips moved, his voice coming out thick, slurred. "My leg . . ."

"Matt, you're awake!" Cat gasped, starting to rise. "I have to get mother and Maria."

Logan held up a restraining hand. "Not yet."

"Why not?"

He didn't answer, instead speaking to Matt. "How does

379

your leg feel? Can you understand me, Matt? How does your leg feel?"

"Leg?" Matt repeated dumbly

Cat understood then. Logan didn't want Olivia in here until after Matt had dealt with Logan's having performed surgery on his leg.

Matt's eyes slid closed, and Cat feared he had passed out again. But then he spoke, the words slow, laborious. "Leg . . . hurts." His brow furrowed. "Strange . . . feels strange."

Cat poured some water into a glass, then cradled her brother's head and held the glass to his lips. He drank eagerly, wanting more when, despite Cat's best efforts, much of the first glassful dribbled down his chin. This time when he opened his eyes, he seemed to have a greater awareness.

"The leg . . . feels strange," he said again, looking at Cat. "What . . . happened?"

"You fell from your horse."

"Horse?" Matt shook his head, as though trying to clear it. "Fell?" For a long minute he lay there, his forehead furrowed in fierce concentration. "Damn," he muttered at last. "I don't remember." He caught Cat's hand, his grip painfully weak. "Where's Maria?"

"Asleep. You've been sick a long time. She's exhausted."

Matt's eyes grew soft, misty. "I'm going to marry her, you know."

Cat smiled. "That's wonderful."

Matt turned toward Logan. "Why are you here?" To Cat his voice seemed more curious than hostile.

"Logan saved your life," she put in quickly.

Comprehension stole over Matt's features, and his

already pale face suddenly turned deathly white. "My leg?" he croaked, looking at Cat. "You let him cut my leg?"

"He saved your life," she said again.

Logan stood. "Maybe I'd better go. I don't want you upsetting yourself, pulling free the sutures."

"No!" Surprisingly, it was Matt who spoke. "I want you to stay."

Cat watched the play of emotions on her brother's face, the shift from anger to betrayal, then finally to a kind of grudging respect. If it were possible for Matt to be open-minded about anything Logan did, Cat could see that he was struggling to do so now.

Logan sat back down.

Cat then told Matt about his accident, the resulting delirium, and the gangrene that had threatened his life. She hoped by doing so she could get him to accept Logan's intervention, hoped, too, that she would jar his memory, that he would recall why he was riding alone to Red Springs in the first place.

Matt took it all in, saying nothing. Then he looked at Logan, his voice steady, calm. "The leg . . . it feels different," he said slowly. "It hurts, but the pain isn't the same. Does that make any sense?"

"More than you know," Logan said. Cat could almost feel the relief coursing through Logan. It never failed to astonish her that Matt's attitude toward him should even matter after so many years of animosity.

"I'm fairly certain," Logan went on, "that once the incisions from the surgery itself are healed your pain will be gone."

Matt blinked, his eyes overbright. For an instant she thought Matt was going to say thank you. Instead, an

381

awkward silence fell over the room. To break it, Cat cleared her throat self-consciously and said, "We still don't know what you were doing on that horse, Matt."

"My God," he gasped. "I remember! You were going to be robbed. Both of you! In Abilene."

Cat frowned. "How could you know that? I haven't even told Maria or Mother."

Matt was agitated now. He spoke quickly. I was riding to warn you. To send a telegram. I heard them planning it. I heard them planning to steal the money."

"Heard who?" Cat demanded, rising nervously to her feet.

"Ryan Fielding . . . and—" He stopped, his eyes filled with a soul-deep pain Cat knew had nothing to do with his leg.

"And me." The voice came from the doorway.

Cat staggered back, as though struck by a blow. "Mother?"

"I wanted this ranch bankrupt," she said. "I wanted it dead." Even as she spoke, Olivia was hurrying across the room to Matt's side. "Oh, my dear, my dear," she half sobbed. "It's so good to see you awake." She sat on the bed and caught his hand in hers. "How do you feel? Are you all right? I tried to stop him. I tried to stop Logan from cutting your leg."

Logan swore viciously, grasping Olivia's wrist. "Never mind the goddamned surgery, Olivia," he gritted out. "Do you have any idea what you did to your daughter? Rafe Latigo almost raped and killed her while trying to get that money."

Olivia's eyes widened with shock. "What are you talking about? You have the money."

"We got it back, Mother," Cat said, her voice shaking,

still unable to comprehend the magnitude of what her mother had done. Numb, sickened, she recounted the robbery attempt.

When she'd finished Olivia was shaking, sobbing. "I promise you, Cordelia, no one was supposed to be hurt. Ryan promised no one would be hurt."

"You thought you could trust Rafe Latigo?" Cat shook her head in bewilderment. "The man's an animal."

"Ryan didn't tell me who would . . . would handle things."

"Handle things?" Cat mocked. "My God, Mother, you plotted to have this done to me!" She felt tears start and fought against them, fearful that if they fell, they would never stop. "I didn't think you hated me that much."

Olivia continued to sob brokenly. "Hate you? Oh, my dear, I could never hate you. I only wanted what was best. I didn't want you giving your life for this godforsaken ranch."

"The ranch? The hell with the ranch. You and Ryan almost cost me my life. If it hadn't been for Logan, I'd be dead."

"Logan!" Olivia spat out the name, turning on him. "It would never have happened, none of it, if you hadn't come here, if you hadn't given her the extension. It's your fault! Your fault!"

Cat swayed, gripping the back of a nearby chair to steady herself. *Your fault, your fault.* The voice, muffled from constant sobbing, it had sounded so peculiar in her dream, indistinct, unrecognizable. Because some part of her had not wanted to recognize it. *Your fault, your fault.*

It hadn't been her father shouting. It had been her mother! Cat sunk to her knees, her emotions roiling. "The dream," she said. "My God, the dream."

383

She felt Logan's eyes on her, but she wouldn't look at him. He would try to stop her, maybe she should stop herself. She felt the shadows hovering, close, so close.

Olivia lifted her gaze beseechingly to Logan. "Don't let her remember, please."

"It's too late, Olivia," Logan said wearily. "Too late."

Cat was in the barn, hearing the storm brewing outside, standing, watching, wishing Logan wasn't crying. Wishing her father wasn't shouting at Logan. And then her mother had come in, screaming, hysterical.

Cat jammed her hands against her ears, trying to shut out the words she had so long tried desperately to remember. The protective wall that had for fifteen years guarded her memory crumbled to dust.

She remembered the words her mother had screamed at her father. "He's not your son! He's my son, mine! You've got no say over him. I was carrying him before I married you! Do you hear me? He's mine. Mine and Jeremy Blackstone's!"

Hadley had slapped her, knocking her halfway across the barn. His face was murderous, contorted. "Whore! You used me! Used me! I thought you loved me. But you were carrying his bastard! Jeremy's bastard!"

Cat had cowered there in the darkness. She didn't know what the words meant, but she knew something was terribly wrong. She remembered wanting to run to Logan, to have him tell her everything was going to be all right. But Logan's face had gone pale, sick.

Instead Cat had whirled and run into the night, into the storm. She'd huddled under a wagon in the driving rain for hours. No one had missed her. Near dawn she'd snuck back into the house wet, terrified. When she'd awakened the next morning, she couldn't even remember why she'd been out in the rain. She'd run to find her mother and father, and though she'd sensed something different about them, she'd thought it was because of Matt's leg, not because of what had happened in the barn.

Jeremy Blackstone's bastard. Cat looked up to encounter Logan's stricken gaze. "My mother and your father?" she murmured.

"I never wanted you to know."

Matt, too, looked stricken. "I don't believe it," he said. "I don't believe any of it." His gaze flicked from Olivia to Cat to Logan, then back to Olivia. "Why didn't you tell me? Why?"

Olivia reached out a hand toward him, as though to smooth back the hair that tumbled across his forehead, but when he flinched away, she let the hand fall back to her side. "I couldn't tell you. I couldn't tell anyone. I didn't even mean to tell Hadley. It . . . it just came out. I was so upset about your leg. I blamed the ranch, blamed Hadley." She closed her eyes. "And I blamed Logan, blamed him for being Jeremy's acknowledged son, his privileged son, while my son had to live in this wilderness."

Tears tracked unheeded down Cat's cheeks. So much pain carried for so long.

Olivia spoke again, her gaze seemingly locked on a past far away, unseen by anyone save herself. "Elizabeth couldn't have children. She sent Jeremy away.

"I went to comfort him. I loved him. We were together six months, and then he went back to Elizabeth. It wasn't long after that I found out I was with child." She wrung her hands in the handkerchief she had pulled from the pocket of her dress. "I was desperate, but I had my pride. Hadley had wanted to marry me for years. I

385

thought . . . I thought it would be all right, that he would stay in Boston."

Cat looked wonderingly at Logan. "You and Matt are half—"

"Brothers," he finished, something indefinable in his eyes.

Matt had turned a ghostly shade of gray.

Cat took a step toward Logan. "You never told your father?"

He shrugged. "It would have broken my mother's heart. Besides, it wasn't my place to say."

Olivia continued to weep. "I didn't want anyone to know my disgrace."

"No wonder she was afraid of your coming back here," Cat said softly.

"I would never have told anyone," Logan said. "Never." He studied Cat critically. "Are you all right?"

"I'm fine," she assured him. "It's more of a jolt for Matt I think."

"I'd like to talk to him alone for a couple of minutes."

Cat nodded, then took a deep breath and walked over to where her mother sat hunched on the bed. Gently, she urged her to her feet, "Come on, Mother. I'll make us some coffee."

"Hadley stole you from me that night," Olivia said, her voice no more than a whimper. "You were never my little girl again. He said I didn't deserve you. He said . . . he said it was God's judgment for my sin."

It'll be all right, Mother," Cat said, her arm around Olivia's shoulders. "You'll see. It'll be just fine." But as she led her mother from the room, Cat allowed herself one last glance at Logan and Matt. She did not welcome the feeling they were once again wary boxers circling in the ring.

Logan could only take Cat's word that she was all right. He could hardly have traipsed after her and made certain. Cat needed time alone with her mother. Just as Logan needed time with Matt.

"You've known all these years," Matt was saying, his tone a mixture of awe and a curious disappointment. "All these years. And you never said anything."

"Hadley asked me not to." Matt was taking it better than Logan had thought he would. But then Matt hadn't gotten nearly as upset about the surgery as Logan would have predicted. Logan felt a long-buried hope flicker to life inside him.

"I know you won't believe me," Matt said, "but I'm not angry. At least not at anyone but myself. I just can't believe you would have kept it a secret after the way I treated you." He shook his head. "I hated you. I hated you so much."

Logan stalked toward the window, his guts twisting, his hopes fading. Always, somewhere inside him, he'd prayed Matt one day would forgive him. His pain at first kept him from hearing the words that followed. When he did, he scarcely dared believe them.

"I hated you for being stronger than me, for being more of a man than me. I hated you for being the kind of son my father wanted." Matt sucked in a deep breath. "Ironic, isn't it? I probably would've done great in Boston."

"Hadley loved you," Logan said softly.

"Sure he did." Matt was unconvinced.

Crossing to the chair beside the bed, Logan sat down. "Don't you dare pull that self-pity crap on me now. After your mother went back to the house that night, Hadley sat in that barn and bawled like a baby.

387

"All he could think about was Olivia trying to take you back to Boston, to confront my father with you. He was scared to death he was going to lose you."

When Matt didn't say anything, Logan continued. "I told him I'd never tell anyone. The next day when he took me to the stage stop, he assured me Olivia wouldn't be contacting my father, that she was too humiliated. But he was already scared about the guilt she was feeling, what it was going to mean to you. She didn't much like ranch life before, after your accident she despised it."

Matt shook his head. "Even I didn't realize how much. My God, Cat could've been killed."

"We'll still have to deal with Fielding." He told Matt about alerting the sheriff to Latigo's possible return, and Matt nodded his approval. They discussed possible traps for both Rocking R men, even as Logan marveled inwardly about the civility of their conversation. It was the longest, and least volatile, discussion they'd had since the day they'd stalked that cougar. And it felt good, damned good.

"I hope Cat's getting things squared away with your mother," Logan said finally, as he reluctantly rose to leave. He didn't want to tire Matt so soon after the surgery.

"Cat's tough," Matt said. "She'll be all right."

"Maybe she's not as tough as you think. At least when it comes to Olivia."

"You in love with my sister?"

Logan stiffened slightly. "That's between her and me."

"You'd be good for each other."

"And how would you know?"

388

"I've learned a lot about love lately. You'd be surprised."

One side of Logan's mouth ticked upward. "No, I wouldn't."

"So, you going to marry her?"

"I don't know that she'd have me."

Matt's eyes grew deadly serious. "I hope that's none of my doing."

Logan looked away, touched by Matt's sincerity, though he didn't fool himself for a minute that any kind of reconciliation with Matt would end the differences between himself and Cat. He had hurt her badly last night.

"I'll talk to her if you want," Matt went on. "I'll talk to my mother, too. I owe her that anyway. She told me her secret. It's time I tell her mine. That she's been blaming the wrong person all these years."

"It was an accident."

Very softly Matt said, "I know."

Logan's eyes burned.

Matt held out his right hand. "There's no reason on this earth why you should forgive me," he said, his voice shaking, "but I'm asking you to anyway. I'm sorry, Logan. Sorry for everything."

Logan swallowed the tightness in his throat, then reached out and clasped his brother's hand.

Chapter Twenty-Nine

Cat paced nervously in front of the fireplace. She could still scarcely absorb all that had happened in the past hour. Of paramount importance, of course, was that Matt was going to be all right. But the thoughts that consumed her were of that long-ago night in the barn and the full measure of the secret Logan had carried for so many years.

Against her will, Cat's gaze flicked to the settee. Her mother sat there, hunched, bereft. Nothing Cat said to her had yet seemed to penetrate Olivia's haze of self-loathing. And in truth Cat had yet to come to terms with what she wanted to say. With a sigh she crossed the room to where Maria stood peering anxiously down the hallway.

"How much longer can they be, *amiga?*" the girl asked. "You asked me to wait, but I cannot bear it much longer. I must see Mateo for myself."

"I'm sorry, Maria. I just think they need some time alone." Cat had told Maria everything, knowing it was the only way to prevent her friend from rushing to Matt's side.

"You are sure Mateo is all right? You were not just trying to shield me, to . . ." Her voice quavered. "I love him so much, Cat."

"I promise you, he's fine."

Maria relaxed a little. "I'm sorry. I know you love them both. I hope for your sake there can be peace between them."

"*My* sake?"

"You do not need trouble between your brother and your future husband."

Cat winced, but decided against telling Maria that Logan no longer had marriage on his mind. Maria had enough to worry about with Matt. Besides, Cat thought hopefully, there were no more secrets between the Jordans and the Blackstones. Logan didn't have to make any more noble sacrifices on her behalf. Maybe they could truly sort things out between them.

"There is someone with whom *you* need to make peace, *amiga*," Maria said gently. Cat followed Maria's gaze to where Olivia sat so forlornly. "She needs you now, more than she ever has."

Cat's shoulders sagged. "I don't know how to talk to her, Maria. I don't know what to say. How could she have put the blame on Logan all these years? And then this business with the herd money . . ."

"Think how afraid she must have been—then and now. Afraid to lose everything—you, your brother."

Cat raked a hand through tousled locks, unwillingly recalling Olivia's anguished comment that Hadley hadn't let Cat be her little girl anymore after that night in the

391

barn. She knew there might never be a better opportunity for openness between them. Didn't she owe it to them both to at least try to talk? To Maria, Cat said, "Maybe you should go on in and see Matt."

Maria nodded knowingly and headed down the hallway, while Cat took a deep breath and walked over to her mother. She sat beside Olivia on the settee. "Are you all right?" she asked softly.

Olivia didn't answer, but a single tear escaped down her cheek.

"Don't cry, Ma," Cat said, feeling her own eyes begin to burn. "Everything's going to be all right, you'll see. Matt's going to be fine. I'm fine."

"Nothing will ever be fine again," Olivia whimpered, staring straight ahead. "Nothing. Matthew hates me."

"Matt doesn't hate you. He could never hate you."

"I've done everything wrong. I didn't mean to, but I did." She gave a sad little sigh. "I've ruined things for both of my children."

"No, you haven't! Don't say that." Cat caught her mother's wrist. "Matt and I aren't blameless, you know. He felt sorry for himself, and I . . . , I know I'm not the kind of daughter you would have wished for." Cat blinked rapidly. "I just wanted you to be proud of me, proud of me for being me."

"Oh, Cordelia," Olivia said, patting the back of Cat's hand. "I am proud of you. Very proud. I wish to God I had learned to stand on my own two feet as well as you have." She wiped at her tears. "I just didn't want you wasting your life in this place. I wanted something better for you, better than what I had. I didn't mean to hurt you. Forgive me, sweetheart. Please, forgive me."

"There's nothing to forgive."

392

Olivia shuddered. "Latigo could have killed you."

"But he didn't. I'm fine, just fine. Logan saved me."

"Logan." Olivia closed her eyes. "My God, what I did to that boy."

"It's over, Ma," Cat soothed. "Don't think about it."

"I'll tell the sheriff what Ryan and I did. I will."

"No, don't you worry about it. Logan and I will take care of Ryan and Latigo."

Olivia straightened a little. "You're in love with Logan, aren't you?"

Cat nodded.

"Then don't let him get away from you," Olivia said with surprising fierceness. "Don't you dare let him get away."

"I won't, Mama," Cat said, half smiling, half crying. "I won't."

They sat huddled together for long minutes, until finally Olivia sat back, brushing at straying locks of brown hair. "I must look a sight."

"You look wonderful," Cat lied.

"I probably look like you do after you've ridden drag for three days."

Cat managed a wry grin, an odd relief seeping through her. "Thanks, Ma," she said. "We couldn't handle changing everything at once." It was then Cat became aware that she and her mother were no longer alone. How long Logan had been standing there she couldn't have said.

"How is Matthew?" Olivia asked, unable to look Logan in the eye.

"Why don't you go in and see for yourself?" Logan's voice was laced with such gentleness that Cat's heart ached with love for him. "He's asking for you."

393

"He is?" Olivia stood, looking fearfully nervous, vulnerable.

"I think he wants to invite you to a wedding."

For an instant Cat feared her mother's disapproval of Matt and Maria's relationship would surface. Instead her mother smiled. "He wants me to be there?"

"He wants that very much."

Her smile now radiant, Olivia hurried down the hall.

Left alone with Logan, Cat felt suddenly awkward, shy. She stood, feeling uncomfortable as his eyes settled on her, a curious intensity evident in their gray depths. "Did everything go all right with Matt?" she managed.

"Fine."

"I'm glad." She gave him a tentative smile, wishing to heaven he'd stop looking at her that way. She was suddenly frightened. Was he thinking of a way to tell her that he'd resolved the last of his reasons to stay in Texas? That he was going home? Her heart hammered in her chest. Would he ask her to go with him?

"Cat—"

Hoofbeats sounded in the front yard. Cat grimaced, as Logan turned and headed toward the window. Whoever had such lousy timing had best not be planning to stay long. She walked up behind Logan and peered over his shoulder.

"My God!" she gasped. "Ryan!"

Logan was already moving for his cane, grabbing it up from where it stood propped against a near wall. The look in his eyes was now cold, savage.

Cat caught his arm as he started toward the door. "Logan, no! We need him alive! We have to hear him out."

"I'll hear him out." Logan was livid. "After I stick

394

this through his gut for what he had done to you."

"Logan, please, he's not worth it."

Ryan knocked, but before Cat could answer, the door swung inward and he strode inside. When he saw Logan, it was as though he'd struck an invisible wall. He stopped, his tongue flicking nervously over dry lips. "Now don't do anything rash, Mr. Blackstone," he said quickly. "I have information you want, information you both want."

Though Ryan had made no threatening move, Cat rushed over and pulled his sidearm from the holster on his hip. When Logan raised the sword, Ryan backed away until he hit the wall.

"Talk," Logan said, pressing the sword tip against Ryan's shirtfront, "or I'll cut your heart out."

Ryan stood stock-still. "I didn't think Olivia would keep quiet for long."

"You leave my mother out of this!" Cat snapped.

"Of course," Ryan said, raising a hand in a placating gesture, "anything you say. I rode over here, because I heard from the sheriff that you two were back. I know what you must think, but Latigo was only supposed to take the money. I swear."

"Is that supposed to make it all right?" Cat demanded.

"I wanted this ranch," Ryan said. "I wanted it badly. I would have done a lot to get it. But not murder, Cat. I promise you, not murder."

"Keep talking," Logan said.

"A lot more is going on than either one of you know. A lot more. Latigo let it slip—"

"Latigo's back?" Logan interrupted, raising the sword tip to Ryan's throat. "Where is he?"

Ryan swallowed convulsively. "I don't know."

Logan pressed harder. A drop of blood appeared at the

end of the sword.

"Watch out with that thing!" Ryan croaked.

"Then tell me what you know about Latigo."

Ryan's words came out in a rush. "He wants me dead. I took every back trail and deer path I could find getting over here. I didn't dare take the main road."

"What are you talking about?" Cat put in. "The man works for you."

"I thought he did," Ryan said. "Until he got drunk a couple of nights ago and . . . Look, I only want to say all this once. And I'd rather say it in front of the sheriff. No offense, but there are things I might have to say that would make me a little gun shy about riding to town with you two."

Cat's eyes narrowed. "Does this have to do with my father? Answer me, Ryan, does it?"

"I'll talk to Toby. No one else. I've already left some interesting bits of information with him. But now I have the missing piece. My bargaining chip, so to speak. What do you say, Cat? Will you ride to town with me?"

"I'll saddle my horse," Cat said, starting toward the door.

Logan barred her path. "You're not going anywhere with him."

"I have to and you know it," she said calmly, though her heart soared at how fiercely protective he looked. "I was hoping you'd come too."

"You can bet on that." Logan herded Fielding toward the door at sword point. "Just in case his newfound sense of conscience deserts him somewhere along the road."

In minutes the three of them rode out, heading on a circuitous route to Red Springs. Ryan kept about three lengths ahead of them, his pace slow, his head swiveling constantly as he searched the trail ahead and behind, obviously terrified of an ambush. Cat held her mare beside Logan's gelding.

"He's scared to death," Cat said, shaking her head at the wonder of it. "He really thinks Latigo is out to kill him."

"It sure doesn't seem to figure," Logan said, scratching his chin thoughtfully.

Cat had the strangest feeling he was about to say more, but changed his mind. Instead they lapsed into a companionable silence. She longed to talk to him about more personal things, but knew it wasn't the time. They rode for hours, going miles out of their way, but even that didn't stem Ryan's mounting unease.

"He's out there," he said, looking back over his shoulder at them. "I can feel it."

"We'll make it," Cat said, hoping to make him less nervous, surprised she should even try. Yet in his way, before her father died, Ryan had been a good neighbor, if not an especially good friend. "We'll get to town and you'll—"

With a sudden violence, Logan hauled back on the reins of his horse, his hand lashing out to grab Cat's reins at the same time. "There!" He pointed. Ahead in a cluster of boulders she caught the sudden movement, sunlight glinting off something metallic. "Hit the dirt!" he shouted.

Ryan started to clamber from the saddle. In the same instant a shot rang out. Cat screamed, as Ryan pitched headlong to the ground.

Even as Logan grabbed at Cat, she tugged her rifle free of its scabbard. The two of them dove for cover behind a fallen tree. "Stay here!" he gritted out.

Cat lay down a steady stream of cover fire as Logan rushed toward the inert Fielding. Gripping the wounded rancher under the armpits, Logan dragged him behind the relative safety of the fallen timber.

"It was Latigo!" Cat cried. "I saw him ride off!"

"I saw him too," Logan said, ripping at Ryan's shirtfront. Whipping off his own bandana Logan pressed it against the gaping wound in Ryan's chest. It was hopeless. Logan looked at Cat and shook his head.

Ryan coughed and blood dribbled from the corners of his mouth. With a desperate strength, he gripped Cat's shirtsleeve. "Tell the sheriff . . . I . . . tell him . . ." His chest heaved. He fought to catch a breath, but failed. His head lolled back, his eyes wide, unseeing.

"Damn," Cat said. "I don't care what he did, he didn't deserve this."

"The man tried to have you killed," Logan said, the irritation in his voice suggesting he wasn't feeling quite as compassionate.

"I believe what he said about Latigo overstepping his orders." She slapped a fist onto the ground. "I don't understand this. Why would Latigo shoot Ryan?"

"Fielding must have outlived his usefulness. Or he knew too much."

Cat frowned. "Knew too much about whom? If Ryan didn't control Latigo, who did?"

"That's what we have to find out." Logan stood. "We'll take Fielding's body to town and talk to Fletcher ourselves."

Cat watched as Logan tied Ryan's body across his saddle. "Why do you suppose Latigo didn't just kill us, too?" she ventured, when he'd finished.

"Maybe three murders would lead too close to his real

boss. Or maybe you and I are supposed to take the blame for Fielding."

Cat cursed. "No one would believe I murdered Ryan."

"Who knows what kind of evidence someone may have planted?"

Cat's eyes widened. "I think we'd better get to Toby."

"Keep an eye out," Logan warned, as he mounted his gelding. "Maybe Latigo will change his mind."

Cat rode with one finger on the trigger of her rifle the rest of the way to Red Springs. It was nearly midnight when they reached town. Dismounting in front of the sheriff's office, Cat hurried over to try the door. It was locked.

When she raised her hand to knock, Logan snared her fist.

"The less noise we make the better," he whispered. "I haven't been able to shake the feeling we're being watched."

Reflexively, Cat looked behind her. She saw nothing. The street was dark, deserted, not even the moon visible in the gloom-shrouded night. "Latigo?" she asked softly.

"I don't know. I just don't want you making yourself any kind of a target."

He manuevered her in front of him, so that his own body served as a shield between her and the street. His matter-of-fact way of risking his life for her brought quick tears to Cat's eyes, which she surreptitiously wiped away. She couldn't let herself be distracted, not even by her love for him. It might cost him his life. He carried no gun.

Nervously, Cat tapped on the door's glass pane, praying Toby was a light sleeper. In less than a minute the door opened. It was obvious from his disheveled appearance that Toby had been asleep, but one look at her and Logan, and he was instantly alert. "What's wrong?" he demanded.

Cat held a finger to her lips as she and Logan hurried inside. Quickly she shut and relocked the door, while Logan scrounged up a match and set a low flame in the kerosene lamp on Toby's desk. The light would likely be visible from the street, but it wouldn't afford enough illumination to give away their positions in the office.

"All right, you two," Toby said. "Out with it. What's going on?"

Cat told him. Toby listened intently, displaying no particular surprise at the news of Ryan's death.

When she'd finished, the sheriff tugged open the middle drawer of his desk and extracted an official-looking document. "This should make things even more interesting," he said, handing her the papers.

Cat squinted at the first of several pages, but couldn't make out much of the writing in the dim light. "What is this?"

Toby hooked his thumbs in the waistband of his trousers. "That, my dear Cat, is Ryan Fielding's two-day-old Last Will and Testament."

"Why do you have it?" Logan put in. "And what does it have to do with Cat?"

"Well, that idea you two had about someone plantin' evidence against you may not be too far-fetched."

"What are you talking about, Toby?" Cat's nerves were fraying. She had no patience with riddles.

"That new will mentions only one beneficiary," Toby said slowly, taking the papers from Cat and flipping to the back page. "Full and complete possession of the Rocking R Ranch goes to Cat Jordan."

Cat gasped. "That doesn't make sense! The man wanted *my* ranch. Why would he leave me *his?*"

"He didn't say," Toby admitted. "But he sure was scared."

"Of whom?" Logan asked.

"He wouldn't say."

Cat paced back and forth across the room. "When people find out about this, they're going to think I killed him, aren't they?"

"Did Fielding say anything at all, Sheriff?" Logan asked.

"Nothing directly," Toby said, "but he did leave this." He pulled a leather-wrapped package from the same drawer. "He said to open it if anything happened to him."

Cat raked a hand through her hair. Ryan's will. A cryptic message and this package. It was as though he had known . . .

She watched as Toby opened the package. He pulled out a piece of paper and unfolded it, a tiny bit of metal falling to the surface of his desk.

Logan picked up the metal, turning it over in his palm. It was about three inches long and had a barbed tip.

Toby held the letter close to the lamp. The more he read, the more his jaw tightened. When he finished, he looked up and regarded Cat levelly. "You'd best sit down."

Cat's heart thudded in her chest. She was grateful when Logan stepped close to put his arm around her. She did not sit down. "Read it, Toby. Please."

Toby read. "'Sheriff Fletcher, on June 2nd of this year I ordered my foreman Rafe Latigo to put the fear of God into Hadley Jordan. I knew Hadley would be on his way to town to wire for an extension on his loan. I didn't want

401

him to get that extension.

"'Latigo confronted Hadley. After an exchange of gunfire, Hadley fell amongst some rocks and broke his neck.'"

Cat closed her eyes, a sharp stabbing pain ripping through her.

Toby continued. "'I believed Latigo's story that Hadley's death was an unfortunate accident, though some part of me wondered that perhaps Latigo had acted out of revenge. He used to ride with that snake-in-the-grass rustler, Barney Jackson.

"'I rode out to where Latigo had staged the body, and I found the spur tip I've enclosed herein. I did not want Latigo connected to Hadley's death, because that link would lead to me. With Hadley out of the way, I saw my chance at the Circle J through Cat.

"'I later ordered Latigo to steal the herd money in Abilene. When I found out he far exceeded my orders, I fired him. He was drunk. He laughed and told me things I hesitate to put in this letter. I fear I have not seen the last of Latigo. Please assure Cat I never meant for things to go this far.'

"It's signed 'Ryan Fielding.'"

Logan swore. "All that cleared his conscience before he met his maker, but it doesn't tell us a damned thing about who's behind all this."

"Ryan did say he had a missing puzzle piece," Cat said. "His bargaining chip, he called it."

Logan looked at her, then looked toward the street.

"Do you think . . . ?" she asked.

"He was coming here. It makes sense he would have it with him."

Cautiously Logan opened the door. Nothing stirred.

402

Quickly he retrieved Ryan's saddlebags and brought them inside. Cat huddled close to him as he pulled out two rolled sheets of paper. Using his cane he anchored one end and unfurled the sheets on Toby's desk.

Cat stared at the topographical maps of the Rocking R and Circle J, fighting back a searing disappointment. "These don't mean anything. I have the same maps back at the ranch myself."

"Maybe not," Logan said, making a careful study of each map. "Maybe not."

Cat watched his fingers trace along a winding line that traversed both maps a line that represented no existing waterway, no road. "What is that?" she asked.

"This is why Fielding died," Logan said softly. "And very likely why your father died."

"I don't understand." She wanted Logan to explain, but he was already grabbing up the map and his cane. She could feel the tension in him, the anger. "Stay here," he said.

"Like hell," she retorted.

He grimaced, but didn't argue the point. "I think you'll want to come along too, Sheriff."

"Wouldn't miss it," Toby said, as they headed out the door. "Just where is it we're goin'?"

Logan spoke in quick, hushed tones to the lawman, and Cat's temper rose. She was certain Logan was only trying to protect her, to keep her from doing something reckless in light of the new information about her father's death, but she didn't like not knowing what was going on.

At first they headed away from the main street, then Logan stopped, seeming to notice something. Keeping to the deepest shadows, they crept along the boardwalk until Logan halted them outside the bank. The shades

403

were all drawn down tight, but Cat caught a hint of a vague glow coming from inside. Dear heaven, was someone robbing the bank?

Toby stepped in front of them. "I'm wearing the badge," he said in a voice that brooked no argument. "I go in first."

Gun drawn, he tried the door. It opened easily. He peered in, then straightened, apparently not alarmed by what he saw. He walked inside. Cat and Logan followed. His back to them, Abner Vincent was hunched in front of the open door to the vault.

"Working late, Abner?" Toby asked in a conversational tone.

Vincent nearly jumped out of his skin. Whirling, he stared at them, wide-eyed, his hand clutching at his chest. "You frightened me, Sheriff," he said, pulling his handkerchief free of his vest pocket to dab at his sweat-dampened forehead.

"Awful late, isn't it, Abner?" Toby went on.

Vincent tried to smile. "Paperwork, you know. It piles up when you have incompetent help. I hope the light didn't alarm you." He looked past Toby, as though seeing Cat and Logan for the first time. He stiffened perceptibly. "What is this, Sheriff?"

Toby stepped closer. "See you got a valise there, Abner. Goin' on a trip?"

"As a matter of fact, yes. After that horrible incident with Leona and Chastity and those vile thieves, I've decided to accompany them to see my wife's relatives in Atlanta."

Toby stepped closer still.

Abner snapped the valise shut.

Cat sensed the tension crackling in the air. Logan had moved off so that he and Toby were actually approaching Vincent from opposite sides. What could this little ferret-eyed banker have to do with any of this?

"What's in the bag, Abner?" Toby asked, still keeping his voice even, natural.

"Paperwork, like I told you." Vincent was sweating more profusely now.

"More likely the money from the vault, eh, Abner?" Logan prodded.

"How dare you, sir!"

Logan halted two feet from Abner's right, Toby positioned himself to the left between the banker and the door to the back room, as though he expected the portly Vincent to bolt for that door.

"Open the valise, Abner," Toby said. "We can get this settled all friendly like."

"I will not! These papers are private business."

"Like these?" Logan held up the maps.

Vincent paled. His gaze flicked almost longingly toward the door.

"Logan, please," Cat said, "what is this all about?"

"The black line on the maps," he said, never taking his eyes from Vincent. "Do you want to tell her, or should I?"

"Tell her what?" Vincent snorted, his bravado ringing patently false.

"Tell her why you had Ryan Fielding killed. Why you had her father killed."

Cat felt her knees buckle, but she managed to right herself, clinging to a chair back for support. "Why?" she cried. "For the love of God, why? What are those lines on

405

the maps?"

"Rights-of-way," Logan said gently, his gaze filled with sympathy as he looked at her. "Projected railroad rights-of-way. Somehow Vincent got wind of it. He wanted the land before anyone else knew. He could drive up the price, make a fortune."

Cat sank onto the chair, her whole body trembling.

"Any time a telegram was sent," Logan explained, "any time any financial dealings were conducted, who knew better what was going on?"

Vincent gave a contemptuous snort, his pompous façade crumbling. "That fool Hadley had to go to outside sources for money. The Circle J would have been mine if you hadn't interfered," he said, looking at Logan. "I was always afraid a man of your background would prove quite inconvenient. That's why I had Yerby and Doakes try to scare you off."

"Your own daughter was on that stage," Logan said.

"An unfortunate accident. Chastity was supposed to have arrived home earlier. She and her mother were diverted to your stage by chance."

"I suppose you're the one who stuck the dagger in my desk," Toby said.

"A crude hint that the Circle J should be allowed to go under." Vincent seemed to be getting some sort of perverse pleasure for regaling them with his cleverness. Cat noted, though, that he again looked toward the door. "I held papers on the Rocking R as well. I'd been advancing Fielding considerable capital in recent weeks. He was anticipating buying you out, Blackstone. Of course, Mr. Latigo was going to steal all of that money, leaving Fielding in considerable debt . . . to me. Unfortu-

406

nately, Latigo never could hold his liquor. He babbled one time too many, and Fielding had to be eliminated. Wasn't it just fine luck that he left his ranch to you, Cat dear?"

Cat's hands were balled into fists. She wished to God she had worn her gun. She wanted nothing more than to put a bullet in that smirking face.

"You've been doing a bit of babbling yourself, Abner," Toby said. "You can finish your sordid little story in my jail."

Toby took a step toward Vincent. Then everything seemed to happen at once. The door to the back room burst open, slamming into Toby from behind. The lawman grunted, collapsed, as Rafe Latigo drove the butt of a Colt hard against his skull. In the same motion Latigo lowered the six-gun and brought it to bear on Logan.

With a shrill cry Cat launched herself at Latigo, but he was ready for her. He sidestepped, driving his booted foot into her leg and sending her crashing onto the floor. Lightning pain burst through her, blackness threatened to engulf her; but she fought it off, scrambling to her feet.

"Stay back!" Logan shouted at her. He had his sword drawn. But Latigo, across the room, was well out of its reach.

"Let's see if that pigsticker can stop a bullet," Latigo snarled, thumbing back the hammer on the Colt.

Logan dove sideways as Latigo fired. In the same heartbeat of time, Cat grabbed up a paperweight from Vincent's desk and hurled it at Latigo's head. She missed, but Latigo whirled, firing a quick shot in her direction. Cat heard the whine of the bullet streaking past her head.

407

It was the instant's distraction Logan needed. Drawing his arm back he hurled the sword like a spear. The honed steel drove six inches into Latigo's chest. Latigo clawed at it like a madman, his gun clattering to the floor, the razor-sharp edges of the steel shredding the flesh from his fingers. He fell forward, jerked once, and lay still.

Cat pounced on Latigo's gun, leveling it at Vincent, who hadn't moved at all. His florid features registered bemusement, as though he couldn't believe Latigo had lost. Logan was bent over the unconscious Toby.

"Is he all right?" Cat asked.

"I think so. He'll have one helluva headache though."

"Are you all right?" she asked, her voice shaking now as the realization of how close they'd come to dying began to sink in.

"I'm fine. Just keep that thing pointed at him."

"Perhaps it's time we discussed this," Vincent said, pulling out a cigar and sticking it between his lips. He then struck a match and lit it.

Cat started to tell him to put it out. Then it came to her. The cigar smoke! "It was you who burned down the barn!" she accused. There had been something peculiar about the smell that night, right before the fire really took hold. But she'd been too groggy the next morning to think straight. "You tried to kill me even then."

"Tried to kill us both," Logan said. "He had the papers for the foreclosure. If I'd died in that fire, he could have done anything he wanted and passed it off as my wishes. The next day was too late. I had them back."

"You're an evil man, Abner Vincent," Cat said. "And I'm going to see to it you pay dearly for all the pain you've caused me and my family."

"I think not," a feminine voice said from somewhere behind them.

Cat whirled. Chastity stood in the room holding a derringer pointed at Logan's head.

"Drop your gun, Cat dear," Chastity purred. "Or your friend will have a worse headache than the sheriff."

Cat did as she was told.

"We'd better hurry, Papa," Chastity said. "Those shots may already have woke up a few citizens of this dreary little town."

"I knew I could count on you, my dear," Vincent said.

She batted her blue eyes at Logan. "I think I should shoot him, Papa, don't you? He dared pick that tomboy over me." She cocked the small gun.

"Chastity, don't!" Cat cried. "Please."

The girl gave no notice she'd even heard. "I'll shoot them both. We'll tell everyone Cat went mad. That she tried to rob the bank in an insane attempt to save her ranch. Blackstone and Latigo were her accomplices. They killed the poor sheriff. But even as he was dying, the sheriff killed Cat." Chastity smiled, obviously pleased with her fantasy. "And then, when things settle down in a day or two, we can still take the money."

Chastity's blue eyes glittered with pure hate. "Say good-bye to your handsome lover, Cat dear. No doubt the only one you ever had."

Cat could see the coiled tension in Logan. If she could get Chastity to shift the gun for even an instant . . . "You'd know all about lovers, wouldn't you, Chastity?" Cat said, looking at Vincent. "Have you ever asked your daughter what she does in that back room, Abner? Who she entertains? And not with cookies and lemonade."

409

"Shut up!" Chastity warned. "You shut your lying mouth!"

"Vicious lies!" Vincent snapped. "I'd expect nothing less from the likes of you. My daughter is as pure of body as she is of heart."

"I'm sure Ryan Fielding could have told you how pure that body is, Abner. Or Latigo. Why do you suppose it took him so long to come to your rescue?" Cat watched the gun begin to waver in Chastity's hand and prayed the girl didn't accidentally jerk the trigger. "Take a close look, Abner," Cat rushed on. "I'll bet she didn't quite get the hooks and eyes straight on the back of her dress. Maybe she couldn't even reach the top ones."

Chastity took an involuntary step backward, as though to keep her father from seeing exactly what Cat had described. Abner went gray, his jaw slackened.

"You bitch!" Chastity screamed, bringing the gun up. "I'll kill you!"

Logan heaved himself sideways, driving into Chastity, sending her sprawling backward. The gun spun away. Vincent lunged toward it. Logan met the banker's charge.

Chastity was up, shrieking, her face contorted. Teeth bared, she lunged at Cat. With a feral rage, Cat drew her fist back and drove it into Chastity's jaw. The young woman howled, screeching as she tasted blood on her split lip.

"I'll kill you!" Chastity screamed. She flailed her arms, scratching, clawing.

Cat eluded the wild blows, waiting for an opening. She saw it and drove herself at her opponent; sending them both crashing to the floor. Cat straddled Chastity's middle, pinioning her arms, immobilizing her. She sat atop her, panting, exhausted, but grinning triumphantly.

Logan trudged over and dumped a beaten Vincent in an unceremonious heap beside his daughter.

The words that spewed from Chastity's mouth might have made Dusty blush.

Cat's smile broadened. She looked at Logan, who was regarding her with a mixture of pride and amazement. "I guess they didn't teach her the finer points of steer wrestling in finishing school."

He chuckled. "Maybe you could use that hold on me."

"I'd like that," she murmured, suddenly all warm inside, despite the utter insanity of the previous few minutes.

She must have said something wrong, because he rose suddenly, busying himself with helping a groggy Toby. Cat's heart sank. Maybe she'd read everything wrong all along. Maybe despite his reconciliation with Matt, Logan still wanted no part of a relationship with her.

Cat's flush of victory faded quickly. She went through the motions, saying little, as Logan and a few hurriedly arrived townspeople helped Toby get the Vincents settled in jail cells.

She was standing on the boardwalk outside Toby's office, staring forlornly at the moonless sky, when Logan came up beside her. "Toby's got plenty of help to guard Abner and Chastity," he said.

She didn't say anything.

"It's still four hours 'til dawn," he went on, and it was then she noticed him twisting and untwisting the haft of his sword. He was nervous. She had never seen Logan nervous before. Though her body was unutterably ex-

411

hausted, her senses grew alert.

"The stage is leaving at eight," he said.

Her heart plummeted. He was telling her he was leaving. No, he couldn't leave. She wouldn't let him.

He had his arm around her waist, guiding her up the street. "Where are we going?" she asked numbly.

"To the hotel. To get some sleep."

Cat noticed the new livery as they crossed to the hotel. She thought of its new hayloft, thought of picking bits of straw out of Logan's sleep-tousled hair. . . .

She walked with him into the hotel, saying nothing as he registered them for separate rooms. Upstairs, she was determined to follow him to his room. Instead, he came into hers.

"I know you're tired," he said, leading her to the bed, sitting her down on it. "But we only have six hours."

"Six hours?" she repeated, not understanding.

"Until the stage leaves."

"Oh, yes, the stage." How could he be so cruel? He was going to count down the hours for her. And then she noticed his eyes, the raw pain in their gray depths.

"Logan, what is it?" She didn't want him to hurt. She never wanted Logan to be hurt.

"I've made a lot of mistakes since I came back to Texas," he said, that odd nervousness again evident in his voice. "The worst likely being coming at all."

She bit the inside of her lip. She wasn't going to cry. She wasn't.

"And there was another stupid mistake. The one where I put my troubles with your family ahead of my love for you. I thought I could never make you believe I could love you enough so that your family's hating me wouldn't matter. I thought you'd end up hating me too."

412

He gripped her arms, his gaze fierce, passionate. "We have six hours left," he said. "And I damned well intend to use every minute of that time to get you to change your mind. To get you to come back to Boston with me."

She blinked, wondering if her exhaustion could be affecting her hearing.

"I asked you a question once," he said, "and your answer was no. And then you asked me to ask it again, and I wouldn't, because I was afraid." He sucked in a deep breath. "Well, I'm still afraid. Scared to death. Because now I want desperately to ask it, but a man's pride can only take so much rejection."

Tears brimmed, spilled over. "Ask me, Logan. Ask me, please."

He cupped her hands in his, his voice hoarse, shaking. "I love you. I love you more than I ever thought it possible to love anyone." His gaze seared her. "Cat Jordan . . . would you be my wife?"

She gave him her answer then—with her body, her soul, her mind, her heart.

Long afterward, sated, replete, she lay naked beside him, reveling in the sweet ecstasy of the moment, and looking beyond it to savor the love of this man with whom she would spend her life, this man who was her life.

"I'd like to think," she said sleepily, teasingly, "there'll be certain advantages to being a doctor's wife."

"I can think of several already," he said, grinning lasciviously.

"I'm serious," she pouted, failing utterly to keep from bursting into a fit of giggles. "For example, I might have questions of a delicate nature."

"How delicate?" he asked, nuzzling her neck with

413

his mouth.

"Like"—she blushed prettily—"how babies are made."

Logan pulled her into his arms, kissing her fiercely, possessively. "You can be sure I'll be right here to answer each and every one," he whispered. "Intimately."

TURN TO CATHERINE CREEL – THE
REAL THING – FOR THE FINEST
IN HEART-SOARING ROMANCE!

CAPTIVE FLAME (2401, $3.95)
Meghan Kearney was grateful to American Devlin Montague for rescuing her from the gang of Bahamian cutthroats. But soon the handsome yet arrogant island planter insisted she serve his baser needs – and Meghan wondered if she'd merely traded one kind of imprisonment for another!

TEXAS SPITFIRE (2225, $3.95)
If fiery Dallas Brown failed to marry overbearing Ross Kincaid, she would lose her family inheritance. But though Dallas saw Kincaid as a low-down, shifty opportunist, the strong-willed beauty could not deny that he made her pulse race with an inexplicable flaming desire!

SCOUNDREL'S BRIDE (2062, $3.95)
Though filled with disgust for the seamen overrunning her island home, innocent Hillary Reynolds was overwhelmed by the tanned, masculine physique of dashing Ryan Gallagher. Until, in a moment of wild abandon, she offered herself like a purring tiger to his passionate, insistent caress!